SELFISH and PERVERSE

SELFISH and PERVERSE
a novel

Bob Smith

CARROLL & GRAF PUBLISHERS
NEW YORK

For my friend Michael in Santa Fe
and my friend Brad in Alaska

SELFISH AND PERVERSE

Carroll & Graf Publishers
An Imprint of Avalon Publishing Group, Inc.
245 West 17th Street, 11th Floor
New York, NY 10011

AVALON
publishing group incorporated

Library of Congress Cataloging-in-Publication Data

Smith, Bob, 1958-
  Selfish and perverse : a novel / Bob Smith.
    p. cm.
  ISBN-13: 978-0-7867-2040-8 (hardcover)
  ISBN-10: 0-7867-2040-9 (hardcover)
  1. Television writers--Fiction. 2. Gay men--Fiction. 3. Los Angeles (Calif.)--Fiction.
4. Alaska--Fiction. I. Title.

  PS3619.M5535S45 2007
  813'.6--dc22

                                                                    2007015718

9 8 7 6 5 4 3 2 1

Interior design by Maria E. Torres

Printed in the United States of America
Distributed by Publishers Group West

The world is a king, and, like a king, desires flattery for a favor; but true art is selfish and perverse—it will not submit to the mold of flattery.

—Ludwig van Beethoven

ONE

Love at first sight makes perfect sense because we're all pressed for time. I was a busy guy and didn't have a spare moment for secret longings, pining from afar, unspoken yearnings, or any of the other old-fashioned pokey trappings of love. I worked long hours as the script coordinator for *Aftertaste*, the Saturday late night television show. And yet, I still tried to read the newspaper every day. I tried to go the gym four times a week. I tried to see my friends on the weekends. I needed to catch up on my sleep, movies, and laundry. I was always fresh out of milk, coffee, and gas. I went to bed every night resolved to finish the novel that I was reading, and I woke up the following morning determined to finish the novel that I was writing.

I wanted to fall in love as swiftly as the term would suggest—my heart dropping from a great height like a heavy stone on an unsuspecting victim. Based on my looks, I had every expectation of meeting someone someday. I was considered attractive; my best friend Wendy Haberman went so far as to tell me that I was handsome but was too "mental" to realize it. My thick light brown hair, worn short on the sides and nonbelligerently spiky on top, won my own unqualified praise; a good haircut could turn my own head. But there was nothing special about my brown eyes or standard fluoridated smile. There's a glitch in my right eyebrow, a scar from falling off a pair of stilts at age ten. (Like I wasn't tall enough already.) Most of my boyfriends thought the scar was kind of sexy until I revealed that my menacing air consisted of mostly being a danger to myself. My nose looked fine from the front, but profile photographs always made me wish it were a smidgen less pointy. (Every type of nose needs a becoming adjective to disguise its appearance; I could live with a beak if I could describe it as aquiline.) My legs were hairy but the rest of my body wasn't; an astrologer at a party once told me this was a common trait of goaty Capricorns. Two years previously, I'd joined a gym and was almost seeing results. I'm sporting abs in a shirtless pic taken at the lake last summer; although I can't see them when I look in the mirror, making me think my body type must be ectoplasmic. My brand-new layer of muscles turned a wire coat hanger into one of those pink satin padded coat hangers ladies use.

At the time my romantic life wasn't my priority crisis. What had me worried was that I was an artsy, thirty-four-year-old man who needed to confront whether I was really talented or just gay. (Too many of my friends misinterpreted the relative novelty of their sex lives as a sign of genius.) My watershed moment of distinguishing a truly rare gift from merely uncommon desires had been building for twelve years when, after having graduated with an English degree from the University of Wisconsin at Madison, I moved from my hometown of Milwaukee to Los Angeles.

Wendy had talked me into moving out to California. She grew up in Beverly Hills and had attended UW because her mother had been a graduate. We had become close in college when we both played small parts in a production of *The Madwoman of Chaillot*. During a tedious tech rehearsal, we sat in the back row of the theater making fun of the other actors and discovered that both of our mothers had died while we were in high school. Wendy's mother had died of breast cancer; mine had died in a car accident. In low voices, we recounted how their deaths had irrevocably changed our lives.

After the rehearsal, Wendy said, "Do you think your mom could give us a lift?" She pretended to catch herself. "Oh, right, sorry." Later when we went out for coffee, I exacted my revenge. While carrying our cappuccinos to the table, I shouted across the cafe, "How does your mom like her coffee? One lump or two?" Unfazed, Wendy yelled back, "One lump should do it!"

We became roommates and eventually I began to think of Wendy as being as reliable as the sun; she would always be there for me, although there were times when I suspected long-term exposure to her could be unhealthy. She was a gigantic woman, six foot three, with a powerful athletic body and matching fee-fi-fo-fum personality. On her left wrist, she wore a charm bracelet that had been her mother's, but on her it appeared about as ladylike as a set of brass knuckles. Wendy delighted in focusing on other people's idiosyncrasies and she reveled in pointing out my imperfections. Apart from an overall disgust with my nerdiness, she zeroed in on my clumsiness, mispronounced words, sprayed saliva, spinach caught between teeth, undone zippers, and other momentary lapses of dignity.

Wendy's father was a television producer, and after our graduation he had offered us jobs as writer's assistants on a sitcom. Since I couldn't decide whether or not to apply to graduate school, I accepted the job without truly understanding the danger it placed me in. The lures of fame and money are often cited as the primary attractions of show business, but the most insidious appeal of Hollywood is that everyone working on a television show or a film, even the lowliest writer's assistant, can be as egocentric as any star. Invariably they begin to harbor delusions about their essential and indispensable importance to the project.

My first day on the job, I was entrusted with delivering scripts to the homes of the cast. I handed over the bound canary-yellow pages to the star of our show directly, not to his maid or personal assistant. He even asked my name and thanked me. Audiences shunned our dreadful program, but I was allowed the satisfaction of honestly believing that without me, there would have been no show that week. And everyone else working on the program, from the limousine drivers to the sound engineers could tell themselves the same intoxicating tale.

I'd made a mistake that no aspiring writer should make; I found a job that plunged me into a world that seemed more interesting than the imaginary world I was trying to create. At first, I had loved being a writer's assistant. It was satisfying to discover that at that age (only twenty-two) I was a powerful and commanding figure. A comedy writing staff is a flock of silly geese—and the writer's assistants lead them. The writers depended on us to properly format their sketches for the script, to fix their computers and printers, to order their food, and most importantly to explain to them how the voice mail system worked.

(The writers were obsessed with their voice mail, and since they were all insecure, when no one called, they interpreted *that* as a message.)

I always assumed these jobs would be temporary—interim employment while finishing my novel—so I moved confidently from bad shows to slightly better shows until landing at *Aftertaste*.

"Script coordinator" was an ornamental title for the senior writer's assistant. But when I was promoted to the position, no one had mentioned that being disingenuous was a requirement for the job. The script coordinator frequently had to reassure a writer that he was funny and that his job was secure, even though indeed he was history; or he had to convince a new cast member who hadn't actually caught fire with our audience that she would be asked back next season. And, on occasion, he would remind the other writer's assistants that their work didn't go unnoticed by the producers and writers who valued their contributions to the show—when in truth, they never thought about the writer's assistants unless a page was missing in a script or a spelling error hadn't been corrected.

I'd held the position of script coordinator for three years and couldn't stay there much longer. The rule in Hollywood is to never appear to be stranded on your stepping-stone job, and I was on the verge of becoming an *old* assistant. My friends believed that I was working on my novel, but for the past six months (let me revise that: for almost a year) I hadn't written a word. I was all talk and no writing. It made me wonder how writers procrastinated in the Homeric era. Did bards of yore talk endlessly about their plans to someday tell a story? My inability to finish my novel terrified me because I was beginning to imagine my brain as a crumpled piece of paper sitting in a wastepaper basket.

Aftertaste was written and produced from a suite of offices surrounding a central anteroom where I worked with the other three writer's assistants. White flat screens topped each of our desks, but we shared a printer, private conversations, and the enmity of the writers. Befitting my position of seniority, I was provided with an ugly half-partition that provided enough cover for my desk to be considered the architectural equivalent of standing naked and cupping your hands over your genitals.

Next to our desks was a waiting area where the cast and crew often hung out during the long workdays. The waiting area was furnished with two sister couches, one pretty and one plain, a cheap wood laminate coffee table and a hulking television monitor that commanded one's attention even when it wasn't turned on.

Ordinarily, I arrived at the office promptly at nine A.M. before the other writer's assistants showed up at nine-thirty. Most of the writers usually arrived in various states of agitation between ten and ten-thirty, giving us a blissful hour free of their questions. But on Monday of the week Dylan Fabizak guest-starred on the show, I was fifteen minutes late because I had to run to the post office to overnight a birthday present to my nephew, Theo.

By the time I arrived at work, Wendy was already seated at her desk, yakking on her telephone as Jeremy Lenahan pulled at a wad of chewing gum in his mouth while reading the current issue of *Fave* magazine. His desk was located next to mine, and from where I sat, determining the tall, gawky Jeremy's gender was similar to taking an eye test where you had to squint to focus on his hard-to-read X and Y chromosomes. A magenta stripe ran down the center of his long, dyed-black hair and Jeremy's eyes were lined with kohl. His spindly biceps were circled by Goth tattoos of chains and barbed wire; whenever he stood up, I always anticipated that they would rattle down to his wrists like bangle bracelets. Jeremy's most masculine feature was his chipped and worn black nail polish, which suggested a hardiness of some kind.

The other writer's assistant, Daniel Reese, was nowhere to be seen, suggesting that there was a slim chance that he might be working.

Needing a second cup of coffee, I walked to the office's kitchen and ran into our executive producer, "Agenda" Lupton. Her real name was Amanda but I'd started calling her Agenda when she posted a large calendar on the wall to mark off the days until her baby was due. Throughout her pregnancy the chic, dark-haired Amanda radiated a maternal glow of resentment. She hated to be kept waiting, and to be kept waiting for nine months, even by her unborn son, was almost unforgivable.

Amanda greeted me with the briefest of smiles—her lips shuddered. The kitchen was too small for two people, and I waited in the doorway while she placed a covered paper cup into the microwave and set the timer for one minute. It always astonished me that Amanda didn't just reheat her soy-milk latte by glaring at it as if the drink had done something wrong.

"Nelson, I need to talk you," she said impatiently, summoning me for our customary Monday morning meeting. I followed Amanda to her office where I stood in front of her desk while she sat down and began scanning the headlines of the trade papers. "Dylan Fabizak has been paroled and he's agreed to be our guest host," she said without looking up at me. "He won't be in 'til Friday. That's fine—he's only in two sketches. He's sober this week, but we can't take any chances. Make sure there's absolutely no liquor in his dressing room. And we need to messenger two copies of the script to his agent." She picked up a marker and turned toward the calendar behind her, ticking off another day of gestation. "Oh, and there's been a change of plans."

I steeled myself for disappointment because when a television producer announces there's been a change of plans, a lie will be told or a promise will be broken.

"I know you asked to leave early today, but the reporter from *Fave* is coming to interview the cast and writers. Chip tries to turn every profile into a fucking exposé. So I need you to warn everyone to watch . . . what . . . they . . . say." She enunciated the last words slowly as if she was speaking to a foreigner with a learning disability.

"That's fine," I said. It was actually a relief to have an excuse to cancel, at the last minute, a coffee date I'd made with a guy I'd met online. It was inconsiderate but I'd already lied to him about my age, body, car, and job and therefore I was comfortable treating him badly.

Amanda's phone rang and I awaited further instructions while she answered the call. I listened to a few minutes of a graphic and whiney conversation with her obstetrician until she swatted the air to signal that I was dismissed. Making my escape, I fled from her office, excited by the prospect of having Dylan Fabizak as our guest star.

Special guest stars appeared infrequently on *Aftertaste* because we weren't successful or prestigious enough to entice major television and movie stars into doing our show. *Aftertaste* was better than our mediocre ratings indicated, but our guest stars were usually limited to the actors our fourth-rated network tried to foist on Amanda from their other programs. (I had my problems with Amanda, but I couldn't deny that she always tried to keep *Aftertaste* a respectable failure.) She resisted the network's pressure and pointed out that the actors she was being offered weren't even good on their own television shows. Amanda told the suits point-blank that she'd prefer to stick with our talented cast rather than have to try to accommodate the needs or demands of a questionable twinkle, her term for flashes in the pantheon.

It was a coup for Amanda to get a genuine movie star like Dylan Fabizak to do our show. Everyone in Hollywood would be interested in seeing his first appearance after his release from prison. I looked forward to seeing him in the flesh after watching him for so many years. Dylan began his career acting in Disney films; then for a time as he grew older he was stuck among the most recent group of boy beauties. He came to my attention when I was a teenager and he began to play sensitive, flawed jocks in made-for-TV movie dramas—the shot-putter with a stutter role. The first time he removed his tank top in a locker room scene, I discovered that he was an extremely talented actor, and henceforth I always watched his movies alone upstairs in my bedroom on my small portable color television.

The rest of the world lagged behind me in appreciating Dylan's gifts until his most recent role, playing a troubled World War II soldier. The film was the one of those gritty-pretty war movies, where the grime-smeared, impossibly handsome soldiers wore bandoliers of bullets like sashes in a beauty pageant. Dylan stormed the beaches of Normandy, and within the first twenty minutes of the film, he shed his innocence and his shirt, making it appear that he was internally conflicted about whether to fight the Germans or go surfing. The small part had earned Dylan critical acclaim and an Academy Award nomination for best supporting actor, placing him in the rarified category of actors who were beautiful and talented.

When I returned to my desk, I announced to Wendy and Jeremy that Dylan was going to appear on the show that week. Wendy didn't seem to care but Jeremy was delighted.

"Did you see his picture in *Fave*?" he asked. Jeremy moaned softly and his eyes rolled orgasmically back into their sockets. "Go directly to jail and become gorgeous! He must have gained twenty pounds of muscle in there. And did you see the barbed-wire tattoo around his bicep? Oh, I'd risk cutting my tongue on *that*."

"Well, I'm not sure we can arrange that," Wendy said. "Because I think he's straight."

"He's not so straight," Jeremy claimed. "At least not from what I've heard."

We paid no attention to him because Jeremy suffered from a bad case of swishful thinking where any man he desired was automatically assumed to be gay.

"I'd be his bitch," Jeremy said dreamily as he walked over to the blue recycling bin and threw away copies of last week's script.

"You're already my bitch, bitch!" Wendy called out.

"Are you in the Manhater 4 Manhater chat room again?" Jeremy asked, returning to his desk.

Wendy raised her right hand and slowly unfurled her middle finger without taking her eyes from her computer screen.

Daniel interrupted their daily feud when he walked to his desk, carrying a cardboard box full of the upcoming show's rehearsal and shooting schedules. Part of Daniel's job was to photocopy and distribute them to the cast and crew every week.

"Wendy, are you talking about me again?" Daniel asked, having overheard her last remark to Jeremy. "I've told you I have a girlfriend."

"No, Daniel," Jeremy answered, "you *are* a girlfriend."

"Shut up, Mary Louise," Daniel said, tossing two copies of the schedules onto his desk.

"Daniels's a big bottom!" Wendy exclaimed, taking juvenile delight in the pleasure of using smutty language. Wendy and Jeremy enjoyed bickering with each other, but Daniel's presence inexplicably turned them into allies who joined in needling him. Sometimes I thought that they were too harsh and reprimanded them, but Daniel told me not to worry about it because he knew that they actually liked him.

"You say big bottom like it's a bad thing," Daniel said, as he tossed copies onto her desk as well.

It was Daniel's last season working at *Aftertaste* as he was starting law school in the fall. He was medium height, tending toward fat, and, as the office's standard-bearer for heterosexuality, utterly confident of his own appeal. People often explained Daniel's amiable personality by observing, "He's from Iowa." You had to give them credit for how they excused their own unfriendliness by turning simple human kindness into a crop with a limited growing range.

Daniel handed me my copies of the shooting schedule, and I told him that he needed to messenger two copies of the script to Dylan Fabizak's agent.

"I thought Dylan was in jail," Daniel said.

"Released for good behavior," I said.

"Apparently," said Wendy with mock sincerity, "Dylan's cellmate in the slammer is a huge fan of *Aftertaste*, and Dylan promised he'd do a guest spot as soon as he got out if Bubba wouldn't make him his bitch. Our ratings are through the roof with the prison demographic—men doing eighteen to forty-nine years."

"He was in for drugs, right?" Daniel asked, turning to me. Around the office, Daniel's inadequate knowledge of show biz gossip was regarded as a serious shortcoming in his education.

"Saying Dylan did drugs is like saying Shakespeare did plays," I replied. "He's been busted for everything. This time he was caught carrying three ounces of coke."

"In Battersea enamel snuff boxes," Jeremy specified, "hand painted with portraits of Sarah Siddons, the eighteenth-century English actress."

"He must be gay," I added. "Or just classy."

The police had taken Dylan into custody, live on the morning news. He had been whacked out on a trail mix of Crystal Meth, Special K, and Ecstasy, standing naked on the corner of Sunset and Crescent Heights, holding a Bundt pan and rambling on about making a birthday cake for God. (One of the fringe benefits of working on a television show was that someone got hold of a copy of the unpixilated video.)

Daniel decided to deliver the scripts to Dylan's agent himself instead of calling for a messenger service because Tamara, his girlfriend, worked at the agency, and he took advantage of every opportunity to see her. There wasn't that much for any of us to do on Mondays so Daniel could afford to blow off an hour. After Daniel left with the scripts, Amanda padded barefoot out of her office and made her way to my desk, holding a glossy black folder in her hand. (She had recently taken to walking around the office barefoot because she said her feet were swollen from her pregnancy.) "Make copies of Dylan's press kit and distribute them to all the writers," she ordered, handing me the folder.

"That is so not his dick!" Wendy declared. She was standing over Jeremy's shoulder looking at his computer screen. Jeremy, it seemed, had gone to *www.starmeat.com* and pulled up Dylan's page. At first I assumed Wendy was unaware of Amanda's presence, until she turned from the computer and said directly to her, "I've seen his dick in the video of the feed from the Christmas bust, and that is so not it."

Amanda strolled over to Jeremy's desk and gazed at the screen. "Ha!" she exclaimed sharply.

Jeremy didn't take his eyes off the screen when he casually said, "He's so totally gay."

"Those rumors have been around for years, Jeremy," Amanda said. "But I'm sorry to say you can't fully claim him as one of your own." She turned back to her office, satisfied she'd ratcheted up the Amanda Lupton mystique a notch.

I picked up Dylan's press kit and flipped through its pages while walking to the kitchen, having decided to eat the chocolate bar that I'd vowed not to eat a half hour earlier. My head was down as I read that Dylan had been born on a ranch in New Mexico, when I collided with a man who had suddenly appeared around a corner in the hallway.

"Whoa! Sorry!"

"No problem," I said, releasing the thick arm I'd grabbed to avoid the full-body slam. My grandmother claimed that you could learn everything you needed to know about a man by bumping into him. A good man would try to catch you while a bad man would try to protect himself. His arms had wrapped around me, holding me tightly, preventing me from falling.

After separating from each other, I instinctively appraised the man attached to the meaty bicep. Also in his early thirties. Handsome. Blue eyes peering out from under a faded red baseball cap. Short rusty hair but not a redhead. Stylish long sideburns. My height, six feet or so. Loose, baggy clothing in fashionable drab shades, the somber palette of greenish-browns that I dubbed "Broccolate." A worn T-shirt with the barely legible logo of "Peter Pan Seafoods" over a solid chest. A black leather band on his left wrist. Shapeless cargo pants unburdened by his slim waist. Hard-worn hiking boots. Each item of his apparel had no particular merit, but, due to some yet-undiscovered process of cold fusion, worn in combination on him, they generated heat.

"Is this Joe Benedetti's office?" he asked.

I told him no and that Joe was in a pitch meeting with the head writer.

Joe Benedetti was one of the most popular performers on *Aftertaste*, and he never let anyone forget that a star has five sharp points. Joe had mentioned to me that his cousin was staying with him for two weeks. "You should meet him," he had said snidely. "He's also a big 'mo." I figured this guy had to be the cousin because Joe's friends were all boneheads who would have shouted, "Watch where you're going!" if they had ran into me.

"Do you know how long he'll be?" he asked.

"It could be awhile," I said, knowing that Joe was the only cast member who wrote most of the characters he played, endowing him with the touchy ego of both a successful actor and a successful writer. If Joe's idea was rejected, an hour of stroking to soothe his injured pride would be necessary afterward. Accepting his idea could take even longer as he fleshed out the character on his feet to everyone's compulsory delight.

"Do you want to wait?" I asked as we continued down the hallway to my desk.

"Sure," he said, nodding.

"There's coffee," I added, pointing toward the kitchen as we passed it. After feeling his hard bicep, I had changed my mind and decided that I didn't want that chocolate bar after all.

"I'm good," he replied, immediately establishing him in my mind as a manly guy who spoke in punchy, declarative phrases such as "get lost" or "blow me."

"Have a seat," I offered when we reached the waiting area.

"Roy Briggs," he said with a smile, offering me his hand.

"Nelson Kunker," I replied, gripping his hand firmly. Roy sat down on the sofa nearest to my desk.

"So, you're a friend of Joe's?" I asked in an exaggeratedly "normal" tone. Pretending to be normal was a fib, but it's a harsh fact that expressing too much individuality means you'll always be single. I loved reading about eccentric characters in novels but understood that in the real world, wearing a monocle will restrict your sex life to masturbation.

"Joe's my cousin," Roy declared. "I'm visiting from Alaska."

The names of certain states held an aphrodisiacal quality for me. An attractive man from Alaska was instantly intriguing while an attractive man from Arkansas could take an entire second or more to captivate me.

"I've always wanted to visit," I admitted, immediately deciding that it was a waste of time to be attracted to someone who lived in Alaska and would be leaving in a week. That was when I first noticed that Roy had a small dark mole on his left cheek and a bleach spot on his shirt.

"I couldn't imagine living anywhere else," Roy said, forcing me to imagine myself living in Alaska.

"What do you do?" I asked, half-hoping that perhaps his job was so boring or disgusting that it would mercifully smother my crush. I've found that asking a man what he does for a living is the simplest method of indirectly asking whether he's happy. When a man answers "I'm just an accountant," you've actually learned quite a bit about him.

"I'm a commercial salmon fisherman part of the year and I'm studying to be an archaeologist," Roy said proudly.

"That's interesting," I said, impressed that he had two adventurous jobs although the second one bordered on overkill. Roy had immediately placed me, as the writer, in the demeaning role of the deskbound, paper-pushing bore in any future relationship. I saw him coming home from work, bearing salmon and gleaming Scythian gold, while over our dinner of freshly caught sockeyes, I told him that I had spent my riveting day trying to figure out another novel way of formulating "he said."

"Are you a fan of the show?" I asked, noticing that Roy hadn't said anything about *Aftertaste*.

"I don't really watch," he answered sheepishly. "Usually, I'm studying." He put a finger to his lips. "Don't tell Joe."

"We're the Loch Ness Monster of television programs," I said. "Everyone's heard of us but sightings are rare."

Our conversation was interrupted when a jowly, fair-haired young man walked into the office. After shoving the last shards from a bag of potato chips into his gaping mouth, he brushed the crumbs from his hands onto the carpet.

"I'm Chip Fiss from *Fave* magazine," he announced. He stood there looking smug as if the name of the magazine alone should have caused us to jump to attention. My face betrayed my irritation that I had to deal with him when what I really wanted to do was keep talking to Roy. I hated when my job interfered with what I felt was my real vocation: getting a boyfriend.

"Let me deal with this," I huffed. I took my time walking over to greet the lumpy, out-of-shape reporter, whom I already thought of as "Potato Chip."

I introduced myself but wasn't too happy as Chip stretched out his arm to offer me his greasy paw. I hesitated to accept it, and he must have realized my distaste because, after glancing at his palm, he indicated with a shrug that it wasn't necessary for us to shake hands.

"Um," I said tentatively, "I heard you want to interview me."

"First, I want to observe," he said brusquely. "Then we'll see about the interviews."

I felt disgusted by my pathetic craving to see my name in print in *Fave.*

"Well . . . it's not like it's my idea," I said irritably. "Agenda mentioned it."

"Agenda?" he asked.

"Amanda," I quickly corrected. Glancing over at Roy, I saw that he had picked up a newspaper from the coffee table and was reading the front page. Wendy was still talking on the telephone, her eyes twinkling because I had screwed up and called Amanda, "Agenda." Jeremy remained intensely focused on his computer screen and was most likely either reading dire environmental news or checking out the macabre Web sites of tattoo artists.

"Listen," Chip said imperiously as he let my slip of the tongue slide, "I want to park on the studio lot instead of a block away. Anything you can do about that?"

"No," I winced, "I'm sorry—only the cast parks on the lot." It was my first insincere apology of the day.

Chip's chip-crusted lips curled into a sneer. "I'll just have to talk to Amanda about it," he threatened, dismissing me with a wave of his hand and heading toward her office. Good luck I thought, knowing Amanda had established the policy that only she and the cast parked on the lot. She might make an exception for him, but she'd certainly resent having, as she had put it, "to revisit the issue."

Intending to resume my conversation with Roy, I mulled over the topics of Alaska, archaeology, and fishing as I walked back to my desk. When I sat down, Roy closed the newspaper and looked up expectantly as if he wanted to speak to me. Suddenly I recalled a magazine article that I had read somewhere.

"I read recently how Eskimo hunters. . . . Is it still okay to say Eskimo?" I asked.

Roy shook his head "no" as he slid down the couch, nearer to my desk.

"Well then, Native Alaskans," I said, "found old stone and ivory harpoons embedded in the blubber of recently killed Bowhead whales."

"It's not accurate to call them harpoons," Roy said. "Without the shaft, they're just stone points."

"But they were once attached to harpoons," I said, thinking that he was being incredibly pedantic.

"Yes," he admitted, "But the points were attached to the harpoons. They're not actually harpoons. Just like an arrowhead isn't an arrow."

"You've got a point," I said, compelled to make a bad joke to stop him from destroying my interest in him completely.

"I've seen them," Roy bragged. He jumped up from the couch and walked over to my desk, facing me directly.

"Can you imagine?" he asked. "Inupiaq hunters haven't used stone points for over a hundred years; they could have been thrown by their great-great-grandfathers!"

I caught a whiff of his wintergreen-scented breath, which added an intriguing physical intimacy to our intellectual connection and also seemed to make him smell vaguely "Alaskan."

"What's the deal with Bowhead whales?" I asked, knowing in fact quite a bit about them. But I sometimes felt bashful about being intelligent and behaved as if my brain were a private part that I needed to conceal. Playing dumb also gave me the opportunity to gaze at the unshaved rusty stubble on his face while he elaborated on the species.

"They have an incredibly long life span—the longest of any mammal."

I uttered a suitable exclamation of disbelief, although the article I'd read had mentioned that fact.

"Some of them could have been born in the middle of the nineteenth century, possibly as early as 1800," he said. "I can't believe you know about this," he added, looking astonished.

For an instant, we were speechless, as we were both amazed to find that our fascination with Stone Age harpoon points was embedded in someone else. My subculture of one had doubled in size. I hadn't consciously chosen to test Roy, but I'd settled upon an obscure story that had struck me as lovely, strange, and haunting. And he got it, right away. His passionate response seemed to promise that whatever peculiar things I dug out of my head, I could trust that he would always understand me.

It was apparent that Roy was handsome and intelligent, but the next thing was to discover if he had a sense of humor.

Roy dipped his head shyly and said that male Bowhead whales were notoriously queer and groups of young males had been observed having stag gangbangs and flipper-waving circle jerks.

"If they live for two hundred years," I said, "then they must have the oldest queens of any species of mammal."

He laughed, revealing a set of flawless white teeth.

"And the nastiest," I added, "if they've been carrying around harpoon points in their blubber for over a century."

"Um, excuse me," Wendy said from behind her desk, "I'm on the phone here with my girlfriend and you're so boring I can't stay awake." She smiled at Roy to indicate that she was teasing us, then exaggeratedly mouthed the words "Thank you" before resuming her conversation.

"You shouldn't have phone sex during office hours," I said to Wendy, trying to remind her, and demonstrate to Roy that I was officially her boss. She glanced at me then began typing rapidly on her keyboard.

"I'm sorry, Reina, I'm just making some notes," she said loudly for our benefit. "I want to be accurate about the time and date because I've been accused of having phone sex by my supervisor here at work. Yes, my lawsuit will demand damages for sexual harassment and damages for discrimination based upon my sexual orientation. I know honey, don't cry. I'm sure we'll get a huge settlement and then we can finally become carefree dykes who travel to Scrabble tournaments with our thirteen rescued cats in our brand-new RV. I'm sure our lawyer can force the company to pay. I'll talk to you later, sweetie. Yes, call your psychiatrist for your trauma."

Roy laughed before I pointed out that she could hardly sue anyone for harassment after she posted my e-mail address to a Web site for men with a diaper fetish. "Three years later, I'm still getting e-mails from Pamperme347."

"You should date him," Wendy advised. "You're always complaining how hard it is to meet men."

"There's no excuse for whaling," Jeremy commented without removing his eyes from his computer screen. "It's murder."

"Whaling's a part of their culture," Roy explained as he sat back down on the sofa. "They venerate whales and honor their spirits before the hunt. It's a tradition that's endured for thousands of years."

"Don't start on animal rights with Jeremy," I warned. "He's a vegan and a PETA member. You'll only get hurt. Or bored. Or both."

Jeremy wasn't about to end his crusade.

"How would you like to be suffocated and have your face ripped open by a hook?" he asked, his appropriately eco-green eyes flashing with self-righteousness.

"Tell me something," Roy said pleasantly to him. "Now the germs in your body are as blobby and defenseless as baby seals, right?"

Jeremy looked suspicious, but Roy forced him to admit that it was true.

"And every minute you're alive your immune system keeps clubbing those germs to death," he said patiently as if he was telling a story to a child. "So logically then, if you're against killing animals, you should kill yourself to save the lives of millions of adorable baby bacteria."

"Thank you!" Wendy chirped to Roy in a sing-song voice. The angry expression on Jeremy's face indicated that he might to be willing to make an exception to killing animals just this once. Wendy rose from her chair and walked over to the sofa.

"Just tell Jeremy to go ahead and have the sex change," she said as she sat down next to Roy. "He's already a big fucking CUNT!"

"It takes one to eat one," Jeremy called from his desk.

Wendy ignored his comment and formally introduced herself to Roy. After they exchanged names and shook hands, she confessed, "I love Alaska. The pot up there's amazing. I spent a summer in Seward getting high on Matanuska Thunder Fuck with my girlfriend Mandy."

"What happened?" Roy inquired politely.

"Ah, we broke up. We didn't have enough in common."

"Did it ever occur to you that maybe it had something to do with you telling people to call her, 'Man' for short?" I asked.

"Yeah," Wendy admitted. "But I never told her to look and sound like Jimmy Cagney."

She shrugged her shoulders and Roy laughed.

"Why do all the women in Alaska look like dykes?" Wendy asked. "Like, I'd be talking to a stocky sixty-year-old woman. She'd have a crew cut and the wind chime earrings. She'd offer to gut my fish or loan me her axe and I'd think, I love the dykes up here. Then I'd find out she has five kids and has been happily married for forty years."

"Sounds like you ran into my mom," Roy said, which made Wendy laugh. He had been admitted into her inner circle, which Wendy's friends visualized as an archery target, placing them within bull's-eye range.

Amanda suddenly came charging down the hall, a familiar sight as she ran to the ladies' room. In her first trimester, she threw up every morning, but for the past three months she had to pee every hour. We needed to look busy.

"So . . ." I said abruptly, "we need to messenger scripts to Dylan's office, and . . ." I trailed off, unable to think of any additional work to invent for Amanda's benefit. Wendy got up from the couch, returned to her desk, and plopped down in her chair. Jeremy began to type on his keyboard, assuming the appearance of working for the sake of Amanda's return trip.

"So, Nelson," Roy asked, "what exactly do you do here?"

After Jeremy and Wendy piped in with "not much" and "very little," I explained what my responsibilities were and then, after thinking about it for a second, revealed that I wanted to be a writer.

Clearly identifying himself as an outsider in Los Angeles, Roy asked me with bright-eyed enthusiasm what I was working on.

"I'm writing a novel," I said, hoping that he wouldn't ask me what it was about. It would have felt far less intimate to pull down my pants and have had sex with him right there than to tell him what I'd been thinking about and intermittently working on for the past three years.

"He had a short story published in a literary magazine," Wendy offered.

"Oh," I said, shifting uncomfortably in my seat, "it was a small magazine, and it was back in college."

"Don't be modest, Nelson," Wendy continued as she crossed the room to Jeremy's desk, stealing back the stapler that he had stolen. "He's a good writer. Although I'm not sure if publishing once a decade could really be called a career."

This was her effort, as a friend, to nudge forward what she imagined to be my budding relationship with Roy. It was also a reminder that both of us needed to move beyond working as writer's assistants.

"What's it about?" Roy asked.

"It's about how a family changes after the mother dies."

"It's not autobiographical," Wendy said sarcastically.

"Sounds like fun," Roy said, deadpan.

"It's actually very funny," Wendy said. "Tell him the opening line."

"I'm trying to parody those overdone coming-out novels," I said, feeling that I needed to explain the opening line.

"Just tell him," Wendy ordered.

"'Todd Greco still felt empty inside even with a big cock up his ass,'" I recited. Roy laughed, which I took for his thumbs up.

Amanda returned carrying a spoon and a carton of peach yogurt then stopped at my desk to say, "We have to get Chip a parking pass for the studio lot." Her tone was neutral, informing me that we would pretend that she had never issued an edict that no more parking passes would be given out this season. She briefly glanced at Roy sitting on the couch and then headed back to her office.

Roy stood up, looked at me, and said, "I guess I should probably get going. . . ." He started moving toward the door.

I panicked at the thought of Roy leaving without my having made some arrangement to see him again. It seemed premature to suggest a date, and I knew it would be impossible to initiate a sincere moment of contact in front of the others. I was fumbling through all the possible ways in which I could use Roy's attempt at visiting Joe Benedetti to my own advantage. "Is there a number where Joe can reach you? Would you like to leave a note?" when Joe came barreling out of the head writer's office.

"Hey, Roy!" he exclaimed. Joe gave his cousin a big hug, all hearty patting on the back.

"Have you met everybody?" he asked, taking a stick of gum from the pack on my desk and then swiping another and shoving both in his mouth. In theory, Joe was a television star, but our program's low ratings meant that he usually went unrecognized by most of the general public. Unfortunately that meant Joe confined his egotistical behavior to work, where everyone acknowledged that he was a temperamental television star, never confusing him with being an obnoxious jerk.

"Roy's from Alaska!" Joe announced between chomps. "He lives in an igloo!"

Raising his fist, Roy said, "Wow. Funny. Are you a comedian?"

"You gonna come to the taping?" Joe asked. "You have to come to the taping."

"Of course I'm coming," Roy replied. "Why do you think I'm here?"

"Oh, right," Joe said, "Nelson, put Roy on the guest list for the taping."

"Absolutely," I said, relieved to know that I'd see him again.

Joe wrapped an arm around Roy's shoulder. "C'mon, let's get breakfast."

"Nice to meet you," Roy said to everyone; then he turned to me. "See you there?"

"Absolutely," I repeated.

"Bring some Matanuska Thunder Fuck!" Wendy called out, as Joe ushered him out of the office.

For the rest of the day I couldn't get Roy out of my head, even though I told myself that we would never become boyfriends. He lived in Alaska, for god's sake. Everyone knows that long-distance relationships never work. But he fascinated me, and curiosity drove me with a force that was almost as powerful as sexual attraction. My infatuation with Roy could turn out to be nothing, but Wendy and I had recently seen a revival of *Citizen Kane*. One of the characters is an elderly man who recalls that fifty years earlier he'd been traveling on a ferry and seen a beautiful young woman in a white dress. She didn't see him, but he claimed that for the rest of his life, not a month went by without him thinking of her. So even though Roy lived in Alaska, I wanted to see whether there was something going on between us. I didn't want to end up like that old man, haunted by the thought that Roy might have been the one for me, regret embedded in my heart like a stone point.

TWO

On Friday nights, *Aftertaste* taped in front of a live audience, and during the afternoon rehearsals we were required to be on the set to record any last-minute changes in the script. Jeremy and I were both looking for a snack at the craft services table when Dylan Fabizak slipped onto the set without any fanfare. He was seated in a folding chair, studying his script before we even noticed him. His short blond hair was greasy, and there were dark circles under his eyes. He looked exhausted but, for extraordinarily handsome men, weariness was a temporary disguise, a prince spending a morning as a pauper. His tight-fitting dark blue shirt concealed his powerful body about as effectively as a tea cozy hides the identity of a teapot; the sleeves were rolled up, revealing thick forearms electric with veins. His chest and arms were meadowed with amber waves of grain, and for an instant I imagined his silo standing adjacent to a well-tended field of wheat.

Pretending that I urgently needed to ask the boom operator working near his chair if he'd seen the director—I'd never spoken to the boom guy in the three years we'd both worked on *Aftertaste*—I edged closer to Dylan and could see long soft eyelashes that complemented his heavy beard, clearly marking him as that most desirable of men, a rugged cuddler. He wasn't perfect though; a constellation of acne scars stippled his left jaw, which would detract from mine and everyone else's appearance, but with Dylan's face, he made it plain that, even on his worst day, when he sported a cluster of ready-to-pop zits, he looked better than everyone else did when their complexions were flawless.

At least I tried to stare discreetly. Jeremy kept tossing his eyes toward Dylan as if he were trying to get his attention by throwing pebbles at his bedroom window.

"If you're done," I said, "go back and put in the changes for the first sketch."

"All right." Jeremy angrily snapped together the three rings of his notebook. His tantrum didn't bother me because he did have work to do and because I wanted a few minutes to ogle Dylan privately before Roy arrived. The day after we met, Roy had called for tickets to the show, and I invited him to have dinner with me before the taping. On taping days, a catered meal was provided for the cast and crew, and we regarded it as an opportunity to pig out on Amanda's dime. Roy had needed to check with Joe before giving me an answer. He thought Joe might be expecting to have dinner with him, and he didn't want to seem ungrateful for his hospitality. Fortunately, it turned out that Potato Chip wanted to interview Joe for his story. They had already agreed to have dinner together in Joe's dressing room on the day of the taping.

My lusting after Dylan was clearly a fantasy. For one thing, he was a movie star and I was a production assistant and that's a Cinderella story with a glass ceiling. I was too far beneath Dylan, too insignificant for him to ever notice me. He was also either straight or bi, and I really only wanted to have sex with gay men. The fantasy of having sex with a straight man never appealed to me, because I was a writer and could complete the narrative and knew I'd probably end up cooking and cleaning for him.

While the camera crew finished placing their equipment, Dylan and I glanced at each other a few times, but he concentrated on learning his lines while I tried to look professional by occasionally shuffling the pages of my script.

It was mortifying when Chip Fiss, the reporter, made a beeline toward me as soon as he walked on the set. On Tuesday, we had become chummy after Chip took me to lunch for my interview, but I didn't want to give Dylan the impression that we were friends.

"Have you spoken to him?" whispered Chip as he rolled a barrel of root-beer-flavored hard candy into his mouth.

I shook my head.

"He looks scrumptious," Chip said as the candy clacked against his back teeth. "Maybe he's cleaned up his act." He sounded disappointed. Perhaps it was my Midwestern upbringing, but I always felt uncomfortable when people relished a ruined reputation or the end of a career as if they were witnessing a glorious sunset. A celebrity's arrest for shoplifting and pompous television interviews were fair game, but I couldn't delight in a star's self-destruction without a twinge of superstitious dread.

Chip had conducted our interview at Chin-Chin, a popular Chinese restaurant. (I usually called it "Double Chin" but possessed the common sense not to mention this to the pelican-necked Chip.) I ordered their famous Chinese Chicken Salad, a dish that was as American as French fries, while Chip ate three orders of Szechwan dumplings, which gave me the unpleasant sensation of watching an animal devour its offspring. When Chip ordered me a beer, I didn't protest even though I had to return to work after lunch. Over three bottles of Tsingtao, I heard all about Carl, his "life partner." I couldn't believe that a slob like Chip was getting man-on-man action. My mind involuntarily flashed on his sex life, but after imagining potato chip crumbs in his bed, I ran from the thought, feeling like a traitor to my sexual orientation for believing, at least in this case, that homosexuality was wrong.

Chip told me at the start of every interview, he deliberately irritated his subjects by talking about himself. He had unintentionally discovered that if he droned on about his boring life, his interview victims would change the topic to anything more interesting, no matter how self-damaging it might be.

Chip became a sought-after entertainment reporter after he figured out that stellar levels of resentment were waiting to be tapped in an industry where actors who were paid millions felt exploited and unappreciated. He assumed correctly that I had to be another disgruntled employee since most of the production assistants on films and television programs harbored artistic ambitions. He asked me if I wanted to write then crowed, before I could answer him, that he was the only entertainment reporter in the history of his profession who had never succumbed to a desire to write a novel or screenplay. He maintained that nurturing an artistic ambition is like raising a tiger cub: sensible people get rid of it before it becomes big and dangerous. Under Chip's disarming interrogation, the first beer made me incautious, the second beer made me rash, and the third beer had me spilling my guts about *Aftertaste*. Since Chip picked up the check, I even threw in how Amanda acquired her nickname.

Three days after my interview, the sight of Chip walking onto the soundstage made me cringe at my behavior. We hustled to step aside when a red-haired camerawoman told us to watch out as she moved her camera to the next set. Chip wandered over to the craft services table to see whether there was anything that he could eat. He claimed he was trying to lose weight by switching to less-fattening snacks, but when he didn't find any Fuji apples or his favorite brand of Finnish licorice, he grabbed a vanilla-frosted chocolate chip cookie.

I frisked myself for my pen. Coming up empty-handed, I dropped to the floor to see whether it had fallen.

"Know where I could get a bottle of water?" Dylan asked from above me.

"Um," I stammered after looking up to his crotch. It was gauche to act starstruck and as I stood up, I pretended to be nonchalant, but I still thought it was unfair that I was the one expected to give a performance every time I met a famous actor.

"There's usually water at the craft services table," I said, consciously remembering to raise my arm when I pointed to its location.

"Oh," Dylan sighed as he gazed in that direction. He needed to walk a hundred feet, and the task appeared to be overwhelming to him.

"I could get you a bottle."

"Would you?" he asked, flashing me an ingratiating smile.

"Excuse me, Dylan," Chip said, elbowing his way between us. "Chip Fiss of *Fave* magazine. I wrote the cover story on "Hollywood's Humbled Hotties."

Dylan stared coldly, unimpressed by this credential. "Am I supposed to thank you for putting me on the front cover?" he sneered.

I remembered the infamous cover: Dylan's widely reproduced mug shot for the Bundt cake arrest. What made the photograph startling was that Dylan faced the camera but made no effort to act or pose. It was Dylan's inability or unwillingness to preserve his image, which conveyed, more than his glassy eyes or stubble-covered face, how completely fucked up he must have been.

Chip refused to accept responsibility for the picture's publication. "I didn't choose the photographs for the story," he said. "And, in case you've forgotten, I did write in the article that you are the most talented actor of your generation."

Dylan grudgingly tolerated him, asking, "Were you the guy who wrote that I had an ass that only comes along once every five hundred years?"

Chip batted his eyes with pride before he corrected him, "What I wrote was, 'Dylan Fabizak has the most marble-worthy derriere since Michelangelo's *David*.'"

"I don't know why you're here," Dylan said looming over the much shorter Chip, "but I don't want any more stories done on me."

Chip backpedaled quickly, a sheen of sweat breaking out on his forehead. "You're not the focus of the piece," he said reassuringly. "It's a story about the people and personalities behind a comedy show."

Dylan didn't have a chance to respond because the stage manager asked the cast to take their places. I fetched Dylan's bottle of water, and Chip rolled another candy barrel into his mouth before walking off the set to make a telephone call.

During the next rehearsal break, I approached Dylan and shyly offered him the bottle. I figured that since he had spoken to me first, the glass ceiling that separated Dylan from a writer's assistant had been transformed into a window of opportunity.

"Thanks," he said, brutally wringing the bottle's neck with a twist of his powerful wrist. "Dylan," he said matter-of-factly as he held his right palm up instead of shaking my hand. The pulsing of his Adam's apple as he rapidly chugged the water transfixed me, and I barely managed to say my name before the stage manager shouted, "Rehearsing!" and everyone on the set stopped talking.

Aftertaste's cast gave the director more problems than Dylan did during the first run-throughs of the sketch. The director had to rein in the cast members who wanted to "improve" their sketches by mugging, funny walks, and goofy voices. When the cast members started adding bits of comic business to the script, the writers referred to it as, "putting gravy on beef stew."

One cast member, Nora, kept flubbing a line. "I'm not needy!" came out as a tongue-tied, "I'm not niddy!" And after repeating her mistake twice, she apologized, "Sorry to keep everyone waiting."

"That's okay," Dylan said, "I'm used to doing time." His remark endeared him to everyone on the set—with the visible exception of Nora.

Dylan appeared to be nervous during the first run-through of his sketch, but he nailed the character during the second take. One of the writers had used an idea of mine about dumbing down the classics. It was a brief parody called "Anton Chekhov's Three Stooges." Curly, Larry, and Moe were living in a provincial Russian village. Curly and Larry wanted to convince Moe to sell their cherry orchard and move to Moscow. Dylan, wearing a black wig, played Moe.

"So you wanna go to Moscow, do ya?" Dylan asked, his eyebrows expertly dancing with barely suppressed fury.

"Yeah, Moe, we want to go to Moscow!" Larry said.

"It'll be terrific!" said Joe, who was playing Curly. "Caviar. Champagne. Goils."

"So you want champagne and goils?" asked Moe.

Both of them replied, "Yeah!" followed by several eye-popping exclamations and arm-swinging gestures to indicate their ya-ya-ya lust.

"I'll give ya Moscow!" Dylan sneered as his face exploded with rage and he rapidly two-finger-forked each man in the eyes then slapped their faces in quick succession with satisfying fleshy-sounding whaps.

My cell phone vibrated in my pants pocket, and I checked to see who was calling me. It was Wendy. She had agreed to signal me when Roy arrived at the front gate of the studio. My attention strayed from the rehearsal as my stomach began to gurgle nervously. I was looking forward to seeing Roy again and turned my back on Dylan to focus on the door to the soundstage.

Wendy and Roy were laughing about something when they walked onto the set. He grinned broadly when he saw me, which made me feel slightly less anxious. Wendy scowled when she saw me, which didn't affect my mood in the least.

"I'll take over," she groused as she slipped the clipboard from my hands.

"Thanks for arranging this," Roy said.

"Roy brought pot," Wendy whispered to me.

"Matanuska Thunder Fuck?" I asked in a voice that carried further than I'd intended.

"Why not tell everyone?" Wendy dipped her head to the left and her eyes shifted in the same direction, indicating that Dylan was standing nearby. Dylan had been reading over his lines, but upon hearing the name of the Alaskan marijuana his eyes narrowed suspiciously as he turned toward us. I assumed that he thought we were gossiping about him, but he didn't appear to be angry when he walked over to us.

"Did I hear someone mention 'Matanuska Thunder Fuck?'" he asked.

After a swift conference with our eyes, Wendy was appointed the spokesperson for the group. "Yeah, this big mouth," she said waving her arm toward me.

"Any chance I can get in on that?"

"Sure!" Wendy said in the overly chipper voice that was part of her arsenal of mockery. "We always provide drugs to the special guests. You want a hooker, too?"

"Yeah," Dylan said, playing along.

"Good girl gone bad?" Wendy said sounding like a waitress taking an order. "She's putting herself through medical school, but she should have a dark side and like getting nasty."

"But she has a heart of gold," Dylan said.

"And tits of plastic," Wendy said. "Let me get right on that."

She handed me back the clipboard and asked me to wait for a minute while she ran to the bathroom. Dylan didn't appear to be in a hurry to leave us, but I was intimidated by his beauty and couldn't think of anything sensible to say.

"How do you know about Matanuska Thunder Fuck?" Roy asked.

"I met a guy from Alaska in prison."

"Roy's from Alaska," I said, hitching my thumb toward him.

"I might make a film up there this summer," Dylan said, looking at Roy with newfound interest.

"What's it about?" Roy asked.

Dylan thought for minute. "A fisherman's life in a small town."

"I fish," Roy said.

"Really? I'd play a fisherman."

The two of them eyed each other warily as the director came over to say a few words to Dylan. Afterward Dylan excused himself and took his place on the set.

"Where do you fish?" I asked Roy.

"Coffee Point. It's on Bristol Bay, across the river from a village called Egegik." He pronounced it as Iggy-gick.

"That's on the Bering Sea," I said sounding like a contestant on a quiz show. I'd assumed that Roy fished near Anchorage. Suddenly a relationship with him seemed to be more implausible. He was on an ice floe drifting hundreds of miles further away from me.

Roy appeared to be pleased. "Down here, most people have never heard of Bristol Bay."

"I'm good at geography," I said, mentally wincing at the sound of my own words. I wanted to impress him with my intelligence, but I also didn't want to come off as a spelling bee champion: L-O-S-E-R.

"Are you a map queen?" Roy asked.

I was still unsure of the process of becoming a queen. Was it a gradual change, or one day would I wake up to find myself metamorphosed into a huge queen? Kafka's Gregor Samsa with a lisp, wearing too much cologne and jewelry, bearing an unnatural fondness for tragic chanteuses and small annoying dogs. I had never thought of myself as a queen of any kind but reluctantly accepted that the description of map queen was accurate.

"I guess I am," I said.

"I like map queens," he said, mollifying me somewhat. "My friend Lloyd reads topographical maps like other guys read porn."

"That could be me," I said. "Something's not right when unfolding a map is more exciting than opening a centerfold."

"I don't know," Roy said. "I think that's exactly the right attitude to have."

He smiled, and it occurred to me that I had passed his geography test.

"Quiet, please," the stage manager yelled a moment before the rehearsal began again. Roy became absorbed in watching the crew bustling around us. I recalled my initial fascination with the windowless subterranean world of a television soundstage. H. G. Wells's novel *The Time Machine* hadn't predicted the future of London; it had predicted the future of Los Angeles. In the artificially lit darkness, crafty Morlocks labored to create shows for simpleminded Eloi audiences. Unfortunately, just like in the novel, the Eloi didn't even realize that monsters were preying upon them.

We watched several run-throughs of the sketch until Roy began to understand that watching good television being made was duller than watching bad television. I saw enough to see that Dylan had a genuine knack for comedy. In his second sketch, "Serf and Turf," Dylan masterfully played a man named Ted who's having dinner with his wife and twelve-year-old son at an authentic medieval banqueting hall. Expecting a lighthearted theme restaurant, they're shocked to discover how authentically medieval it really is. Dylan is disturbed when hungry street urchins fight for scraps as the hunchbacked busboy empties trenchers onto the floor. The toothless crone of a hostess casually stomps on a live rat and the surly waiter recommends the special of the day: Pig Snouts in Honey. Dylan calms his wife who's anxious to leave when the restroom turns out to be a slop jar, and they're splattered with blood when a kitchen wench slaughters chickens at the next table. After being prevented from leaving because of an imposed quarantine—Table Six is dead from the plague—Dylan's wife uses her cell phone to call for help. A waiter cries out, "The witch speaks into a silver clam. To her Dark Lord and Master, Satan!! No witch shall live!" Dylan springs to his wife's defense as she's tied to the stake and a pyre is built. "She's not a witch! She's a good mother, a wonderful wife, and a considerate customer. She always tips generously!" His wife adds, "Yes! I always leave ten percent!" The restaurant's staff becomes enraged and shouts, "Ten Percent?!! Kill the tithing-tipping witch!!" The headwaiter orders armed guards to seize Dylan and his son. They're offered a choice, "If you give allegiance to this devil's strumpet, then you'll be burned as witches, too!" Dylan glances at his son. The sketch closes with them joining the mob in shouting, "Burn her!"

Dylan made us laugh, but he earned the highest accolade on the show because he also made the normally stolid crew laugh. The writers always maintained that the crew never laughed at anything.

Wendy returned to the set, carrying a bottle of water and a banana. She said to Roy, "I would've brought you something, but I wasn't sure what you wanted." She gave me a look that prompted me to offer to run and get something for Roy. After taking his order, I left him with Wendy who began to regale him with horror stories about previous special guest stars on the show.

In one corner of the soundstage was a long table covered with a gross amount of candy, potato chips, and other forms of crap. (Chocolate-covered pretzels seemed to have been created by a mad dietician, a Dr. Frankenfood, determined to unnaturally unite sweet and salty snacks.) It was almost as if the production of a television show required ingesting the same amount of unhealthy junk foods that audiences gobbled down while watching television at home. Yogurt and fresh fruit were offered but overall the ratio of healthy to fattening corresponded to a maraschino cherry on a hot fudge sundae.

Joe was helping himself to a cup of coffee when he spotted me.

"So you're having dinner with Roy," he observed leeringly as I selected Roy's banana. "You'd better watch out, Nelson. If you're not careful, you might end up a mail-order bride. Roy's determined to remain in Alaska, but he says the boyfriend pickings are slim up there. So he's going to import one."

"Really?" I said, feeling that Roy's interest in me had lost some of its luster. I didn't want to think that I was his first choice because I was his only choice. I had assumed that Roy felt the same mysterious connection between us when we had discussed the harpoon points, but he probably became excited because he thought my interest in Alaska demonstrated a willingness to consider moving there.

"He's going to Boston next month for a wedding," Joe said as he grabbed a handful of tortilla chips. "If you don't work out, he'll probably grab someone there."

"Is he that set on staying there?" I asked, thinking sadly that our relationship was going nowhere, which appeared to be an actual location equidistant between Los Angeles and Alaska.

"He's hard core. He loves Alaska. He's pissed that I've never visited. He said that when he returns home from a trip, he always thinks, 'I can't believe I get to live somewhere people dream of visiting all their lives.' So if you're thinking about dating him, you'd better buy a pair of snowshoes."

Joe rushed off because he needed to change into his costume for the next sketch. I walked back to the set, convinced now that our chances of becoming boyfriends were nonexistent. What would I do in Alaska? I was having trouble finishing my novel in Los Angeles but suddenly the blank pages appeared to be snow-covered as I tried to imagine writing in Alaska.

When I returned to the set, Roy thanked me as I handed him his banana and bottle of water. An unexpected rush of optimism allowed me to push aside my doubts and tell myself that anything could happen. It wouldn't be awful if Roy and I became friends, the second runner-up position in the Mr. Right pageant.

"Go to dinner," Wendy suggested when the rehearsal resumed. "You can watch this later during the taping."

"You hungry?" I asked Roy.

"Always," he said, smiling.

I told Roy that I needed to stop by the office to check my messages and glance at e-mail before we went to dinner. I was planning on neglecting my job that day but I was conscientious about appearing to have a work ethic. My preferred form of white-collar crime was stealing time from my job because, like slipping a watch into a pocket, it was easy to conceal. During working hours, I covertly made phone calls to friends and family, checked my e-mail frequently, and used the photocopiers to print everything from party invitations to resumes for more exciting jobs that still paid nothing.

While walking down a narrow hallway to the exit, Roy glanced suspiciously at me, before putting on an expression of mock outrage. "Are you following me?" he asked, repeatedly looking over his shoulder while he walked faster. I increased my pace to keep up with him. He hurried to an exit and quickly closed the door behind him. Once we were outside on the lot, he raced to get away from me. Walking briskly ahead of me in the alleyway, he constantly jerked his head back in my direction to see whether I was gaining on him. I found myself pulled into his joke, charmed by his earnestness, impressed that he managed to pull off acting silly with beguiling conviction. He kept up the ruse until we reached the production office building.

The office was on the second floor, and as I headed toward the stairs, Roy suggested that we take the elevator. It sounded odd because

I already thought of Roy as the robust type—a throwback to the frontier, when men didn't need to exercise because in the course of a busy day they bounded up gangplanks, forded rivers, and climbed stairs.

After the doors closed, Roy flicked a switch to stop the elevator, grabbed my shoulders, and kissed me. I was surprised but tried to act cool and respond with a calm ardor as if I'd been expecting his kiss for days. I wanted him to think that I was a sexy stud and kissed handsome men in elevators all the time, although my beating heart sounded like it was trying to tell him otherwise. My first rational thought was a feeling of elation that I hadn't misinterpreted the signals that he liked me. Our kiss was passionate, a long-term commitment of more than ten minutes, a sign that he wanted to get to know me better and was beginning the process by exploring the inside of my mouth. My second thought was a feeling of relief that Roy was a good kisser. Kissing a man seemed to tell me everything I needed to know about him: Roy was gentle, passionate, strong, loving, playful, and brushed and flossed regularly. My third thought was the crotch tingling realization that we were going to have sex because I'd discovered that most of the time, at least with gay men, if you make it to first base, you've scored. Roy tasted slightly salty as if working as a fisherman had imbued him with brine. His beard was rougher than it appeared, and I enjoyed the sensation that my head was a match being struck repeatedly against his face. I briefly wondered whether my breath smelled bad but could still taste an extra-strong breath mint from a half an hour ago. My worries faded away the longer we kissed. It never failed to astound me that someone whom I didn't know—and who didn't know me—could make me so happy merely by pressing his lips against mine.

Roy had me backed up against the rear of the elevator, but after a few minutes of being the recipient of his kiss, I decided that I should make an effort to take the lead. I slowly maneuvered him against the wall. In the turnabout, Roy accidentally patted my crunchy jelled hair, and we both snickered, as if the revelation that I used hair care products was the first of many intimacies we would share. Our reverie was completely broken after we heard an elevator cable creak and we pulled away from each other to listen. Was someone waiting for the elevator, the only elevator in the building?

Roy threw the switch and, as the car came to a stop on the second floor, we impulsively kissed again and were lip-locked when the doors opened, revealing Amanda impatiently tapping a pen against a script. Waiting for the elevator had turned her face into a fencing mask, expressionless and ready for combat. During her pregnancy, Amanda had become an easy-to-topple fertility figure, and she had been compelled to use the building's sluggish elevator. She hated waiting for elevators because she resented any form of transportation where she couldn't travel first-class or order the driver to step on it.

"I was kept waiting for this?" she asked shrilly.

"Sorry," I offered feebly as we scurried out of the elevator. I was embarrassed that she had caught us kissing but also couldn't help feeling proud that she had caught me making out with a very handsome guy.

"That's helpful," Amanda mocked as she stepped inside the elevator. Her mouth opened as if she was about to say something else when a puzzled look crossed her face. The elevator doors closed before she could speak again.

"That's not good," I muttered, trying to guess how and when she would punish me for making her wait. Paradoxically for someone so impatient, Amanda could wait weeks for the right moment to bring up the subject again, preferably in a large group to maximize my embarrassment.

Roy looked shaken by our encounter with Amanda.

"I'm sorry," he said, "I didn't think we'd get caught by your boss."

"Don't worry about it," I said, surprised to find that I wasn't afraid of the consequences of kissing on company time but was more upset that the moment had been spoiled.

Roy shook his head back and forth slowly. "Dude, you're on her shit list."

I imagined a stationery pad with Amanda's Shit List embossed across the top of the page and my name handwritten in block letters below. And I'm ashamed to admit that I'd lived in Hollywood long enough to wonder whether having my name at the top or bottom of the list was better placement.

"I don't care," I said defiantly. "I don't plan on being here forever." As the words came out of my mouth, I understood that I was making a vow. I was determined to make this my last season working as a writer's assistant.

Jeremy was in the office working on his computer when we stopped at my desk to see whether I had any messages. There was an e-mail from my brother reminding me that our father's birthday was in two weeks. I jotted down, "Dad's birthday" on a blue adhesive note pad, peeled it off, and pasted it next to the other notes attached to the edge of my computer screen. Over the course of a typical week, my computer bloomed with blue petals—an overgrown, artificial forget-me-not.

I quickly tried to hurry Roy out of the office when Jeremy began another lecture about animal rights. He had recently launched a one-man campaign to convince local drag queens to forego wearing artificial leopard, tiger, and zebra skin fabrics. "It's a form of exploitation." Ditto for feather boas and beehive wigs. "Beehives are technically manmade," admitted Jeremy, "but they're symbols of their slavery." And he wouldn't be caught dead in a pair of fishnet stockings. He released us after we promised to read his self-published brochure entitled "Green Queens."

Outside on the studio lot, walking alongside Roy, the misty air felt clammy against my face. The sun shone through a lingering layer of fog, and the hazy light seemed to be a camera trick designed to make the city appear prettier and softer than it really was. I suddenly envied Roy's unabashedly patriotic attachment to Alaska, because my love of Los Angeles was indivisible from what I loathed about the city. Of course, I praised the balmy California climate that made farmers boast that it was possible to grow anything from artichokes to sequoias. But the Golden State's bounty reproached languishing as a writer's assistant while millions of other transplants flourished. It was a fallacy to think of Los Angeles as a la-la land because the city was inhabited by hard-driving, practical men and women with the plain common sense to think that if two heads were better than one, then why not have two faces?

Turning the corner of a soundstage, we ran into Dylan who appeared to be lost.

"Where are they serving dinner?" he asked.

"We're headed that way, if you want to follow us," Roy said.

Of course I was thrilled that Roy had asked Dylan to join us. Is there a gay man who doesn't want to be seen in the company of two total hotties? But as much as I liked their handsome faces, they also fascinated me. Dylan was a talented artist—two words that always excited me—and Roy saw the world through an artist's eyes. They seemed to embody my most romantic desire: after we had amazing sex, I'd be burning to talk to them.

Dylan walked beside us, not saying anything until I complimented him on his performances. Then he perked up and thanked me. "I give most of the credit to the wigs," Dylan said modestly. It was the first time I had ever walked with a movie star. It was fascinating to observe how people stared when they recognized him. He deflected their attention by keeping his eyes unfocused like a blind man's. As we passed by soundstage #23, Dylan pointed toward it.

"When I was a kid," he said, "I worked on my first film in that building with Marilyn Quattrini."

Marilyn Quattrini had been a talented comic actress and notorious party gal who made a handful of films in the early '80s. She'd died tragically in a golf cart accident and, after the publication of a best-selling tell-all biography, had become a cult icon—her name a byword for drinking, drugging, and eighteen-hole fatalities.

"One day, after we finished shooting," Dylan said, "I saw her walking back to her trailer with a slice of pizza in one hand and a glass of vodka in the other. When she reached her trailer, she realized that her hands were full and couldn't open the door. Instead of setting down her drink, she took the slice, wrapped it around the door handle and turned it."

"Now that's a real drinker," Roy said.

"It's *Sophie's Choice* for the boozy," I declared. "Which do I spare? My heart or my liver?"

"How much do you want to bet that she ate the slice once she got inside?" Dylan asked.

"She probably dunked it in her drink to kill any germs," I claimed, which made Dylan laugh.

We continued walking when Dylan suddenly asked, "So you have some pot?"

Roy glanced at me, passing the buck with his eyes. I considered lying but said impishly, "Maybe. . . ."

"Well," Dylan said, "I wouldn't mind, if anyone decides to . . . you know, I just want to put the word out . . . in case . . . if someone wants to . . . I'd be interested." Dylan poked around the subject of drugs as if his tongue were a needle trying to find a vein.

Neither of us spoke up. I waited for Roy to say something, and he later admitted that he had expected me to say something. The inherent conviction that we could depend upon on each other to save us from making a stupid mistake was, more than even our physical attraction, a sign that we were destined to become boyfriends.

Dylan asked Roy, "Does Alaskan weed grow extra large like those hundred-pound cabbages in the midnight sun?"

"Not to my knowledge," Roy replied. "I've never seen thirty-foot pot plants exhibited at the State Fair."

"We could smoke a joint in my trailer," Dylan suggested.

Roy shifted uncomfortably, and I sensed that he wanted to say something. He glanced at me, his eyes signaling his intention to speak but not seeking my permission. "Don't take this the wrong way," he said, "but should you be smoking pot?"

"Should any of us?" Dylan asked, as he pulled at the collar on his shirt drawing attention to his thick neck. His grin had the chilling effect of a wolf baring its capped teeth.

Dylan moved between us and draped his heavy arms over our shoulders while we walked. He started to knead the flesh on my right shoulder, which wasn't painful but wasn't relaxing. It was an invitation—you scratch my back and I'll scratch yours—and also a form of intimidation—watch your back.

Dylan's voice became seductive, "C'mon, how often will you have a chance to get high with a movie star?" We both received another affectionate squeeze.

"You're pushing it," Roy said, but Dylan just chuckled.

The hand resting on my shoulder almost felt reassuring and although I knew it was reckless, I wanted to get high with Dylan. When I was a boy and got in trouble with a friend, my mother would ask, "If a friend asked you to jump over Niagara Falls would you?" I would shrug and say, "No" because I was too young to answer her with a question of my own, "Is the friend hot?" It was a crucial detail because beauty impaired my judgment. While I believed that a writer should be an authority on life, a witness to human joys and sorrows, Dylan's face and body made it hard to distinguish between gathering life experience, essential for a writer's work, and stupid blundering.

"Maybe you should wait until after the taping?" Roy cautioned.

"Wait a minute," Dylan said indignantly. "I don't want to get fucked up. I just want to stay loose."

Roy looked at me as I tried to make up my mind. I decided that smoking one joint wouldn't undermine the show. On some level, Roy's concern struck me as a case of the pothead calling the kettle a bong. I was impressed that we were going to get high with a famous movie star and thought that deep down Roy also had to find it exciting. I wanted to show Roy that life in Hollywood could be as adventurous as life in Alaska. I had moved on from daydreaming about moving to Alaska; my new fantasy was that I would make Roy want to move to L.A.

"All right," I said, "let's go to your trailer."

"You're sure about this?" Roy asked softly.

I shrugged slightly and nodded. I felt anxious but I was tired of playing it safe as a writer's assistant. If I was ever going to get a boyfriend and become a writer, I needed to take a few risks.

"Oh, he's sure!" Dylan said jubilantly. We walked back toward the soundstage and he released his grip on my shoulder only seconds before opening the door to his trailer.

THREE

D ylan announced himself as a neat freak when he set down his
scripts in the trailer. He carefully placed them so they lined up
precisely at a ninety-degree angle to the corner edges of the counter.
Dylan saw us staring and explained, "When you live in a prison cell,
you can't afford to be sloppy." He told us to take a seat at the kitchen
table. Underneath a newspaper on the banquette, he was disgusted to
find a neatly folded pair of white boxer briefs and a still sweat-soaked
tank top. "Sorry about that," he said as he shoved them into a gym
bag. No apology was necessary I thought as I idly wondered what
Dylan's used briefs might bring on eBay, then dismissed the thought
as pervy. I slid across the banquette and Roy sat down next to me.

Dylan removed an appointment book and a large unopened fruit basket from the tabletop. Hanging off a hook on the bathroom door was a dry cleaning bag holding two dark blue shirts. Dylan asked me to hand him the script sitting in front of me. I read the title, "Violet Cryderman." Sitting next to an ashtray and a pack of cigarettes, I was surprised to see a brand-new paperback of J. R. Ackerley's *My Father and Myself.*

It was a wonderful book, but I never expected Dylan to be reading it for two reasons. First of all, he didn't strike me as a reader. I'll admit that I was prejudiced, but generally men with great chests don't use them as a bookrest when they're in bed. Secondly, it was also the unapologetic memoir of a gay man who discovered that his father probably had a homosexual relationship when he had been a guardsman in the British army. The book made me think that Dylan must be gay. When heterosexual men curl up with a book about a man who saw some action in the military, most of them would prefer not to learn that it had been romping with a sugar daddy.

"Are you reading this?" I asked, pointing toward the book, curious to know what Dylan thought of it.

"Yeah," he said, as he cleared a seat for himself on the other banquette by removing his gym bag. "The prison librarian recommended it because I'm thinking about writing about my father." Dylan walked to the other end of the trailer. "I don't know exactly what I'm going to write about him," he added as he placed the bag on the bed. "But I'm thinking about it."

I was ridiculously romantic about books, and seeing that Dylan owned a relatively obscure memoir that I revered immediately suggested that we were soulmates. It was confusing because I also believed that Roy was my soulmate since he shared my love of the harpoon point story. My soul appeared to be a bit of a slut, hooking up with a frequency that would make a call girl blush.

"What do you think of it?" I asked, thinking that I might be able to determine Dylan's sexual orientation by getting him to discuss the book.

"It's a twisted story, but I like it," Dylan said. "The father's a trip. It just goes to show you. You never know who might be gay."

I couldn't tell if Dylan was trying to be coy about his sexuality. He sounded unconcerned as if the subject didn't really interest him. I wished Wendy were there because she would have bluntly asked, "Speaking of that, are you a homo?" I hadn't read the book in years but expressed my admiration for a scene where the father remains unexpectedly composed when Ackerley brings home a male friend for dinner and the friend is wearing mascara.

"Don't ruin it for me," Dylan warned. "I'm not that far yet."

Having been forbidden to talk about the book further, I was vexed that the subject of his sexual orientation had been snapped shut.

Dylan opened the refrigerator and took out a bottle of water for himself.

"You want something to drink?" he asked, holding the door open to allow us to see the selection of beverages. "There's water, sodas, and I brought beer. I knew they wouldn't stock any alcohol for the addict. I don't know why people think if you're addicted to one drug, you're addicted to all of them."

"Most addicts aren't picky," Roy said matter-of-factly.

Dylan glared at Roy for a second but then appeared to force himself to smile.

"You're a hard-ass," Dylan said.

"My first boyfriend drank," he said without apology as he took a can of beer and opened it.

"What about you, Harrison?" Dylan said as he waved his hand toward the drinks.

"It's Nelson," Roy corrected, which prompted an apology from Dylan. I tried to cover my embarrassment and reassert my dignity by choosing a diet soda, feeling virtuous for having some self-control, refraining from drinking alcohol during working hours, limiting myself to smoking pot.

"C'mon, Alaska," Dylan said to Roy as he took the seat opposite us. "Where's that Man-fuck pot?"

Roy removed a drawstring leather pouch from an inside jacket pocket. The pouch contained an intricately carved wooden pipe in the shape of a whale and a small, gray 35-millimeter plastic film container.

"Sweet pipe," Dylan observed.

"I bought it in Vancouver," Roy said while filling its bowl. "It's wooden so it passes through airport security."

Dylan smiled at Roy. "Well, the next time I fly with drugs I'll have to remember that." Then he winked at me.

"Sorry, dude," Roy said sheepishly, which made Dylan laugh.

"That's all right," he said, handing him his cigarette lighter. "I should have known I'd be searched that day. Drug-sniffing dogs bark when they see my photograph."

Roy lit the pipe, took a hit, and then passed it to Dylan. I rarely smoked marijuana and when it was my turn, I coughed violently, the smoke leaving my lungs like rocket exhaust, throwing me back against the banquette.

"Take it in slowly," Roy cautioned.

The phrase hung in the air and we looked at each other wordlessly and then began to laugh.

The next time I coughed, Roy teased, "You're wasting good pot!"

"I could get high off what you're not using," Dylan added. "I should put my mouth over yours and inhale." He grinned at me, and I was relieved that another round of coughing covered my flattered blushing.

The pipe was passed around again until it burned out. Roy pulled out his lighter and Dylan cupped his hands around the bowl to shelter the flame. Watching them, I became absorbed in how intimate they looked. It occurred to me that it wasn't necessary for Dylan to shield the flame; it wasn't as if gale-force winds were blowing inside the trailer. He seemed to want to get closer to Roy. Then I remembered that Dylan had winked at me. A wink is flirtatious. It's practically saying, just imagine me shutting both of my eyes when we sleep together. Then I looked at Dylan again and thought that perhaps his focus was actually on the marijuana. Perhaps the pot was making me paranoid.

"If I take this part," Dylan said to Roy, nodding his head in the direction of the script lying on the counter, "I'd like to ask you a few questions about fishing."

"Now?" Roy asked doubtfully.

"Why not?" he said, before taking a deep hit off the pipe. When Dylan inhaled, it looked as if the buttons on his shirt were going to pop off, which was an incentive to keep smoking.

"Are you out on your boat all winter?" Dylan asked.

"I don't use a boat, and I don't fish all year. The season for sockeyes is in June and July. I use a set-net. I fish from shore."

"That's what my character does! I wasn't exactly sure what a set-net is."

"You hang a net off the shore—it sits in the water or sets—sets, I guess." Roy was at first perplexed and then amused by his last remark, which let me see that he was high. "The fish are swimming toward the river and they get caught in the net. Then you go out in a small boat—I use an inflatable raft—and you pick the fish out of the net."

"I'd like to see how that works."

"Well, if you're out on the Bering Sea and stop in Egegik this summer, look me up."

"You'd let me come out and fish?"

Roy was taken aback when he realized that Dylan was serious. "I'd have to think about it."

"I'd drive out. I like to research my parts."

"You can't drive out. You fly out. You have to take two planes."

"If you let me come out there, I'll bring pot for you and all of your friends."

Roy chuckled. "Well, that might be expensive. Alaskans like their pot."

"What do you do the rest of the year? Besides working out."

Dylan glanced down at Roy's chest, but he did it without leering. I couldn't tell if he was hinting that he'd like to get his hands on it or just doing that straight guy thing where it's okay to compliment another man's body if it can be received as a high-five instead of copping a feel.

"I'm in school—studying archaeology."

"How'd you become interested in that?" I asked.

"There's an archaeological site on my family's island," Roy replied. "When I was ten, my parents were digging a foundation for a new house when they discovered some old house pits. My mom's a teacher, and she arranged for a dig to be conducted. That summer I worked with the archaeologists and became obsessed. That was all my mom needed. She loaded me up with every book on the subject."

"Wait a minute, back up," Dylan said. "Your family owns an island?"

"Part of a small island. We have the only private inholding. The government owns the rest of it."

"I thought you were an unspoiled backwoods boy," he said. "Now I discover you're the country squire."

Roy scoffed at his description.

"Hardly," he said. "My dad's a fisherman and my mom was a schoolteacher. My grandparents homesteaded the island back in the thirties. We really only use it during the summers."

"I thought your mom fished," I said.

"She's retired from teaching but she still fishes."

"What about your dad?" I said noticing that he hadn't said much about him. I'd observed that most people favored telling either mom or dad anecdotes. It almost seemed to be an inherent trait like being right- or left-handed. I was a dad man myself, because after my mother's death I'd become extremely close to him.

"My parents are divorced," Roy said, his voice becoming grave. "I don't see my dad that much. We're not that tight."

"I hear ya," Dylan said to Roy. "My old man's a prick."

I suddenly felt that having a likeable father was somehow shameful.

"Is it because you're gay?" I asked Roy, wondering whether an occupational hazard of being a fisherman might be believing that you're Jesus Christ.

"I wish," Roy said. "But my brother Pete's straight and he's not close to him either. I've tried with my dad. His life revolves around fishing. Sometimes I think we had our season with him."

Losing your parents while they were alive almost seemed to be a more devastating loss than having them die.

"Did you do much research before you played Leon Cardenas?" Roy asked. Before Dylan was busted, his last performance was playing

Leon Cardenas, a charming, psychotic drug dealer in the film *Shooting*. In one horrific scene, he killed a chef with a food processor.

"I researched drug dealers," Dylan said as he relit the pipe. "It was the first time I'd ever tried coke or crystal meth." He smiled grimly. "That was a mistake."

"That part made you famous," I said, mortified for sounding like a fan.

"Not famous," Dylan said, shaking his head. "I went from being an unknown actor to being recognized and confused with other actors named Dylan."

"I remember you in that made-for-TV movie," Roy said, "where you played that shot-putter."

"Shhhh," Dylan said, putting his finger to his lips. "We don't talk about that."

Roy and I simultaneously quoted a widely ridiculed line of stuttering dialogue from the film—"M-m-my homework's finished!"— which caused us to laugh hysterically.

"Like I haven't heard that one," Dylan said mildly before taking another hit off the pipe.

"Now you can play all sorts of criminals," I said chuckling. "You've researched jail."

The two of them looked at me strangely.

"You all right?" Roy asked. His face generously signaled that he was willing to be embarrassed for me if I was incapable of doing it for myself.

"Nelson's fried," Dylan declared.

My face grew warm. Dylan had alluded to his prison sentence in conversation, but he hadn't spoken about it directly. And here I was joking about it. I was concerned that I'd hurt his feelings. Though I didn't consider that he'd spent almost a year in jail; an ex-con was probably tough enough to handle a little ribbing.

"I shouldn't have brought that up," I said, feeling humiliated.

"Why not?" Dylan asked. "Everyone else does. I never really understood the power of fame until a police officer asked me to sign an autograph while I was handcuffed. He had to unlock them before I could sign it, and as soon as he did, all of the other cops asked for autographs, too."

"At least he didn't ask you to sign your mug shot," I said.

"Or ask me to pose for it with them," Dylan said as he took another hit off the pipe.

"How'd they treat you in there?" Roy asked as he opened another beer.

Dylan suggested smoking another bowl before answering him. "The inmates teased me all the time, but it was never a problem. Whenever we watched television, they'd always ask me if I knew the performers. It didn't matter whether the show was in black and white. They'd point to Marlene Dietrich and ask, 'You ever work with that skinny bitch?'"

Dylan picked up his water bottle and took a swig.

"I broke a guy's arm in there after he stole my drugs," he said as he took another hit off the pipe. Dylan incarcerated the smoke in his lungs and didn't parole it until long after Roy and I had taken hits. "I wouldn't have made it in there if I couldn't have gotten high. My boyfriend could always get something."

My eyes widened at his confession that he was gay. This was hearing it from the horse's mouth. I couldn't wait to tell Jeremy.

"Fooled you," Dylan said. "C'mon, you think I'd tell you that I'm gay?"

"Straight guys wouldn't joke about it," Roy said shrewdly.

"Yeah, but I'm an actor," he said.

"Which is another way of saying that you're a professional liar," I said.

"It should be against the law for an actor to tell a lie offstage," Roy said, "in the same way professional boxers can't fight outside the ring."

Dylan got up from his seat and walked over to the fruit basket and tore open the cellophane covering. He picked through the items until he found a jar of cashews.

"I'm not just a good liar," Dylan boasted, "I'm a perfect liar." He opened the jar, taking a handful of nuts before setting it on the table. "Do you know how to tell a perfect lie? The secret is to always tailor your lies to other people's flaws."

"What do you mean?" Roy asked.

"Well, last week," he said while eating the nuts, one at a time, "I blew off dinner with my friend Mark. I didn't even call to cancel. The next day I called to apologize, but I couldn't tell him the truth—that sometimes he bums me out. So I tried to think of a lie that he'd believe. Well, Mark's a whore. He sleeps with anyone. So I told him, 'I'm sorry. I should have called but I met this hot chick and. . . .' Before I could say another word, he said, 'Don't apologize! If it had been me, I'd have done the same thing. Where'd you meet her?' It's almost foolproof. If a friend of mine's materialistic or greedy, I'll tell him a lie that involves money, like: 'Sorry, my car broke down and the repairs are gonna cost me a thousand dollars.' If a friend of mine's fat, I'll use food as an excuse. 'Sorry, I missed your show. My agent took me to Spago for dinner and he insisted that we stay for dessert.' Trust me, fatso will say, 'Oh, that's all right. Did you have their plum tart?' It works every time."

There was a loud knock on the door of the trailer. We immediately froze and stopped talking. Dylan looked confused.

"Dylan, its Amanda. I'm sorry to disturb you."

We waited for Dylan to respond. He stalled for time by shouting, "I'm getting dressed!" as he pointed to the bathroom. We managed to move quietly inside and closed the door behind us.

"Can I meet you down on the set?" Dylan yelled back to Amanda.

"I'm not going to scream through the door," she said. "I need to talk to you right now. I've gone into labor and I won't be here for the taping."

"All right," Dylan said, "give me a second."

We heard a squeaking noise from the back of the trailer as Dylan opened a window to let in some fresh air.

"It will just take a minute," Amanda said pleasantly. The handle of the door clicked and Dylan's footsteps could be heard scrambling to prevent her from entering.

"Oh!" she cried out.

"I got you!" Dylan shouted before a moment of breathless silence. "Are you all right?" he asked.

"Yes," she stammered. "That step is steeper than I thought."

"Sit down," Dylan said.

"What's that smell?" she asked. "Are you smoking pot?"

"It's incense."

"Don't lie to me!" she snarled. "We're taping in two hours!"

Roy and I were pressed against each other—his back felt amazingly solid—and I became aroused. Moving backward to adjust myself, I knocked a tube of toothpaste to the floor, causing a soft plop.

"Who's in there?" Amanda screamed.

"My cat," Dylan said calmly. "I closed the door because I know pregnant women aren't supposed to be around litter boxes."

In my opinion, he sounded like a perfect liar. But Amanda wasn't buying it.

"Give me a fucking break," she said. Amanda banged on the door with her fists, startling us, causing Roy to jump and knock over a bottle of mouthwash.

"Whoever's in there," she said addressing us, "you're breaking the law, and I'm going to call the police."

After we stepped out of the bathroom, Amanda moaned, "Nelson?" She clutched her stomach with both hands. It took me a moment to understand that her pain was due to a contraction and that I wasn't the cause of it. She walked over to the banquette and sat down. "What's with you today?" she asked as she tried to find a comfortable position on the seat. "First, I find you sucking face in the elevator, and now you're getting stoned in the guest star's dressing room. You're too old to be having a second freshman year."

She finally seemed to give up trying to sit in a ladylike manner and let herself slouch. Her face was pale, and her nose and forehead were shiny with perspiration. She looked nauseated.

"I'm really disappointed in you," she said with a pained expression.

She did appear to be genuinely hurt by my behavior. I hadn't expected that reaction from her and felt deeply ashamed.

"You owe me an explanation," she demanded.

I couldn't tell her that I wanted to impress Roy with how exciting life in Los Angeles could be. The alternative explanation, that I wanted to hang out with a hottie movie star, was equally unpalatable. I chose to sound stupid instead of appearing shallow. "I don't know," I said. "I just got carried away."

"Who the hell are you?" she asked Roy.

"Roy Briggs. I'm Joe's cousin."

He actually stepped forward to offer her his hand but withdrew it after he saw her contemptuous response, shaking her head back and forth.

"Goddammit," Amanda said as she glared at her swollen belly. She sounded frustrated that she couldn't order her assistant to postpone meeting her son until tomorrow. "Can you even do the show?" she asked Dylan, while grimacing from another contraction.

"Yes."

"I don't have a choice," she said. "Get whatever you need from here right now. You're going to the set. You're not leaving there for the next two hours. A security guard will be watching you the entire time. Even if you have to take a piss!"

Amanda picked up an unopened bottle of water from the table, stared at it as if the thought of drinking it disgusted her, then set it down again.

"I asked them to come here," Dylan said.

"Yes," she snapped, "And they could have said, 'No.'"

I was impressed that Dylan was willing to take the blame for us when there was a knock on the door. Amanda lifted a slat on the closed blinds and peered out the window. "Shit," she said. "It's Chip." She didn't say another word as she tried to decide what to do. I glanced at Roy who raised his eyebrows.

"Do you think he's going to want to write about this?" Roy whispered to Amanda.

"He's not going to find out!" she said through gritted teeth.

"I know," Roy said sadly, "but these things have a way of getting out."

It shocked and gratified me when Roy spoke up, and I waited to see what Amanda's reaction would be. She certainly didn't want it revealed that Dylan got high before taping her show. It would call her judgment into question for being the first person to hire him after he'd been released from prison.

She rubbed her stomach but remained silent. The knock on the door was more persistent the third time.

"Dylan, I can hear you in there. It's Chip Fiss, I need to talk to you."

"We'll wait here while you lead him back to the soundstage," she whispered to Dylan.

"Just a minute, Chip," Dylan shouted. "I'll be right out." He hastily put some clothing into a small duffel bag and exited the trailer. We could overhear him speaking to Chip and I was impressed by his performance. "Hey, Chip," he said, "I wondered if you were ever going to get around to interviewing me. I was starting to think you didn't like me anymore." Dylan then added gratuitously that Chip's shirt looked loose on him. "Have you lost weight?" he asked. Chip fell for it and chirped, "Four pounds since last week!" I had a hunch that Chip would have his shoulder massaged while they walked to the soundstage.

The next few minutes passed interminably, and Roy and I stared at each other, trying not to make eye contact with Amanda. I was afraid that I was going to be fired, and being stoned on pot made me feel both despairing and euphoric. The unnatural combination of those two incongruous emotions made me suspect that I was too wasted to under-stand the consequences of what had happened. I veered from panicking over whether I would have enough money to pay next month's rent to calmly planning what office supplies I would steal since I'd have more time to write. I decided to take a box of felt-tip pens, a stack of legal pads, and a carton of paper for my computer printer. I'd already stolen all the software and stamps I wanted.

Amanda winced periodically from the contractions. Roy finally asked her if she needed anything. "I need to have this baby," she said, a slight smile appearing on her lips. Roy asked if she was expecting a boy or girl.

"A boy," she said.

"Have you picked a name?" he asked.

"Charlie," she said. "I didn't want one of those ridiculous first names that sound like last names. Like Clinton or Whitney."

We waited until we were certain that Dylan and Chip were gone. "It should be fine now," Amanda said finally. Struggling to rise to her feet, I offered her my arm, and she gratefully accepted it. I attempted to take the heavy bag that she was carrying from her hand. She started to argue with me but I said firmly, "Let me," and she released the bag.

"Thanks," Amanda said weakly. "My car's not too far away."

We walked slowly to her car. She had trouble finding her car keys in her purse. She was sweating, and a strand of her usually perfectly-groomed hair fell down across her forehead. I thought she looked as if she was going to throw up or pass out.

"Let me drive," I said.

She looked me in the eyes as she considered the idea.

"I don't want you to drive if you're stoned."

"I'm not anymore," I said, telling her the truth.

A glimmer of a smile appeared on her face as she handed me the car keys.

"I'll come with you," Roy said, but I insisted that he should stay behind. He argued with me for a few minutes, but I convinced him that it would make things worse if he disappointed Joe by not attending the taping. I told him that I would meet him on the soundstage when I returned to the studio.

"Are you all right?" he asked. "I feel awful about this." He looked deeply upset and his display of contrition touched me.

"Can we finish this love story a little later? I don't have time for this."

Roy helped Amanda get in the front seat of the car. She could barely strap the seat belt across her abdomen.

Once I pulled out of the studio lot and began driving to the hospital, Amanda cursed every time we hit a bump or pothole or had to stop for a red light. She called the hospital to demand that someone should be waiting for her at the emergency room entrance. She argued with the person and after winning the battle, closed her cell phone and slipped it back in her purse. Then she told me that she wanted me to drive her car back to her house in the Hollywood Hills. She would give me cab fare to get back to the studio.

"You know, Nelson," Amanda said while we waited for a light to change, "I made you the script supervisor because I thought you were smart and responsible." She paused to take a breath. "Chip told me about your nickname for me. It was really stupid to tell him that in an interview. Although I can appreciate how the name fits."

"I'm sorry," I said. "It didn't start out as something mean. It started out as a silly joke."

She shifted in her seat, puffing and wincing as another contraction hit her.

"You're the one who needs an agenda," she said. "I know you've claimed to be working on a novel, but if this behavior is any indication of your discipline—"

She didn't bother to finish her thought as she groaned from another contraction.

"Drive faster," she ordered.

After I parked the car, Amanda and I walked to the emergency entrance. She opened her purse and took out two twenty-dollar bills. Handing me the money, she told me to use it as cab fare. An orderly was waiting for her at the emergency entrance with a wheelchair.

"Thank you for driving me," she said before the orderly wheeled her away. "And Nelson, I want you to clean out your desk tonight."

FOUR

In a moment of excessive pride, I handed back the cab fare and car keys to Amanda. My reasoning was that getting fired was humiliating, but getting fired and then taking money from your boss to go clean out your desk was degrading. Amanda actually seemed miffed that I wouldn't do her one last favor.

When I arrived back at the studio, after a very expensive cab ride, I found that Amanda had called ahead and told the guards at the front gate not to admit me. She left a message that they would pack up my things and ship them to me. Of course I didn't have Roy's cell phone number with me. It was on a post-it note on my computer. I called Wendy and left a message on her cell asking her to tell Roy what had happened. (I knew that I wouldn't reach her during the taping because leaving your cell phone turned on during a taping was something that a writer's assistant did only once.)

I considered waiting for Roy in my car in the parking lot, but it was only 7:30 and the tapings almost never finished before 10:30. I didn't think I could handle three hours with nothing to distract me from brooding on the crushing thought that, in addition to not being able to finish my novel, I was now a failed writer's assistant. And I was fired for getting high on the job, sophomoric behavior that couldn't be excused because I had graduated from college twelve years ago. I knew from experience that rehashing my depression in a sealed apartment would bring my self-loathing to a satisfying boil that I could keep rolling for days by binging on junk, solitary tippling, and wasting more time that I couldn't afford to lose by flipping through hundreds of channels of crappy television.

At eleven o'clock, I was thinking of going to bed when my telephone rang.

"Hello."

"I can't believe you smoked that pot without me!"

"Hi Wendy."

"What's wrong? Are you still stoned?"

"No, I got fired."

"You got fired! Oh now I really hate you. I wanted to be out of *Aftertaste* before you! Are you all right?"

Her question sounded as if we were doing a conference call with her multiple personalities and the sweet, sensitive one had spoken up.

"I'm fine."

"Do you want me to come over? I have a date with Reina but I'll break it."

I hadn't met Reina yet, but Wendy was always guarded about her new girlfriends. It was impossible to take offense about her secrecy though, because I'd decided long ago that lesbians were a tribe like the Hopi. They welcomed visitors and loved to share their crafts and culture but they were never going to reveal their deepest mysteries to outsiders.

I told Wendy that she should go out on her date. I knew she would have canceled it if I'd asked, and she wouldn't have bitched about it, either. She was capable of acts of generosity that were as oversized as her neediness.

"This is the best thing that could have happened to you," she said before mentioning that Dylan had killed on the show; the audience had loved him. Then she handed her cell to Roy.

"How are you?"

"I'm okay. Although I did get fired."

"Oh that sucks. Shit, I want to see you."

"You can come over," I said ambivalently. I wanted to see Roy but having my first sex with him after I'd been fired sounded unpromising. It's bad enough wondering whether you'll be sexually adequate but throwing into the mix whether I could afford lube and condoms was an anxiety that I didn't need.

"I want to see you, too, but Joe's giving me grief about not spending enough time with him. I'm really sorry. But do you want to go to the La Brea Tar Pits with me tomorrow? I've never been and I've always wanted to see them."

I couldn't believe that I hadn't thought of that! Of course, an archaeologist would love seeing one of the most famous fossil sites in the world. And it was located nearby. For the first time that evening I felt optimistic. There was still a chance to show Roy that Los Angeles had a lot to offer him.

Roy picked me up at noon, and we had lunch and then worked out at my gym. We didn't arrive at the tar pits until almost three-thirty. We parked on a side street and while putting quarters into the meter, I observed, "My friend Glenn calls this neighborhood, 'Pits Adjacent.' Roy didn't understand the reference because he was unfamiliar with Los Angeles real estate terms. I explained that in Los Angeles real estate advertisements any house for sale within twenty miles of Beverly Hills was always called, "Beverly Hills Adjacent." So Glenn suggested that the neighborhood surrounding the La Brea Tar Pits should be called "Pits Adjacent."

"Keep working on that one," Roy mocked, wagging his eyebrows. I laughed because explaining a joke turned bad poetry into worse prose.

As we walked the sidewalk to the park's entrance, I noticed that the wind had picked up and gray clouds had filled the sky. The palm trees swayed drunkenly, and leaves and papers blew across our path.

"It feels like rain," Roy said. I agreed with him without bothering to explain that in Los Angeles the threat of rain was like the threat of an earthquake; it was always possible but, on any given day, it was unlikely to happen.

The La Brea Tar Pits, the Los Angeles County Museum of Art, and the Page Museum share an entire city block of parkland. Surrounding the park is an elegant ten-foot-high green painted fence that deterred trespassers like a snotty personal assistant; it looked formidable and pretended to have more authority than it really possessed.

"It's too bad that they had to build the art museum here," Roy said as we entered one of the gates. "They should have left the area more natural."

The art museum's buildings towered over the tar pits, which made it seem that all of Los Angeles's cultural and natural attractions had to be shoehorned into one block.

"It's so wrong," I said. "It seems to be saying that LA's an artistic deathtrap."

The park was almost empty. Even on sunny days, the park was never crowded but the overcast sky seemed to have deterred other Pleistocene buffs. We decided to check out the Page Museum first because it closed at five. I insisted on paying for Roy's admission because I wanted to treat him and also to ensure that he'd always remember that his first visit to the tar pits had been with me. The main exhibit hall displayed mounted skeletons of the Columbian Mammoth, the Shasta Ground sloth, and other mammals that had been recovered from the tar pits. It was immediately apparent that Roy was enjoying himself because as we walked through the museum, he talked excitedly about America's lost megafauna.

"You know these animals wouldn't have been afraid of men because they evolved without them."

"Just like the animals in the Galápagos," I said, remembering a nature special that I'd seen on television.

"The first Americans must have thought they were in Meat Heaven," Roy said as he read the ground sloth's plaque. "They ate their way down the Americas."

"How can we be sure?" I asked as we looked at a holographic reconstruction of a Native American woman, based upon the only known prehistoric human skeleton found in the tar pits.

"The last mammoths on Earth lived on Wrangel Island off Russia until four thousand years ago," Roy said. "If climate change killed the species, they should have died, too. But they weren't wiped out until men arrived. We ate them."

"What about the Neanderthals, did we kill them off?" I asked.

"They could have been wiped out by an epidemic but I think we killed them," Roy said as we moved over to look at a glass display case filled with mounted prehistoric skeletons of condors, which oddly reminded me of chicken bones.

"We hate members of our own species who look slightly different from us. I'm sure we would have been extremely hostile to another species of humans that looked very different from us."

"It's too bad they're extinct," I said. "Neanderthals were hot. An entire race of mesomorphs. I read in *National Geographic* that their bones and muscles were like modern weightlifters."

"They also had that brow ridge," Roy said, tapping his forehead. "I'm not sure that's a turn on."

"It is to someone," I said confidently. "I'm sure there's a Bony Ridge M4M chat room somewhere."

"With one lonely guy waiting for a computer literate Neanderthal to instant message him," Roy said, making me laugh.

"He'd probably lie about his Stone Age on his profile," I said, showing off for Roy's benefit. "He'd claim to be Neanderthal but actually be an older species like Homo Erectus or Australopithecus."

Roy laughed, which was enormously satisfying.

We came to an interactive display where visitors were challenged to pull a steel piston out of a pool of tar. Roy and I took turns as each of us struggled to raise the piston a foot. It was much harder than I had imagined and I could see how impossible it would be for an animal to escape from a tar pit once it became entrapped.

"A woman recently wrote a scientific paper suggesting our stories about dragons and other mythological beasts were probably inspired by ancient people finding dinosaur bones." Roy said as we moved to another display case of small mammal bones. "And I've been thinking that perhaps our legends about Minotaurs and other beast-men might be garbled memories about our first contact with Neanderthals. They must have appeared to be monsters."

"So the Neanderthal unibrow became the one-eyed Cyclops?" I asked.

"Something like that," he said. "We wouldn't forget meeting Neanderthals. And since there's a good chance we killed them, it's nice to think they might have lived on in our stories."

"That makes sense," I said, impressed by his reasoning. "But how do you prove it?

"You can't. You could make a case if you could prove that Neanderthal bones were once thought to be the remains of a Minotaur by the ancient Greeks."

Next we examined a wall in the museum that had a spectacular display of a hundred dire wolf skulls that had been recovered from the tar pits. They were mounted in rows of fifteen against sheets of yellow Plexiglas.

"That would be a great look for my apartment," I said seriously.

Roy looked at me dubiously. "If I went to your place," he said, "and saw a hundred dire wolf skulls mounted on your wall, I'd be out of there."

"Would you think I was a werewolf?"

"I'd think you were a freak."

His response seemed reasonable, and I smiled.

"I want to see the cave paintings at Lascaux someday," Roy said as we examined an artistic rendering of all the prehistoric animal species in the museum crowding around the tar pits as if it was Happy Hour back in the Ice Age.

"The real cave? Or the fake one?"

Roy's face widened with amazement. "The real one. You get points for knowing that they have a fake one."

I preened for a minute, letting it sink in that he had his own trophy boyfriend—unfortunately more of a trivia whiz than a triathlete.

"I thought they don't let people in Lascaux anymore," I said as my brain's search engine pulled up a memory of a magazine article. "Our breath causes mold on the paintings."

"They still let in a few people," he said. "But you need to receive special permission from the French government. My fantasy is that I'll write a letter explaining that I'm an archaeologist from Alaska, and I'll receive permission. Europeans aren't impressed by Americans but they're still impressed by Alaskans."

"Wouldn't it be funny if cave paintings were just early to-do lists?" I joked. "'Hunt bison and deer, kill horses and mastodons, avoid lions and bears.'"

Roy smiled but remained engrossed peering into the windows that displayed the usually behind-the-scenes workshops and labs that were part of the museum tour.

"I've always wanted to find an arrowhead," I said as we looked at a desktop covered with small piles of discolored fossil bones. "I read a story about Thoreau; he was hiking in the woods with a friend who said, 'I've always wanted to find an arrowhead.' At that exact moment, Thoreau bent down and picked up an arrowhead. Then he handed it to him. I love that story."

"Why do you love it?" Roy asked, his blue eyes alight with curiosity.

His question surprised me and I had to think for a moment. "It makes Thoreau almost sound supernatural," I said. "And it's a very optimistic story. It suggests the world is full of wonders. Just keep your eyes open." Then I grinned because the real reason occurred to me. "I guess I really love that story because I want to find an arrowhead."

"There are still places where you can do that," Roy said. "Last summer, I was hiking in Northern California, in redwood country, walking along a river that I knew once had huge runs of salmon. On an impulse, I decided to see if I could find anything. I looked down at my feet and there was a beautiful rectangular stone anchor about the size of my fist. It had a square shaped notch cut neatly at the top. The area was littered with dozens of stone fishing tools. Anchor weights and net stones in all shapes and sizes. Most of them beautifully crafted. I was in a state park, and the other tourists were oblivious. They were stepping right on them. Everyone was looking up at the redwood trees, ignoring anything at their feet. Which is a good thing, because they'd all be gone by now."

"I'd love to see that," I said, admiring how adventurous Roy's life sounded.

We were the last people to leave the museum at closing time, after spending almost an hour looking at books in the gift shop.

"Do you smell the tar?" Roy asked excitedly when we walked outside. "Or I guess I should say asphalt." Inside the museum, we had read that the pits were actually filled with asphalt, the lowest form of crude oil. It was technically incorrect to call them "tar pits" because tar was a man-made substance.

I said that I could smell it also.

"Somehow I didn't expect that," he said. The sky was dark gray and it definitely looked like rain. A gust of wind rattled a trash can as we strolled into the park. The head of a large plastic mastodon came into view. Its trunk was lifted in the air as if it was warning the rest of the herd about our approach.

"In this light, it almost looks real," Roy observed.

"It's probably made out of petroleum, so in a sense it is prehistoric."

"I wish we could get closer," Roy said as we approached a tar pit. All of the tar pits were enclosed by chain-link fences. They reminded me of a derelict motel pool. A gas bubble sat on the surface of the oily water. The bubble didn't appear to be inflating or deflating and its sturdiness was mildly disgusting.

I leaned against the gate in the fence, absentmindedly pulled against it, causing the lock to snap open with a loud click.

"Someone didn't do their job today," Roy said.

We looked at each other then looked around the park. No one was nearby, so we decided to step inside. We cautiously made our way to the edge of the pool.

"Be careful, the ground's soft here, " Roy warned as he stepped carefully toward the tar pit.

I suddenly recognized the strong aromatic smell of black sage from hiking in the Santa Monica mountains. I leaned over to inhale the bush nearest to me, taking in its heady medicinal scent.

"You've got to smell this," I said stepping forward to break off a leaf of the plant for Roy. As I reached out, my left foot slipped on a patch of mud and my sneaker plunged into a warm viscous liquid. From above me I heard a rustling noise coming from the tops of the trees, the sound of rain hitting the leaves. I looked up as the first big cold drops splattered my head and shoulders, and a downpour immediately followed. I tried pulling my foot out but there was an ominous sucking sound before the fresh smell of tar wafted to my nose.

"Shit!" I exclaimed.

"I'm getting soaked," Roy said as he sought cover under a tree. He hadn't noticed my predicament.

The tar gripped my foot with antediluvian force. As I struggled to remove my leg, I lost my balance in the tug of war and tried to regain my footing by moving my right foot forward to what I thought was solid ground. But the heavy rainfall had covered the surface of the tar pit with a layer of water, obscuring its boundaries. My misstep produced another ominous slurp followed again by the aroma of tar.

"Roy!" I yelled. It had to be hundreds of years since the last frightened mammal had cried out from a tar pit.

"Let me come and get you." Roy said as his alarmed face registered that I had fallen in a tar pit.

"Oh my god!" I said.

"Don't move."

"I'm not moving. I'm stuck."

"Are you sinking?"

"Yes," I said, thinking that being swallowed by a parking lot was a particularly cruel way for a Southern Californian to die; being entombed in a tar pit would be like being stuck in traffic for eternity.

"Don't get near me!" I shouted when Roy stepped toward me. "I don't want you to be trapped." I sounded as if I'd had a sudden breakthrough in therapy.

"Maybe I can pull you out. See if you can reach me."

My feet were slowly subsiding in the adhesive ooze when I tried to reach Roy's outstretched hand. I had a vision of seeing my skull added to the dire wolf specimen wall in the museum.

"Is there rope in your car?" Roy asked.

"I don't carry rope," I snapped. "I live in a city."

"I'm trying to help you," he said patiently.

The rain continued to fall, and I realized that I really was sinking and began to feel terrified.

"Roy, what should I do?"

"We've got to get help."

Roy told me later that he was afraid, because visitors to Anchorage sometimes walked out on the mudflats surrounding Turnagain Arm and became mired in the muck. They often drowned when a three-foot wall of water called a bore tide rushed in. He couldn't help thinking of an Anchorage urban legend that a man had been pulled apart when a helicopter tried to yank him out. And tar had to be more tenacious than mud.

"Do you have your cell phone?" Roy asked.

"Yes."

"Call 911."

I removed my cell phone from my jacket pocket and while punching in the numbers, I realized that I might be arrested for trespassing. But the gurgling sound around my knees reassured me that spending a night in jail would be preferable to dying in a tar pit.

"Hello, 911." A woman with a deep steady voice and a soothing Southern accent answered my call.

"Hi. I'm, um, I'm . . . sinking in the La Brea Tar Pits. No, this isn't a joke. I'm really stuck and I'm sinking. I'm being serious. No, we're not supposed to be here. Um, I mean, I'm not supposed to be. Is this being taped? It doesn't matter. I'm right behind the museum. There's a big mastodon. No, don't hang up! It's fake. It's made out of plastic. It's part of the exhibit. Listen to me; this isn't a prank call. I really need some help immediately. My name's Nelson Kunker. Okay, I'll stay on the line."

"She's calling the fire department," I shouted to Roy who had walked outside the fence and found a newly planted sapling. He began pushing and pulling at the tree until it toppled over with a loud crack. The rain had let up, turning into a misty sprinkle. A few people in the park had sought protection under a tree and they were pointing toward

Roy, who was vigorously swinging the sapling back and forth trying to break it off at the base of the trunk. A dark-haired man started walking toward us and suddenly my stomach felt like it was sinking faster than the rest of my body.

"Roy, you have to go," I said when he returned carrying the sapling.

"I'm not leaving you," he said holding the sapling out for me to grab.

"I might be arrested for being in here. You can't afford to be arrested at the La Brea Tar Pits."

"I don't care. I'm not leaving you."

He reached out to me with the sapling, and I grabbed hold of it. He tried to pull me out but couldn't gain enough leverage.

"You're going to be an archaeologist," I said. "This won't look good on your resume."

There was a slurping gulp as I slid in further. Standing outside the fence, a man was talking loudly into his cell phone while the sound of fire trucks could be heard approaching on Wilshire Boulevard.

"Let me try something," Roy said as he directed me to hang onto the sapling. "Are you okay if I drop the tree for a second?" he asked.

"Yes," I said as he proceeded to let go of the sapling. A large California sycamore grew next to the tar pit, and one of its main branches extended out over the pool. Roy walked over to the tree and scrambled up the trunk—climbing that tree would have taken me hours—and crawled out onto the branch.

"Roy, get down," I said, "I don't want you falling in."

"I won't fall in," he said with manly disdain, while shimmying closer toward me on the branch.

"All right," he said straddling the limb. "Can you swing that up to me?"

I was able to do it, but the exertion caused me to sink three more inches.

"Hang on tight," Roy said as he pulled on the sapling. It seemed to be working as my rate of subsidence slowed down.

"I think I've stopped sinking," I said, "but you should get out of here."

Of course, I would have despised him if he had deserted me then.

"Will you shut the fuck up," he said through gritted teeth while straining to keep me from slipping in any further.

I heard a helicopter circling above us. Looking up in the sky, I'd expected to see a police helicopter but my heart sank when I recognized the familiar logo of the Channel 7 News Team.

"All right," I said, finally abandoning the idea that he could leave me. "If anyone asks, you don't know me. You came to my rescue. Okay?"

"Yes, all right," he said, puffing from the exertion of holding me up. "Just shut up."

The Channel 4 News Team arrived minutes later. Outside the fence, I could see a blonde-haired woman reporter, talking into a microphone as she faced a camera. Even though it was very windy, her petrified-looking hair didn't move. She turned toward me and shouted over to ask me if she could interview me. A cameraman stood next to her and I could see a glowing red light on his camera.

She asked my name.

"I'm a little busy right now," I said.

She asked again.

"I'm not giving you my name," I said. I was tempted to ask Roy to throw his coat over my head but didn't, a decision that I came to deeply regret later.

"Was this a suicide attempt?" the reporter shouted.

"Oh yeah," I said sarcastically. "I wanted to take my time."

The firemen arrived, interrupting my interview. The fireman in charge was in his late thirties. He had black hair and a moustache, broad shoulders, and looked like he should be Mr. January on a firefighter calendar. The Channel 2 and Channel 7 news teams arrived and set up their cameras outside the fence. Now it sounded like two helicopters were circling above me. Mr. January told me not to worry. They needed more leverage to pull me out, he explained. But first, they would have to cut down the fence behind me to bring in a bucket ladder.

In the meantime, Mr. January set up two firefighters on either side of me. He had Roy climb down from the tree and then told me to let go of the sapling. He threw a Frisbee (!) to me, which was attached to a rescue harness. Embarrassingly, I dropped the Frisbee twice before finally catching it. I sank in up to my waist struggling to get the harness on. Mr. January was incredibly patient and told me to calm down and take my time. Finally I managed to put the harness on. The firemen on either side of me had rigged up poles, connecting them to the harness, almost like a swing set, preventing me from sinking in any further.

Roy walked over to side of the tar pit, and his head looked like a pincushion as reporters thrust microphones into his face. There were now four news teams on the scene since the Spanish language station's news crew had also shown up. A large crowd gathered outside the fence, and police officers were setting up a line with yellow barrier tape. Several press photographers asked the officers if they could cross the line to take pictures. They were given permission to step forward and began snapping away.

My cell phone rang, playing the theme from *Shaft*, causing Roy along with the firemen, the reporters, and the rest of the crowd to laugh. Since my hands were free, I fished it out of my shirt pocket again and flipped it open, immediately recognizing the name and telephone number on the screen. I punched the talk button and said, "Hi."

"All right, are you retarded?" Wendy asked. "How the fuck did you get stuck in the La Brea Tar Pits?"

"You're watching me?" I asked, knowing the answer but still unable to believe what was happening to me.

"You're on all the local channels," she said before pausing. "Oh my god." She sounded genuinely alarmed. "You're live on CNN." She paused again. "And FOX and. . . ." She paused before saying, "MSNBC has a commercial—No, they're flashing Breaking News—there you are. Why don't you wave to me?"

"You're being mean," I said but waved anyway. At that point a further loss of dignity appeared to be impossible.

"I'm sorry," Wendy said as she tried to be compassionate. "What can I do? Are they going to be able to get you out? Oh my god. Do you realize CNN goes all over the world?"

"You're not really helping," I said, trying not to imagine millions of people following my story with the same cliff-hanging suspense that audiences had shown waiting to hear about the fate of coal miners trapped in a cave-in or a little boy who's fallen down a well.

"They interviewed Roy," she said. "He claimed to be walking by and heard your cry for help. What's up with that?"

I explained that I didn't think an archaeologist should be caught breaking into a tar pit.

"That was thoughtful of you," she said. "He looked so handsome on TV. And how about him climbing up that tree for you? You can never break up with him. You need a butch man in your life. He can act as your full-time lifeguard."

She was the only person who could make me laugh in that situation.

My phone's screen lit up again indicating that I had another call waiting. I recognized the name and Wisconsin number. "I've got another call," I said. The hissing sound of an acetylene torch burning started up behind me. They were cutting down the fence to allow the bucket ladder to reach me.

"It's my dad," I said, "Call me later."

It never occurred to me that Wendy would mock my last instruction to her when we reviewed the events of that day later.

"Tell him hi," she said before I punched the talk button.

It should have occurred to her that I would mock her last instruction to me when we reviewed the events of that day later.

"Nelson, are you all right?" My father sounded frantic.

"I'm okay, Dad."

"Who were you talking to? And why are you waving and laughing?"

I explained that Wendy had called me, and he immediately said to tell her hi. My father and Wendy adored each other. Whenever he came to visit me, the three of us would go out for a steak dinner and martinis, and they would sit there, getting tipsy, discussing me for hours as if I weren't there.

"Why aren't those firemen doing anything?" my father asked.

"I think they're trying to get me out without getting stuck themselves," I replied.

Teams of five firemen on either side of me took turns as two of them stood on step ladders, keeping me aloft while the other firemen loitered near the fence, waiting for another team of firefighters to cut through the park's outer fence and the chain-link fence surrounding the pit itself.

"I wish they'd hurry up," my father said. "This makes me want a cigarette."

My dad hadn't smoked for over seven years. "Don't start smoking again," I said.

A tall man in a green baseball cap in the now large crowd held up a handmade sign that said, "Free the La Brea 1!" Several of the cameras turned toward the asshole. It annoyed me because the park had been almost empty a few minutes before. A few museum officials dressed in suits and lab coats were talking to the firemen, and my father must have seen them, too.

"Are you going to need a lawyer?"

"I'm not sure," I said as an unbidden joke appeared in my thoughts. "Maybe to handle the movie rights."

"This isn't funny," he said sternly. "I'm worried about you."

I heard the unmistakable clang of the first fence falling. Then they set to work on the chain-link fence with bolt cutters. I heard every sharp plink as they snipped away.

"You don't know how much it scared me to realize it was you," my father said, his voice quavering slightly. "You don't expect to turn on the TV and see your son on CNN. Unless he's the president or something."

I thought his last observation was hilarious but didn't mention it. "I'm sorry, Dad," I said. "It was an accident."

"Well, I hope it was an accident!"

"It was."

"Is your friend there?"

"He's here," I said. "I didn't want him to get involved but he stayed with me until the firemen came."

I had talked briefly with my father about Roy on the first day we had met. My father had called to remind me about my nephew Jarrod's graduation from preschool and, feeling giddy, I blurted out how Roy and I had connected over the story of the Bowhead whale harpoon points. This was unusual because I normally liked to wait until I'd had several dates with a guy before talking to my dad about him.

My cell phone rang again. I assumed it was Wendy calling me back but saw an unidentified local number with a 310 area code. I had no idea who was calling because not very many people had my cell phone number.

"Dad, someone's calling me."

"Take the call," he said abruptly in his usual manner. He always volunteered to hang up as if his calls were never important to me.

"Dad, don't hang up."

"That tar's going to be a bear to get off," my father said practically. "Call me if you need anything. I'll talk to you later."

"I will," I said.

"I love you," he said. After the death of my mother, my father ended every telephone call with my brother and me by saying, "I love you." It never sounded perfunctory and always moved me.

"I love you too." I pressed the talk pad. "Hello?"

"I didn't want you to think I'd deserted you."

Scanning the crowd, I saw that Roy had borrowed a cell phone from someone. I was impressed that he had already memorized my telephone number. He smiled when our eyes met.

"I didn't think that."

"I'm not going anywhere," Roy said.

I made a bad joke: "I'm stuck with you."

"Always with the jokes," he said dryly. "And yes, you are."

FIVE

After an hour of strenuous tugging by two brawny firemen arrayed on each side of me in bucket ladders, the crowd cheered and flashbulbs went off when I was finally extracted from the tar pit with a sloshy pop. My pants and sneakers remained mired in the tar, artifacts for future archaeologists. For years afterward complete strangers never tired of reminding me that seeing me dangling in the rescue harness in my underpants, made me look exactly like a dirty-diapered infant in a baby swing.

Setting my feet upon terra firma again, the crowd roared once more, and I acknowledged their cheers with the abject modesty that my situation deserved. Roy and Wendy rushed forward to wrap me in an old army blanket as reporters shouted questions, which I ignored. Wendy had been watching the television coverage and, when she saw Roy standing by himself in the crowd, she drove down to keep him company. She barely had time to say, "You need to enter the Witless Protection Program. You'll need a new identity after this," before waiting police officers surrounded me.

The museum didn't press charges. The lock on the gate shouldn't have been open and they accepted that their negligence left them liable for large blundering mammals. My father suspected that they might have been afraid that I'd try to sue them. But I figured they thought my public humiliation was sufficient punishment. The police officers appeared to be relieved that they didn't have to arrest me, as they weren't too eager to put my goo-covered body in the backseat of a squad car.

It took hours to clean me up. One of the museum's paleontologists took pity on me and let Roy and Wendy work on me in the back room of the museum. The skin on my hairy legs was rubbed almost raw from all the scouring required to remove the gunk. (Thankfully, my underwear shielded my pubes and Johnson.) Wendy tried to get the tar out from under my toenails but quit giving me a pedicure after an hour of picking.

"Your feet can't be shown in public for the next six months," she announced.

Roy and I didn't get back to my apartment until close to midnight. As we walked to my car, he said straightforwardly, "I hope you don't have cats; I'm allergic."

"No," I said, relieved that we had entirely skipped discussing whether we were going to spend the night together. I was grateful that I didn't have to go through the usual coy routine of asking him up for a drink, and I was also relieved that Roy still wanted to sleep with me. I also considered that an archaeologist might get a kinky thrill from having sex with an artifact removed from the La Brea Tar Pits.

I lived in Hollywood, close to West Hollywood, and my apartment building was a charming architectural fraud that looked like a castle. It was befitting because most of the residents were either queens or noisy Russian immigrants, whose frequent loud arguments I couldn't understand although I liked to imagine that they were disputing each other's claim to be the last of the Romanovs. My landlord maintained that Charlie Chaplin had once lived in my building. I heard these assertions all the time: James Dean or Marilyn Monroe lived here and there. My theory was that people in Los Angeles told these ghost stories to bolster their courage: "I'm not going to fail. I live in a city where other unknowns have become stars."

There were twenty-seven new messages on my voice mail. I stopped playing them back after Roy and I listened to my cousin Donny telling me that he was watching me at an airport bar in Seattle. He held out his cell phone and had everyone in the bar yell out, "Hi, Nelson!" Other callers included my father's next-door neighbor, Mrs. Mattea, who said sweetly that I should have my own TV show because I looked so handsome. My ex-boyfriend Brent also called. He lived in Philadelphia and excitedly informed me that he and his perfect new boyfriend Steven, a handsome doctor, were watching me together. Great, I thought, as my remaining self-esteem slid under the surface of the tar. One of my writing professors from Madison had left the message: "Nelson, remember there are no bad experiences, just bad writers." He was wrong, and I would have forcefully told him that if he'd spoken to me directly.

My apartment was clean but it was far from being a showplace. Basically, my decorating philosophy was that an ugly room could be vastly improved simply by bringing home a beautiful man. My furniture was garbage-picked finds, hand-me-downs from friends, or possessions that I disliked but couldn't afford to replace.

"You have a lot of books," Roy said as he looked at the three book-cases lining the living room walls.

"It's an addiction," I said, thinking that if reading was an addiction, I had started with the recreational drug of comic books before moving on to the hard stuff.

Roy commented on my worn paperback trilogy of *The Lord of the Rings* sitting on a shelf. I confessed that it was one of my favorite books. It was a relief to find out that he loved the books also.

"You know what I've always wondered," he said. "Why did Frodo have to walk to Mordor? Why didn't Gandalf just have the eagles fly the ring to Mount Doom in the first place?" He pointed out that an eagle had rescued Gandalf from Isengard and that an eagle could have easily flown over the volcano and dropped the ring in. I was flabbergasted but had to agree with him. I had read the book several times, seen the movie several times, but had overlooked that obvious defect in the plot.

It should have ruined the book for me, but it only made the story better. It was hilarious to think that Professor Tolkien had labored for ten years over his masterpiece, reading it out loud to several other Oxford dons, but no one had pointed out that gaping hole in his Ring. It delighted me because Roy had actually made us part of the story. My appreciation of the book now included being told that the whole thing was bogus, and if the supposedly wise high-elves and wizards had used a little common sense, Frodo could have skipped the Mines of Moria and Shelob's Lair.

"I'm going to have to be careful about letting you read my other favorite books," I said. "You'll read *To Kill a Mockingbird* and then tell me that you've found evidence that Atticus overlooked, proving conclusively that if he had been a better lawyer, he could have won his case."

"Don't think I'm not working on that."

I inched closer to Roy on the couch, in preparation for kissing him.

"Do you read much?" I asked, trying to make the question sound casual although his answer was important. Experience had taught me not to expect to find a hunky bookworm who read as much I did, but I wanted to make sure that Roy was open to opening books.

"All the time," he said, which made me smile. "But right now, I only have time to read books for school."

"What do you read for fun?"

He thought about it for a minute. "I read a lot of nonfiction," he said.

"No novels?" I asked, thinking that I should definitely kiss him because he had initiated our first kiss.

"Not lately," he said, twisting his thick lips into shapes as he tried to recall one. "When the movies came out, I read *The Lord of the Rings*. Then last summer, I read *A Confederacy of Dunces* and *A Home at the End of the World*. They were great. And I also like to read graphic novels."

Roy passed my entrance exam. I could work with Tolkien, John Kennedy Toole, and Michael Cunningham. Of course, I secretly planned on becoming a bookworm bully, forcing him to stick his face in all of my favorite novels. His love of graphic novels was worrying but I thought maybe we could find common ground in Michael Chabon's *The Adventures of Kavalier and Clay*.

"It looks like you read all the time," Roy said. "I'm impressed."

"Don't be," I said. "Reading flatters everyone. The dullest person on earth never has to fear that a book will lose interest in *him*. A book never tells a reader, 'I'm not in the mood or get your hands off me.' A book is always willing to put out, day or night."

I didn't mention that it had occurred to me that reading novels could really fuck you up though. Sometimes I worried that no relationship with a real person would ever be as satisfying as my relationships with the characters in *A Glass of Blessings* or *Down There on a Visit*.

Roy grinned. "Shall we turn the page?"

I kissed him, and we boned up and started removing our clothes as if we'd tried them on at a store and both agreed that they looked awful. We eventually moved into my bedroom and that night Roy did things with my equipment that made me feel that I needed to reread my owner's manual. Every man I had ever had sex with always seemed to be more experienced than I was. It didn't matter whether they were younger or older, whenever I slipped on a condom, I couldn't shake the feeling that I was wearing a dunce's cap.

On the scale of uptight to fully dilated, I was cautiously adventurous, willing to try anything that didn't require calling an ambulance or consulting a lawyer. Almost immediately, Roy found what I called my sweet spot, an area on the nape of my neck, and he puckered up and leaned on my doorbell. It curled my toes and made me shiver with eye-rattling ecstasy. I almost told him to stop but was afraid that he would. I'm embarrassed to admit that I might have even moaned. It was a cartoon response that only needed steam shooting out of my ears and thumping hearts circling above my head to be complete.

At one point I had to tell Roy to relax and slow down because it felt like he was beating my sword into a plowshare. Roy talked about sex directly, which I found liberating, slightly shocking, and a huge relief. He gave explicit directions or offered gentle suggestions without the slightest hint of reproach or superiority. Roy wasn't a jokey guy but his succinct descriptions of longing made me laugh. That night he whispered in my ear, "Treat my nipples cruelly but be kind to my cock and balls."

Afterward, Roy fell asleep before I did. His right arm was draped lightly over my back and his legs touched mine, making me think, just before I fell asleep, that my passage from childhood to adulthood was simply realizing that a security blanket worked better with two people snuggling under it.

Early the next morning my friend Vanessa called from Brooklyn. She left a message that my tar-smeared body was on the cover of *The New York Post*. New York newspapers never lost an opportunity to illustrate that life in Los Angeles was absurd and my picture was headlined, "Total Asphalt!"

Roy and I were still in bed, and I kept catching an occasional whiff of elusive peek-a-boo BO that had to be coming from one of us. I screened the next call but picked up to talk to Wendy.

"Is he still there?"

"Uh-huh."

"How was the sex? Does he have a big dick? Is he blowing you right now?"

"Great. I guess. And no."

My answers were technically correct although seconds before Wendy had called Roy had started stroking the back of my legs.

"Now remember honey, when he's just about to come," Wendy said in an assumed motherly voice, "you stick a finger up his ass so he does it real hard." *We* shared a long-standing fantasy about how the stage mother of a porn star would impart maternal advice to her son.

"Meet me for brunch at Food Rink in half an hour?" she demanded. The imperative question was Wendy's contribution to

English grammar. She asked it with the implicit understanding that there was only one correct answer. It deserved its own form of punctuation, which I envisioned as a question mark with two pendulous dots to symbolize Wendy's balls. "You'll get to meet Reina," she added.

"Do you want to meet Wendy for brunch?" I asked Roy. He had draped his delightfully heavy leg over mine and I felt incapable of making any decision as the prospect of impending sex eclipsed inessentials like food.

"In an hour or so," he said while stroking my back.

"We'll be there in an hour and half," I said as he wrapped his arms around me.

"I'm hungry now!" she whined. "Meet me there in forty-five minutes."

"No," I said firmly as my resolve stiffened after Roy slipped his hand down my underwear. Unfortunately for Wendy, I had gone through a sexual dry spell during the past six months, and I would have had no difficulty blowing off kings and presidents.

"Gross," said Wendy as she conceded defeat. She could browbeat me into doing almost anything but grudgingly acknowledged that gay male sex was the one thing that she couldn't do better than anyone else.

"I'll give you an hour and a half. As if you need that long," she sneered. "Don't be late!"

FooDrink, or Food Rink as everyone called it, was the restaurant that my friends and I could agree upon when we couldn't agree on any other restaurant. The cuisine was Southern Californian, which meant that classic American, Asian, Italian, and Mexican-style dishes had either unnatural implants or liposuction to improve their taste or augment their appearance. The turkey meatloaf was free-range and studded with organic sun-dried tomatoes, the pizzas were called "skinny-crust," which sounded better than the alternative, "shallow," and with your bison burger, you could opt for a small salad instead of fries, which I liked to think of as a side of prairie. FooDrink's menu was home-cooking if you were raised by two gay dads.

Since cheap good restaurants attracted the young and good-looking, FooDrink was always crowded. I was surprised to see Wendy standing by herself when we arrived.

"Where's Reina?" I asked.

Wendy scowled. "She's on call this weekend." She explained that Reina was a veterinarian and worked at a fancy animal hospital in Culver City. She had been called in to work.

"Look how perky Nelson looks," Wendy observed to Roy. "Sex acts like a makeover on him. You wouldn't know that only hours ago he had been up to his waist in tar."

I accepted the compliment but didn't say anything although I was aware of the effect and was tempted to joke that having someone sit on my face actually took years off it.

Wendy had put her name on the reservation list and we waited on the sidewalk for our table.

"Oh, my fucking god!" She suddenly shouted. Wendy stared at a newspaper inside a vending box. "Do you have any quarters?" she asked urgently, searching her pockets. "Shit," Roy exclaimed as he followed her eyes. I was overcome with disbelief when I saw my tar-smeared face on the front page of the *Los Angeles Times*. "A Sticky Situation" read the caption. Wendy put six quarters into the machine and removed a copy of the paper, quickly turning to the mercifully small article on the front page of the California section. It gave my name and briefly reported the circumstances of my "incident."

"Uh-oh," Wendy said ominously. "It's an Associated Press photo. This could be on the front page of every newspaper in the country."

"I didn't think this would be considered that big a news story," I said.

"Of course, it's news!" roared Wendy. "You're the biggest thing to happen to the La Brea Tar Pits in ten thousand years."

"Are you okay?" Roy asked as he placed his hand against the small of my back.

"Not really," I said, having suddenly lost my appetite.

"At least it's a good picture," Wendy declared as she examined the photograph. I looked closely at my picture and had to agree that I looked handsome and sort of butch. If the headline were different it's possible that I might have been mistaken for an oil-rig roughneck. Human vanity is capable of infinite feats of expansion, but I would always regard that moment as my personal benchmark.

"You do look sort of hot," Roy said consolingly.

I smiled grimly. "Well, that makes it all worthwhile."

"In other circumstances," Wendy said as her sympathy waned, "people wouldn't think you were an international laughingstock."

The host called her name and led us to our table. I wanted to leave but Wendy convinced me that obsessing about the newspaper article in a restaurant would be preferable to obsessing about it at home. I stared at the menu while Wendy advised Roy on which items were worth ordering. She usually ordered their vegetarian cheeseless pizza—with chicken—and then asked the waiter to organ-grind shredded Parmesan cheese over the top of it. Surprisingly, she wasn't trying to be difficult but was merely asserting her birthright as a native Angelino to change any dish on any restaurant menu to suit her current dietary whims, restrictions, or ethical qualms.

"Excuse me," the waiter asked after I placed my half-order for the chopped salad. "Did I see you on CNN this morning?"

"Uh, um . . . I . . . don't know," I stammered.

"You're fucked," Wendy said, shaking her head. "They replay their stories every hour during the weekend. All over the world!"

Suddenly I felt that everyone in the restaurant was staring at me. The other diners were engrossed in their meals and conversations but I couldn't overcome the sensation that I needed to hide.

"I love the food here but I hate that it's so fucking noisy." Wendy complained after the waiter took away our menus.

"Last year," Roy said. "I was visiting my friend John in Salt Lake City. We were in this loud bar, and John said, 'Last week my friend Albert burned his arm pretty badly. He had to have skin grafts.' So I asked, 'How'd he do that?' John said, 'He was burning wigs in his back-yard with gasoline.' I thought that was a little strange. 'Why was he burning wigs?' I asked. John shouted, '*Weeds*! Not wigs! He was burning weeds.' I thought he had said, 'wigs.'"

"I've heard of a guy *sounding* like a queen," Wendy said. "But that's the first time I've ever heard of a guy *hearing* like a queen."

"I love it," I said, temporarily distracted by his story. "You thought it was normal that a guy would be burning wigs in his backyard."

"Yeah, with gasoline," Roy said, mocking his own credulity. "I thought his friend was a crazy drag queen quitting the business."

"So he torched his wigs to insure that he could never go back to doing drag," Wendy suggested.

"Do drag queens ever quit?" I asked.

"No," Wendy said. "That's their triumph and their tragedy."

"I know a drag queen in Seattle who's in his seventies," Roy said. "He's had a stroke and open heart surgery but he still does drag."

"Do you think he went through rehab to learn how to walk in heels again?" I asked.

It occurred to me then that Roy was a good storyteller. When you think about it, and I did often, storytelling is a skill that everyone needs to develop. In every couple, both parties need to take turns as Scheherazade and learn to hold each other's interest as if their life together depended upon it. A thousand and one nights is less than three years, hardly any time at all, really, and I felt *The Arabian Nights*, in addition to being classic literature, could also be regarded as the first marriage manual. A man who could tell a good story inherently promised that he would never bore me and that our lives would be an adventure worth retelling.

Unfortunately, I started to brood upon a character I had authored, one who had captured the imagination of the entire country: Nelson Kunker, the tar pit guy.

"Don't mope," Wendy said. "If I had your talent, I'd be thrilled that someone fired me from a job that was holding me back. Now you can finish your novel. And who knows? The tar pits might be material for your next book."

"Thanks," I said. "But it takes more than a pep talk to make someone forget that he's had a really bad day, especially if his bad day has been televised as breaking news on all of the twenty-four hour news networks. It's okay. Let me feel shitty for twenty-four hours."

"All right," Wendy said. Our drinks arrived, and she began to tear open a packet of artificial sweetener for her iced tea. There was a funny remark somewhere about Wendy and artificial sweeteners but I was too depressed to think of it.

"What about you?" Roy asked Wendy. "Do you want to write, too?"

Wendy nodded the shameful acknowledgment that intelligent people in Los Angeles gave when they confessed to the urge to write. It was slightly more respectable than confessing to the urge to act and regarded as slightly less pretentious than confessing to the urge to direct. Confessing to the urge to produce was usually considered to be a sign of insanity or of a rich second husband.

"But I don't want to write novels," she said. "I want to write for television."

"What are you working on?" Roy asked.

"We wrote some sketches together," Wendy said with a nod toward me. Almost a year ago, Wendy had spent an hour formatting a sketch that she described as, "The worst piece of unfunny shit" and had started one of her, "I can write funnier crap than this" rants. It had been her third rant that week, and I dared her to write something better because I thought she could. She surprised me by asking if I wanted to team up with her. Writing sketches was tempting because it was a genre where anything over six pages was considered too long. I had stopped working on my novel and thought that completing something might inspire me to get back to my book. Over the next two months, we wrote ten sketches by staying after work and working on the weekends. I was satisfied with them. They were funny but I had left it up to Wendy to get us a writing job.

"I want Amanda to read them," she said, "but she's been such a cunt since she got pregnant that I held off. And now's certainly not a good time to give them to her."

"One of our sketches is about . . ." I started.

"Don't jinx it!" Wendy shouted, stopping me midsentence.

"You're superstitious?" Roy asked.

"Just about my work," she said. "I don't want to end up as virga."

"Virga?" he asked. "Isn't that what they call falling rain in the Southwest that evaporates before it hits the ground?"

Wendy and I were astounded that he had heard of the obscure word.

"All right," she said. "You're a little too smart, archaeology-boy."

Roy accepted her compliment with a bemused grin.

"Virga is Wendy's term for wannabe artists who never accomplish anything," I clarified for his benefit. I found it difficult not to think of myself as virga, and my unfinished novel as a rain of letters that evaporated before hitting the page.

On Monday morning Wendy called to tell me that Chip's article about *Aftertaste* had appeared in *Fave*. Wendy had assumed my position as the script coordinator, and she reported that Amanda was furious. (She was working from home since the birth of her son and called Wendy about fifty times a day.) The story was entitled "The Comedy Agenda of *Aftertaste*," and its centerpiece was a hatchet job of Amanda in which my nickname for her was made public. It was unfair to her and I was sorry that I had provided Chip with his cheap shot.

Wendy also called me that afternoon.

"I have some bad news," she said ominously. "Joe pitched a new character this morning: The Tar-Pit Guy."

"No," I said as I imagined Joe expertly parodying my flat-voweled Wisconsin accent.

"Yes," Wendy said. "Amanda's given him the go-ahead to write it up."

My notoriety only increased during the next week. I had struck the national funny bone, and on Monday several late night talk show hosts put me in their opening monologues. To my horror, I was also recognized everywhere. Idiots, who probably couldn't have named the current vice president, called out, "Tar pits!" when they spotted me at convenience stores and gas stations. Just as I started to hope the commotion was starting to die down, I would hear "The Tar-Pit Guy" used as a reference on a morning radio show or news footage of me would be aired on a special called *America's Most Embarrassing News Stories*.

The following Saturday night, Wendy, Reina, and Roy came over to my house to watch the Tar-Pit Guy make his debut on *Aftertaste*. Joe did a perfect imitation of my Midwestern accent and even managed to hint that the character was gay without actually making him effeminate. No one in the room laughed until Wendy exploded when the character's cell phone rang and it was *Larry King Live*. Then we all laughed. I was mortified but admired Joe's skill and admitted that the character was funny. I'd always admired the sophistication of the ancient Greeks because they had a god Momus, who was the god of blame, mockery, and criticism. Naturally, Momus was also regarded as the patron of writers and poets. He seemed to have inflicted a punishment on me that was perversely fitting. I liked to think that I was extremely funny and very intelligent and suddenly everyone considered me to be hilariously idiotic. It was like a comedian actually dying from the fall after slipping on a banana peel.

"He wants to make the Tar-Pit Guy a recurring bit," Wendy warned.

"I really have to go into hiding," I said.

"It'll die down," Wendy said. "Unless the character catches on."

"Why don't you come up to Alaska for the summer?" Roy suggested. "No one's going to recognize you up there."

I looked at him to see whether he was serious. "I mean it," he said, as if he sensed my skepticism.

It did sound appealing, but going to Alaska for the summer violated the first commandment of gay life: Thou shalt not move to another state to be with someone whom thou barely knowest. It was crazy, but it also seemed to be sensible. Roy wasn't a jerk, and neither was I until recently. Undoubtedly every gay man who quits his job and moves from California to be with a guy he met online from New Jersey tells himself the same thing. I looked to Wendy to see what she thought.

She shrugged.

"Just for the summer! You can't move there!"

Roy and I had another week together in Los Angeles before he returned to Alaska. Proof of our immediate intimacy was that after spending only two nights with him I lost my usual pee-shyness and could take a leak while he stood next to me brushing his teeth. We spent the next seven days and nights together talking constantly. We talked on the phone. We talked in the car. We talked during meals. We talked in bed. We tried to cover everything in a week. Childhood reminiscences, high school traumas and triumphs, job histories, brutal yet affectionate capsule biographies of our siblings that we would have never repeated to them, superficial and astute psychological analyses of our parents' behaviors. We revealed political beliefs (mutual incomprehension about Gay Republicans), spiritual beliefs (each of us had experienced a "paranormal experience"—a UFO sighting for me and a ghost sighting for Roy), and exchanged litanies of passions: favorite foods, favorite books, favorite painters, favorite movies, and tastes in music. We recounted our respective sexual histories and listened to each other's love stories with the calm detachment of anthropologists, the horrified countenances of pious churchgoers, the prurient curiosity of innocent bystanders, or the rib-tickled satisfaction of a theater audience, depending upon the number of positions assumed, roles played, devices employed, body parts engaged, or partners involved. (Roy had me beat in that department, as his tally was two threesomes and a fourgy.)

By the time Roy departed for Anchorage, I felt confident that going to Alaska for the summer wasn't completely insane. I was going just for the summer. I wasn't uprooting my entire life although I tried to suppress the thought that I didn't really have much of a life to uproot.

I couldn't leave immediately with Roy because I needed to raise some cash and try to sublet my apartment. I decided to hit my father up for the money because he was a successful plumber and always joked that he was flush with cash. I settled upon a loan of fourteen hundred dollars as I thought borrowing that amount sounded more frugal than asking him for fifteen hundred. My father wasn't stupid; he was always reading history and science books, but I was dim and operated under the assumption that if I ignored something obvious it remained invisible to him, too.

My plan was to suggest that I wasn't going to Alaska for a vacation; I was going there to work on my novel. My father respected hard work, and he wouldn't notice that I didn't want to work for the money that would allow me to work on my novel. At first my father seemed confused about what exactly I wanted the money for.

"I'm not giving you money for that," he said. "I saw something on the Discovery Channel that said it's the most dangerous job on Earth."

"That's crab fishing on the Bering Sea," I said.

"Bristol Bay's out near the Aleutians," he warned. "The Japanese invaded there during the war." After my mother's death, my dad spent two years watching programs about World War II on the History Channel. He knew more about D-Day than Eisenhower did.

"He doesn't fish on a boat," I said, explaining that Roy fished from the shore with a net, prompting my father to ask several technical questions that revealed my ignorance about salmon fishing.

"How do I know you're not just going to spend this money on wacky-tobacky?" he asked.

I had told my father that I'd been fired from *Aftertaste* for smoking pot on the job. It was completely stupid of me but my father always said that there was nothing I couldn't tell him and I took him at his word.

"I've learned my lesson," I said. "And I've started back in on the novel."

This was true. After my asphalt dunking, I was so desperate to re-establish some self-esteem that I reread what I had written and was pleasantly surprised to find that I liked it. I set my alarm to wake up at eight every day to write and actually did.

"Well, I'm not that smart but tell me something."

This was always a dangerous prelude to being clobbered by his sagacity.

"Isn't being an artist a job? Don't artists have to wake up and work every day? Picasso painted every day. He didn't wait for inspiration. He worked."

Sometimes I envied friends of mine whose parents discouraged them from becoming artists. They warned their children being an artist wasn't practical or undermined their confidence by reminding them that they were trying to succeed in an extremely competitive profession with a high rate of failure. My father never did that. He supported me in whatever I chose to do. But his "unconditional" support came with one condition: I had to do my best. I couldn't fail because I was what I would call a "slacker," or what he would call a "butt-sitting bastard."

My father didn't respond favorably to my working-on-the-novel ploy, and I had no backup plan. I knew he liked what he heard about Roy, and out of desperation I reminded him that Roy had suggested that I come to Alaska. It wasn't my idea.

"How are things between you two?" my father asked.

"Um," I said. "They're good."

"Roy sounds squared away. The only thing I like about your plan is that I think he'll keep you out of trouble."

After I came out to my father, I went through a short-lived militant phase and had told my father that he always talked to my brother about the women he was dating but that he never asked me about the men I dated. That was a huge mistake. I gave him entrée into prying into all aspects of my life and into giving me unsolicited observations about my behavior. I had nightmares that one day he was going to push me aside and demonstrate how to give a proper blow job because I was doing it all wrong.

"Will you lend me the money?"

"No," he said.

"I'll pay you back."

"Let me finish."

I tensed up because "let me finish" signaled declarations of opinion in which my father ended discussions by presenting incontrovertible facts.

"You need to get your life together," he said without rancor. "I'm worried about you. You got fired for smoking grass, then you take a dip in a tar pit. You're too old to be asking me for money—for this. You want to go fishing, great. Figure out how to pay for it. You claim you want to write, but as far as I can tell you don't. Do you make time for it? You say you want a boyfriend. Show him how much he means to you by working to be with him. Figure out how to get to this Iggy-place. Follow through on something. It sounds like Roy knows what he's doing with his life. Can you say the same thing?"

My father spoke calmly, which made his words more searing. He patiently explained the current workings of my life in the same genial manner that he explained how black holes functioned or vents at the bottom of the ocean released plumes of scalding gases. He and I shared the same ability to effortlessly remember strange information, and he related the events of my recent life as if they were historic facts; and since the subject matter had always fascinated me, his words would be impossible to forget.

"I hate to say this," he said, "but why would Roy want to be with a man who can't figure out how to spend the summer with him?"

My father ended the call by saying, "I love you."

"I love you, too," I said, my shame covering me like a heavy blanket.

SIX

On rainy days when I was growing up in Milwaukee, I used to leaf through my grandfather's old leather-bound atlas and the world appeared to be a work of fiction. Place names such as Alaska, Mongolia, and Yap were as far-fetched and fabulous as Lilliputia, Middle-earth, and Oz. I'd never traveled beyond the contiguous United States before—Ontario doesn't count as foreign in Wisconsin—and when my plane began its descent into Anchorage, flying over the snow-covered mountains and dark waters of Cook Inlet, I felt a wild surge of exhilaration.

Roy had bought my airline ticket, but I had insisted on paying him back. My money situation had improved because Wendy's girlfriend

Reina sublet my apartment for the entire summer after her roommate threw her out. The ex-roommate was Wiccan, and she went ballistic when Reina lit a candle that was only supposed to be lit on the vernal equinox. The summer solstice was in two weeks, and I planned on observing the occasion with a private ceremony thanking the Goddess for alleviating my financial plight by creating crazy lesbians.

Roy lived a block away from Delany Park, in a historic Anchorage neighborhood where log cabins were built next door to small houses from the thirties that reminded me of art deco igloos.

Roy's sunny second-floor apartment shamed me, because while my television was propped up on garbage-picked glass bricks, his spotless place was furnished with slick vintage Scandinavian furniture that he'd bought before it became collectable. Roy claimed that Danish Modern worked in Alaska because it was made at the right latitude. His apartment was starkly beautiful but possessed an austere, unsettling quality. It reminded me of a doctor's waiting room. Every chair was a place to sit comfortably while you waited to hear bad news.

"Scandinavian furniture's sort of the logical outcome of twentieth-century design," I said while stroking my hand across a desk chair's nubby turquoise fabric. "Mission furniture designed by agnostics."

"Did you think I sat on logs?" Roy asked.

"No, but I have a theory that if a man can't choose a good bed, then he'll be no good in the sack."

"Not from my experience," he said. "I've had great sex in dorm rooms."

It had been three weeks since we had seen each other and the topic of sex was clearly on both of our minds. I continued to elaborate and improvise on my theory about how interior decoration reveals a man's sexuality. "If a guy's apartment is too busy with knickknacks and other junk," I claimed, "when he kisses you, he'll heave his tongue around your back teeth like a wet seal trying to clamber onto a rocky shore."

Roy stuck his tongue into my mouth and proceeded to clamber onto my rocky shore. It was my first sarcastic kiss. Dropping any pretense of continuing to discuss kissing in theory, we proceeded to lip-grinding smooching. Roy led me into his bedroom, where I observed that he did know how to choose a good bed. It was severely modern and looked as if it had been built for a monk who had renounced everything but his sense of style.

Unfortunately after quick and passionate sex, we didn't have much time to lounge in his bed because we were meeting Dylan Fabizak for an early dinner.

Dylan had arrived in Anchorage two days earlier and immediately called Roy to ask him again if he could go salmon fishing. Roy had put off giving him an answer, but during their conversation he mentioned that we had tickets that night to see his best friend Alex Nevak's one-man show. Alex was a Yup'ik storyteller and both Dylan and I had asked variations of the same question: What the hell's a Yup'ik?

"The Yupiit are Native Alaskans," Roy explained. "They live in Western Alaska and speak an Eskimo language, but salmon fishing and seal hunting are more important to their culture than whaling." To Roy's dismay, Dylan asked if he could tag along. Roy wasn't thrilled about spending my first night in Alaska with Dylan but he was glad to help Alex fill another seat. We were having dinner with Dylan before the show at the Kalikat Bakery.

The Kalikat Bakery is a bakery, restaurant, and gourmet grocery store located a few blocks from Delany Park. Famous for what Roy called their manly muffins—broad shoulders, narrow waists—steam billowed constantly from the bakery's exhaust vents, making the gleaming modern building appear capable of dispensing cappuccinos from the downspouts of its gutters.

For the citizens of Anchorage, the Kalikat Bakery was a beloved landmark, reassuring them that they lived in a cosmopolitan city and had access to hot and cold coffee beverages of varying hues and potencies, mustards of many nations, and daily copies of *The New York Times*. Purchasing a latte every morning was deemed a civic obligation, the money supporting a worthy local cause—the preservation of Anchorage's café culture.

Dylan walked into the bakery wearing a becoming pair of matte-silver eyeglasses, immediately stoking my fantasy of a porn magazine called *MENsa* that would be devoted entirely to four-eyed beefcake.

"Nelson, it's great to see you again," he said warmly. It thrilled me that Dylan Fabizak remembered my name until I realized that Roy had probably refreshed his memory. "This is perfect," Dylan said while reading the menu hanging above the counter. "I love these self-serve places; you don't have to tip anyone." His remark branded him as a cheapskate but I didn't think much of it because it reinforced my Midwestern prejudice that the more money a person had, the more likely he was to be a Scrooge. We placed our orders, paid the cashier, and then waited until our numbers were called.

I examined Dylan's white thermal T-shirt, which, in addition to displaying every contour of his muscular body, revealed dark tattoos bleeding through the light fabric. Two angel's wings were tattooed on his shoulder blades, their teal blue feathers peeping out from underneath his collar. While Roy and Dylan discussed the best hiking trails in the city, I entertained myself imagining that the barbed wire encircling his huge left bicep was a constant nuisance, continually snagging and tearing his shirts.

A dark-haired, bearded man in a black leather jacket kept staring at us while we waited for our orders. At first I assumed he recognized Dylan. Dylan must have thought the same thing, because he sighed and tensed up expectantly when the man approached our table. But the man ignored him and spoke to me.

"Excuse me," he said. "Did I see you on the news?"

My face flushed, and I nodded my head.

"I knew it was you!" he brayed. "The guy in the tar pits, right?"

"Yes," I replied tersely, hoping that he would go away.

"Did you do jail time for bustin' in there?" he asked in a loud voice. An elderly woman wearing a strand of pearls, seated at the next table, overheard him and hastily shunted her coffee cup nearer to her tray.

"No" I said in a near-whisper.

"Back off," Dylan said. It wasn't apparent to me whether he was coming to my aid or angry that the man had failed to recognize him.

"Dude," Roy said pleasantly, "we were having a conversation."

The man apologized and returned to his table, pointing me out to the frumpy overweight blonde-haired woman seated across from him.

"The good news is that you can live down anything in Alaska," Roy declared. "The state motto on our license plate should be: Bury Your Past."

I offered a quick smile that looked as if he had asked me to demonstrate the expression.

"Sorry," he said. "I thought we could joke about it."

"Not yet," I said as the man in the leather jacket returned with the woman in tow. He asked if they could get a photograph with me. Roy gave him a dirty look, but I didn't know what to say and mumbled, "Okay." The man handed the camera to Dylan, instructing him on how to operate it. Dylan shrugged and asked us to stand closer together before snapping a picture of me standing between my two awestruck fans. The couple thanked me profusely, then the woman asked Dylan for his autograph and a photo. He was happy to oblige her and I manned the camera while he put his arm around her shoulder and smiled.

After our fans returned to their table, a server brought us our food. I shook my head and announced, *"Now* we can joke about it."

Dylan admitted that he had wanted to call me when he had realized that I was the Tar-Pit Guy. "I couldn't believe it," he said. "I kept thinking, fuck, I thought I had bad publicity. How will this guy ever live this down?"

"Hey," I said, "at least I wasn't on drugs, and they didn't videotape me naked."

Dylan grinned sinisterly. "That's what makes it so humiliating. You don't even have the excuse that you were high. And you have to admit that I look really fine naked. Right?"

He appeared to be appeased when I granted him that.

"So what's the deal with you two?" Dylan asked. "Should I be expecting a wedding invitation?"

Roy and I shifted in our seats. We hadn't even started referring to each other as boyfriends (we were still officially telling people that we were dating), and more importantly we hadn't gotten around to exchanging pivotal declarations of I love you. (From my experience of man-on-man love, I think that phrase should be dubbed, "the words that dare not speak their name.")

"We haven't talked about it," I said, convinced that a soft, tubby cherub doesn't rule love between men. Gay men had forced Cupid to shape up. He became a gym-hardened leader, demanding unquestioned allegiance as he guided us on our hunt, warning that a single, careless word such as *love* or a sudden movement toward cohabitation could startle our quarry. We covertly stalked each other, lying in ambush, waiting patiently—sometimes for years—for Cupid's signal that it was time to loose an arrow, knowing that men only had a single shot.

"I can't imagine living up here during the winter," Dylan declared before shoveling in a mouthful of salad. "Isn't it dark all the time?"

"Yeah," Roy said, "It's dark all the time. During the winter, it's like the back room of a sex club. There's a lot of groping; it's totally hot. You'd love it. It's the perfect place for Hollywood closet cases."

Dylan's face changed color and he looked angry.

"That was uncalled for," he said, "I was just asking a question."

I didn't understand what had prompted Roy's spiteful outburst, though I was fascinated by it. It was so unexpected that it confused me. Maybe Roy wasn't as nice as I had thought. He saw the appalled expression on my face.

"I'm sorry," he said. "I guess I'm oversensitive. Everyone assumes that we travel by dogsled or live in igloos. I've actually met Americans who don't even know we're part of the United States."

Roy went on to say that Anchorage's winters were comparable to other northern American cities like Chicago or Minneapolis. "The sun returns as quickly as it departs. By March it's already staying up until nine o'clock. Although after a long winter, icicles start to look like prison bars."

His choice of words had to be deliberate, and I couldn't understand why Roy was trying to provoke Dylan, but this newly aggressive side of his personality intrigued me.

"Well, I couldn't live up here," Dylan said. He made a face to indicate that the prospect repulsed him.

"Well, I couldn't live in L.A.," Roy said. "The traffic's so bad, it takes an hour to go anywhere."

"Oh, that's brilliant," Dylan said. "You actually noticed that Los Angeles has heavy traffic. Next you'll tell me that we have earthquakes. Oops, so does Alaska. Look, people in L.A. can handle being bored in traffic because that's the price they pay for living in a city that's not boring. You'll never be stuck in traffic in Alaska; you'll just be stuck in Alaska."

"L.A.'s ugly. We live in a beautiful place."

"Ugly place, beautiful people or beautiful place. . . . I don't know about you but I have no desire to fuck a forest."

"I should have said 'natural beauty,' not Botox-injected."

"It's too isolated up here," Dylan said. "I need to be exposed to new things. New people. New ideas."

"As far as I know," Roy responded, "you can open a book anywhere. Or have your personal assistant read it and do coverage for you." He raised his hands and mimed quotation marks. "That is what they call it, right?"

His comment infuriated Dylan. "I bet I read more than you do," he said. "Last year, I read two books a week."

"Well, some of us weren't lucky enough to be sentenced to a year of reading time," Roy said.

I started to think that they hated each other. Dylan was supposed to be trying to convince Roy to take him fishing but had only succeeded in making him angry. And Roy had become bitingly sarcastic. I decided to try to remedy the situation. Dylan was about to say something else when I blurted out, "Did the prison have a good library?"

He appeared to change his mind and answered me instead of responding to Roy.

"I worked in the library," he said. "I loved the librarian, Miss Facos. She's a tiny woman, barely over five feet, but she's not afraid to tell the biggest, scariest cons to be quiet. When word got around that she called the warden's office about an overdue book, the inmates started calling her, 'The Enforcer.'"

"What types of books were most popular?" I asked.

"Just what you'd think," he said. "Police procedurals and murder mysteries. There was always a waiting list for *Sherlock Holmes* and *In Cold Blood*. The librarian took a liking to me and assigned me to work the check-out desk. I got a kick out of trying to help every inmate find the right book. To loners, I'd recommend *Robinson Crusoe* or *Desert Solitaire*; to drug dealers, I'd suggest *Naked Lunch* or *Confessions of an Opium Eater*. To crooked lawyers, *Bleak House* or *To Kill a Mockingbird*. To murderers, *Double Indemnity* or *Crime and Punishment*. But I had my rules. White supremacists were limited to checking out *Mein Kampf* once every six months; violent sex offenders weren't allowed to read *A Clockwork Orange,* and I wouldn't loan out *Lolita* to just anyone."

"What'd you read?" I asked.

"Well, after reading several recovery memoirs, I told the librarian that I loved Chekhov's plays, and she insisted that I had to read his stories and especially his letters. Have you read them?"

"I haven't," I replied.

"You should. His letters make him come alive. Some of them are so beautiful."

Dylan smiled and took a bite of chicken. He added, "She also suggested that I read Joe Orton's plays because he started out as an actor. And she had me reread Shakespeare because he was an actor, too. After that I read everything she recommended."

Involuntarily picturing him lying in his prison bunk, shirtless, reading *Entertaining Mr. Sloane* started to give me a stiffy.

"One of my favorite books was cowritten by an actor," I said. "It's called *Diary of a Nobody*. The authors were two brothers, George and Weedon Grossmith. George performed in Gilbert and Sullivan's plays."

Dylan nodded politely but didn't say anything. I expected that reaction because *Diary of a Nobody* was a book that nobody I knew had ever read. It was mentioned in *Brideshead Revisited*, and after reading that Evelyn Waugh thought it was one of the funniest books ever written, I'd bought and read it. My reading tended to proceed like a row of falling dominoes, one book leading me to the next.

Roy looked at his watch. "We have to leave, or we'll be late."

His truck had an extended cab with a backseat, but Dylan asked me to scoot over because he wanted to sit up front with us. Roy looked puzzled as I slid over next to him. "I want to see the sights," Dylan explained as I was wedged between the two of them. Their legs pressed against mine, and someone's jacket smelled like pine needles, but I couldn't tell whose. To make the tight squeeze more bearable, Dylan reached his left arm around my shoulder, resting it along the back of the seat. Roy reached over and placed his right hand on my thigh, convincing me that touching should be listed first as the primary ingredient in the formula for happiness.

Like every first-time visitor to Alaska, I marveled aloud that at eight o'clock at night, the sun hung in the sky as if it were three in the afternoon. It almost seemed as if the sun was a tourist, too, and was completely disoriented from changing time zones after having traveled all day.

"I'll give you this," Dylan said. "Anchorage is nicer than I imagined."

"I was thinking the same thing," I said as we looked at the city's skyline against the backdrop of the mountains. We drove down Sixth Avenue running parallel to Fourth Avenue, Anchorage's Main Street, where a row of small- and medium-sized skyscrapers were neatly lined up like cereal boxes on a shelf. I imagined a yawning King Kong waking up, selecting a building, then pouring office workers into a bowl, or maybe grabbing a handful to eat as a snack, right out of the box.

The Fourth Walrus, Anchorage's struggling alternative theater company, was located in a former elementary school on Fourth Avenue that served as an arts center for a struggling children's theater, a struggling ballet company, and a struggling art gallery. The atmosphere of the arts center was depressing. Hallways were lined with cheaply printed posters promoting upcoming events—photocopied posters inherently promising the derivative—and the school had the stifling air of an infirmary for the arts, a hospice for organizations with fluttering pulses and unhealthy balance sheets.

As we took our seats, Roy raved about Alex's work, which he said combined traditional Yup'ik storytelling with performance art. It sounded dreadful but I kept my mouth shut. The introduction of performance art to the indigenous peoples of Alaska sounded like another in a long line of historic disasters inflicted upon them—a calamity comparable to the devastation wrought by the introduction of alcohol and influenza.

My expectations were low but the clever title of the show appealed to me: *Caribourgeois*. Alex appeared on the bare stage of the former school auditorium wearing a black T-shirt and black jeans. He was slim with shoulder-length black hair, a moustache of trimmed cat whiskers, a hawklike nose (real-deal aquiline), and a long, neatly incised scar running down his left cheek. It was reasonable to assume that the curious looking gash played a role in his choice of a career as it begged for an explanation. He was handsome but it took me a moment to see that because his scar made him appear threatening—until he smiled.

"Tonight I'm going to sing a traditional song of my people," Alex announced in a lilting voice while lighting a small candle. "It's a ceremonial song of renewal that we reserve for special occasions." He began to slowly sing in Yup'ik, the recognizable verses of "Happy Birthday to You." The guttural, ancient-sounding Yup'ik words sounded hilarious sung with the familiar melody. But after the audience laughed, Alex continued to sing, his voice gaining in power, until the song became moving, transforming "Happy Birthday to You" into something primordial and profound.

Traditional Yup'ik tales about the relationship between men and animals inspired most of Alex's stories, but a note in the program explained that Yup'ik storytellers didn't merely recite traditional stories but were expected to tell of their own experiences. So that night Raven prowled the parking lots of supermarkets, Eagle hung around the docks, and Bear foraged in garbage dumps.

Within minutes Alex convinced me that a man changing into an animal could be a garden-variety supernatural event. While portraying an animal, Alex's voice and body assumed cartoonish attributes as he demonstrated an expert's knowledge of their natural behavior. It was like watching Daffy Duck reveal, between sibilant monologues, that he was a real bird, perhaps a surf scoter or another black duck, as he used his bill to preen his feathers and search for parasitic mites. In the middle of Alex's performance, while Raven sweet-talked Bear into opening a clamshell fast-food container, a member of the audience accidentally dropped something metallic that made a loud clattering noise. Alex reacted in character, jumping in a manner that suggested a startled bird lifting off the ground and fluttering a few feet.

Alex ended the evening by retelling the story of the salmon people. It was a Yup'ik tale of a fisherman who's transformed into a salmon and learns to see men from the salmon's point of view. The story started out comically as Alex explained salmon have long been held up as a poignant symbol of the reproductive urge, extolled for their perseverance in their quest to spawn. But he identified with the returning salmon as another insanely driven species that was prepared to endure any sacrifice and overcome every hurdle to get their rocks off.

"Swimming upstream is grueling," he said, "but watching my weight and exercising four times a week for the entire span of my adult life, all in pursuit of maintaining my sexual desirability, is no piece of cake either."

As Alex continued with his story, he explained the salmon was so hungry for love that he couldn't eat, and the fisherman was so hungry for food that he couldn't love. We watched as the man slowly transformed into a salmon. Alex's hands and feet began to twitch, stroking the air slowly like fins moving through water. Then Alex conveyed what he called "the horny salmon" in a man's body along with a "hungry man" in a salmon's body through a virtuoso series of oscillating facial tics and balletic motions of his hands and limbs.

"When the man becomes a salmon, his heart almost breaks from feeling the full force of the salmon's desire," Alex said. "And the salmon realizes for the first time the misery of a starving man."

Raven then mocked the salmon, "You'd solve both your problems if you'd just give your heart to the two legs/no wings for dinner."

To the audience's delight, the salmon's mouth, which had continually opened and closed as water passed through its gills, for an instant assumed the fishy version of "Oh! That's a great idea!"

The salmon achieves his quest for love by allowing himself to be caught by the starving man. The moment could have been played farcically, but Alex showed the gaunt-cheeked man's initial astonishment and then his teary-eyed gratitude.

To honor this expression of love, the man vows to retell the story of the salmon's gift to every generation. "It's a love story that's been told for thousands of years," Alex said before adding an aside. "One of the things I love about my job is that I get to promote interspecies love to right-wing conservatives and they don't even realize it."

Alex ended the evening by suggesting that nonnative Alaskans should tell traditional stories about their relationships with their traditional foods. He pointed out that it was dangerous that we showed no respect for the natural world that sustains our lives. "Although," he admitted, "it might be hard to make the legend of the Doritos people into a story that anyone would care about."

When the curtain came down, the audience burst into a long, sustained round of applause, and Alex came out and took the first of three curtain calls.

"So what did you think?" Roy asked as we walked up the aisle of the theater.

"He's great," Dylan said. "I didn't know what to expect."

"He's fantastic," I gushed. "I loved when he told the story about the spider and casually mentioned that her name was Charlotte."

In Alex's retelling of several traditional Yup'ik tales, he often made sly references to other animal stories such as *Goldilocks* and *Little Red Riding Hood*. He even alluded to Chekhov's *The Seagull*, Orwell's *Animal Farm*, and Alfred Hitchcock's *The Birds*.

"I liked the part where his mother's cleaning under his bed and discovers that Charlotte wrote, 'Alex is Gay' in her web," Roy said.

"I especially liked that he never mentioned it again," Dylan added.

"It never occurred to me that every culture tells animal stories," I said, while thinking that we needed a spider to spell out whether Dylan was gay or straight.

After the show we waited for Alex in the hallway while he met his fans and even autographed a few programs. I could see our three reflections in the glass of a trophy case and quietly celebrated my unexpected victory over singleness. Roy and Dylan appeared to be especially tall and large standing in a former elementary school—two giants, the lead and his understudy, brought in for a special production of *Jack and the Beanstalk*.

After the last of his fans departed, Roy introduced us to Alex and we offered him our congratulations.

"I told you not to worry," Roy said, smiling proudly.

"The middle part needs some work," Alex said, "but I thought the opening worked well."

"I'll never hear 'Happy Birthday to You' in the same way again," I said. "And I loved how Raven jumped when you heard the noise in the audience."

"Thanks," he said. "But something's not right with the wolf story."

"What have I told you?" Roy said with asperity.

"Accept a compliment and shut up," Alex said. "It's not that easy."

"Yes, it is," Roy argued. "Don't second-guess yourself."

"That's what acting is," Dylan declared. "It's second-guessing done with total conviction."

"I tried to explain that to him," Alex said. "But he's never been on stage."

"Oh, don't get all artist-y with me," Roy said. "You work intensely for a few hours. It's like a doctor performing surgery. You don't hear them going on and on about their concentration and focus."

"It is the same thing," Alex maintained. "A doctor performs surgery. If he doesn't get it exactly right the patient dies. It's the same with an actor, if he doesn't get it exactly right, he'll die on stage."

"Well," Roy said, tiring of their dispute. "All I know is that you didn't die tonight. You were great."

Alex shrugged noncommittally, and after he gathered his bag from backstage we headed outside to Roy's truck. Alex had asked Roy for a ride home, and he and Dylan climbed into the backseat of the cab. "You have to meet Graham," Dylan said to Alex, telling him about the director of his film. "He'll be here in a few days and one part still hasn't been cast. I think you'd be perfect for it."

Alex thanked him, commenting, "That's really generous of you."

I glanced over at Roy and caught his eye. He looked abashed for having treated Dylan so harshly at dinner and nodded to indicate that he might have been wrong about him.

"He really needs to hire you," Dylan said excitedly. He asked him for his telephone number. Alex handed him a business card that said "Alex Nevak, Storyteller." As someone who found it difficult to become a novelist, I wanted to know how he became a storyteller.

"Alex," I asked, "how did you get started?" I never tired of hearing the self-creation myths of gay men who were artists. They tended to follow the same general pattern, differing only in their genres: The proud confession that he knew when he was eight years old that he wanted to be an artist, after reading the book, listening to the recording, or seeing the play, movie, painting, or photograph that changed his life. Or the unexpected revelation in high school or college, when the spotlight, klieg light, desk light, strobe light, skylight, or flashbulb appeared over his head depending upon whether he realized that he wanted to be an actor, singer, dancer, comedian, film director, writer, rock star, painter, or photographer. Hearing their struggles made it less painful when I declared, "I'm a writer," and listeners reacted with the fixed smiles and expressions of polite interest that social courtesy requires when speaking to small children, the senescent elderly, and aspiring artists.

"My great-grandfather was a storyteller," Alex said. "At first I told our traditional stories without embellishing them, but something was missing. My grandmother helped me though. One time I forgot to turn out a light, and she reminded me to show the lamp the respect that it deserved. We believe there's a nonhuman person inside of everything: animals, trees, stones—even lamps. That was my inspiration. I needed to honor the spirits inside modern Yup'ik life. I wasn't showing respect to snowmachines, microwaves, washers, dryers, you name it. Sometimes I think that's why the Yupiit love television so much; it reinforces our most ancient beliefs, because we can actually see the people inside the lamp." Alex appeared to be dumbfounded by his observation. "I've got to remember that," he said to himself. He quickly dug a pencil and small notebook out of his knapsack and jotted down the thought.

"I love that you make your living doing this," Dylan said. In the program for *Caribourgeous*, Alex's bio stated said that, during the summer, when he wasn't salmon fishing, he performed on cruise ships in southeast Alaska, and that during the winter, he performed in community centers and schools across the state.

"I'm barely lower-middle class," Alex responded, "but somehow it all comes together."

"How were your shows in Seattle?" Dylan asked. The program also noted that Alex had performed the show in Seattle for two weeks before his limited-run in Anchorage.

"Great reviews, small crowds," he said with a shrug. He sounded disappointed but not apologetic or ashamed. "You'll love this," he added enthusiastically. "I bought a digital camera at an electronics store and the salesperson was a near-miss. How great is that?"

"A near-miss?" Dylan asked.

"Transgendered guys who get breast implants but keep their dicks," Alex said.

"We're slashing more than just prices!" I exclaimed.

"She offered me a two-year warranty on parts and labor," Alex said. "And I wanted to ask her if she got the same deal."

"Wouldn't it be great if her name tag had "Larry" crossed out with "Linda" penciled in below?" I asked. I'd expected to feel shy around Alex after Roy's build-up, but we hit it off immediately because we spoke the same language: jokes. We were able to follow each other's flights of fancy with the instinctive grace of flocking birds.

"Did you meet anyone in Seattle?" Roy asked.

"Yeah," Alex said listlessly.

"Whenever Alex performs out of town he always gets laid," Roy declared.

"Not always."

"Yeah, right," Roy said. "Whenever we go out to bars together, he always splits with some dude, and I'm left a whorphan."

"I left you a whorphan that one time."

"What about the time in Boston?"

"I forgot about him," he allowed.

"How did you guys meet?" I asked.

It was obvious that they were once-fucked buddies, because they both flinched slightly as if they experiencing the simultaneous aftershock of an ancient orgasm.

"We met in Egegik," Alex said. "My family's originally from Bethel, but my uncle married a woman from Egegik and he set nets there. My first summer out there, I was a total Eskimo hottie, and Roy had to have me."

"Don't forget he's a storyteller," Roy cautioned. "And that's pure fiction."

"That's the legend that my people tell," Alex said.

"We became friends," Roy said. "And at the end of the season, we took a sauna together and basically came out to each other. We slept together once but decided that we'd make better friends than boyfriends. At least, that's the legend that my people tell."

"You see," Alex said grandly. "There are many different legends but ultimately they all tell the same story."

"Are you finished?" Roy asked impatiently.

"Roy don't be tack-a-turn," Alex teased before offering an explanation for his deliberate mispronunciation. "Roy once dated a guy who mispronounced taciturn as tack-a-turn. We loved it because he was pretentious."

"He wasn't that bad," Roy protested.

"He had china plates hanging on his walls," Alex proclaimed with an air of confidence that no further argument would be required.

"Did he have one of those granny-fag apartments?" I asked, "where you walk in and think, Oh, we better be quiet during sex, we don't want to disturb his grandmother. Then you discover that he lives alone."

"Fuck you all," Roy said after he laughed.

"He had stuffed animals on his bed," Alex revealed.

"Oh, God," Dylan said. "I have more respect for men who sleep with real animals."

Roy stepped on the gas, causing us to scream like teenage girls as we were thrown back in our seats. The massive truck became a charging rogue elephant scattering Mustangs and Impalas to the far sides of the road.

"We should show them the salmon fishing on Ship Creek," Alex suggested to Roy, who nodded his head in agreement and turned down a side street. Ship Creek skirted downtown Anchorage, and every night in June hundreds of people lined up along its banks to fish for king salmon, the largest and most prized species of salmon.

There wasn't any parking near the creek, and we left the truck at a dock and walked over to the nearby stream. The sun was starting to set over Cook Inlet, and the sky had turned lurid tie-dyed shades of red, orange, and yellow.

"Look at your shadows," Roy said as he pointed toward our feet. Our shadows were pulled from our bodies, casting behind us on the asphalt for thirty feet, forming a textbook image that could be used to illustrate short summers followed by long winters.

"What causes that?" I asked.

In the far north, Roy explained, light hits the Earth at a sharp angle, and the distortion was caused because the light had to travel through more of the atmosphere. His ready answer impressed me, reiterating my belief that one of the reasons I required a boyfriend was to halve my ignorance and double my chances of understanding the world and myself.

The entire length of Ship Creek, below the dam and fish ladder, up from where the stream emptied into Cook Inlet, was lined with fishermen, standing wader to wader, fishing lines whizzing into the water. I imagined the fish cowering below as the rain of hooks fell from above.

"It doesn't seem very sporting," I said as we began to walk along the bank of the creek. "It must be like swimming through a barbed wire fence."

"I never thought of that," Roy said.

We watched a large woman on the bank of the creek cleaning a fish. Her motions were automatic and habitual like a secretary slicing open a letter. After glancing at the worthless contents, she dumped them into the creek and kept the valuable envelope.

Suddenly a large king salmon, almost three feet long, roiled the surface of the creek, briefly shooting out of the water, panic flashing from its scales. At the sight of the fish, men, women, and children on both sides of the creek began casting and recasting their lines, a group effort to weave an impromptu net.

"All that fish wants to do is get laid," Dylan declared, "and hundreds of men want to kill him."

"That's my life in a nutshell," Alex said.

"Can you imagine having to go through all of that just to fuck?" Dylan asked.

"Thank God we have masturbation," I said. "Salmon would become extinct if the males ever learned to jerk off."

"Imagine always having to return to your childhood home to have sex," Alex said.

"*Humans* would become extinct," I said.

"What about the salmon that gets rejected?" Dylan asked. "It has to happen."

"That could be a children's book," I said, "Sammy the Blue-Balled Salmon."

"Mommy," Alex said in a child's voice, "read me the part again about how Sammy got stood up after swimming upstream for a thousand miles."

"Don't forget the gay salmon," I said, suddenly inspired. "He swims upstream struggling against the current and the Christian right. Salmon have no margin of error. They reproduce once and then they die. They can't sexually experiment or go through a phase in college. What if the gay salmon doesn't realize that he's a . . . queen salmon."

I looked to Alex if see if he thought the name worked and he nodded his head as if to say that it would suffice for now.

"When it's time to fertilize the eggs," I said, further embellishing the idea, "suddenly the queen salmon's not that enthusiastic. But he goes through with it because that's what salmon do. Then, just as he finishes, he spots a trophy-size piece of salmon beefcake and thinks, 'Oh my God, I'm gay!'" I abruptly flipped my head sideways, lolling my tongue, to illustrate the fish going belly up. "Too late!" I shouted.

"In our stories," Alex said, "the salmons' bodies are said to be canoes they leave on the shore when they've finished their journey upstream."

"That's a beautiful image," I said.

"Do the salmon people have to live and dress as a salmon for a year before the change?" Dylan asked.

"The fin implants are really expensive," Alex answered, not missing a beat.

"That's one way to update all those fairy tales." I said, assuming the demeanor of a librarian reading a story aloud. "The Ugly Duckling had to undergo psychological counseling, daily injections of hormones, and a series of painful operations, but eventually he became a beautiful swan."

"Although, to be honest, " Alex said as he added the closing line, "everyone could tell that he had once been a duck."

Roy pointed to a group of salmon in the creek, milling about at the bottom of the fish ladder. He explained that they were conserving their energy before trying to ascend the steps. Describing a group of fish as a school suddenly made sense, because they appeared to be a gang of loitering juvenile delinquents—some of them with intimidating, scarred fins—daring each other to make the first move.

Dylan and I fell behind as Alex and Roy walked ahead of us. Alex began telling him a story, and Roy whooped with laughter while Dylan moved closer toward me.

"I was surprised to see you guys were still together," Dylan said candidly.

"Why is that?" I asked, bristling to what sounded like an insult.

"You don't seem cut out for each other," he said with a shrug.

"And why is that?"

"You're funny," he said. "And he's . . . *Roy.*"

I laughed, which was disloyal, but then I defended him. "Roy has a great sense of humor, but he doesn't crack jokes, he. . . ." I had to think for a moment to describe how he made me laugh. "He can be silly but always remains perfectly logical."

Dylan didn't appear to be impressed.

"You need someone more devilish," he said, "someone who's going to bring out the bad side of Nelson." If a member of my family or a close friend had suggested that idea, I would have dismissed his or her statement as absurd. But Dylan didn't know me at all and therefore his pronouncement took on the authority of an oracle. He looked directly at me, and I noticed for the first time that his eyes were a greenish brown hue; it figured that his eye color would be trendy Broccolate. "You've never done anything really rotten before, have you?" Dylan asked. "If you're going to be a great writer, you need to tap into your dark places."

"That's a new one," I said. "Being evil will broaden my outlook on life."

"See? That's what I like about you. You're funny."

I felt flattered that Dylan thought I was funny. And I also started to think that he couldn't be straight because he was definitely flirting with me. When we caught up with Alex and Roy, Dylan left my side and wedged himself between them, draping his arms across their shoulders.

"So what's it going to be?" he asked. "Are we all going fishing? C'mon you gotta let me come fishing."

Roy tugged at his watchband, pulling at it until his watch spun around completely to the opposite side of his wrist. Whenever he was nervous or uncomfortable, Roy fiddled with his watch, giving the impression that he was trying to restrain himself from checking to see why time was passing so slowly.

"I don't have a big place," Roy said. "I'm not sure there's room for you."

"I'll sleep on the floor," Dylan suggested. "I'll sleep on you. I'll sleep on Nelson. I'll sleep on both of you. Whatever it takes." It didn't take a genius to discern a sexual proposition beneath his glib tone. "You're not going fishing without me," he said playfully.

"Let me think about it," Roy said forcefully.

"But you're not saying no?"

"I'm not saying no."

His answer made Dylan smile confidently as if he was assured of eventually winning Roy's assent.

Roy and I had discussed my going fishing with him, but I went back and forth on my decision. I really was confused. I'd come to Alaska to see whether our relationship would lead anywhere, knowing that it could lead to me moving to Anchorage. I also wanted to finish my novel and see if my writing would amount to anything. It was possible that I would write every day while Roy fished, but I was afraid that I'd spend the three weeks goofing off. I didn't want to take a chance that I would stop writing again. I was broke and unemployed and my father's lecture had convinced me that I couldn't waste any more time. The problem was that I wanted to go fishing because it sounded like fun, and I was determined to renounce having fun. I didn't want to behave stupidly anymore. I had to get to work.

My objective in life was clear in my mind: I wanted everyone to leave me alone—without being single or lonely. Do I contradict myself? Very well then. I contradict myself. I am large, I contain multitudes. You really have to hand it to Whitman: no one has ever written a better definition of being totally mental. But, then, he was a crazy queen, too.

Wendy and I had stayed in touch by e-mails and telephone calls and I had tried to discuss with her whether I should go fishing with Roy. She had immediately suggested that I was subconsciously trying to sabotage our relationship. All of my friends think they're intelligent and sophisticated, but they're convinced that inside each of us lurks a secret mastermind who's plotting to ruin our lives. And they have the temerity to think this clandestine boogeyman is based on sound scientific psychology. You really might as well just believe in demons as the cause for misfortune.

Dylan turned toward me. "Are you coming with us?"

"No, he isn't," Roy snapped.

"Why not?" Dylan asked. "We need you out there."

"I'd like to go," I said, "but I don't think I can afford to be out there for a month. The flight's expensive. . . ." My explanation petered out lamely, and it occurred to me that the secret to the salmon's amazing drive was that they lacked the ability to talk themselves out of swimming upstream.

"It's only for three weeks," Dylan said. "C'mon it'll be an adventure. You have to come. We're not going without you."

"It does sound like fun," I said, smiling, deciding that Dylan had to be gay. Straight men don't hold eye contact that long.

"Oh, it'll be fun," he promised, wrapping his arm around me and giving my shoulder a quick squeeze.

Roy's eyes met mine like we were strangers passing on the street, quickly moving on without revealing anything. He kept walking and his face didn't betray what he was thinking, which proved that the Yup'ik story was true. Men change into salmon all the time; we had become the salmon people, moving silently, keeping our thoughts to ourselves, driven by love but unsure whether we'd find it.

SEVEN

We had our first fight, or what I like to think of romantically as our first hiss, after I told Roy that I'd been hired at the Kalikat Bakery. It was a part-time job, working about thirty hours a week, but I'd earn enough money to get me through the summer.

Roy's pale face flushed. "How much money are you going to make serving coffee for three weeks?" he asked. He had a point; taking a job to make lattes almost seemed to be the opposite of taking responsibility for your life.

"The money's not great, but I can write every day," I admitted, before telling him once again about the conversation I'd had with my father.

"You can write out there."

"I know, but I just got back into it. I'll have to drop everything to get ready and then once I'm out there I'm sure we'll have fun. I'm just afraid that I'll stop for a day and then that will turn into two days then two weeks, two months, and two years. I don't really have a rational reason. I just think that going out there now would be doing something stupid."

I wasn't being completely honest with Roy. After I'd arrived in Anchorage, the extra hours of sunlight seemed to assure me that I had time each day to do everything that I wanted to accomplish. What I hadn't expected was that I actually did what I set out to do.

There was an element of irrationality to my fear that I would stop writing again. But I was thirty-four years old and deeply afraid of making another misstep. I had already experienced being trapped in a job, bogged down with my novel, suffering a death so slow that no one noticed that I was gradually sinking into my grave.

"My writing's going well here," I said. For me, that imprecise phrase meant that each day I was eager to get back to work. Supposedly if you let a monkey pound away on a typewriter long enough, the odds are that eventually by chance, he'll write the *Iliad* or *Odyssey*. My work method was similar to that. I spent time each day chimping away on my computer, but unlike our primate kin, I could recognize when by chance I produced a word, phrase, idea, character, or scene that made me think I was one step closer to accidentally producing a book.

"You'd like it out there," Roy said bitterly as he picked up an archaeology journal and began to read. I observed how easily the idea that you don't want to talk could be communicated. When Roy was angry or in a bad mood, he became stealthily quiet, an assassin choking his words from behind. On the other hand, perhaps he was communicating with me, since the simplest method of telling someone exactly how you feel is to make that person feel as shitty as you do.

"Roy . . ." I said, trying to find space in his closet for my empty suitcase.

"What?" he snarled. The first snarled "What?" between a couple is always a milestone. It's the most succinct contraction in the English language, abbreviating the phrase "What do you want now?" to a single hostile word.

"Nothing," I replied. We had each retreated into our skulls, the prehistoric caverns where men live brutishly, huddled around pain as if it was a warm fire.

I was at a disadvantage fighting with Roy because throughout my life, my behavior, feelings, or thoughts continually led me to believe that I must be crazy. But I never thought Roy was crazy, or at least that he was crazy about the same things as I was. (A couple with matching neuroses is like a couple wearing matching outfits: it's cute for about the first five minutes.) One of the reasons I was attracted to Roy was that compared to me, he was sensible and competent. If he was angry with me, then part of me assumed that he had a legitimate reason to be enraged. How could I ever win an argument with him when I was fighting with one hand pointing at myself?

Roy put down his archaeology journal, rose from his seat, and walked over to the closet and wordlessly began to move boxes around, removing a crate filled with hockey skates and a bin loaded with camping equipment to make room for my suitcase. When he finished, he stared at me, his expression solemn while his body visibly relaxed.

"It pissed me off that you were so eager to come fishing when Dylan asked you."

"I wasn't eager," I argued.

"You got all girlish," he shot back.

"I didn't get all girlish," I said, suddenly sounding awfully girlish.

"'It does sound like fun,'" Roy said, his face assuming the ready-to-smile position. He was an accomplished mimic and impersonated my response with devastating accuracy, skewering my Great Lakes pronunciation of fun as "fuh-n" and caricaturing my fawning expression.

"I didn't say it like that," I said, my face assuming the ready-to-smile position.

"Yes, you did," he said before repeating, "It does sound like fun" which made me laugh. Our silly arguments shared 98 percent of the same DNA as our serious disputes, but like the differences between humans and chimpanzees, that slight variance was significant.

"I was just being polite," I said, thinking that I was telling him a white lie, which I thought of as a jockstrap covering an embarrassing truth. I could easily resist Roy's entreating me to come fishing, because he was already hooked on me. But I didn't want to say no to Dylan because he evoked a fantasy that I wasn't ready to let go of.

"Are you going to let Dylan come with you?" I asked.

"Would you mind if I tell him no?"

"No," I said, relieved that we weren't fighting anymore. "It's your business. I don't know anything about fishing." Honestly, I thought it was the best thing to do, because I didn't want Roy spending three weeks alone with him. In addition, I assumed that if Dylan and I stayed in Anchorage, we would probably see each other again. If I'd worked with numbers as quickly as I calculated social situations, I would have been a billionaire before I turned twenty-five.

"I don't want to babysit another addict," Roy said. His first boyfriend, Derek, was an alcoholic, and Roy had told me that one night he drove home drunk, passed out in the driveway, and then almost froze to death. "Also my mom will be out there and I don't want him OD-ing in front of her," he added.

I hadn't met Roy's mother, Dee, yet. Since I had arrived in Anchorage, she'd been in Portland visiting Roy's brother, daughter-in-law, and Isabella, her first grandchild.

"I don't think he's on drugs now," I said, not really having any experience with addicts but thinking that if Dylan was using heroin, it should be sold as a skin care product because his complexion was radiant.

"I don't want to be responsible for him," Roy declared.

He made me promise that I'd reconsider my decision not to come fishing with him, making me regret taking the job at the bakery.

"If I quit now," I said, "people will think I'm flaky."

"I have news for you," Roy said, finally allowing himself to smile again. "You are flaky, but in your case it's another word for adventurous. It's one of your better qualities."

My first job in Alaska wasn't exactly what I had envisioned when I left Los Angeles. I never saw myself as a logger or fisherman, but it was impossible to come that far without entertaining the possibility that I might find a job that was intrinsically Alaskan. I consoled myself with the observation that lattes were as emblematic of the Pacific Northwest as eagles and orcas. I tried to imagine myself as a legendary figure in a tall tale—a diminished Paul Bunyan whose prodigious strength resided in his ability to brew a mighty powerful espresso. His coffee was so strong that one sip kept the man on the moon awake at night.

I could honestly claim that I worked outdoors since the newest hire had to sweep and pick up litter in the parking lot. My work was hard and physical: the distinction between blue-collar and white-collar jobs in America having been reduced to whether you're paid to sit or stand. I was a blue-collar worker because I stood and rang up orders on a computer instead of sitting and placing orders on a computer. My job was also demanding. People could actually taste the difference between skim milk and one-percent and became steamed if I tried to pull a switcheroo. My work could even be considered hazardous as it involved using potentially dangerous equipment. On my first day, I scalded my thumb while heating half-and-half for a macchiato. Keeping a level head, though, I avoided a blister by immediately plunging my thumb into an iced javanilla.

The morning crew at the Kalikat Bakery was a free-spirited group made up mostly of college-age students who fell into two types: intellectuals who could argue about the objectivity of history as a written construct but needed to be reminded to screw the lid on the blender, and less ambitious students who thought Voltaire was the name of a comic book supervillain. The rest of the staff was comprised of slackers who sought out no-brainer jobs or members of Anchorage's small group of aspiring artists, baby-faced bohemians getting ready for the big move, not to New York or Los Angeles, but to Seattle.

The staff made me feel welcome after I'd earned their respect when I worked through my first shift with a scalded thumb. I demonstrated that I could remember six different drink orders without having to write down the confusing variations in milk fat or caffeine content. And I had shown that I could handle obnoxious customers by deceitfully insulting them. "Do you prefer heavy foam or light foam?" I'd ask with a false smile. The customer thought I was being considerate, but the question was intended to alert the staff to another kook who needed a psychiatric evaluation to discover why he was so anal about his coffee order.

After work I either went to the gym or spent several hours writing on my laptop at the bakery. If anyone else was writing there, the odds were slight that he or she was working on a novel or a screenplay. The writer was more likely to be working on a first-person account of surviving a bear attack. Anchorage's bookstores devoted entire shelves to purple-prosed volumes of bear attacks, which led me to believe that establishing your credentials as a writer in Alaska required having a limb gnawed on by a grizzly. However, as evidenced by the books, the bears never mauled anyone's writing hand.

Dylan remained in Anchorage ostensibly because he was researching his part—and because the director of his film asked him to help with the auditions for a few small parts that hadn't been cast. Dylan usually arrived at the bakery around noon or later to order his daily large skim latte. He had a distracting habit of idly scratching his stomach while standing in line. He lifted his T-shirt, revealing a glimpse of taut flesh and raked blond hair that always hit me like a double espresso. The staff was not impressed that I was on a first-name basis with a movie star. It was pointed out that Dylan never left a tip in the jar near the cash register. The tip jar was a point of contention at the bakery because it had a handwritten sign taped to it that read, "Tipping: Good Karma." The staff was insulted when Dylan said it sounded like we were threatening that if our customers didn't tip heavily in this life, in their next incarnation, they'd have to work a minimum wage job making lattes.

I had finished my morning shift and had started staring at my computer screen but I wasn't aware that Dylan stood behind me until he read over my shoulder from the page I was rewriting.

"'Vander refused to let me continue drinking instant coffee, which he described as a magic trick that doesn't work for anyone.' Hey, that's pretty good! Is this your novel?"

"Yeah," I said.

"You might want to rethink the name 'Vander' though."

I smiled. "You're probably right." Vander was based on my first boyfriend Brent and hearing Dylan say it aloud convinced me to find a simpler name.

"How much longer are you going to work?" Dylan asked as he sat down at my table.

"A few more hours."

"Do you want to go for a hike?"

"With you?" I asked incredulously.

"Yes, with me," he said, mocking my disbelief. It's sad for a would-be novelist to admit, but I couldn't imagine why Dylan wanted to hike with me. (I sometimes think the primary reason novelists write fiction is due to a compelling need to invent lives more exciting than their own.) I decided that Dylan didn't know many people in Anchorage and that he was starting to feel bored.

"Uh, sure." I felt like a hypocrite for immediately abandoning my novel for Dylan, after having told Roy that I wouldn't even consider the possibility of stopping work on it for him. But I easily excused my duplicity by telling myself it was just for an afternoon of hiking as opposed to three weeks of fishing. I had also planned on going to the gym that afternoon, and hiking would substitute as my workout for the day. I liked to pretend my values were superior to the politicians whom I routinely vilified, but found that in my own life I justified dishonesty like a presidential press secretary.

"We were auditioning all morning," Dylan said. "I'm starved. Do you mind getting me a sandwich? I don't have any money on me. I didn't have time to stop at a cash machine."

I resented that Dylan assumed that he could use me as his errand boy. But I didn't say anything because I had a soft spot for extremely handsome men, a spot that grew harder as I got to know them better. Dylan waited in his rental truck while I went inside the bakery and spent my last ten dollars on a bottle of iced tea and a smoked turkey, arugula, and tomato sandwich with cranberry mustard on focaccia. After returning with Dylan's meal and climbing in the truck, I asked him how Alex's audition had gone. Dylan had kept his promise and set up Alex's audition for the director of *Violet Cryderman*.

"So many one-man-show performers are one-trick ponies, but he can act," Dylan said as he pulled out of the parking lot. "And I don't think he'll read too much on screen."

"What do you mean?"

Dylan removed his right hand from the steering wheel and rapidly tipped it back and forth. It offended me that he was using that hoary, outmoded sign language to indicate Alex's homosexuality. It was practically the same as accusing him of being a ye-olde-damned sodomite.

"His character's straight," he added.

"Alex isn't queeny," I argued. Dylan's homophobia angered me, but I was also irritated that he had driven past two banks and several cash machines without stopping.

"He convinced an audience that he was a wolf, an eagle, and about a dozen other animals," I said. "I don't think he'll have a problem convincing people that he's straight."

"He sold you," said Dylan. "But then you're his friend."

I was tempted to point out that friendship didn't mean that I was oblivious to my friends' faults. I knew their flaws better than I did my own.

"I barely know him," I said. "He's talented though. I hate when artists refuse to admit when another artist's good. If they can't do that, then how can they distinguish what's good in their own work?"

"I didn't say he wasn't talented," Dylan said grinning. "He's just not as talented as I am. I think it's important for artists to have huge egos." He lifted his sunglasses to signal that I was being teased.

"You've got a point," I said, thinking that I needed to lighten up. We drove in silence for a minute, neither of us having much to say to each other. From my experience working at *Aftertaste*, I knew the easiest method of starting a conversation with an actor was to ask him about himself. But in Dylan's case, I was also genuinely curious about him.

"What made you want to become an actor?" I asked.

"You might find this hard to believe, but I've always liked attention," he said with a smirk. "But I began to see acting differently when I was a teenager. It opened up an entire world of feeling inside of me. My mom remarried and her new husband was a sick fuck who loved to bad-mouth me. But I didn't feel I could say anything against him, because I didn't want to cause trouble for my mom. So I just shut down. Acting allowed me to let out my anger. I became addicted to experiencing feelings." He smiled knowingly. "And I'm aware that being addicted to anything isn't necessarily healthy for me."

I smiled, acknowledging that I was aware of his pharmacological history but I was unable to think of any response that wouldn't sound like, "Yeah, that's true. You are one fucked up motherfucker."

We drove to one of the entrances to Chugach State Park and my eyes were drawn to the looming mountains in front of us. I kept staring at the mountains that surrounded Anchorage in the same guileless manner that a tourist in Hollywood would gape at a legendary movie actress.

At first glance, the mountains also gave the impression of everlasting youth, but a closer examination revealed that they were ancient. The lovely vibrant green skin and striking profile caught my eye, but further scrutiny revealed the surgical scars of bare rock that girded the surface and held the assemblage of parts together. Adding to the effect of an aging beauty were the receding patches of winter snow that looked like dabs of wrinkle cream that had been applied too generously.

"Acting's the best job in the world," Dylan declared as we entered a pricey neighborhood bordering the Park, where ski-lodge sized houses had spectacular panoramic views of Cook Inlet and downtown Anchorage. "It's a complete emotional life without any consequences or responsibilities. I can portray a noble, brave man without risking anything besides my dignity. And if people believe my performance they'll attribute those qualities to me. On a good day, I start to fucking believe it. And I can play a horrible villain, the lowest, most evil human scum, and if I do my job well, people will love me even more. I can't lose."

His eyes glittered as he spoke. Listening to him, I realized that like many artists Dylan had found a subject, acting, where he could talk endlessly about himself in the guise of discussing his craft. He was dull, but my tolerance for a bore was contingent on whether I wanted to sleep with him. If a man gave me a boner, he was automatically entitled to use my dick as a microphone and drone on about himself in a manner that I wouldn't have tolerated in anyone else.

Dylan continued to drive uphill until we reached a turnoff to a small gravel-covered parking lot. We had the park to ourselves, as there was only one other car in the lot. After parking the truck, Dylan reached for a pack of cigarettes on the dashboard, lighting one for himself before offering me one.

"I don't smoke," I said before we got out of the truck.

He shook his head disapprovingly.

"See? You're too good. We need to change that. Great artists are in touch with something vital and dangerous," he said. We walked to a scenic overlook and could see the city of Anchorage far below us. I scanned the horizon for Denali but it was hidden behind clouds.

"I once met Uta Hagen at a party," Dylan said as we started walking on a trail with dense brush on either side of us.

I knew she was a celebrated teacher of acting but Dylan informed me that she had also originated the role of Martha in the original Broadway production of *Who's Afraid of Virginia Woolf?*

"When I met her, she was in her eighties, but you wouldn't have known it," he said. "She made a pass at me, so I made out with her just to say that I did."

I grimaced and said necking with an eighty-year-old woman sounded gross.

"Some of the best things in life sound gross," Dylan said. "But adults learn to see through that subterfuge."

I wasn't sure whether Dylan had gone to college but his use of the word subterfuge suggested that he had, leading me to ask him where he had studied acting. He told me that he had graduated from UCLA's theater program but claimed that his best acting teacher was his father.

"I learned how to act from hearing him tell lies," he said. "He truly was a bullshit artist. He used to lie to my mother about where he had been last night and lie to her about what he had done with his paycheck. He lied to me about why he missed my baseball games, my plays, my birthdays, and almost every holiday. He used to tell me the most beautiful tragic stories. There would be tears in his eyes and his deep voice would become thick with emotion. But after a while I understood that he was giving a performance. He was gifted. He used to take a puff," Dylan brought his cigarette to his lips and inhaled causing the tip to blush. "When he exhaled, the smoke used to curl out of his mouth as if he was divulging a secret." Dylan released a stream of smoke that slowly snaked out of his mouth like a serpent.

It was the height of the season for wildflowers and stands of red and yellow western columbine, dark blue Jacob's ladder, and budding magenta fireweed grew alongside the trail. I asked Dylan to stop for a minute while I searched for chocolate lilies, the flowers that I was most curious to see after reading about them in an Alaskan wildflower guide. Underneath a bush, I found three growing together in a clump.

"They're supposed to smell disgusting," I said, before stooping down to sniff a brown lily. It smelled musty, as if the effort of blooming had caused it to perspire.

Dylan also bent down to smell the flower.

"It's smells like sex," he said. "You know what my definition of great sex is?"

"What?"

"The next day you jerk off thinking about it."

"What's your definition of bad sex?"

"That's easy," he said. "When someone gives you a piece of ass but they save the best piece for themselves."

Dylan snapped the lily from its stem and held it to his nose.

"Don't—" I said, stopping myself because bemoaning the loss of a wildflower would make me sound priggish.

"Don't, what?"

"Pick the wildflower," I said trying to sound as if picking wild-flowers in a state park didn't bother me. I assumed everyone knew that you're not supposed to pick wildflowers, because my father had been telling me that since I was a boy.

"They're flowers," Dylan said. "They'll be dead in a week. You have to learn to accept that pretty things don't last very long."

"You're pretty," I said. "Do you want your check-out to be rushed?"

"Do you think I'm a pretty flower?" he chuckled. "Do you want to smell me? I might be a little funky." He gave his armpit a cursory whiff.

"Do you have to make everything about sex?" I asked with sham outrage. "We were having such a nice time!"

"Everything's about sex," said Dylan as he reached out and tapped my lips with the lily. "This flower just wanted to get humped by a bee."

"Because of you," I said, "it probably died a virgin."

"That's why you need to get it while you can," he warned. "You never know when you'll be picked."

"So Death is just a queen in a floppy hat randomly snipping flowers with a pair of gardening shears to make a bouquet?"

It made more sense than the standard image of hooded Death carrying a sickle. A sickle is used to harvest a crop when it reaches maturity, while I knew that Death plucks people of all ages with the impulsive greed of a tourist picking wildflowers.

"Are you calling me a big queen?" Dylan asked.

I shrugged. "Is there something you want to tell me?"

He smiled. "I'm an actor. I can be whatever the part requires."

"I'm taking that for a yes," I said. Dylan just grinned again. He twirled the lily in his hand before letting it fall to the ground. We left the brushy part of the trail and entered an immense, windswept, treeless valley. The vegetation looked arctic, mostly green mosses and lichens, and it appeared that if we waited a few minutes a glacier would return shortly.

I'm in Alaska! That thought had come to me unbidden several times since my arrival. It was jolting, because it was accompanied by thrilling spasms of happiness.

"And I'm supposed to let you go fishing with Roy?" I asked half-seriously.

"I'd already be going fishing with Roy, if he was interested in me," Dylan said. "Believe me, I know when someone's interested in me."

He stared directly at me, leaving me with the impression that he was talking about me.

"You flirt with everyone," I said.

"I'm not flirting with you," Dylan said, holding eye contact until I had to turn my head, suddenly aware that I was flirting with him.

"If I was flirting with you," he said, "I'd find an excuse to touch you." He gently reached out to brush my cheek with his hand. "Mosquito," he said devilishly. "Or I'd accidentally find a way for you to touch me." He lifted my hand and slipped it under his shirt, running my palm across the cobbles of his hairy stomach.

"But I'm not flirting with you," Dylan said, letting my hand fall. "I want you to do me a favor. You have to convince Roy to let me go fishing with him."

I'd never cheated on a boyfriend before but wondered if there was any special exemption to fidelity for a once-in-a-lifetime star-fuck.

"I don't know if I have any pull with Roy about his fishing," I said. "I've never been out there. I don't know anything about it."

"You've got pull with him," Dylan argued. "He's your boyfriend."

I told him that his chances of going weren't good. Roy was adamant that he didn't want to be responsible for him. "To be honest," I said. "Roy's concerned that you're going to use drugs."

Dylan looked dismayed and shook his head. "I don't blame him," he said. "But I'm not using anything stronger than a little pot every now and then. You can reassure him on that."

I nodded, wondering whether that was sufficient to convince Roy to take him fishing. In Wisconsin we had always considered smoking pot to be using drugs.

Dylan and I walked the trail for several yards before he spoke again.

"You're a fellow artist—I'm an actor and you're a writer—and I think you know better than anyone what it's like to be an artist in trouble. I saw your picture in the tar pits. You understand what it's like to have people think you're irresponsible and to be judged for your mistakes. Imagine what it's like to have people think that you're so fucked up that you need to be locked up."

"I'm not comparing myself with you," I said, "but I've also been on the cover of the *L.A. Times*."

Dylan nodded sympathetically. "I want to do a good job on this film," he said. "I have to prove myself again. I need to be great, or I'm fucked. I know it sounds all Hollywood to say that I want to go fishing to prepare to play the role of a fisherman. But that's how I've always worked. I immerse myself in a character until I feel confident that I know him and his world. I want to know how he stands, loves, hurts, hates, and laughs. Even smells. When you write a novel, you must feel you need to know your characters and their world completely before you can write about them."

"Well, I'm writing about my family," I said, "so I've done the research."

Dylan's face became set with impatience.

"You don't always have to entertain me," he said. "I'm talking about something important."

I considered whether I had been trying to entertain him but decided that I'd actually just been thinking out loud. "I wasn't *trying* to entertain you," I said. "You said something and I said the first thought that occurred to me. I never have to think of something funny. It just pops in my head and shoots out my mouth. It's like you. Maybe you're not trying to be flirtatious, you just *are*."

I thought Dylan might smile at my comparison, but his face remained chiseled and fixed like a statue's.

"Just admit that you like to make me laugh."

"That's part of it. But you just accused me of not being serious and now I am. I think my being funny is mostly about entertaining myself.

It's a way of having fun or avoiding thinking about something sad or depressing or hopeless."

Then I confessed that I'd always mocked the idea of pretentious actors getting into character but I could see that writers also had to get into their characters in a similar manner. I liked to believe that I knew whether my characters woke up grumpy or perky, whether they liked to cuddle or roll over after sex, whether they voted Democratic or Republican, and whether they liked their coffee black or with just cream or cream and sugar or whether they had recently cut back on coffee because of the caffeine.

"I'm sure you've needed to research something for your novel," said Dylan.

"I'm writing about my uncle's dairy farm where I spent the summer after my mother died," I said. "On my last trip to Wisconsin I made a point of visiting him to see the setting again and remind myself about how he and my aunt lived."

I didn't mention to Dylan that the main challenge I had in writing the chapter was trying to re-create the irreconcilable feelings of confusion I felt from being depressed about my mother's death, along with the intense exhilaration I enjoyed when I had my first sexual affair with one of the hunky farmhands who liked to skinny-dip in the pond at the end of the day. I felt intensely guilty like a mourner at a funeral who becomes aroused by the size and power of one of the pallbearer's arms.

"Researching a character has almost become a superstition with me. You're a writer—do you have any superstitions about writing?"

"When I write in the mornings," I said, "I usually have a cup of coffee but I only like to drink from one blue mug. It's kind of a talisman with me."

I had brought the stupid coffee mug with me to Anchorage, hoping that it would help me to continue working on my novel.

"I knew you'd understand," Dylan said. "An artist's confidence is fragile, and going fishing with Roy will help my performance. It doesn't matter whether it's just in my head because every act of imagination starts in your head. An artist has to suspend *his* disbelief before he can get an audience to suspend *their* disbelief. I'm not going out there to sleep with anyone. I'm going out there to work."

"I try to do everything in my power in order to make my work better," I admitted as I recalled the years of writing I'd already put in on my novel.

"I know," Dylan said. "It makes you see how the first artists were regarded as shamans because they were in touch with something larger than themselves."

"No," I said. "The first artists were regarded as shamans because they had more experience at praying desperately than anyone else in their tribe."

Dylan laughed. "Was that for me?" he asked. "Or just your head popping?"

"It's about a fifty-fifty split."

"So you'll talk to Roy?"

"I'll talk to him. But I can't promise anything."

Dylan's face filled with gratitude, and he grabbed me by the shoulders. "Thank you," he said leaning in close enough to kiss me. I was taken aback but didn't pull away.

"I could kiss you," he said as he leaned in close to my face, close enough for me to feel his breath on my lips, then he suddenly released me. "But I don't want you to think I'm gay."

"You might not be gay, but you're definitely a cock-tease."

He grinned at me before turning back to face the trail.

EIGHT

On Saturday night, I decided to broach the subject of Dylan going fishing with Roy because we were going to see him that evening. Lloyd Arnedahl and his partner of nineteen years, Don Pryor, were close friends of Alex's and Roy's, and they threw a welcome-to-Alaska party for director Graham Lemoore, Dylan, and me. According to Roy, Lloyd and Don gave the best parties in Anchorage, and anyone worth knowing in Alaska knew one or both of them. I was going to be meeting most of Roy's friends for the first time and so I dressed with extra care, wearing my current favorite shirt, a black short-sleeved dress shirt that promoted me like a publicist. I also wore my new pair of black Blundtstone boots. They were an unnecessary recent purchase but Roy had encouraged me to buy them. (Why is it that deep down, I really only trust the opinion of people who see me naked regularly to tell me what to wear?) Roy also appeared to be nervous about our debut as a couple, changing his shirt moments before we left the house. He removed his new red short-sleeved shirt and replaced it with his new dark blue one.

"Which one do you like better?" he asked and I told him the blue one. It made his eyes look more strikingly oceanic. I thought about how lucky I was to be going to a party with the man whom I would most like to meet at a party.

Lloyd and Don lived around the corner from us, and we walked to their small green house on Tenth Street bordering Delany Park. On the way, I said, "The other day Dylan asked me to talk to you again about taking him fishing."

Roy looked annoyed, crinkling up his lips. "I'll tell him tonight that he's not going."

"You know," I said, trying to sound diplomatic, "he explained to me that going fishing would really help him with his part."

"Really?" Roy sounded skeptical. "What do you think?"

"I don't know," I said, shaking my head. "He feels that he needs to prove himself again. I can understand that. Didn't you say that the state motto should be 'Bury Your Past'? Everyone deserves a second chance. Even movie stars."

Roy's face softened and after a reflective pause, he offered me a deal. "If you come fishing, I'll take him."

I grinned because Roy seldom tried to manipulate me.

"Just think about it," I said, feeling that I'd fulfilled my obligation to Dylan.

"I'll think about it, if you think about it."

"All right," I promised, although I told him that I doubted that I would change my mind. We arrived at the white picket gate to Lloyd and Don's front yard, which burgeoned with blooming lilac bushes.

"Nelson, welcome to the Great Land," Don said, shaking my hand as we entered their house. He appeared to be amused by his own hyperbole, but I couldn't detect any irony in his deep mellow voice. Don had silver hair, a sharp nose, and a neatly trimmed beard. He was a tall, fit, fine-looking older man who appeared to be in his midfifties. At that time I still considered all older men, and anyone over forty plummeted into that category, in the same detached manner that I regarded beautiful women. Their beauty was like the sunshine in winter: I could see the light but didn't feel the heat and my appreciation remained dispassionate.

We were the first guests to arrive, and Lloyd greeted us in the living room. He was a short, powerfully built man with a broad coarse face. His twisted broken nose made him look like a thuggish boxer until he said, "Nice to meet you, Nelson." Then his languorous drawl insinuated that the last time he put up his dukes was when someone disparaged Gwen Verdon's dancing in *Damn Yankees*.

Lloyd and Don had a museum-quality collection of Alaskiana displayed in their living room. I inquired about the collection, and Lloyd said that he was a doctor and during the early seventies, he had worked all over Alaska in remote villages. Most of the collection, he explained, was gifts from grateful patients. He showed me several wooden Yup'ik masks, including a rare one of Mickey Mouse made in the 1930s. In a glass-fronted case was a group of dark, discolored prehistoric harpoon points and fishing hooks carved from bone and ivory, which looked like the tartar-encrusted teeth from a fierce imaginary beast. Mounted above the fireplace was a long spiraling mastodon tusk. The tusk had washed out of a river up north and was an extremely valuable and extravagant gift from a miner after Lloyd saved his life.

"Eventually, it's all going to the museum," Lloyd declared, as a waiter dressed in a white shirt and long black tie entered the room. He was bearing a silver tray holding four glasses of champagne. Roy and I each took a flute as Don and Lloyd reached for the remaining glasses.

Don held up his glass to propose a toast. "To new friends," he said. After we repeated the phrase, clinked glasses, and drank, Don excused himself to check on the caterer. Once Don was in the kitchen, Lloyd announced, "I just want to warn you that tonight I'm getting completely plastered. I'm a champagne *fiend*! I can drink champagne forever. And when I get a few flutes in me—watch out. I can't even go to wedding receptions anymore. All I can remember, from the last wedding I went to, is the first forty-five minutes. After that, I was told that I wandered from table to table—my tie askew, my shirt undone—and I kept asking the other guests, "Are you finished with that bottle?" Oh, it was not a pretty picture! That's why I don't do wedding receptions anymore."

Before meeting Lloyd, I used to think the soliloquies of Shakespeare's characters were stagy and contrived: real people don't explain their motives and behavior with overly dramatic monologues. But Lloyd convinced me that big queens are masters of the dying art of the soliloquy. And Lloyd was a big queen. In Alaska, vastness is prized and just about every glacier and national park is described as being larger than Rhode Island or Delaware, the teaspoon and tablespoon of Alaskan measurement. Listening to Lloyd, I became convinced that he was the biggest queen in our biggest state, a giant who caused cocktails to shake in their glasses from the booming tread of his mincing feet.

"Oh, look at me," Lloyd bemoaned, after catching his reflection in a mirror hanging on a wall. "You know you're an adult when you look in the mirror and think, I look tired. Then it dawns on you that, no, I don't look tired, I look old. It wouldn't matter now if I slept for a solid year. No matter how much sleep I get from this point on, I'm never going to look better than I did when I was completely exhausted at twenty."

Roy and I smiled awkwardly, but neither of us had a response to his lamentation.

"How old are you?" I asked. The obsession some older men have with their own youthfulness is almost as creepy and repulsive as pedophilia.

"How old do you think I am?" he said threateningly as if he was going to challenge me to a duel because he'd look five years younger from a distance of forty paces.

"You'll be in serious trouble if you're wrong," Roy warned.

"Fifty?" I ventured.

"I'm forty-eight," Lloyd said crisply before taking a restorative swig of champagne. He took it as an article of faith that he looked younger than his age because his body was muscular and not fat. But Lloyd overlooked that since he had turned eighteen, he thought of himself as wise beyond his years, which was duly reflected in his face. It was unfortunate that I had to inform him he looked his age but I excused myself with the thought, 'Don't fish for a compliment if you don't have any bait.'"

"Of course, you have nothing to worry about," Lloyd said to me. "How old are you? Twenty-six?"

"Thirty-four," I said.

"I loathe you," he said benevolently. "Where are you from?"

"I grew up in Milwaukee but live in Los Angeles."

"And how do you like Anchorage?" he asked.

I could practically see Roy's ears twitching as he waited to hear my answer.

"I like it," I said, explaining that Anchorites, or whatever the citizens of Anchorage called themselves, were the city's worst boosters. Anchorage possessed most of the amenities of modern American cities: from a great newspaper to an excellent art museum to a gay bar where it was possible to hear a song that wasn't originally released on vinyl. But Anchorites, including Roy, talked about Anchorage as if they were trying to sell you a cubic zirconium by talking up its platinum setting. They bragged and cringed in the same sentence, "We're five minutes from the best parks in the world, but we don't have an IKEA and I wish we had a decent Uzbek restaurant," I made it a point of saying.

One of the selling points of Anchorage was that it didn't have an IKEA. American cities could afford to shed a few pounds of sprawl, and the lack of several national retail chains made Anchorage seem sensibly less bloated than other cities. Anchorage could take its place alongside Sydney, San Francisco, or Seattle as one of the great cities of the Pacific, but it didn't know it yet. It was still the unspoiled, handsome boy from the sticks who was charmingly unaware that he could model. "Does the thrill of living here ever wear off?" I asked.

"It hasn't for me," Roy said, before taking a sip of his champagne.

"It took me awhile to fully appreciate Alaska," Lloyd admitted. "My family moved up here when I was twelve because my parents thought the world was going to end. Well, no wonder; they lived in Utah! The world ended there years ago, but no one's told them yet. From Utah, we moved to Idaho, then to Washington, then finally up to Alaska. We lived out in the bush. On forty acres. One hundred ten miles from the nearest road. I was angry with my parents for years because they told us we were just going camping."

"Are your parents still worried about the end of the world?" I inquired.

"No," he said. "Now all they worry about is their grandchildren."

The doorbell rang as other guests arrived. Lloyd greeted everyone loudly, taking time to give each one a brief monologue before moving on to the next guests. When Lloyd was out of hearing range, I turned to Roy and launched into, "I'm a champagne *fiend!* I can drink champagne forever. I can't even go to wedding receptions anymore. The last wedding I went to . . ." continuing until Roy began to shush me as he laughed.

The room became crowded and Roy introduced me to several of his friends. Tall, good-looking Matt was also studying to become an archaeologist. He had a scraggly beard, blue eyes, and light brown bed-head hair. When I discovered that he was from Santa Cruz, I eventually thought of him as surfer-Jesus. He and his beautiful wife Belinda immediately invited us for a barbecue the next night. Roy's friend Val was a petite, playful blonde-haired lesbian. They had grown up together in Homer, and she worked as a linewoman for the telephone company. "So this is the famous Nelson," she declared, nodding approvingly as she looked me up and down. "All Roy could talk about after his trip to L.A. was Nelson, Nelson, Nelson." Roy looked embarrassed but also kind of proud, and I noticed that he didn't deny her statement.

Val invited us to go out on her boat the next day, offering to show me an islet that she called Birdshit Rock. "I've seen tufted puffins there," she said, trying to tempt me with the teddy bear of seabirds. Evidently Roy had been talking to his friends about me quite a bit. They knew that I had worked at *Aftertaste*, that I was a writer working on a novel, and that I liked to birdwatch. Val also let slip that his friends were aware of my tar pit fiasco when she said, "I promise that we won't get stuck in anything," Her face immediately revealed that she was worried that I'd take offense and everyone looked at me to see my reaction. I smiled to signal that I was no longer sensitive about the subject. I also learned that Roy must have told Matt about how we had connected over the harpoon point story.

"Starting in the fall," Matt said, "I'm going to be working at the museum in Fairbanks. You two should come up, and I'll show you one of the points."

Roy's friends were determined to like me because he did, and their extension of friendship made me feel welcomed and also the victim of a benign conspiracy. It was flattering and disturbing because I immediately liked his friends and understood that Roy wasn't just introducing me to them, he was offering me a life.

Two older women with gray hair walked up behind Val, the thinner of the two women tapping her on the shoulder. Val turned her head and shrieked, "When did you get back?" Their reunion caused Val to drop out of our conversation, allowing Belinda to say, "We're going to check out the buffet. We didn't have dinner."

Roy and I looked at each other to see if either of us wanted to join them. We weren't hungry, as I'd brought home two orders of lasagna from the bakery that we'd polished off.

"We might grab something later," Roy said, giving Matt and Belinda permission to leave us. They headed into the dining room while Roy and I remained standing in a corner of the living room holding our drinks.

"Your friends are great," I said.

"They are," Roy said. "Matt and I are working on a grant proposal together." He explained that they wanted to do a test dig in an unglaciated area in the Alaskan peninsula, searching for signs of the first Americans.

Lloyd's boisterous welcome announced Dylan's arrival at the party. Don came out of the kitchen wiping his hands on a dishtowel as Dylan looked around the room. His blond hair was damp and he wore a black silk shirt and blue jeans that miraculously turned fabric into flesh.

After saying hello, Dylan had a question for me.

"When do you usually go to the gym?" he asked.

"After work," I replied. "Usually around one-thirty." That afternoon, I'd discovered that Dylan had joined my gym. He had startled me when he leaned over my head while I was bench-pressing. "Come on," he barked as he spotted my last set. "It's all yours. C'mon. Muscle it up! Get a big chest." He was being facetious but his deep commanding voice did make me do two more reps than I'd ever done before.

Lloyd signaled a passing waiter to offer Dylan a glass of champagne.

"We should work out together," Dylan proposed as he lifted a glass from the tray. "Having a work-out partner helps motivate me."

Roy's back stiffened slightly, and I didn't respond immediately because I knew that I shouldn't sound enthusiastic about working out with Dylan. Roy went to the gym every morning at seven A.M. because during the day he worked at the university's bookstore, and he hated going to the gym after work when it was crowded. We'd discussed working out together, but I told Roy that I did my best writing first thing in the morning, which had ruled out our becoming workout partners.

"I could help you pack on some size," Dylan said, looking at my chest and arms with the business gaze of a farmer checking out a cow. "You'll be my protégé. I'll turn you into an irresistible stud."

I laughed politely as visions of pumped up grandeur immediately played in my mind while I tried to suppress the thought of us showering together after our workouts.

"You wouldn't mind that, would you, Roy?" Dylan added.

Roy glanced at me then looked at Dylan. "Nelson looks fine to me," he said. "But if he wants to become muscle-bound, it's up to him."

He wasn't that much smaller than Dylan and his disparagement of muscle-bound men could only be heard as taking a shot at a thickly muscled movie star.

"You don't want to get too muscular," Don cautioned. "Men's bodies have become like SUVs. They're built for six but rarely have more than one passenger."

"Well, I disagree," Lloyd said. "Men should get as big as possible while they're young. You need to start out as a mountain if you don't want to end up a troll hill."

I had to admit that Lloyd had an extraordinary physique. He sported a set of baseball biceps that were remarkable on a man who most likely threw like a girl.

"We've got to make some decisions," Dylan said to Roy. "Do I stay here and work as Nelson's personal trainer or am I going fishing with you?"

"It's not a tourist area," Roy warned.

"I don't want to sightsee," Dylan said. "I want to fish. It would aid my process if I understood your process."

The actor babble caused me to cringe inwardly, but everyone else appeared to be indifferent to it.

"You'd have to bring your own food," Roy said. "It's rough out there."

"*Rough?*" Dylan said sarcastically, "I was in prison for a year."

Everyone, including Roy, chuckled at his remark.

"So am I going?" Dylan asked.

"You can come," Roy said without enthusiasm. Dylan let out a whoop of joy.

"I don't want to be responsible for you," Roy declared. "I don't want you doing any drugs."

"You don't have to worry about that," Dylan said.

Roy's change of heart made me suddenly uncomfortable. When I looked over at him, he raised his eyebrows once, gesturing that he wasn't very happy. Dylan raised his champagne to propose a toast.

"Here's to fishing," he said.

Roy reluctantly clinked his glass against Dylan's and then said, "Here's to good fishing." The rest of us raised our glasses and murmured, "To good fishing."

"You're not coming?" Dylan asked, turning to face me.

"Well," I said, suddenly thinking that I would go nuts wondering what the two of them were doing out there. Roy's face became stiff with pent-up anger, and he turned away from us to speak with Don. Lloyd, I noticed, kept his focus on Dylan and me.

"That's too bad," Dylan said.

"You must go with them," Lloyd insisted. "You're being offered a chance to experience the Bristol Bay fishery firsthand. It's something that most people—even most Alaskans—never experience. I would think a writer would jump at the opportunity."

Lloyd's voice had become steely, and the physician writing a prescription had momentarily supplanted the champagne fiend. His face was stern and I felt a sudden pang of uncertainty.

"You'll regret staying here," Lloyd added, offering me his grim prognosis of my three weeks alone in Anchorage. Well-meaning people often start a conversation with a writer by saying, "You'll find this interesting." Nine times out of ten, the subject being proffered isn't worthy of anyone's attention. But Lloyd's conviction that it was my duty as a writer to see Coffee Point for myself was the strongest appeal that anyone could have made to induce me to go fishing with Roy and Dylan. Lloyd didn't change my mind, but I was shaken by his certainty that if I stayed in Anchorage, I would miss out on an experience that could be vitally important to me as an artist.

The front door opened and Graham Lemoore arrived with Alex. Lloyd and Don raced to greet them, and Alex eventually brought the film director over to meet us. Graham was in his early forties, dark and intense looking, gauntly handsome, carrying barely enough flesh to pass for attractive. During the introductions, I noticed that Graham avoided looking at or speaking to Dylan.

After I shook hands with Graham, Alex added, "Nelson's from L.A."

"Really?" he asked. "What do you do?"

"I'm a writer."

Graham's face assumed the soulful countenance of a film director praying fervently that he wasn't about to be asked to read my screenplay. But Graham was also puzzled by something and intently studied my face.

"Have we met before?" he asked.

"No," I replied.

"I know you from somewhere," he said.

"You might have seen me on the news," I said quietly. "The La Brea Tar Pits."

It was my fate to accept that like the dire wolf, the Columbian mammoth, and the Shasta ground sloth, I would forever be associated with the La Brea Tar Pits.

"That's it!" Graham exclaimed. "What brought you up here?"

I jerked a thumb toward Roy. "My boyfriend." It was the first time I'd used the word in four years, and it felt satisfying to employ it again.

"And what do you do?" he asked, addressing Roy.

"I'm an archaeologist."

"Interesting," Graham said politely.

"He's also a salmon fisherman," Dylan blurted out. "I'm going fishing with him."

"I'm not speaking to you," Graham hissed, causing Dylan's face to turn red. The sudden hostility was shocking, but Graham resumed a placid expression as if his display of anger had been for the camera and it was time to move on to the next scene.

"So you're the fisherman?" Graham said to Roy.

"Yeah," he replied.

"Are all three of you going fishing?" he asked.

"No," Roy answered. "Nelson's staying here to work on his novel."

Graham wasn't paying attention to Roy's answer because he became distracted when a pretty dark-haired young man walked into the room. He stared at the pretty man until the pretty man's lips curtsied a hello. Graham had no response but said wearily, "My boyfriend Thatcher."

Thatcher was in his midthirties, and his overly plucked and trimmed eyebrows marred his pretty face. They looked like two centipedes wearing fifty matching pairs of panty hose. Sprouting under Thatcher's lower lip was a patch of hair that made him look as if he had eaten pussy for dinner and dribbled a bit on his chin.

Graham hastily excused himself before walking over to speak to Thatcher. A few minutes later, Graham's raised voice could be heard above the conversations in the room. I couldn't understand what he was saying but his cheeks were two unfurled sails, waiting to catch a scream. Graham repeatedly used his hands histrionically as if he was conducting their argument with an invisible baton. Thatcher, ten years his junior, poked the air with his index finger as if he was trying to test its hardness. Graham made a final cutting motion with his hands.

"Well, where were you?" he shouted above the din in the room. "I don't care who can hear me!" Instantly aware that everyone in the room was watching them, they formed a huddle of loud whispers as if they had suddenly decided to conceal that they were arguing.

"Never fight with your boy toy in public," Alex declared.

"He's a little old to be a boy toy," Dylan said.

"He's practically a collectable," I said.

"Is he an actor?" Roy asked.

"He's a wactor," Dylan replied. "A waiter slash actor. But I think his days of working at either career ended once he found a wealthy boyfriend."

"Everything I know about men I learned as a waiter," Lloyd declaimed, shaking his head back and forth with infinite patience. "If someone on a date undertips, he'll stiff you at some point in the relationship, too. If he splits the check with surgical precision, then you can be sure he's figured out what everyone in life owes him. If he's suddenly in a big hurry to leave, you can be sure that he'll rush off as soon as he's finished with you. But if he lingers over the meal, leaves a big tip, and makes a real effort to talk, you have a shot at real happiness."

"Dear, I think you've had enough champagne," Don declared as he reached out and took Lloyd's glass from his hand. "You become too cynical when you drink."

Lloyd agreed and switched to mineral water by grabbing a glass from the tray of a passing waiter. There was a lull in the conversation, and a baby-faced man in his thirties wearing a red and black plaid flannel shirt, took the opportunity to approach Dylan. "Excuse me," he gushed. "I just wanted to say that I'm huge fan of yours." The man's boldness seemed to encourage other fans in the room, because a chubby man in his early twenties stepped forward to speak to Alex, and a throng of their admirers soon surrounded the two stars.

Don looked into the dining room and said, "I'd better tell them to put out the other turkey." He left and Lloyd motioned for us to follow him because the area near the bar was getting crowded. As we walked to the other side of the room, a tall, thin man wearing a shapeless stained pink dress and a frayed blonde wig strolled by us.

"Somehow I didn't expect drag queens in Alaska," I said in a low voice.

"Why not?" roared Lloyd. "There are tired people everywhere."

He waved at an outlandishly tall woman across the room.

"That's Kate," he said. "We love her. Every year she auctions her services to raise money for the community center: A Dyke with a Chainsaw for Two Hours. The bidding's always fierce."

Lloyd led us to a sheltered alcove located between two bookcases. To my surprise, he read mostly literary fiction. When I asked him what book he was currently reading, he named the latest Philip Roth. Lloyd explained his method of choosing a novel. "If it's too hard, too thick, or too long, I know it's going to give me more pain than pleasure. Of course, when I was younger, I was willing to try everything once. If I started a book, or a man, I'd always finish him. But now, if I'm not enjoying myself, I just roll over and go to sleep."

A copy of *The Professor's House* by Willa Cather caught my eye and I pointed the book out to Roy. "It's the perfect novel for an archaeologist," I said, telling him that the middle section of the novel contained a moving story about two cowboys finding a cliff dwelling in the Southwest.

Lloyd immediately pulled the book from the shelf and pressed it into Roy's hands. "Take it," he said. "I'll never read it again, and it will give me more shelf space."

Roy thanked him and then pointed to a large triangular-shaped stone that sat on a side table.

"Do you have any idea what this is?" Roy asked me. The stone had a pie wedge neatly cut from its upper right-hand corner. It appeared to be a fossil cheese but I guessed correctly that the stone was a prehistoric anchor weight for a fishing net. The incision looked freshly made as if the carver had finished working on it moments ago.

For the next half hour, we listened to Lloyd as he covered varied topics with forms of unilateral address. He ranged from commentary, "Men in drag either look like a trashy trophy wife or the scorned first wife. It's always one or the other" to a sermon, "Monotheism was a huge mistake. Who wants a God of all trades, master of none?" to a catty remark, "Donna's always sitting on a barstool. We call her, 'The Stationary Dyke.'"

"Oh, damn it," he said abruptly as he looked across the room. "Don's talking to Heidi Puerta. He told me to rescue him if he got stuck talking to her. Heidi's a doll, but by the end of the evening she gives you a headache."

He hurried to save Don just as Dylan signed his last autograph and made his way over to us.

"Do either of you want another champagne?" Dylan asked, holding up his empty glass while glancing at our empty glasses.

"I'm a champagne *fiend*!" I declared. "I can drink champagne forever. I can't even go to wedding receptions anymore. The last wedding I went to . . ." I repeated the monologue verbatim, actually enjoying the rhythm of his language, before I explained to Dylan what Lloyd had said.

"Have you noticed that big queens always sound like they're giving out clues to the world's most difficult crossword puzzle?" I asked. Roy and Dylan stared blankly, prompting me to clarify my statement. "All night Lloyd's been making pronouncements that sound like crossword puzzle clues," I explained before citing two examples: "I'd do him in a minute." and "Never go there in August." They laughed as they grasped the concept. Then we began to play an improvisational party game as they quoted several examples that they'd heard Lloyd say. Finally, we just started making up our own queeny pronouncements. We laughed harder as each of us kept adding clues to our unsolvable puzzle:

Across

1. I'd do him in a minute.

3. Never go there in August.

5. It's the *only* brand of Vodka.

7. They call that a city?

11. Absolutely the best way to make chicken.

13. Could you see him hunting? I don't think so!

15. I've been saying that for years.

17. She's the one actress that I feel can do no wrong.

19. It's better than Xanax.

Down

2. She hasn't made a good movie since *Chinatown*.

4. I can take him for twenty minutes. Tops.

9. It's sort of become my trademark.

10. Apparently, he's *huge*.

12. Don't get me started on that.

14. I tried it once. Once was enough.

17. Let's not go there.

18. Was that bitchy?

In case you're stumped, the correct answer to 1 Across and 10 Down was Dylan Fabizak, but Roy and I didn't tell Dylan that. After we ran the joke into the ground, I asked Dylan how he knew Lloyd.

"I don't know him," he said. "I was invited because he's a friend of Graham's."

Hearing Graham's name mentioned by Dylan made everyone glance awkwardly at each other as we thought of the scene that had occurred minutes earlier.

"I'm glad to be going away for a few weeks," Dylan admitted.

I suddenly felt like an actual champagne fiend as I realized that I urgently needed to find the bathroom. I excused myself and headed off. When I came out of the bathroom, Graham was waiting for me in the hallway.

"Can we talk?" he asked, tilting his head toward the back door, signaling that I should follow him outside.

It was after midnight, and the sun had set but the sky never darkens completely during the summer in Alaska. A soft, gray glow remained overhead as if someone had left a door ajar and the sun was a light burning in another room.

"Don't let your boyfriend fish with that fucker," warned Graham, assuming correctly that I would understand which fucker he was referring to.

"He slept with my boyfriend and he'll sleep with yours," he said. "They fucked in the bed that I paid for and then stuck me with a tab for room service. Don't trust him."

Graham raked his hands through his long, shaggy gray hair.

"Dylan couldn't get a job with his record," he said ruefully. "His agent was begging for parts. No one wanted to hire him because insurance companies wouldn't post a production bond for him. But I took a chance on him because I think he's talented. I believe in him. Now I'm supposed to direct that fuck when I don't even want to look at him."

He unlocked his car and opened the door but remained standing.

"On my last picture," he said, thinking aloud, "the cast stopped speaking to each other, so I had to bring in a therapist to work out their issues. Maybe I can fly her in again."

"You needed a therapist for the cast?" I asked.

He nodded. "There's an entire specialty built around resolving workplace conflicts."

"Things like, 'He stole my theatrical gesture,'" I said. "Or, 'She keeps upstaging me.'"

"Or, 'He fucked my boyfriend,'" Graham said bitterly.

He got behind the wheel of his car and honked the horn twice. "Don't trust him," he warned. Thatcher immediately came running out of the house and hopped into the passenger side, acknowledging me with a quick guilty smile.

They drove off and I returned to the house. I ran into Dylan in the kitchen. He looked chagrined that I caught him wolfing down a piece of turkey.

"Thanks for putting in a good word with Roy," he said. "I wouldn't be going fishing without you." I smiled but didn't say anything. I was willing to take undeserved credit for Roy's change of heart even though I still had no idea what had caused it.

"My biggest problem isn't the drugs," Dylan confessed. "The drugs mask the real problem. I'm a sex addict. I think about sex all the time. 24/7 inches. My dick's always nudging me: check out this guy. I used to try to convince myself that I didn't have a problem. I never denied fucking hundreds of guys, but I rationalized it by telling myself that I was an artist with a stronger than normal desire for beauty. Well, my shrink pointed out that I fucked plenty of ugly guys, too. Hell, I couldn't argue with his reasoning. I've learned to accept that I'm a sex addict and someday—if my higher power's willing—I'll learn to control it."

It was satisfying to hear Dylan disclose that he was gay, but I'm ashamed to admit that hearing that he was also a sex addict didn't rouse my sympathy. I understood that sex addiction is a real problem, but it was hard to think of it as a serious problem because I wasn't sure what distinguished a sex addict from a normal man. Unless normal men just think about sex all the time while sex addicts actually have sex all the time. The more I thought about it, the more I came to see that it was unfair for an extremely attractive sex addict to let other people know of his addiction, especially since I suspected that Dylan knew that I was jonesing for him. All of a sudden I didn't feel comfortable about Roy spending three weeks alone in the wilderness with a self-confessed sex addict. It was too easy to imagine Roy becoming the monkey on Dylan's broad back.

Dylan moved closer to me and reached out affectionately to pat my shoulder. "I owe you," he said.

I remembered that he owed me ten dollars.

"Hey, do you have the ten bucks for the sandwich from the other day?"

"I thought it was seven."

I reminded him that I'd also bought him an iced tea. I never could understand why cheap people are willing to blow their reputations for generosity for the measly price of a sandwich. Dylan scowled as he took his sweet time searching for ten dollars in his wallet. But I refused to feel uncomfortable and waited patiently until he handed me the money. I needed all the cash I could get because I was going fishing with them.

NINE

O ur small airplane crossed the tree line after a short stop to re-
fuel at the airport in the town of King Salmon. Along the entire
west coast of Alaska, tundra hugs the frigid waters of the Bering Sea and
the spruce trees diminished to the size of candles until they guttered out
completely as we approached Coffee Point. Lakes abutted ponds and
the sodden land separating them appeared to be a green cobweb that
could be swept away with the swipe of a hand. I kept scanning the
ground below on the remote chance that I might see a brown bear
loping beneath us.

My pilot was Lloyd, the champagne fiend, and I'd been uneasy
when he offered to fly me in his Cessna to Coffee Point. It was hard to

believe that Lloyd had been a pilot in the Air Force, but Don insisted that it was true. Lloyd's generous offer had saved me from spending the rest of my meager savings. The price of an airline ticket from Anchorage to King Salmon would have cost more than my ticket from Los Angeles, and flying directly to Coffee Point also saved me from having to hire a bush pilot for the last thirty-five mile leg of the trip. Dylan and Roy had flown out six days before us, but I had to wait because Lloyd had volunteered to work at a health clinic and couldn't get away until the end of the week.

For the entire three-hour flight and one-hour refueling stop, Lloyd regaled me with tales from his former life as a barfly. ("You know I'm almost fifty, and for all this time—for all these years—I never knew until recently that you're supposed to tip strippers when they talk to you. I knew that you tipped them when they're on stage and you approach them. But whenever a stripper was standing next to me, rubbing his dick on my leg and squeezing my ass, I thought he was just being friendly.")

As we prepared to land, the airplane crossed the Egegik River in a wide arc, flying over the village of Egegik, which looked as if its slapdash buildings and houses had been delivered that morning. We recrossed the river and circled over Coffee Point, which from the air appeared to be a shantytown constructed from the boxes and crates that neighboring Egegik had been shipped in. There were hundreds of fishing boats waiting around the mouth of the River and offshore along the coast. The returning salmon didn't have a chance, I thought.

The landing on the gravel runway at Coffee Point was smoother than I had expected.

"Have you got your passport?" boomed Lloyd as we rolled to a stop. "Because you've left America. Even Alaskans consider this to be the boonies. You know how people always talk about being in the middle of nowhere? Well, Coffee Point is on the *outskirts* of nowhere."

Lloyd helped me unload my bags. Then he reached into the fuselage and pulled out a large two-handled shopping bag and a small brown paper bag. "Don and I put together a survival kit for you," he said before removing a small tightly rolled plastic bag from his jacket pocket.

"Matanuska Thunder Fuck," he said, handing me the bag. "I have a pal who grows it up in Palmer."

Lloyd then handed me the small brown bag.

"Don sent these for you and Dee," he said. Dee was Roy's mother who I was going to meet for the first time.

I opened the bag and saw two pint-sized mason jars filled with dark red preserves.

"Raspberries from your garden?" I asked.

"No, they're nagoonberries."

"Sounds like something hanging from your nose."

"Quite the opposite," said Lloyd, "nagoonberries, *Rubus arcticus*, are also known as wineberries. They're almost unheard of outside of Alaska. They grow in the wild and possess a sweet, delicate, almost winey flavor. Nagoonberries are the rarest and most delicious member of the raspberry family. I'm a nagoonberry *fiend*."

At first I had been angry when I heard that Alex had told Lloyd about how I'd taken to repeating his champagne-fiend monologue. I thought Lloyd would be offended, but he had jokingly accused me of being a viper nursed at his bosom, a thought I tried to repress as I'd recently glimpsed his nipple rings while he was doing yard work. In my company, Lloyd had taken to making occasional references to being a champagne fiend, which tickled me. I loved when a private joke became a toy to be shared among friends, a word or phrase that could be brought out and played with at any time.

"Don wants Dee to make nagoonberry ice cream for you. It will change your life! The other jar is from me. Late at night when you're stoned and get the munchies, here's what you do: toast some English muffins—there's a package in the bag—then spread them with real butter—there's butter in there, too—then smear them with a big dollop of nagoonberry preserves. It's heavenly. When you're completely fucked up, it's better than the finest pastry."

"You sound like the host of a cooking show for potheads," I said.

"Oh, Nelson," he sighed, "that would be my dream job!"

Lloyd then opened the large shopping bag, reached in and pulled out a pair of Xtra Tuffs, the rubber boots that are as indispensable to life in Alaska as sunglasses are to life in southern California.

"You'll need these," he said.

"Lloyd," I said, deeply moved by his generosity, "thank you."

"We couldn't send you out in the bush without a pair of Xtra Tuffs," he said. "It would be irresponsible on our part."

"You're the first real friends I've made . . ." I began.

". . . who are over forty?" Lloyd interrupted before I could finish my sentence.

"No, I was going to say, 'in Alaska.' But that, too."

"Age isn't important in the long run," Lloyd said as he helped me move my luggage a safe distance from the runway. "I have friends who are younger than me and friends who are older than me." Lloyd opened his eyes wide as if his statement had astonished me. "Yes, Nelson, there *are* men older than me. I think of everyone alive when I'm alive as my contemporary. It doesn't matter whether a person's one or one hundred, if we're both breathing; we already share a lot in common."

Lloyd's conversational soliloquy didn't require a response, but I smiled before I frowned.

"I thought Roy would meet me," I said looking around at the seemingly vacant fishing camp.

Roy had been overjoyed when I told him that I'd decided to come with him to Coffee Point. He even let out an "awesome!"

"What made you change your mind?" he had asked.

"I didn't want you spending three weeks in the wilderness with the world's hottest sex addict," I'd confessed.

Roy had laughed, which wasn't the reaction I'd been expecting.

"Well, I didn't want to leave you in Anchorage with the world's sexiest personal trainer," he'd admitted.

It seemed an amusing "Gift of the Magi" moment until I asked Roy if it demonstrated that we didn't trust each other.

"I trust you," he'd said, "but I don't trust you with him."

When it appeared that no one was going to meet me, Lloyd asked, "Do you want me to stay? I'd hate to leave you stranded out here, although you have steaks and pot, so you'd be welcome anywhere in the bush."

Roy had brought out all of our canned, bottled, and dry food to Coffee Point, but Lloyd had suggested that I bring the makings of a banquet. Since we'd have plenty of salmon, I'd bought the best steaks I could find, plus salad greens and loaves of crusty olive bread from the Kalikat Bakery.

"I'll be fine," I said, knowing that Lloyd wanted to hurry back to Anchorage because he and Don had tickets to a concert that night. But after saying that I'd be okay, I realized that I believed it. I wasn't sure where my wellspring of self-confidence issued from but, having muddled through a tar pit, I assumed I'd probably survive the tundra.

Lloyd said good-bye with a handshake instead of the more fashionable hug between men. It was the one thing about him that was old-fashioned.

"Have fun out here," he advised as he climbed inside the cockpit. Before closing the door, he shouted, "You're having an adventure, don't forget that!"

I watched Lloyd depart before I carefully packed the jars of nagoon-berries in my backpack and exchanged my sneakers for my Xtra Tuffs. Standing up, I looked around. A strong wind snapped a signal flag hanging on a pole. The sun on my chest encouraged me to remove my jacket, but the brisk wind on my back cautioned against it. The weather was idyllic by the standards of Bristol Bay, because it wasn't raining.

A collection of run-down looking buildings stood nearby but I didn't see or hear any people, even though it was two-thirty in the afternoon. In the opposite direction was the gently rolling treeless tundra where low bushes were growing in the swales. Off in the distance, across the river, I saw a snowcapped mountain on the horizon, which I would later learn was Mount Peulik, an active volcano.

A dirt road looped away from the airstrip, but I couldn't see it from where I was standing. I decided to hike across the short expanse of ground that separated me from the nearest building. Stepping onto the spongy turf, I discovered that the seeming expanse of low grasses were a series of tussocks, each one having a different moisture level and load-bearing strength. I wobbled unsteadily with every step I took, and it was difficult to keep my balance carrying a heavy backpack and three unwieldy duffel bags. By the time I realized my error, it was too late. Retracing my steps would have required the same amount of effort as continuing forward. Several times my Xtra Tuffs puddled deeply into the mud, bringing back vivid memories of the tar pits, and I was sweating heavily when I finally reached solid ground again.

The roar of the four-wheeler's engine could be heard long before the squat miniature dune buggy bolted from a bank of shrubs along the road. The blond-haired driver waved his arm at me as he towed a small trailer that bucked and swayed, kicking up clouds of dust. I watched as Dylan raced toward me and felt a pang of disappointment that Roy wasn't driving the four-wheeler, but I also relaxed for the first time since I'd boarded the airplane in Anchorage.

Dylan skidded to a stop and raised his oval, yellow-lensed sunglasses. "Need a lift?" he asked, grinning at me. His form-fitting red, long-sleeved thermal shirt made it seem that Hercules was offering me a chariot ride.

"Yes," I said as I threw my duffel bags into the trailer. I'd decided to wear the backpack to protect the precious cargo of nagoonberry preserves.

"How'd you know I was here?"

"Roy told me to listen for your plane. He went to buy a new battery for his truck, but he should be back in an hour."

Dylan patted the seat behind him.

"Get on."

There wasn't much room, but I climbed aboard. Once I was seated, I couldn't decide where to put my hands. The most sensible thing would have been to act like a motorcycle passenger and put my arms around his waist, but that seemed too forward and intimate. There were two small plastic handles on the sides of the seat and I tried gripping them.

"Hang on to me," he ordered. "This thing bounces and I don't want to lose you."

I placed my arms loosely around his waist.

"Grab me," Dylan said impatiently. "Pretend you're a biker chick, and I'm your old man."

"I'll cut you, motherfucker!" I said, snarling in character as I grabbed hold of him. I don't believe that I was cynical or jaded, but I'd come to accept that whenever a gay man delves into his feminine side, he's invariably a hard woman.

Dylan gunned the thumb throttle on the four-wheeler, and I was thrown backward and grabbed him tightly around the waist. Scooting closer to his broad back, I caught a whiff of perspiration and dandruff shampoo, a combination of odors that I thought could be sold as a scented candle, if it were marketed right.

We took off down a sandy lane, and when I felt in danger of falling off, I hugged Dylan as if he were my boyfriend. He turned his head back to smile at me, and the exhilarating sense that I'd embarked on a grand adventure was inextricably combined with the furtive thrill of touching Dylan's body.

Coffee Point was a jumble of aircraft and boat hangers, small houses and storage sheds at the headland on the north shore of the Egegik River. The small fishing camp sat on a bluff twenty-five feet above the ocean and the mouth of the river and enjoyed an expansive view of bleak grandeur. But, during the winter, I thought Coffee Point and Egegik must feel tied to the shore like men lashed to the mast of a storm-tossed ship.

"Welcome to your shit hole for the next month," Dylan said when we arrived at our house. It sat amongst cabins and shacks that stood at haphazard angles to each other along the sandy road as if a meeting of houses had been called to discuss forming a street but nothing had been decided. The rickety two-story shack made me imagine that during a sudden downpour, Roy had to quickly choose to seek cover by either opening an umbrella or building a house. Apparently, at Coffee Point, the preferred method of finding shelter from the rain was building a house because it took less time. Our house was built out of a hodge-podge of materials: unpainted plywood panels—weathered gray by the winter winds and rain—sheets of rusting, corrugated metal and peeling batten boards, roughly painted a drab rust-colored primer.

The houses of Coffee Point were funky and dilapidated, but they had the larky air of run-down summer cottages, whose beachfront setting considerably ameliorated any suggestion of poverty as almost every house had a million-dollar ocean view.

A basketball hoop mounted on a metal pole outside our front door distinguished our shack from its neighbors. Stacked next to every house were the ubiquitous large white plastic totes labeled with black marker, "Ice Only" or "Water" to distinguish them from the totes used to haul salmon to the cannery's weigh station. Ropes and ladders hung on the outer walls of storage sheds, and blackened, rusting barrels of diesel fuel and gasoline were sprinkled around Coffee Point like toxic chocolate jimmies. A portable diesel generator chugged away down the road, supplying electricity to our house and our immediate neighbors.

The numerous dogs of Coffee Point lay strewn in yards and seemed less like pets than abandoned pieces of equipment. The only proof that the dogs were alive was when they occasionally jerked their heads over their shoulders, snapping their jaws dementedly at the air, biting at mosquitoes but making themselves appear to be hounded by unseen enemies.

"Wait till you see the inside," Dylan said as he lifted the heaviest bag from the four-wheeler's trailer. "It's better than my prison cell but not by much."

I grabbed the other two bags and followed Dylan inside the doorway where a small heater puffed away, and I was immediately enveloped by the fuggy smell of coffee, diesel fuel, and men.

The first floor was a sunny main room with a kitchen and dining area and an adjoining small bedroom and bathroom. A bright blue enameled stove from the sixties or early seventies stood next to a five-foot long butcher-block countertop. Underneath the kitchen sink was a small dormitory-sized refrigerator. The view of the ocean from the kitchen window was blocked by the large well-constructed sauna that Roy's brother Pete had built. Two mismatched chairs sat next to the small, wooden kitchen table, which had "Roy Rules '84" and other juvenile graffiti carved into its surface.

Sheets of cheap, wood-grain paneling in various colors covered the interior walls. At the top of the walls where the paneling would normally have been cut or sawn, the sheets had been bent and pressed, extending the walls into a coved ceiling.

Dylan pointed out his small bedroom. Thumbtacked to the door was a poster of the Marsden Hartley painting "Madawaska—Acadian Light Heavy." I'd seen the original in the Art Institute in Chicago and came away thinking his portrait of a handsome bare-chested boxer is a masterpiece. The painting is startling because it's such an unflinching self-portrait of Hartley's desire.

"Do you like my poster?" asked Dylan.

"He's one of my favorite painters," I said, recognizing that the man in the picture could be Dylan's dark-haired twin. I was impressed that Dylan knew Hartley. He was a hero of mine: for his artistry, for his living honestly as a gay man between the World Wars, and for even choosing to replace his unpleasant first name of Edmund with the splendidly dreadful name of Marsden.

"I don't know much about art but I know a hot guy when I see one," Dylan said, holding my gaze until I began to suspect that he wasn't talking about the painting. "I'm reading that book you recommended, too," he said. *"Diary of a Nobody.* I'm not sure if it's as good as you made out, but Mr. Pooter's a real character."

I was flattered that Dylan had actually bought the book. I admitted that the last thing I had purchased in Anchorage was the one-volume copy of Chekhov's letters that he had recommended.

"Since we're next to Russia, he seemed like the perfect author to read," I added.

"Your room's up here," Dylan said, pointing to a steep set of stairs leading to the second floor. The treads were covered with light gray carpeting, and Dylan informed me that it was mandatory to take off your shoes before climbing them. I followed him up the stairs to a large, immaculate white-painted room with three enormous picture windows that offered views of the beach and river. Built underneath the windows, about a foot off the floor, ran a ledge that also served as a window seat. A sculptural piece of misshapen driftwood was displayed in front of the largest window. In addition, collections of rocks, antique glass fishing floats, and other beach-combed treasures were neatly laid out in baskets and shallow bowls. A row of books and DVDs ran underneath the ledge.

Along the windowless back wall, built into an alcove, was an inviting-looking double bed covered with a patchwork quilt. A dark blue curtain could be pulled shut across the alcove to block out what I thought must be the almost constant light.

The only furniture in our bedroom was a battered metal office chair and a desk that had been built from a collection of mismatched boards. I walked over to the desk and saw that it faced south, offering a view of the river and snowcapped Mt. Peulik in the distance. A sheet of notepaper sat on the desktop, held down by a beautiful dark gray oval stone. Roy had written in red ink, "Dear Nelson, Welcome to Coffee Point! This is your desk! xo love, Roy."

After reading his note, I felt momentarily dazed with affection as if Roy had dropped his heart from a great height, hitting me like a heavy stone.

"This is great," I said to Dylan, looking again around the room and thinking how close I had come to staying in Anchorage.

"It's not bad," he said in agreement. Then he said, "It's warm in here and I don't know how to shut off the heater." He began to pull his T-shirt over his head but it became entangled in his arms. "A little help here," he said through his shirt. I walked over and gave the shirt a tug, unveiling his torso.

"Thanks," he said with a cocky grin as I memorized the size and shape of his nipples and charted the love trail that led down from his navel.

"There's a raven's nest in an old airplane hangar down the road," Dylan said as we climbed back down the stairs to the kitchen. "You've got to see it. There's nothing more evil looking than a nestful of baby ravens. It's like something out of a fairy tale."

He walked over to open a window and let in some air. I'd hung my backpack on a chair and, as Dylan struggled with the window's stubborn sash, it gave way suddenly and he recoiled, accidentally bumping the chair, knocking the backpack to the floor. A sharp clink of glass startled me. I hurriedly emptied the contents of the backpack onto the kitchen table, afraid that he'd broken the jars of nagoonberries. They were undamaged, but while I checked to see whether anything else had broken, Dylan picked up the rolled, plastic bag of Matanuska Thunder

Fuck that I'd set on the table. A rubber band had snapped and the bag
had started to unravel.

"What's this?" Dylan asked.

"Lloyd gave it to me," I said, remembering that Roy had been
adamant that he didn't want Dylan using drugs.

He opened the bag of pot and sniffed the contents appreciatively.
"Maybe we should give it a try."

"I don't think we should."

"When the cat's away. . . ."

"The cat's dating one of the mice," I said firmly. "Roy said if you
do drugs he'll put you on the next plane."

"Smoking pot's not doing drugs," Dylan said. "I'll protect us from
your boyfriend."

He removed a package of rolling papers from his back pocket and
began to roll a thick joint on the table. I watched anxiously as he lit it,
inhaled, and then offered me the fattie. I took the joint from his hand
and moved toward the bathroom because I'd decided to flush it down
the toilet.

"Don't do that!" Dylan shouted as he realized what I intended to
do. He grabbed my shoulder, then wrapped his arms around me. I tried
to pull away from him but he held me fast. His warm bare chest pressed
against my back as he held me tightly. He tried to pinion my arms by
grabbing my wrists but I moved my left hand and grabbed his thick
forearm in an attempt to free myself. The soft hair on his arms tickled
my palm, and I could feel muscles flexing and ridges of prominent veins.
I was immediately aware of how attractive our situation might have been
under different circumstances.

Our eyes met, and Dylan smiled, wrapping his other hand around
my fist. He began to slowly pry the joint from my fingers. I struggled

to break his grip as he whispered in my ear. "You don't want to do that." I could smell the remains of a chocolate chip cookie on his breath. The joint began to burn my finger and thumb and I dropped it.

Instead of picking up the joint, Dylan spun me around and kissed me. I was startled but went with the smooch while I tried to decide what to do. It's always a bad idea to debate the merits of kissing someone you desire while in midkiss, because two balls can outvote one brain. He shoved his hand down my pants and gripped my now hard dick. Then his tongue shot into my mouth like a transplanted organ being rejected by his body. I broke off the kiss just as the door opened. Roy walked into the kitchen. The smoke hanging in the air formed an actual cloud of suspicion. I was still locked in the shirtless Dylan's embrace. Roy looked confused then he became angry.

"Fuck," he exclaimed.

TEN

It's a matter of conjecture on how I actually injured myself—clumsiness often demands more acrobatic agility and perfect timing than gracefulness—but I believe that when Roy walked in, Dylan released me as I pushed him away, and I lost my balance and fell. The edge of the kitchen table clipped me in the temple with a thonk that sounded as if my head was being tested for ripeness.

"That hurt," I moaned as my eyes teared up from the intense pain over my left eye.

"You're bleeding!" shouted Dylan when I turned to face them.

"I can't believe it," I said as a trickle of blood ran down my forehead and dripped onto my shirt. Stunned by my own ineptitude, I stood motionless, trying to figure out what I should do.

"Hang on," Roy said before hurrying to the sink and returning with a clean dishtowel. He tried to stanch the bleeding, but the cloth soon turned crimson. Roy looked worried while Dylan appeared to be nauseated and moved away from me.

"We'd better go see my mom," Roy said.

"I don't want to meet her like this."

"She'll know what to do."

"Is there anything I can do?" Dylan asked, staying outside of my bleeding range, obviously repelled.

The amount of blood scared me—my blue shirt was soon drenched—but Roy's composure assured me that I'd be all right. Dylan said he'd stay behind and clean up the kitchen floor, although he looked a little queasy at the thought of it. Roy's face was resolute as we walked out of the house.

"Will you grab the jar of nagoonberries?" I asked, remembering Lloyd's gift.

"We'll get it later," Roy said as he walked next to me, his arm resting on my back, ready to catch me if I fell.

"Please," I said with the plaintive whine that either touches a boyfriend's heart or irritates him depending upon circumstances that neither party can predict. Since it wasn't in Roy's nature to deny a request from a man holding a bloody towel to his head, he reentered the house and returned with the nagoonberries. Waiting for him, I kept thinking that every mother of a gay son worries about AIDS, and a new beau dripping blood on her kitchen floor would be a graphic representation of her worst nightmare. I'd anticipated meeting Dee under the normal circumstances of initial uneasiness allied with the inherent confidence that we'd eventually like each other.

I was concerned about my injury but could multi-tsk-tsk my anxieties and worry about what Roy thought when he found me standing in the kitchen with the half-naked Dylan, while tormenting myself with frantic speculation about what Roy's mother would think about me when she saw that I was bleeding.

A pot of geraniums struggled to survive outside Dee's small red house. Posted near the front door was a "No Vendors" sign whose dry wit made me feel welcomed. We entered the mudroom, and seeing the shoes and boots neatly lined up in a row, I carefully wiped my feet on the doormat. Roy opened the inside door and shouted, "Mom!" as we stepped into her kitchen.

"She doesn't lock up?" I asked as we waited for a response.

"No one does," Roy said. "Locked doors are dangerous in an emergency. If you need to borrow something from a neighbor, you walk in and take it."

"You actually trust your neighbors," I said. "That's not right."

I had tried to make a little joke but Roy stared at me as if I'd suffered brain damage.

"Usually you can trust people out here," he said as he roughly pushed me through the door. The sting of his sarcasm made me momentarily ignore my aching forehead. Roy wasn't going to let me forget that even though I was bleeding, he had also been wounded.

Dee's kitchen was filled with the tantalizing aroma of two freshly baked cherry pies. I tried to avoid dripping blood on the yellow linoleum-tiled floor and attempted to behave like a considerate guest and bleed in a discreet manner near the doorway. I took in the red painted cabinets, a full-sized refrigerator that had to be forty years old, and a chrome-legged kitchen table with six matching chairs that held court in the center of the brightly lit room. Above the sink was a large picture window, and I could see the masts of fishing boats peeking over the sill.

"Mom?" Roy called again.

"I was wondering when I'd meet him," said Dee Briggs as she entered from the adjoining room. She carried a paperback in her left hand, and her face had the blank-page expression of someone who had been deeply engrossed in reading. "I was thinking you were either ashamed of me or he was butt-ugly."

Dee appeared to be in her early sixties. She was slim and wore her long gray hair tied back in a ponytail. She wasn't wearing any makeup but did have on a pair of dangling silver and black opal earrings. She hobbled across the kitchen with a stiff deliberate gait that indicated her right foot or leg hurt her.

"Look how you're walking," Roy said shaking his head reproachfully.

"Don't start," she warned. Roy had told me that they had been arguing for months because he thought his mother was too old to fish by herself and needed to hire a crewman. She'd told him to mind his own business. Roy actually thought she should give up fishing entirely but knew she wasn't ready to hear it. He'd also admitted that he'd miss her if she stopped coming out to Coffee Point.

"Well," Dee said calmly after she acknowledged that I was bleeding, "you're not butt-ugly but I'm sure you've looked better." She ignored my apologies and told me to sit at the kitchen table while she examined my cut. Roy was ordered to get a compress out of a kitchen cupboard and a bottle of hydrogen peroxide from a cabinet in the bathroom.

"You might need stitches," Dee declared as she leaned over me, examining my injury, giving me an opportunity to meet her right breast. She placed my hand on the compress and told me to apply pressure to the wound. I began to bemoan my clumsiness, but Dee interrupted my whining and told me to reapply pressure to the wound.

"Don't tell me that you're stupid on our first acquaintance," she said to me while washing her hands. "I take people at their word."

I interpreted her severe look as a statement that she wasn't in the habit of dealing with fools, which was intimidating because I hadn't broken the habit of being one.

"Accidents happen," she said while drying her hands. "You'll go back and tell everyone you got mauled by a bear."

"A two-inch gash?" Roy sneered. "Our bears can do better than that."

"Did you know Roy's grandfather was a bear guide?"

"How does someone decide to become a bear guide?" Roy said to no one in particular.

"A hunter was nearly disemboweled by an angry bear," Dee said as she picked up a microphone, which was attached to a small radio transmitter. "My father tied his guts back in with a wire then dragged him out of the bush on a stretcher."

"Is everyone in your family tough?" I asked, thinking that I couldn't imagine my grandfather leading a party of golfers out of a sand trap.

"Just the women," Dee said. "The men think they are."

"Hey, I'm tough," protested Roy.

"You're reliable," she said. "Don't confuse that with toughness. Your grandfather would never abandon an injured man but after your grandmother died, his grief killed him within a year."

We observed a moment of silence to honor the ability of a man to die of grief. Dee's father's death reinforced my belief that every life story is a tale of survival. Bears will never attack most of us, but experience mauls everyone eventually and most of us do live to tell the tale.

"I read that in the early sixties a Soviet doctor in Antarctica had to operate on himself and remove his own appendix," Roy said. "Now that's a real man."

"Would a real man know how to sew?" I asked.

"You'd call him a sissy for using a needle and thread on himself?" he asked. I grinned and shrugged, giving him the point.

Dee spoke into a microphone to someone named Mary in Egegik about my condition. They discussed whether we should travel across the river but Mary responded that she'd come to us in her skiff. Dee signed off and turned to me.

"You're reading Barbara Pym," I said, noticing the cover of the book, *Excellent Women,* which Dee had placed on the kitchen table.

"You've read her?" she asked.

"Every novel," I said. "She's one of my favorite writers."

"One of my ex-students badgered me into trying her," Dee confessed, "I usually don't read novels but I've enjoyed hers."

"She's really funny," I said.

"And sad, too," Dee said. "She portrays lonely women with great dignity."

"There was a time when I couldn't seem to get a date," I said. "And I found reading about the lives of plain unmarried women comforting." Roy and his mother looked at me oddly, making me glad I hadn't mentioned that sometimes I fantasized if spinster were spelled "spinsta" it might acquire a newfound cachet.

Dee picked up the jar that I'd set on the table and read the hand-lettered label.

"Who brought the nagoonberries?" she asked.

"Nelson," Roy said.

"Lloyd and Don sent them for you," I explained, not wanting to take credit for their gift.

Dee sighed fondly. "Lloyd and his nagoonberries. That was awfully generous. He doesn't often part with them."

"He's a nagoonberry *fiend*," I declared, before recounting once more my initial meeting with Lloyd. Roy had already heard me tell the story of the champagne fiend several times but there's a tacit agreement between most couples that they'll listen dutifully to each other's favorite anecdotes and stories repeated ad nauseum. The term life-partner had come into vogue to describe couples, and it really was fitting when used in the sense of a vaudeville act where two people shared the same bill and had to endure hearing the same performance over and over.

Dee listened to my champagne fiend monologue, but she didn't smile.

"A more sensible man wouldn't have offered to fly you out to Coffee Point," she pointed out. Ashamed of my ingratitude, I tried to explain that Lloyd amused me because his passions were both absurd and glorious. I was tempted to add that I'd been similarly entranced when her son talked about the stone harpoon points found embedded in the blubber of bowhead whales.

While we waited for Mary to arrive, Dee asked if we wanted a piece of cherry pie. We both said yes and she cut large slices. I noticed hanging on the wall a family portrait taken thirty years ago. Roy wore every four-year-old's gleeful smile, boasting about his own adorableness, while Dee's frosted hair was a Harvest Gold color that matched her kitchen appliances.

"When did you first come out here?" I asked as she handed me a plate and a fork.

"It was my son Pete's idea," Dee said as she sat down with us at the kitchen table. "He was twelve and begged me to let him come out fishing with a friend. I thought he was too young to go, but it sounded kind of appealing. I had the summer off from teaching, and my husband was going to be away fishing. On an impulse I decided that we should all go."

"Our first few seasons we lived in tents," Roy said, shaking his head in disbelief. "I don't know how we ever lived in tents with the wind out here. Once during a storm, we had to tie some of the buildings here to these big Cats—road graders—and run them all night in the opposite direction of the wind to keep them from blowing away."

Forty minutes later, there was a double knock on the door. Dee opened it and a short dark-haired woman entered. Mary carried a brown leather valise of medical supplies bearing the insignia of the Red Cross. Her long, straight black hair was tucked under a Yankees baseball cap and her hooded navy blue sweatshirt had, "Stitch N Bitch" printed in white letters on the front.

A teakettle began to whistle, and Dee hobbled across the kitchen to take it off the burner. Mary immediately looked down at her leg.

"What's wrong with your foot?" she asked.

Dee winced slightly as she poured hot water into a teacup. "I hurt it fishing," she said curtly.

"What happened?" Mary demanded.

Dee glanced guiltily over at Roy. She looked as if she didn't want to discuss what had happened in front of him. "The boat fell off the trailer and landed on my foot. It's the first time that's ever happened."

"You didn't tell me that!" Roy shouted. Dee's mouth moved as if she was going to yell back at him, but she refrained from saying anything. It appeared that being tack-i-turn ran in the family.

"You'd better have me look at it," Mary said.

"I'm not the patient, Mary," Dee said crisply.

Mary set her valise down on the kitchen table. She glanced at me and said, "He'll live. He's still bleeding." Then she looked back at Dee. "Most of my cases are two-for-one deals. I go to treat one patient and usually find another one who's in worse shape."

Mary ordered Dee to take off her boot.

"You're starting to live up to your sweatshirt," Dee said.

"Do you like it?" Mary asked, smiling for the first time. "It was a gift from the staff at the regional headquarters. They said that I was, by far, the bossiest community health practitioner in southwestern Alaska. I've come to think of it as my uniform."

Mary placed her hands on her hips and stared at Dee, waiting for her to remove her boot. Dee sighed and began to unlace it. "I thought Natives were supposed to respect their elders," she said.

"We used to until you taught us to think of them as old people," Mary replied. She stared at Dee who returned her gaze until they both laughed. Dee began to remove her boot and sock. The top of her foot had a large, ugly purple and yellow bruise. Roy's face turned an angry red color as he hissed, "Shit." His face became fixed with determination. "That's it," he said. "I'm going to call Pete if you don't hire a crewman."

"Don't use that tone of voice with me," Dee scolded.

"You're too old to keep doing this by yourself," Roy said bluntly.

Dee's face became equally set as her son's. "I'm not giving up my permit," she declared.

"I'm not asking you to give up your permit," he said as his anger faded. He smiled as he thought of something.

"Why don't you hire Nelson?" Roy suggested. "He needs the money, and you need the help." I shot Roy a look of anger that was as quick as a bullet but not nearly as effective in silencing him; I thought he should have run his proposal past me first. It seemed that he was setting me up to fail again and also putting his mother and me on the spot. Dee looked surprised, but she didn't seem as irritated as she had before.

The two of us exchanged skeptical looks. I felt that she saw a scrawny fish that should be thrown back.

"Did you talk this over with Nelson?" Dee asked.

"What's to talk about?" Roy replied.

"Your father always said that," Dee said sharply, "before I divorced him."

"It's obvious that it's good for both of you."

His statement enraged me. I was fuming, but of course I didn't want to act pissed off in front of strangers who were meeting me for the first time. One of the drawbacks of decisive people is that they often extend their authority to telling other people what they should do. I was sick of it. Roy decided that I should go to Alaska and then insisted that I should come out to Coffee Point. I had explained to him that I wanted to work on my novel. I didn't want to fish. But I also didn't want to be seen as the guy who doesn't want to fish. I felt trapped like a salmon in a net or a clumsy man in a tar pit.

"What do you think, Nelson," Dee said, "Do you want to crew for me?"

"I'd like that," I said as my stomach churned. I looked at Roy. "But I want to make sure that I'll have time to work on my novel."

"You'll have time," Roy said. "And you'll go back with some money in your pocket."

The prospect of earning money placated me somewhat, but I was angry that Roy had made a major decision for me without discussing it with me.

He wasn't taking my writing seriously. Perhaps he didn't think being a writer was a real job. When he worked he used his hands to dig up artifacts and to catch fish—even I had difficulty thinking of typing as manual labor.

"All right then," Dee said to me before she offered Mary a cup of coffee and a piece of pie.

Mary refused the pie but accepted the coffee. Then she turned to face me. "Let's see what's going on with you." She removed the compress from my head but her expression didn't change. She poured disinfectant from a bottle on a cotton pad and then warned me that it might hurt before cleaning my wound. It stung, but I didn't flinch, determined to preserve a semblance of dignity. I often felt that I participated in Manhood by maintaining my membership at the lowest possible level; I remained affiliated with the organization by paying the nominal fee each year, but they gained nothing from my support because my dues barely covered the administrative costs of enrollment. Trying not to fidget, I asked Mary about the Alaskan Native Medical Service. She explained that the federal government had established a system of community health practitioners to provide health care to remote villages without doctors. The health practitioners were trained for eight weeks and then sent back to their villages with an encyclopedic textbook that covered every sort of medical problem from acne to schizophrenia.

"You mean if someone walks in with chest pains," I asked. "You go to your book and look up chest pains in the index and then turn to page 68 and follow the directions?"

"Yes," Mary said with a smile. "We can also talk to a doctor by radio."

"And that works?"

"We'll see," she teased.

"A friend of Lloyd's wrote the textbook," Roy said. "He and his partner are doctors. You should meet them. Their idea of a fun vacation is to vaccinate people against polio in India."

Mary cleaned out the cut, which started bleeding again, and then she instructed me to keep applying pressure to the wound. She stood up and looked over at Dee.

"Dee, can I speak to you privately?" she asked. Mary's face looked grave as they walked into Dee's office.

"What's she doing?" I whispered to Roy.

"I have no idea," he said.

It made me suspect that Mary had discovered an inoperable tumor and wanted to discuss with Dee how to break the news to me. The two women's faces looked grim after they returned from their brief conference.

"You don't need stitches," Mary announced when they returned. She placed a pressure bandage over the cut and tightly wrapped my head with gauze. I was instructed to leave the bandage on for two days then change it. She said that she'd come over to look in on me in three days. The gauze wrapped around my head made it appear as if I'd undergone brain surgery.

"I thought you looked familiar," Mary said to me as she packed up her medical supplies. She explained that she had watched my rescue from the tar pits on television. I'd mistakenly assumed that traveling to the Bering Sea would place some distance between the La Brea Tar Pits and me. But I learned that even Egegik and Coffee Point had television. It made me wonder if Natives on remote islands in the South Pacific with access to satellite news were building effigies in my image.

"You gotta be more careful," Mary said dryly. Her succinct delivery of this sound advice made everyone laugh.

I nodded.

"I'll try," I promised.

ELEVEN

Roy asked me what the hell Dylan and I had been doing as soon as we started to walk back to our house. I snarled back, "What the hell were you doing back there?"

He acted like he had no idea about what I was talking about.

"Are you bipolar?" I snapped. "Because you switch back and forth from know-it-all to dummy. You forced me to crew for your mother!"

"Don't change the subject."

"I wasn't doing anything," I explained. "Dylan kissed me."

"It didn't look like nothing."

"Don't make decisions for me without talking to me first!"

"You had a choice."

"No, I didn't! What was I supposed to say, 'Look old woman, you're gonna have to lug those fish yourself because I'm a delicate artiste. I'm here to write my novel and fuck your son.'"

"I don't know if that's still in the picture."

I explained that Dylan and I had started fighting when I attempted to throw out the joint and one thing led to another. Roy immediately set me straight that, like most Alaskans, he didn't care if Dylan or anyone else smoked pot.

"He can't keep it in his pants," Roy said. "I should put him on the next plane out of here."

Dylan wasn't at the house when we arrived. Roy immediately tore open a box of chocolate truffles I had brought and began scarfing them down.

"You don't seem that upset about it."

"What am I gonna do? He wants to sleep with us."

"Us?"

"Me," Roy acknowledged. "And I guess you, too."

"Did he hit on you?"

"Are you jealous?"

Roy grinned, revealing a glob of chocolate stuck to one of his incisors. I was mad so I decided not to mention it.

"Yes," I said. "When did this happen?"

"A few days ago in the sauna. He asked if he could blow me and I said no. Then he asked if we could jerk off together. I said no again. Then he asked me if he could jerk off while feeling up my thigh. I was too tired to argue and told him not to make a mess."

"You what?"

"He likes my legs."

Roy's legs were thick and powerful.

"That's worse than a kiss. You had sex with him."

"I didn't have sex with him. I didn't do anything."

"You could say the same thing if he had fucked you!"

Roy tried not to smile.

"You didn't tell me this."

"Hey," Roy said. "Just because I have a boyfriend doesn't mean I still can't have a private life."

I let that pass because it seemed unfair not to allow him to have a private life when I was in the midst of obsessing about mine.

"Don't forget I like your legs, too."

"Well, you're special. You can grope me and jerk off anytime you want."

Same-sex jealousy is inherently twisted. In comparison heterosexual jealousy is straightforward; a straight man's self-regard will never be called into question because the other man fucking his wife isn't interested in doing him, too. (Well, for most straight men that's true.) No doubt, if Roy had fucked Dylan, I would find it upsetting and kind of hot. A small part of me—located approximately between my navel and upper thighs—would be envious because Dylan turns my crank. How mental is that? I believe that, on some level, the degree of every gay man's jealousy depends on whether he thinks a guy is sexy and whether he has a chance with him, too. It would be horrible to discover your lover fucked a guy you'd enjoy fucking but could never get; it would be like being spurned twice.

"We're stuck with Dylan for now," Roy said. "At least we know he's a sex addict so we can deal with it."

"You know we're probably the only two gay men on the planet who'd think that's a problem?"

Roy nodded.

"I need to check my net. C'mon, I'll give you your first fishing lesson."

"You're being bossy again."

"Ow, my finger has a cramp," Roy suddenly exclaimed, waving his hand theatrically as he pretended to suffer a muscle spasm that caused his middle finger to become erect.

"You can stay here but Dylan's coming with me," he said. "There won't be anyone to suck face with."

I wiggled my two middle fingers at him.

Dylan met us outside. He'd walked down to the cannery's weigh station and had smoked a joint with the crew. He began to put on his waders and started to giggle as the wind wrapped them around his legs.

"This is like wearing a full-body condom," he complained.

"Well, you are a total dick," Roy said as he and I set two plastic totes on the back of his truck. Dylan wasn't sure how to take his comment but decided that he was joking and smiled. I was certain that Roy wasn't joking.

A rank, fishy odor overwhelmed me when I opened the passenger door of the truck. The seats in the cab were saturated with years of seawater and salmon.

"It smells like a mermaid skank," I said, unable to ignore the putrid stench but trying not to sound prissy.

"It smells like salmon ass," Dylan declared as he piled in the seat beside me.

"That's the smell of money," Roy claimed as he started the engine. I suggested driving with the windows rolled down but Dylan vetoed it.

"The mosquitoes make you more miserable than the smell does," he said sensibly. "You won't notice it after awhile."

"You'd have to be dead not to notice the smell," I said but discovered after a few days that he was right.

Trucks arrived at Coffee Point as different makes, but the isolation created the perfect conditions for natural selection, and after a few years every truck adapted to the harsh environment and resembled a single, rusting, dented species of wreck. Roy owned an orange and white 1974 Dodge Power Train that bore Washington license plates that had last been legal in 1997. His truck had been brought out on a barge, and since it was only driven on a few miles of beach roads, registering his vehicle with the state of Alaska wasn't a priority. Roy treasured his truck, because the V-8 engine could muscle though the sand while loaded down with a ton of salmon and, at the start of the season, usually needed only minor tinkering to get it running after sitting out all winter.

"Did you cut off the side rail?" I asked as we drove down the bluff. I assumed that the missing right section of the truck's bed had been removed to make loading and unloading the plastic totes easier. Roy guffawed, shaking his head. "It rusted off," he replied. "Although it does look like I removed it."

Down on the beach, Roy pointed out a pile of junked rusting trucks and even an old school bus. "Trucks never leave here," he said as we drove by them. "This is literally the end of the road. My family owned most of those. Driving past them is sort of like looking through a family photo album."

"I feels like poor white trash," Dylan said in a hillbilly accent. "We lives in a shack, we haves a junkyard right outside our front door. Nows I just need to sleep with someones in my family."

Dylan was wearing a float coat and a jacket and had secretly slipped his hand underneath my thigh and gripped me tightly as he spoke. His face remained impassive and he looked straight ahead as he repeatedly squeezed me. I let him grope me because it was enjoyable and because I figured that later I could also claim that I didn't do anything either.

The wide sandy beach served as the road linking Coffee Point and the cannery. Roy's set-net site was three miles away from his house and while driving down the beach we hit a bumpy, furrowed stretch of sand covered with dead salmon. A long-tailed jaeger glided motionlessly in the brisk wind over the eyeless fish—the jaeger's thin, streaming tail feather making it look like a malevolent child's kite.

"Do the birds peck out the headlights on the trucks, too?" I asked, having noticed that most of the trucks at Coffee Point, including Roy's, were missing one or both headlights.

"It sure looks like it," Roy said. Set-net sites lined the entire beach every three hundred feet and as we drove, he pointed out salmon caught in the nets, their flapping tails splashing at the surface of the water. Several trucks, coming from the opposite direction, passed by, and Roy always waved to the driver. The identical uniform for all of the fishermen, men and women, was a baseball cap, waterproof float coat, gloves, and waders, which made them as indistinguishable in appearance as the salmon they caught.

I noticed that running along the top of the bluff, white signs were posted above each permit holder's section of beach.

"What's with the signs?" I asked, feeling delightfully offshore from my own experience because everything about Coffee Point was new and strange.

"We have to display our permit numbers," Roy explained. "The Department of Fish and Game has to be able to read them from offshore."

When we arrived at Roy's site, we stepped out of the truck and looked up at his sign high above the shore.

"Your sign's chartreuse!" Dylan exclaimed.

"I thought I'd gay it up," Roy said proudly. He was the least campy of men, and when he emitted a tiny fairy shriek, somehow it seemed fresh, sexy, and original.

When I saw Roy's set-net for the first time, I finally understood the term "picking fish," because catching salmon with a set-net was similar to taking down laundry from a clothesline. Only the laundry was wet, slimy, and alive, struggling to escape because cleaning was a death sentence. A hundred yards offshore and forty feet apart from each other, two buoys supported two pulleys near the surface of the water. Two old automobile tires resting on the beach marked the locations of two more pulleys. The fishing net was attached to a yellow line, which ran through the four pulleys to form a rectangle. The pulleys were secured to their positions by something Roy called "screw anchors," which he thought were also used to stabilize or install telephone poles. He admitted, "I'm not exactly sure which."

Roy moved his net by attaching the yellow line to his truck by means of a jumar, the same metal tool rock climbers use to securely fasten a rope. By driving his truck backward and forward, Roy could pull his net in or out of the water. All of the fishing nets sat in the water on the left side of their rectangle, nearest to the mouth of the river, right in the path of the returning salmon.

Most set-net fisherman picked fish from their nets in aluminum boats or skiffs, but Roy used an old life raft that appeared to be held together by its patches. Dylan helped him carry the raft down to the water, but Roy excused him from further crewman duties because he said he could keep me company.

We stood on the shore and watched while Roy paddled out to pick fish.

"Have you heard about salmon sharks?" Dylan asked. "They can be twelve feet long and are known to hang around the mouths of rivers waiting for the salmon. Imagine finding one of them in your net."

It was easy for me to imagine reaching into the water as the gaping jaws of a shark swallowed my arm. The sound of the waves breaking on the shore began to taunt me with "wuss" repeatedly as I continued to have doubts about becoming Dee's crewman.

Lying astride his raft, Roy paddled out with his hands, which were encased in long-sleeved rubber gloves, because the water was cold enough to keep seafood fresh. Working his way along the length of the net, Roy used a wrench-sized, wood-handled iron-picking hook—it looked like a prehistoric dental tool—to extricate salmon entwined in the net by their gills, throwing them into the bottom of his raft.

"You know what I feel like doing right now?" Dylan asked after the two of us had stood quietly for a few minutes.

"What?"

"Taking you to that shack so we can fuck." He pointed to an abandoned cabin on top of the bluff.

My uncertain smile indicated that I didn't think he was being serious while my heart raced as I considered the possibility that he was. "Don't pretend that you're not interested," he said, removing his gloves slowly.

His unnerving confidence disturbed me and I jumped when Dylan suddenly reached behind my neck and slipped the tag of my shirt under the collar. "That's been bugging me for the past hour," he said, amused that I'd been startled by his touch.

The casual intimacy of the gesture sent a chill down my spine, and I thanked him for keeping me looking presentable.

"You don't need my help," he said. "You look good." He bent down to pick up another branch. "You know, earlier, during our scuffle,

I had a feeling you started to enjoy yourself. Remember when you grabbed my forearm? You kind of panicked when you realized you liked pawing me. Right?"

I saw no point in denying his supposition. "Yes," I admitted as a victorious grin spread across his face. Instead of feeling embarrassed that my interest in Dylan was so transparent, I was relieved that it had been acknowledged. It would have been humiliating if he hadn't picked up on it.

"It was sexy. I'd never seen you so passionate. For the first time, it made me curious about your writing. I want to read your novel." He leered at me. "In bed. After we've fucked, of course."

"I have a boyfriend," I declared. It was meant to be a statement of principle, but came out sounding like Roy was an obstacle to be overcome.

"You have a boyfriend now. And he likes that you're . . . um . . . reliable." He spoke as if politeness prevented him from calling me boring. "But I can tell that you're not as experienced as Roy."

"You don't know that!" I protested, while inwardly agreeing with him.

"Don't even try. If you were experienced, we would have fucked today."

His disarming logic caused me to laugh in agreement.

"But you never made a move, because you were afraid that I might not be interested or that Roy would find out. That kind of thinking will prevent you from ever becoming a good writer, let alone a great writer. An artist needs talent, but he also needs courage and passion. I'm a good actor because I take chances."

I allowed myself to smile.

"Our fucking will make you a better writer," he said with utter conviction.

"Really? Because I think working hard and writing well will make me a better writer."

One of the mysteries of the world is that no one has ever adequately explained how great art is created. There are legendary creation stories but they all explain the birth of Picasso's *Les Demoiselles d'Avignon* about as well as Genesis explains the creation of the world. Unfortunately, because the process of artistic inspiration doesn't seem to be scientifically explainable, it means that any crackpot theory can be considered valid.

"People joke about artists having big egos, but we need them. An average-size ego would never survive the economic uncertainty, self-doubt, and flops that every artist has to endure. Then there are the critics. Everyone makes fun of flaky actors or kooky painters but it takes guts to be an artist."

I mentioned that a stockbroker at a party had once said to me, "You want to be a *writer*?" His contempt had made me furious.

"An acting teacher of mine once said that, 'Nothing inspires more malice than holding onto youthful ambitions past the age when others have shed theirs,'" Dylan said.

I was relieved that we'd stopped talking about sex and had returned to the cozy familiarity of grousing about the odious hardships of an artist's life. Of course, we successfully ignored that we discussed this staple topic while walking along a beach in a spectacularly beautiful and exotic setting.

"What would you do if I kissed you now?" Dylan asked, as he glanced out at Roy in the water. "Right in front of him? I think you'd let me kiss you long enough to form a memory and then break it off. Then for the rest of your life you'd jerk off to that snapshot. You're never going to be good at anything, if you keep visiting your life and returning with souvenirs."

I considered kissing him to prove him wrong, but Roy was returning to shore and I could imagine how it would hurt him. It occurred to me, not for the first time, that perhaps I would never become a writer. Although I failed to consider that being able to imagine convincingly someone else's heartache suggested that Dylan was wrong.

"You're a good kisser," Dylan said. "I like how writers kiss. Well, good writers. Bad writers kiss like they're on the cover of a romance novel. They sell it too hard. If you had the guts right now, we'd go to that shack and you'd let me remove your clothes. Then when you started to shiver, I'd kiss you down the length of your body. I'd pay particular attention to that special area you have right here." He pressed his finger against the nape of my neck. It felt warm against my skin as he held it there. I knew that Roy had to have told him about my sweet spot. It wasn't a secret, but somehow it disappointed me that he had shared it with him. I suddenly felt unhappy and wanted Dylan to stop trying to seduce me. I vowed that if I ever decided to rewrite mythology, I'd make Cupid a member of an immortal guardian race, similar to the elves in *The Lord of the Rings*. They would form an army of bodyguards dedicated to using their arrows to defend our hearts from the onslaughts of love and desire.

"Think of me as a crash course in your sex education," Dylan said gleefully. "My dick could be your Harvard and my ass could be your Yale."

"What's my major?" I joked.

"You have to pick one."

"Can't I have a double major?" I asked when Roy shouted, "I need some help!" He had returned to shore and was trying to drag the heavy raft, loaded with fish, out of the water.

"Don't wait too long," warned Dylan as he went to give him a hand. "I'm interested now, but I'm not in the habit of waiting for men to grow up."

He smiled to show me that he wasn't trying to be hostile, and I nodded to indicate that I'd heard him.

Dylan helped Roy toss the heavy, over two-foot-long sockeyes into the plastic totes on the back of his truck. When I tried to assist them, Roy stopped me. "You need a crewman's permit," he said. "You're not even allowed to pick up one fish."

Before resetting his net, Roy consulted a booklet of tide charts. If the tide was going to be low, and he didn't allow for it, his net would be left high and dry, leaving his fish to spoil on the beach. If the tide was going to be high, Roy would try to set his net as close to the shoreline as possible, because the returning fish swam near the coast as they headed toward the river.

Roy usually checked his net an hour after the tides changed, twice each day, but when the fish were running, he needed to check his net four times a day, sometimes more. His habit was to check his net first thing in the morning, then around noon, then around six or seven, and finally before sunset at around ten-thirty. Driving back and forth to his site and delivering salmon to the weigh station could add another four hours to his day.

The three of us piled in the truck and we drove to the cannery's weigh station that was located a short distance up the river, because every inch of beachfront was filled with set-net sites. Stapled to a plywood wall of the weigh station's one-man-sized shed, next to an industrial scale, was a hand-lettered sign that gave the current price the cannery was paying for a pound of salmon—55 cents. Roy and Dylan delivered close to two thousand pounds of sockeyes or "reds," as they were commonly called. It was a large catch and would have been the norm ten years earlier, but since the Bristol Bay fishery crashed in the late eighties, big hauls were regarded as fluke bonanzas.

"Who's the daddy?" Dylan asked.

"That's Aaron," Roy said.

I never learned the last names of the men who ran the weigh station, but Aaron was in charge of the crew. He ran the weigh station with the assistance of Derrick and Walt, two buddies whom he had recruited in their hometown of Boulder.

Aaron was a solid, heavyset guy in his early thirties with dark hair, and his gold wire-rimmed eyeglasses lent him a scholarly air as he wrote down the weight of each fisherman's catch.

The three of us agreed that fair-haired Derrick was gorgeous. "He needs a good haircut though," Dylan said. "Then I'd fuck him." Derrick seemed oblivious of his chiseled profile and godlike physique. He proved once again that the legend of Narcissus falling in love with his own reflection is told with a misplaced emphasis on his extraordinary beauty, when it should be told as a cautionary tale about the perils of being exceptionally stupid.

Walt was a lumpy young man with a shock of unkempt brown hair. "He looks like an intellectual." Dylan said. "Maybe he's a writer." Walt wore a pair of outrageous, oversized green plastic sunglasses that made him look goofy without making him memorable. I was willing to bet that in any group photograph, his name always eluded people.

Visitors to Coffee Point were rare and tourists were nonexistent, and the friend of a friend was a binding tie in the isolated community. Dylan and I earned the weigh station crew's immediate respect and friendship for having traveled so far to see Roy.

When the crew discovered that I was a writer, they assumed that I was going to write about Coffee Point, and what I found intriguing was that all of them believed that it was a subject worthy of a writer's attention. What impressed me the most was that everyone at the weigh station, after meeting me once, remembered my name, even though I wasn't a business contact who could help anyone's fishing career.

As soon as we pulled into the weigh station, Walt began to shovel crushed ice over the fish in the back of the truck while Derrick used a forklift to unload the white plastic totes. When a tote was lifted, long jets of blood poured from the drainage holes drilled in the four corners of the container. Derrick drained the tote over the sand, and, for a few seconds, legs of blood formed a grisly table. Then the tote was deftly placed on the scale, and Aaron marked down the weight on his clipboard. Roy also wrote down the weight and date in a notebook. The fishermen were paid at the end of the season, and Roy kept his own record of what he was owed, because even though he trusted Aaron, he didn't trust the cannery. Once the totes were iced and weighed they were loaded onto a flatbed truck and driven down the beach five miles to the cannery.

After they'd finished with Roy's catch, Aaron, Derrick, and Walt approached the cab of the truck and surrounded the driver's side window. "We're asking everyone the question of the day," Aaron said. "You guys want to give it a shot?"

Roy glanced at me, and I gave my consent by raising my eyebrows, while Dylan signaled his assent with a nod of his head.

"We're game," Roy said.

"Let's hear it," Dylan said.

"Have any of you ever been in a fight?" Aaron asked. "A real fight with punching."

We sat thinking about our replies for a few seconds before anyone answered him.

"In high school, I fought Eric Huggett," Roy volunteered. "He gave me a cut lip, but I gave him a black eye."

"I was in a fight in the eighth grade," I said, bowing my head toward the driver's side window. "I was suspended for three days. But when the teacher broke up the fight, I wasn't losing."

I was relieved that I could answer the question without embarrassing myself.

Dylan leaned over me and said, "I broke a guy's arm in prison. He deserved it, too."

I didn't want violent friends, but I was proud that Dylan and Roy were a couple of ass-kickin' butt fuckers. As the crew listened to our accounts of schoolyard battles and a prison vendetta, disappointment seeped into the three men's faces.

"Are you hearing stories from guys who've lost teeth or had broken beer bottles waved in their faces?" I asked, picturing fishermen brawling in waterfront bars.

"No," Aaron said. "We're not asking guys we think have been in a fight. We're asking guys we're not sure of."

We groaned as we registered the implicit insult. Our manhood had been weighed in the balance and came up a scrotum short. It was common knowledge at Coffee Point that Roy was gay, but the subject was almost never discussed. It was generally regarded as an undesirable character trait that in Roy's case could be overlooked because he was a good fisherman. He was friendly, worked hard, and always willing to lend a hand. He spoke up, articulately and briefly, when he had something to say at the annual meetings with the cannery representatives, and most of the fishermen were indebted to him because anyone who asked could use his sauna.

Roy's attraction to men fell under the broad amnesty of commonly known, privately joked about, character flaws of other Coffee Point fishermen: Dee was stubborn and didn't like to be told what to do. Karen

Corelli had emphysema but didn't believe that her chain-smoking had anything to do with it. Joe Motley had been divorced five times because he was a pussy hound. Milt Farkas was a boozer who reeked of peppermint schnapps. Captain "Hoot" Barlow never had the same crewmen each summer because of his notorious temper, and Roy Briggs sucked dick.

"Aaron," Dylan said, "it was nice to add, 'a real fight with punching.' in case we didn't know what type of fight you were talking about."

"What did you think we'd say?" Roy asked. "I was bitch-slapped once by my boyfriend!'"

"Let's hear about your fights," I challenged.

They protested that they weren't trying to insult us. Aaron explained, "It's not about you being—" He skipped lightly over the word *gay*, because sometimes even saying the word felt queer to straight men as it came out of their mouths. "We thought you were too nice to fight."

"That's more insulting," Dylan said.

"We can be pricks," I laughed.

"Come back later this afternoon," Aaron offered.

"We're baking cookies!" Derrick said with too much enthusiasm.

"'We're baking cookies!'" mocked Dylan. "He's definitely never been in a fight."

Derrick stoically endured his fair share of ribbing until Roy glanced at his watch and announced that he wanted to get going.

"I'm gonna walk back," Dylan said as he opened the door of the truck and got out. He walked over to speak with Aaron and Derrick.

"He's already figured out that Aaron always has great pot," Roy commented as we drove away.

Back at the house, Roy switched on the old clock radio in the kitchen. Part of every salmon fisherman's routine was listening to the announcements from the Alaska Department of Fish and Game about which fishing regions were open or closed. The state tried to preserve the salmon fishery by allowing enough fish to return up river to spawn, and that meant that during the season, there were times when no fishing was allowed. The length of the closures could be for half a day or several days depending upon how the fish were running.

There was only one radio station on the dial at Coffee Point. It transmitted from Dillingham, and since its mission was to serve everyone within its listening range, the station played an eclectic range of music from the Beach Boys to Irish sea chanteys to Native Alaskan groups like Pamyua.

Roy insisted that we had to listen to the radio station's most popular program. "If you really want to understand rural Alaskans," he said, "you should listen to *Open Line*." The program was offered as a community service, and people were encouraged to call in to make announcements for anything. Roy was a superb mimic and offered as an example his impression of an Alaskan Native announcing, "I got dogs for sale. The mom bites, but we're hoping the pups don't take after her."

A telephone could be heard ringing in the background as the host of *Open Line* came on the air. The phone rang continuously for the entire hour. Ben from Naknek made the first announcement. "If anyone needs a free babysitter for the summer, I'd be willing to help out," said a gravelly voiced man who sounded as if he suffered from a brutal hangover. "You can try calling me at my sister's." He gave a telephone number before hacking up a loogie on the air, "Or leave a message for Ben at the Naknek store. I'll get back to you as soon as I can."

"That's a horror story waiting to happen," I said. "Who the hell would want Ben to babysit their kids?"

"Boo Boo from Ekuk has called in," the announcer said, "He wants to wish a happy birthday to his Aunt Happy."

Boo Boo from Ekuk began to sing "Happy Birthday to You" in Yup'ik.

"It's just like Alex's show!" I exclaimed. Roy sang the tune along with Boo Boo, and I was impressed that he knew the words in Yup'ik.

A whale had washed up on shore near Dillingham and many listeners called in asking for whale blubber recipes. A man named Fred called in to say, "My mom always prepared it the German way by boiling it in hot water with some salt."

"I'm gonna call in and give my recipe for whale enchiladas," I said.

"Someone would probably want it."

After the call-ins were completed, the radio announcer began to read various announcements that people had previously called in.

"Gus Bereshkov has a fishing boat for sale. He's willing to talk price as the engine needs work."

"The Naknek Knickinack Knockers basketball team wants to thank everyone for helping with their fundraising drive to go to Hawaii." Then he addressed several messages to people in the listening area, starting with, "Linda in Manokotak wants to wish her husband Rob a happy seventh anniversary."

I shared my fantasy that people would have the announcer tell people things that they didn't have the guts to say in person. "Joe from Ugashik wants to tell his wife Connie that he did it with her sister, Carol. Sorry about that. . . ."

"Quiet!" Roy shouted.

I stopped speaking just as the announcer said, "To Roy and Nelson at Coffee Point, we have a message from Wendy in Los Angeles." Roy beamed at me, thrilled that he'd pulled off his surprise. "Listen, you big queens," the announcer read, sounding as if he were sending a greeting to an exiled royal family, "I'm arriving on Friday afternoon. I know

Nelson's a slob, but please make sure the house is clean or you'll regret it. Love, Wendy."

"Did you know she's coming?" I said, flabbergasted and elated by the news.

Roy nodded. "We worked it out before I left. I wasn't sure if we'd hear her message though. I was hoping that we would."

"I've missed her," I said. Since I'd left Los Angeles, we had talked on the telephone or e-mailed each other almost every day but I did miss her. I valued her opinions—Roy called it "abusive honesty"—and while her typed insults were entertaining, they weren't nearly as satisfying as her face-to-face derision.

"She's missed you, too," Roy said. "Although she worded it differently. 'I'd better come up there to make sure the fucking klutz doesn't kill himself.'"

I asked him where she would sleep, as there weren't any spare bedrooms in our house.

"She's staying with my mom."

"Why do you hate your mother?"

TWELVE

"We need to get sauna wood for tonight," Roy announced early the next morning.

No trees grew within thirty miles of Coffee Point, but the shoreline was littered with driftwood, and gathering fuel for the sauna's stove was a routine chore.

"Can't we do it later?" I asked, before suggesting putting off gathering what Roy called "sauna wood" until later that afternoon.

"Don't procrastinate," Roy said.

"But I have to," I claimed. "Procrastina, goddess of delay and deferment, is one of my enshrined household gods."

"Yeah, I've noticed," Roy said amiably.

"She's an easy god to worship because she doesn't take offense when you fall behind on your daily offerings to her."

"The woodbin won't be filled by magic," Roy declared. I disputed his assertion, arguing that procrastination is a strongly held belief that a miracle will occur and the car problem will go away, and the tax returns will be filled out.

"Procrastination isn't shirking responsibility," I insisted, "it's an expression of divine faith."

"No wonder you haven't finished your novel," he said, before grabbing my ass and ordering me to move my butt.

"We'll get it done faster if Dylan helps," Roy suggested.

Dylan was reading a copy of *Fave* magazine from 1999.

"Does it take three people?" Dylan asked, shrewdly sidestepping the charge of laziness by branding us with it.

"It does if you want to take a sauna tonight," Roy said tartly.

"Can I at least finish the article?" Dylan whined.

"No," Roy said.

When Dylan spoke about acting, he was in the habit of saying, "It's about the work," which was galling because he was naturally lazy. On the rare occasions when Dylan was forced to pitch in, after all manners of abeyance were exhausted, he possessed the slothful man's ability to volunteer for the easiest job; when wood needed to be chopped, Dylan would gladly offer to dice onions.

I began to wonder if Dylan's claim of being a sex addict wasn't partially attributable to his inability to refuse any opportunity to lie down for a while. In another example of the unfairness of life, and my own propensity for shallowness, instead of losing my respect for this lazy muscle man, I discovered that I didn't really have any strong objections to having a hunk lounging around shirtless. His habitual indolence actually increased his desirability, as I couldn't help imagining that he wouldn't have the energy to fend off a determined pursuer. Dylan tired easily, and I was willing to bet that he'd be a pushover and put out rather than try to fight me off. I considered the possibility that he might be a lazy lover and behave as if getting an erection was heavy lifting but decided that bedding him would give me more than enough vim to make up for any deficiencies in his vigor.

In fairness though, Dylan enjoyed and sought out tasks that required brief showy feats of strength. He relished being the pivotal last man to grab a truck's bumper when its wheels were spinning in the sand. He'd take charge, ordering everyone to push on the count of three, and then after the truck was freed, he'd accept everyone's praise of his strength.

While Roy was starting up the four-wheeler, Alex stopped by for a visit. He lived across the river with his uncle in Egegik but frequently drove his skiff over to visit Roy and Dee in Coffee Point.

"Look at you," Alex said, appraising my appearance. "You've been here a day but you already look like a fisherman; it looks like you haven't washed in a week."

We never bathed in the mornings, preferring to spend our days dirty until we washed in the sauna before going to bed. "It's okay not to take a bath in Alaska if you're going outside," Roy claimed. "It's the perfect environment for lazy, dirty people." I expressed doubt whether the chance to enjoy poor personal hygiene in a pristine environment would ever replace Denali as a tourist draw, but I found that living in a condition of feral grubbiness had its compensations. Getting dressed in the mornings was a breeze once I realized that, out in the bush, utility took precedence over fashion, and staying warm was more important than looking hot. I could wear the same shirt for a week without inviting comment and mixed colors and combined patterns with a disregard that hitherto I'd reserved for the homeless and the insane.

"Is that Roy's shirt?" Alex asked.

"Yes," I replied.

"You're really a couple," he observed. "Once you start wearing his clothes."

"First get in his pants, then wear his shirts," I declared.

"Is the ink stain to let people know you're a writer?" Dylan asked, waving his hand toward my shirt pocket.

"Yes," I said. "It's easier than carrying a quill pen around and looking tortured."

I'd been cold that morning, and Roy had offered me a green and gray flannel shirt from his pile of clothing on the floor. Although, before letting me put in on, he thoughtfully advised giving the shirt a sniff test. (We never did laundry at Coffee Point as Roy refused to pay the exorbitant prices charged by the service at the cannery. Socks and underwear were hand washed, but nothing else would be properly cleaned until we returned to Anchorage.) I found the shirt satisfactory—it smelled musty but didn't reek of BO, mildew, or salmon—until I saw the large black ink stain on the front pocket. When I started to remove the shirt, Roy stopped me. "Coffee Point's my burial ground for clothes," he explained before assuring me that a stained shirt could be worn with confidence in a community where every garment had reached its final rinse.

"Nelson looks hot," Dylan said as he pulled on a pair of work gloves. "The stubbly beard. The rugged clothes. Put in a few more months at the gym and you could do porn."

Roy couldn't restrain his eyebrows from dancing skeptically as he completed attaching the trailer to the four-wheeler.

"You don't think I could do porn now?" I asked, feigning outrage at his display of disloyalty.

"Honey," he said sweetly, "don't take this the wrong way but anyone can *do* porn, whether anyone would buy it. . . ."

"Damn," I said. "Doing porn was going to be my fallback career."

"There's a niche market," Alex said. "Fishermen porn."

"You like my big pole, don't you?" Dylan asked, lowering his voice to a register employed exclusively by gay male porn stars. "Yeah, swallow my big nightcrawler."

"'Swallow my *worm?*'" Alex said doubtfully. "You need to rethink that."

The ambiguity of being praised and mocked was confusing, but two years of therapy had convinced me that my sense of identity operated like thesaurus software. My virtues were embedded with immediate links to their antonyms, but I finally understood that use of the built-in feature was optional. If someone called me "handsome," it wasn't necessary to automatically click and scroll down to perceived flaws such as, "birthmark shaped like Florida on my right shoulder" or "broad shoulders offset by skinny legs." I didn't attribute Dylan's praise to lust but to an actor's powers of observation. He'd noticed that since arriving at Coffee Point I was no longer worried about how I looked, because I had no choice in the matter. Vanity's a form of stress—worrying about our appearance is probably the chief cause of frown lines—and my looks had probably improved, because I'd stopped fretting about them.

Alex offered to help us gather sauna wood, and the three of us walked alongside the four-wheeler as Roy drove slowly down to the beach. It was low tide, and sandbars had emerged offshore and in the mouth of the river. The beach had doubled in size, and the wet sand looked newly made—a last-minute revision of God's. A few dead salmon floated at the waterline, having washed out of a net or fallen from a passing truck. Overfed seagulls stood sluggishly nearby, bloated by the surfeit of food. A jaeger hovered overhead, bobbing up and down in the wind as if it had trouble staying aloft after weeks of stuffing its face.

Roy parked the four-wheeler, and Dylan immediately offered to take charge of the kindling. I was asked to handle small branches and Alex, presumably due to his years of wood-gathering experience, was authorized to gather the larger branches. Roy assumed responsibility for the logs. His instructions were scientifically precise, and after he held up representative examples to illustrate the difference between a stick and a twig, we accused him of being a size queen.

Keeping the sauna stove supplied with firewood eventually became my sole responsibility. Gathering wood became a game for me, and Roy compared me to a scavenging seagull when I'd shout for him to stop the truck to allow me to pounce upon an especially choice branch or log. I loved beachcombing for wood, as it allowed me to perform a useful task while still permitting me to daydream. I imagined pieces of timber floating down the rivers of Alaska, though the discovery of a particularly gnarled old branch, bearing the scars of a brutal history, suggested that it might have escaped from the far-off forests of Siberia.

As we began to search the sand for wood, Roy invited Alex to dinner the following night. "We're having a welcome-to-Alaska party for our friend Wendy," he explained.

"Is she staying with us?" Dylan asked, immediately confirming my suspicion that he disliked her. He appeared to be relieved when Roy said that she would be staying at his mother's.

"What's she like?" Alex asked.

"She doesn't miss a thing," Roy said.

"You know how God is omniscient," I said. "Imagine if he was an unbearably rude lesbian who judged you every day. That's Wendy."

"What he's saying," Dylan explained as he picked up a large twig, "is that she's a bitch."

Roy repeated the radio message that she had sent us and Alex laughed.

"She's also a writer?" he asked.

"For television," I said, dropping a branch when my hand touched something slimy.

"Maybe she'll write a part for a handsome Yup'ik actor," Alex said.

"The competition must be fierce for those parts," Dylan scoffed. "I mean, how many Eskimo Pie commercials do they do each year?"

Alex's eyes narrowed before he said, "Who were you calling a bitch?"

Dylan didn't object to this description and merely smiled. Alex followed Roy toward the base of the bluff, where bigger pieces of wood had been deposited during last winter's storms. And we searched the middle shore, where smaller pieces had been left at high tide. Alex soon had Roy laughing, and I felt a twinge of jealousy at their closeness with a corresponding sense of relief that someone else shared the responsibility of keeping him happy.

"Guys, come here!" Alex shouted. He and Roy were standing over something on the beach that they wanted to show us.

We dropped off our wood at the trailer before walking over to them.

"Look at this," Alex said as we approached. He pointed down to a group of green gemlike plants necklaced through the sand. Delicate thimble-sized yellow and white flowers capped quatrefoil, triangular shaped leaves. The pale green leaves diminished in size as they ascended from the base of the plants, making them look like jade pagodas.

"That's sea purslane," Alex said. "The leaves are high in Vitamin C. Arctic Explorers ate it to prevent scurvy."

"Let's look for iceberg lettuce," Dylan sneered. "Then we can make an Eskimo salad."

Alex frowned and asked, "What the fuck's your problem?"

"I'm getting into character," Dylan claimed.

"Well, if he's an asshole," Alex snarled, "you've nailed him."

"He's bent out of shape because we put him to work," Roy said as he began sifting through the pile of wood in the trailer, discarding various pieces that didn't meet his standards.

"Try eating Native foods before you mock them," Alex challenged.

"Serve him Stink heads," Roy said.

"What are they?" Dylan asked.

Alex explained that fermented salmon heads were a Yup'ik delicacy. They were aged for several days in grass-lined pits until they developed a gelatinous consistency. By all accounts, the pungent stench and taste of stinkheads were unforgettable.

"Have you tried 'em?" Dylan asked Roy.

"I don't eat food with the word stink in its name," he said pleasantly.

"You eat blue cheese," Alex said. "It's stink milk."

Roy conceded the point.

"I've eaten worse things," Dylan said. He delivered his comment to me with a knowing flick of his eyebrows.

"My uncle's making a batch," Alex said, raising a log then placing it back on the sand. "I'll make sure he saves you some."

"Sounds great," Dylan said, again catching my eye. "I'm open to new experiences."

I'd noticed that, for every piece of wood Alex gathered, he picked up another piece, which he then carefully returned to the ground again.

"Are those pieces too wet?" I asked, suddenly unsure whether the wood I'd gathered was dry enough. Almost everything at Coffee Point was damp to the touch and I'd decided that if the wood didn't feel like it needed to be wrung out before being placed in the trailer, that it was dry enough to burn. But I didn't want to hear later that I'd screwed up again.

I held up a branch. "How do you tell when it's too wet?"

"What?" he asked, sounding lost in thought.

"You're not taking every piece." I said, extending my arm to point to the branch he had dropped.

"Oh," Alex mumbled without offering any further explanation.

"You're selecting them," I said while setting my sauna wood in the trailer.

"It's not that," Alex said. "I used to collect firewood with my grandmother and she always had me overturn a few pieces. She said the wood becomes uncomfortable sitting in the same position."

I didn't say anything because showing concern for the comfort of a piece of driftwood struck me as both unspeakably lovely and endearingly silly. Easing the pain of a branch or a twig made limiting our compassion to the living sound uncharitable. Our culture is based upon our lack of empathy for things; we never consider the feelings of our possessions. We use them like whores. They're there to service us, because we paid for them. And when we're finished with them, they become trash to be put out on the street. I was tempted to ask Alex if a culture that believed that you needed to consider the feelings of everything held any advantage in understanding the emotions of people.

"Oh, Christ," Dylan said, catching my eye. "Now we've got to be nice to inanimate objects."

"That's his point," Roy said impatiently. "There are no inanimate objects. Everything has a soul. Yup'ik hunters used to decorate their tools and weapons—not for their own pleasure—but to make their equipment happy."

"Fuck that," I said, eagerly trying to make Dylan laugh. "I'm not going to fluff my pillow to make it more comfortable."

Dylan laughed as he reached for another branch lying on the ground.

"That's all I need," he said. "To become codependent with the entire universe."

Dylan bent down to carefully tuck a branch under a blanket of seaweed. He looked over to see if I was watching him.

"There you go," he said, patting the seaweed gently. "All comfy."

I chuckled at his ridiculous behavior.

Dylan asked Alex, "Did your grandmother say, 'Sticks and stones will break my bones, but I bet they have their reasons'?"

"Go fuck yourselves," Alex said lividly. We stood for a moment, stunned by his rage, as he stormed down the beach toward the river. Roy was also furious and stared at me with openmouthed astonishment.

"Can't he take a joke?" Dylan asked.

"He can take a joke," Roy said, his mouth tight-lipped with anger.

"He jokes all the time," I said weakly.

"Not all the time," Roy snapped. "He didn't have to tell you about that. You insulted his grandmother."

Roy hurriedly wrapped a tarp around the wood in the trailer, tying it down with bungee cords, which he pulled tight as if he was trying to strangle something.

"I thought writers are supposed to be observant," he said to me, shaking his head in disgust, before climbing aboard the four-wheeler and taking off.

"Don't worry about them," Dylan said as we watched Roy ride down the beach. "They'll get over it. We'll apologize."

"What good's an apology," I declared, feeling that we had proved that there were exceptions to the Yup'ik belief that everything has a soul.

"Depends on the apology," Dylan said.

"What makes yours so special?" I said, thinking that his arrogance had become repulsive.

"I'll fuck him," he said smugly.

"Is that your answer for everything?" I asked.

"It is for some people," he replied.

"Alex isn't an idiot."

"No, but he's a man."

I moved to get away from Dylan because he was making me feel more ashamed of myself.

"I could tell you were showing off for me," he said, coiling his arm around my shoulders, which I immediately batted away. "You deserve an apology, too. Maybe, I'll apologize to you and Roy together. It will be a joint apology." Dylan pointed to his dick in case I didn't get the pun. "That's it. You'll get to sleep with me but you won't be cheating on Roy."

His condescending tone of voice implied that a man who hadn't had a threesome was lamentably behind in his education. I was lousy at emotional math and couldn't figure out whether a threesome with Dylan and Roy would create twice my usual anxiety about sex or whether it would be halved.

"Roy's not into that," I said uncertainly.

"That's not what I've heard," Dylan declared. "He told me stories about Seattle. He's done a few things that I hadn't even considered."

Dylan misunderstood me because I hadn't spoken precisely. I should have said that Roy's not into that now. He'd admitted that when he'd lived in Seattle, he'd indulged in the usual recreational drugs, late night partying till dawn, and had been willing to try almost anything or anyone once.

"Roy moved back to Alaska to get away from that," I said repeating what he had told me.

"We all say that sort of thing," Dylan said patronizingly. "But that doesn't mean he doesn't still want to party."

"We never go out in Anchorage."

"Because it would make him miss Seattle. I don't go out to bars because I hate them; I avoid them because I love them. Is the sex between you two good?"

The most disgusting but accurate title for a porn movie about my sex life would be *Seeds of Doubt*. I thought we had a good sex life, but trying to assess the quality of our sexual satisfaction as a couple, without speaking to Roy, was futile.

"If you're not sure, it probably isn't," Dylan declared. He looked startlingly handsome in the soft morning light. He bent over and picked up a smooth palm-sized stone off the sand. He rolled the stone back and forth in his hand as we walked silently down the beach. Suddenly Dylan stopped and stared down at his feet. "A dead duck," he said sadly.

The body of a male Spectacled Eider was nestled behind a tuft of sea grass. I told Dylan the name of the species and its sex, trying to sound casually matter of fact, hoping I didn't come across as dull and pedantic. "They're endangered," I added, strangely pleased by the discovery of a rare dead duck. It was debatable whether my enjoyment of the discovery of an odd duck's corpse was a sign of my increasing maturity or the result of the loss of my innocence. Sometimes I imagined my innocence falling from the top of an hourglass, filling the lower half with maturity.

"It must have died recently," Dylan said, as the duck's body showed no signs of decay.

"See the spectacles?" I asked, unable to contain my excitement. Surrounding the bird's eyes were oval white patches, outlined by black rings.

"I didn't think they lived around here," I said, puzzled by its unexpected appearance at Coffee Point. Dylan resumed walking, and sensing that his interest in imperiled sea ducks was exhausted, I refrained from mentioning that the Spectacled Eider breeds on the North Slope and in the Yukon delta and the population had been reduced to five thousand pairs. I wanted to tell Roy about the duck, and that brought on renewed remorse. A fellow nerd, he would've shared my curiosity about whether this was the first sighting of a Spectacled Eider at Coffee Point. Helping me find the answer would intrigue a man who possessed an abiding interest in prehistoric stone tools and whose idea of enjoyable bedtime reading was a new academic article about flaking chert and lithic wear patterns.

One of the great attractions of homosexuality is that, after becoming an avowed member of a community of people with passions out of the norm, it frees you to declare an allegiance to other minority tastes and enthusiasms. Once a man musters the gumption to declare his secret longing to be fucked hard by a brute of a man, it becomes much less daunting to overcome his reticence a second time, and admit that he has a ridiculous, deeply held yearning to learn how to crochet or see all of the operas of Rimsky-Korsakov. For me the most unconventional thing about being gay was discovering that talking about my sexual desires with an acquaintance frequently felt less intimate than talking about my hobbies and interests.

The nebbishy thrill of seeing a rare bird, albeit a dead duck, was imbued with sadness as I also mourned the loss of Alex's regard and

Roy's respect. I wasn't attempting to build an entire Chekhov play about my encounter with a dead duck, but at that moment, trudging the beach with Dylan, it mirrored my general experience of being alive. My excitement was genuine, even when it was based upon an absurdity, but it retained an ineradicable melancholy.

"How'd you become an expert on ducks?" Dylan asked with a slight touch of mockery.

"I'm not an expert," I protested. "I read an article about them in the *Anchorage Daily News*. I'm a duck dilettante."

"We both like nature. Maybe we can become duck buddies," he leered.

"No more talking about sex," I ordered, "I'm cutting you off. You're a sex *fiend*."

Dylan laughed and then accused me of lacking compassion toward the victims of addiction. "I'm a captive of my genitals," he claimed.

"All men are captives of their genitals," I said, unmoved by his appeal for sympathy. "And we're all victims of the Stockholm Syndrome."

Dylan didn't understand my reference and I explained that it was a psychological term used to describe when hostages become attached to their captors.

"I'm very attached to my conjoined twins," Dylan said, patting his crotch affectionately.

"You're on final warning," I said, menacing him with a stare. He heaved a theatrical sigh, rolling his eyes to signal his willingness to change the subject. He told me that he was a member of the Nature Conservancy and had lent his name to several environmental groups, although his marquee value as a celebrity do-gooder had diminished since his arrest and jail term.

"Yes," he said with assumed weariness. "I'm another movie star who drives a hybrid gas/electric car."

"Let me guess," I said. "You want to buy a ranch in Montana and build a huge solar passive house?"

"Nope," he said, "I'm from New Mexico. My dream house would be in Tesuque, north of Santa Fe."

I forgot that he grew up there, having read his bio, and asked him where in New Mexico.

"On a ranch in the boot heel," he said. "My parents split up when I was nine. Then my mom and I moved to L.A. I spent most of my childhood on horseback. Did I tell you that I might do a movie playing Oscar Wilde on his trip out west?" He chuckled at the thought. "My Dad will be excited about me making a Western. Till I tell him that I'll be playing the biggest fag west of the Mississippi." He shook his head. "But he might like the movie because Oscar drank like a real man and never backed down from a fight."

I grinned, telling him that I agreed with his assessment of Wilde's character.

"Have you always been interested in nature?" Dylan asked as he zipped up his sweatshirt.

"Yeah," I said. "When I was in the sixth grade, our teacher suggested celebrating Earth Day by picking up litter on the way to school. I was eager to help clean up Mother Earth, but my mother was horrified by the prospect of me picking up used condoms or hypodermic needles. She insisted on packing me a bag of garbage to carry to school. I brown-bagged my litter. I was afraid that the teacher would find out, and she'd think I was trying to pass off household trash for real litter."

"I can see you proudly dumping out a bag of neatly folded garbage. You must have been a total geek."

Dylan spoke affectionately, but he assumed that I'd taken offense at his comment when my expression changed to bewilderment. I reassured him that I was thinking of something else. I'd never told Roy about my Earth Day garbage ruse and suddenly I felt that, by telling Dylan, I'd cheated on him.

Dylan impulsively threw the rock in his hand far out into the surf.

Contemplating the idea that everything has a soul, I pitied the stone as it plunged into the dark cold water.

THIRTEEN

R oy didn't look up or speak to us when we returned to the house. He sat at the kitchen table, drinking a cup of green tea, reading a back issue of the journal of the Alaskan Anthropology Association. He turned a page, revealing a black-and-white photograph of a collection of spear points. Dylan had gone into his bedroom and closed the door. I poured myself a glass of water. The unnatural hush convinced me that someone could make millions inventing a spray that eliminates tension in a room. An outmoded digital clock radio sat next to the stove, and a slow whirring noise preceded the rotation of the minute wheel from three to four. It reminded me of my brain, another still functioning device from the Seventies, straining to keep up while I tried to decide what I should do or say.

Roy's ex-boyfriend described him as "tack-i-turn," but he didn't mete out silence as a punishment. If I'd spoken to him, he would have answered me. His brooding concentration conveyed the sense that each of his feelings was painstakingly crafted. Unfortunately Roy seemed to be an emotional perfectionist and sometimes I wondered if he would ever finish any feeling that he felt was worthy of public display.

My stomach gurgled and I decided to make a peanut butter-and-jelly sandwich. Dylan returned from his bedroom, bare-chested, a towel draped across his shoulder, carrying his razor and a can of shaving cream. We exchanged guilt-stricken glances as he headed toward the bathroom. I put two pieces of sourdough bread into the toaster and grabbed an open jar of peanut butter from a shelf. Unscrewing the lid released a soft whoosh of air.

"That's from last year," Roy warned without lifting his head. "Or the year before."

"Where's this year's?" I asked, recalling that we'd purchased a large jar.

"It broke," he said. "A bag fell off the four-wheeler."

I took a tentative whiff of the jar's contents. "It smells fine." The peanut butter had spent the winter in an unheated house on the shore of the Bering Sea. It probably thawed out a week ago and was as well preserved as most of foods in our refrigerator back in Anchorage. I decided to brave it and spread some on my toast.

"Suit yourself," Roy said, raising his sad eyes to meet mine. He appeared to be resigned to my death but would mourn my passing.

"Do you want a sandwich?" I asked, hoping to reestablish his good-will by offering him food now and sex later. I'd never known Roy to be anything but docile and contented after dinner and an orgasm.

"You try it first," Roy challenged.

I made a show of biting into my sandwich, chewing and swallowing, then stared at my watch and waited.

"Don't toast my bread," he said after I failed to succumb to peanut butter poisoning.

"That's pure sugar," said the clean-shaven Dylan when I opened a jar of cherry preserves for our sandwiches. Ironically for an ex-con, Dylan watched his calories like a prison guard; there were never any successful escapes to his washboard abs.

"That's a first," I said. "An ex-heroin addict sneering at sugar." From the corner of my eye, I saw Roy trying not to smile.

"Sugar's harder to quit than heroin," Dylan declared. "And I know because I've been addicted to both."

He took a package of salmon and a bag of salad greens out of the refrigerator. Dylan had arrived at Coffee Point without bringing any food (I'm not counting his two cases of protein drinks) but had arranged to have fresh meat and vegetables flown in once a week and paid a Filipino woman at the cannery to supply him with fresh salmon fillets.

"Sorry, I can't share this," he said, spraying olive oil into a frying pan. "I still owe my lawyers a bundle and need to watch my pennies."

We'd made him dinner and breakfast from our supplies, and I was outraged that he wasn't going to offer us any of his lunch after we had shared our food with him. Roy appeared to be amused by his lack of generosity and resumed reading his magazine. Dylan must have noticed that I was taken aback by his open refusal to share his food, prompting an explanation.

"Money's always been an issue with me because my mom had to use food stamps when I was growing up," he explained as he turned on the burner underneath the pan.

Dylan deserved credit for giving us the heads-up that he was a cheap bastard, but I've never understood the modern fallacy that offering a psychological disclaimer for a flaw makes it less objectionable. If Charles Dickens wrote *A Christmas Carol* now, Scrooge's haunting wouldn't result in a change to his behavior. It would simply help the selfish miser understand how he became callous and greedy. The old skinflint would let Tiny Tim die, then have the insolence to explain to the Cratchits that his avarice and indifference were the product of deep wounds that he suffered as a child and young man. He'd cheerfully plead for their indulgence, because he'd also been a vulnerable boy in a harsh and pitiless world.

Roy quietly brought his mug over to the sink and rinsed it out. I handed him a plate with his sandwich and received a mumbled thanks.

"We'll check the net again around six," Roy told Dylan before moving toward the stairs.

"All right," Dylan said as he sprinkled some of Roy's sea salt on a sizzling salmon fillet.

"I'm taking a nap first," Roy announced. Since fishermen worked hard for several hours and then had to wait several more hours before working hard again, daily siestas were a custom of Coffee Point. Roy looked at me to see if I was going to join him. I was relieved that he wanted to associate with me and picked up my plate and followed him up the stairs. We sat down on the built-in window seat underneath the large window that faced the beach. The sky was overcast except for a small opening in the clouds where a ray of sunlight shone down on the water, illuminating a group of fishing boats. "That's so beautiful," I said. "And cornball. It looks like a kitschy seascape painting called 'The Blessing of the Fleet.'"

Roy picked up his sandwich. "It's called a 'sucker hole,'" he said.

I scrunched up my face because I wasn't exactly sure what he meant.

"It misleads you into thinking that the weather might clear up." Roy enjoyed teaching me the arcane lingo of Alaska, and I knew that he wouldn't have mentioned it if he was still angry with me.

"I'm sorry about today," I said, hoping to receive my own blessing.

"Don't apologize to me," he said, before biting into his sandwich.

"I don't want Alex to hate me."

"He'll get over it," Roy mumbled through a mouthful of peanut butter. "He's been mad at me before."

"I got carried away with Dylan."

"You know that he likes you."

"He told you?" I asked, thinking that sounded improbable.

Roy sighed and shook his head. "I was talking about Alex," he said. "Not your new boyfriend."

"I knew that," I fibbed.

"You have a crush on him."

"No. I don't."

Roy's face became unyielding and he stared at me until I relented.

"Maybe a little," I confessed. Of course I had a crush on Dylan, but didn't feel then that it was proper to talk about my love life with my boyfriend. I trusted Roy with my body but still wasn't completely at ease talking to him about my feelings. I was afraid that he'd hurt me or I'd hurt him—forgetting that when Roy manhandled my balls, all I needed to say was, "Not so rough," and he'd be gentler. I'd put my balls in Roy's hands, so why not trust him with my heart? I had to believe he'd show all of my delicate body parts the same consideration.

"You should have a crush on him," Roy said. "He's been flirting with you. Has he hit on you?"

"Yes," I said, not ready to admit that he had recently proposed fucking on the beach.

"He's been asking a lot of questions about you," Roy said before taking another nibble from his sandwich.

"What did he ask?" I said, waiting impatiently for him to finish chewing his food. Roy was the world's slowest eater. Honestly, I could have finished an intravenous meal in the time it took him to eat a god-damned cracker. Sometimes I wondered if he ever got hungry for dinner before finishing his lunch. I'd previously thought his daintiness was endearing but was starting to sense that I could squander my youth waiting for him to finish a simple salad.

"All sorts of stuff," Roy shrugged, after finally swallowing the mouthful of sandwich.

"Like what?" I demanded, wanting to know everything that Dylan had asked him, wishing that I could download Roy's entire memory like a computer's.

"Where you're from. How we met. What you write about."

"Really?" I was genuinely surprised because whenever Dylan and I had talked, it had been mostly about him.

"Is that why you started hitting the gym?" Roy asked, giving my left bicep an affectionate tap. "Are you getting in shape for him?"

"What?"

I refused to believe that Roy felt threatened by Dylan. Then I decided that I was being inconsiderate. No wonder Roy was "tack-i-turn." He confessed his feelings, and I promptly dismissed them because I had trouble believing that a handsome man had any problems or insecurities that couldn't be resolved by looking in a mirror.

"I came out here because I thought he'd hop on you," I said.

"He wants to sleep with me, but he's intrigued by you."

Roy's eyes sparkled, and I sensed that sex was in the offing. I'm not sure if we released pheromones or whether I picked up on his slightly elevated pulse rate or his eyes lingered on me for a millisecond longer than usual. It might have been the situation. The same dramatic principle that insists that a gun should never appear on a stage if no one's thinking of firing it also applies to placing a bed in a room with two lovers. I picked up a bone that was displayed on the windowsill and nervously turned it over in my hands. The joints were almost nonexistent, and the tapered ends were unbroken. The bone was shaped like a baseball bat.

"Do you know what that is?" Roy asked.

"No."

"It's an oosik," he said, wheeling the word over his tongue. "The penis bone from a walrus. When I was ten, my brother convinced me that I had an oosik. He told me, 'That's why they call it a boner.'"

"Did you think yours was retractable?"

"I was completely gullible. See these?" He pointed toward a bowl of iridescent green glass balls. "They're floats from Japanese fishing boats." He picked up one and handed it to me. The glass was riddled with trapped air bubbles and the uneven surface was dimpled. It looked like a memorial to haste.

"They used to wash up on the beach all the time," he said. "My father told me that during World War II Japanese submarines used them for an emergency air supply. If they ran low, he said they'd bust 'em open. He claimed that when you opened one, you could still smell cigarettes and sushi from the glass blowers' breath. He must have laughed for about ten minutes when I told him I took a hammer to one and didn't smell anything."

It was then that I began to see that Roy's passion for archaeology was tied to his charming affection for his own past. He could talk about the history of the last emperor of the Incas with the same immediacy that he could relate a story about his first time riding a bicycle. He stood up and motioned for me to crawl into bed with him. A light rain began to patter the windows and roof as we stripped down to our underwear. Getting under the covers during the middle of the day, with his warm body beside mine, was wildly cozy. Roy must have felt the same way because he hugged me tightly and grunted, "Sweet."

We kissed, which suddenly made me remember my conversation with Dylan on the beach. I gently pulled away to ask, "Did you tell Dylan about my neck?"

"Sorry," he said with a smirk. "I think I did."

"How'd that come up?"

"We had a few beers, and I told him how you insisted on my leaving you in the tar pits. Then he started talking about what his ex-boyfriends liked in bed." He winced. "And I might have mentioned what my boyfriends liked."

"Oh, that's nice."

"Did you know he dated Owen Eglington?"

Roy's favorite television show was a science fiction series about a team of space explorers in the twenty-second century. Owen Eglington played the science officer on the program, and we both agreed that he was a total space stud.

"Now you'll really want to sleep with Dylan," I said. "He's one degree removed from sleeping with the guy you have a crush on."

"Dylan wants you," he declared.

"He wants us both," I said. "At the same time."

"He mentioned that," Roy said noncommittally.

I didn't know what to say next. I wanted to know what he thought before venturing an opinion.

"How do you feel about that?" Roy asked in the monotone of a therapist.

"I don't know," I answered. "It kind of creeps me out, but it's also kind of exciting to have a movie star wanting . . . us."

"Kind of exciting?" He slipped his hand under the waistband of my underwear. "Your oosik likes that musclebound tattooed whore."

"Well, he has those big arms," I said while gripping Roy's thick arms. "And those big pecs," I said, moving my hands to his chest. "And that hot ass," I said, squeezing his butt.

"He's hot, but his dick only points one way," Roy said, pointing toward himself. "I prefer brainy guys." He ran his hand roughly through my hair then wrapped a heavy thigh across my leg. "It's your call."

"Threesomes are sad somehow," I said. "Aren't they something older gay couples do to spice up their sex life?"

"I don't know that many older gay couples," Roy said, "besides Lloyd and Don."

We both smiled at the idea of Lloyd and Don having a threesome.

"It seems to me that older gay men try to preserve sputtering relationships by adopting a baby," I said, thinking of two guys I'd met at a party in L.A. "Which is a platonic threesome."

"Or becoming duo daddies to a series of younger men," Roy added.

I yanked down Roy's underwear.

"Threesomes aren't sad when the three guys are hot!" Roy declared.

I laughed. "You're right."

"We need an answer for him," Roy said seriously. "He'll bring it up again."

"I don't need him," I said honestly, because at that moment I was satisfied.

"You're sure?" His face was inches from mine, and I caught the faint scent of peanut butter on his breath. "Years later I don't want you taking it out on me because you missed out on sleeping with Dylan Fabizak."

"Do we have to decide now?"

"That settles it," Roy said while grabbing me, pulling me closer to him. "Let's not make a habit of this. We're not sleeping with every movie star who wants a threeway."

He prevented me from saying anything else by kissing me forcefully on the mouth. We wisely dropped the subject as it seemed pointless and rude to discuss having sex with someone else while having sex with each other.

At six o'clock Dylan and Roy went out again to pick fish. I tried to work on my novel but kept thinking about them working together, which made me restless. After an hour of fruitless pecking at my laptop, I decided to walk down the beach. I'd walked halfway to Roy's site when it started to drizzle, and I heard a truck tooting its horn behind me. Dee pulled up next to me and leaned over to open the passenger door.

"C'mon," she said. "It's too wet to walk." I climbed inside her truck, admitting that I was starting to feel cold.

"Did you buy your crewman's permit at Bud's today?" she asked after we began to move again.

"No," I said, briefly considering offering her an excuse but deciding that she wouldn't cut me any slack for sleeping with her son.

"Let's stop and get it," she suggested, turning off the road to park at the only shack built below the bluff, directly on the beach. As we got out of the truck, Dee shook her head. "Bud will make a big fuss when he finds out that you're crewing for me. We're the last of the old timers."

After fishing at Coffee Point for more than forty years, Bud Getzka had retired, but he still returned each summer for the fishing season. To keep busy, he worked a few hours a week running the mailroom at the cannery and also sold crewman permits at his shack on the beach. His combination store and house was built on pilings, and I ducked my head to enter as the doorframe had buckled. The roof of Bud's house was constructed of sheets of green fiberglass, filling the room with a verdant light that made everything look mildewed. The place smelled of pipe tobacco, fish, and damp canvas, odors that could be the building blocks of a cologne called "Old Salt." Guarding the cramped room was a mean, fat, ginger-haired tabby sprawled on a pile of old newspapers. The cat let Dee pass but hissed at me, bristling his fur but being far too sedentary to arch his swaybacked body.

"Don't mind Captain Ahab," Bud said to me from behind a desk piled high with papers. "He's eighteen years old and hates anyone young. Only wrinkled hands can pet him."

Piles of moldering fishing equipment barricaded Bud's desk, and he stood up and maneuvered around a heap of life jackets to shake my hand. Bud was a stout man with white hair and a white beard, but he moved gracefully around numerous obstacles to reach me. His face was ruddy and deeply lined, and Bud looked so stereotypically nautical that I was willing to bet that he must have an anchor tattooed somewhere on his body. A calendar from the current year was stapled to the wall above his desk. It was June but the month displayed was April, and the bikini-clad model's picture had faded in the near-constant light, making her and the calendar look years out of date. We stood in an island of open space next to a dust-covered glass case of native handicrafts. Resting on top of the case, stacked like firewood, was a basket filled with oosiks.

Dee teased Bud about the clutter, and he blamed the mess on her refusal to marry him.

"Even if we were married, I wouldn't pick up after you," she declared, causing him to laugh. After I filled out the crewman form, Dee paid my permit fee because I didn't have the ninety dollars in cash on me.

"I'll take it out of your pay," she proposed even though Bud offered to let me pay him back later.

"She'll take it out of your hide," Bud said.

"Oh, don't listen to him," Dee remarked as we prepared to leave.

The rain was coming down harder when we left Bud's, and the wind had picked up. As we drove down the beach, Dee told me that the following summer, before the season started, she wanted to take the Alaska ferry and visit the Aleutians. "It's one of the few parts of the state that I haven't visited. . . ." Her voice trailed off suddenly as her face drained of color. She was looking out at Roy's raft bobbing in the surf about forty feet from the shore, trapped against his net. We couldn't see him or Dylan. Something was wrong, because Roy would never leave his raft untended. I was aware of the pilot light of fear that always burns in my chest, ready to kick in at a moment's notice.

Dee stepped on the gas pedal, and I was thrown back in my seat. As we raced past the side of Roy's truck, I saw him lying on the beach. A soaking wet Dylan was kneeling in the sand next to Roy's body desperately administering CPR by placing his lips over his mouth. The first gutwrenching blow of panic was followed by the sickening nausea of dread. "Oh, no," cried Dee in a near whisper. She slammed on the breaks and was out of her truck in an instant. I followed her, and we watched as Dylan worked on him. Water dripped down my face as the rain came down harder. I felt numb from the cold and my terror. I thought of my mother's death and was afraid we were standing upon the shore of a vast ocean of pain that we would have to cross. Just as I lost hope, Roy made a retching noise and coughed up water.

Dylan supported Roy's head as he opened his eyes. Before I could rejoice Dee yelled, "Nelson, get the blankets behind the seat in the truck!" Then she ordered them to strip off their wet clothes. Roy's and Dylan's teeth started chattering, and their hands were so stiff from the cold that we needed to help them remove their jackets and boots. When they hesitated to take off their underwear, Dee shouted, "Don't be foolish! Take everything off!" as she ran back to restart her truck. Dylan did as he was told, while I helped Roy remove his underwear as he tried standing up. I immediately wrapped woolen army blankets around their shoulders.

Dee had turned the heat in the truck to high and Dylan and I helped Roy walk over and climb inside. I left them and went down to the water to try to bring in Roy's raft, knowing that he didn't have a replacement for it. It was twenty feet from shore and I could see that the water wasn't too deep. I quickly stripped down to my underwear, and ran out into the icy waves to tow the raft to shore.

"Nelson!" Dee shouted. "Leave it! Leave it!" The water was freezing but only came up to my waist, and since the bottom was sandy, I was able to dash in and out. I began to shiver immediately and Dee grabbed another blanket and wrapped it around my shoulders. "Get in the truck," she ordered. "You fool." She smiled and shook her head before tipping over the raft to dump the catch out onto the beach.

"I can't believe you did that," Dylan said after I returned to the truck and squeezed in beside Roy.

"We m-m-might have been able to bring it in by pulling in the net," Roy said haltingly.

"I didn't know," I said feeling like an idiot. "I didn't want you to lose your raft."

Roy didn't say anything, but he took hold of my hand as we watched Dee secure the raft to a tire rim embedded in the sand. Her hair was dripping wet, and I rolled down the window when she walked over to the passenger side of the truck.

"You'll follow me back," she said handing me Roy's keys.

"I can't drive a standard," I said, thinking that I wasn't Roy's boyfriend so much as I was his second appendix, something useless, that at any moment could turn into a potentially life-threatening problem. My teeth were chattering but I felt the warm flush of humiliation. Dee looked at me with pity.

"We can't leave his truck here, the tide's coming in."

"I can drive," Roy insisted.

"No," Dee said firmly. She looked down the shore for someone to help us, but the sudden squall had driven the other fishermen off the beach.

"I'll drive back," Dylan said before he stepped out of the truck from the driver's side. His blanket barely covered his crotch.

Dee ordered him to get back inside.

"I'm okay," he said. "I'll follow you. Let's go, it's cold."

She handed him the keys and then climbed into the driver's seat.

"Mom, I'm sorry about the scare," Roy said as we started down the beach.

"What happened?" Dee asked as she brushed a dripping lock of hair from her forehead. I could see that her hand was shaking.

"We went out in the raft together. I was reaching for a salmon when Dylan bumped into me, and I fell off."

Dee kept checking her rearview mirror to make sure that Dylan was still behind us.

"Somehow my boot got caught in the net and I couldn't get it out. Dylan dove in just as I passed out. I'm glad he's strong. He said he had to rip the net to get my foot out."

"Have you ever fallen over before?" I asked.

"No. I don't go out when the water's rough. I don't know how to swim."

"Are you kidding?" I couldn't believe that I possessed a skill that Roy lacked.

"Lots of Alaskans don't know how to swim," Roy said. "It's not like we spend our summers tanning at the beach."

"Lessons," Dee hissed, sounding like it was a topic that had been discussed many times in the past. "You're taking them as soon as you get back to Anchorage. You scared me to death."

Roy turned to look at her. "Are you all right?"

"No!" she said fiercely. "I've seen fishermen down on the beach. Most of the time they don't get up."

We drove in silence, and I offered up a little prayer of thanks to my nebulous deities as I squeezed Roy's hand. Dee stepped on the brake and the truck halted. She watched the rearview mirror intently.

"What's wrong?" Roy asked.

"Dylan stopped." Her eyes remained fixed on the mirror.

Roy and I turned around in our seats. Dylan had pulled over and opened the door of the truck. He got out and then abruptly heaved over and threw up.

"The poor guy," Dee said, "I shouldn't have let him drive. This was traumatic for him, too."

Suddenly I felt as if all three of us were going to cry. Dee's eyes glistened as mine teared up and Roy sniffled and gripped my hand tighter. After a minute, Dylan held up a hand to indicate that he was all right. He got back inside the truck and started it up. Dylan's vulnerability had moved me intensely because for the first time since we had met, I didn't see him as a movie star or a hunk, I saw him as another man. I thought of Shakespeare's line about man being a poor bare forked animal. Then my mood abruptly altered because I thought Dylan would appreciate the irony that he didn't have to give a performance to bring us to tears; he just had to be himself.

"It's a shame about my catch," Roy said when we started moving again.

"You can get more fish," Dee observed.

"The bears will get 'em," he said.

Dee was silent as we drove down the beach and up to her house.

"We can fix your net tomorrow," she announced after she parked. "You don't want to miss out on a day when the fish are running."

I offered Roy a hand getting out of the truck, and he began to shiver again in the rain and wind.

"Nelson, you're taking driving lessons tomorrow," Dee said decisively as we entered her front door. "Be here at seven in the morning, and don't be late."

"All right," I said meekly, knowing that I would be on time.

FOURTEEN

W hile shaving the next morning it occurred to me that Roy owed his life to a cheapskate who expected to be repaid if he bought you a fifty-cent newspaper. I tried not to focus on the quarter-pound of flesh that a sex addict would demand as compensation for saving your life. Dylan was on my mind since I didn't have to be quiet getting ready in the bathroom for my first truck-driving lesson. There wasn't a chance of me waking him because he had spent the night in Egegik "apologizing" to Alex.

Shortly after dinner, Dylan had walked down to the water and hitched a ride across the river. Dylan's belief in his own irresistibility was enviable and vile; he thought that all he had to do was twirl his dick around like a magic wand and all would be forgiven. His show of remorse angered me because I felt a genuine sense of repentance and didn't like Dylan's cynical treatment of Alex. Although part of my resentment stemmed from my envy that I couldn't just offer my ass as a catchall apology. I had told Roy what I thought about Dylan's "apology" but he told me not to worry about Alex.

"He comes from a long line of hunters," Roy said. "He's the last man I'd try to outfox."

Promptly at seven, I knocked on Dee's door and she waved me into her kitchen. "Did you eat anything?" she asked, squinting at me as if my inability to drive a standard proved that I was unable to feed myself. I was ravenously hungry, which was unusual for me because I never ate first thing in the morning. Dee offered me a plate of freshly baked blueberry scones, and I wolfed down two of them and then shoved another one in my coat pocket for later. My unexpected hunger brought back a memory of my mother's funeral when, after the graveside service, we went to my Aunt Sue's house. My face burned with shame when Aunt Sue had pointed out to the assembled mourners that I ate two large helpings of her baked ziti. Roy's close call proved once again that an encounter with Death stimulated my appetite almost as if the grim reaper's bony face was a reminder that there'd be a long wait between your last meal and the next one.

A thick fog covered Coffee Point when we headed out, obscuring buildings and trucks, making me feel that the sun was waiting for coffee to brew and wasn't fully awake yet. Dee suggested heading down to the abandoned cannery along the river for my first driving lesson because the beach road dead-ended there. "We want to give you room to screw up," she said practically, tempting me to respond that I doubted whether all of Alaska was large enough to fully contain my ineptitude.

As we approached the river, a blond-haired man in a blue jacket emerged from the mist. He ambled alongside the road, and we waved as we recognized Dylan and drove past him.

"What's he doing out at this hour?" Dee asked as I watched Dylan recede into the fog in my side-view mirror.

"He spent the night in Egegik with Alex," I said, wondering if Dee would fill in the blanks about their sleeping arrangements.

"I thought Alex was angry with you and Dylan," she said.

It was embarrassing to learn that she had heard about our shameful behavior. It didn't surprise me though because I knew that Alex was close to Dee and sometimes visited her in Homer.

"Did he tell you what happened?" I asked.

She nodded. "I saw him walking back from the beach. He looked upset and I asked him what was wrong. He called Dylan a *terpak*. Then said you were one, too." She explained that it was a Yup'ik word that means, "Big Anus."

I explained to her what had happened, trying to let her know that I understood that there were no mitigating circumstances and we had behaved like oversized assholes.

"The really awful part is that I actually think that rearranging driftwood to make it more comfortable is beautiful," I said. "It's so generous that it actually becomes cosmic."

"So, in addition to being inconsiderate," Dee said, "you lied to Alex and yourself."

"Yes," I said, thinking that she could add cowardly and selfish to her list. I had hurt Alex's feelings simply because I wanted Dylan to like me.

"We were trying to be funny," I said lamely.

"Humor's like fire," Dee said. "It can either warm you or burn you."

"You're right," I said, feeling that Dee could give my father a few lessons in the art of dismantling the illusions of Nelson Kunker. "I have to apologize to him."

"And apologize to all that driftwood."

I knew when Dee made a joke that at least she had forgiven me.

"Oh, yeah," I said. "They can really hold a grudge."

We parked near the derelict cannery, which looked haunted in the fog. Small clouds hung on its crumbling walls, and I almost expected to see the ghosts of long-departed salmon flickering through the broken windows or hear the spectral rattle of cans moving down the long-silent assembly line. After I switched seats with Dee, she briefly explained the principles of driving a standard.

I tried to follow her instructions exactly and started the engine, letting out the clutch slowly while gently pressing on the gas pedal until we stalled. I panicked and immediately slammed on the brakes, causing Dee to lap dance after she spilled her coffee. "Go easy on the brakes," she said patiently while wiping off her jacket with paper towels.

I apologized and restarted the engine, following the same procedure until we stalled again. And again. And then another time for good measure. It was frustrating and humiliating, and every time the engine died, I muttered, "Sorry. . . ."

Dee told me bluntly to quit fussing. "Are your first drafts perfect?" she asked. "No. They probably stink, but you go back and rewrite them."

She accepted my frequent mistakes with stoic indifference. She had taught history to junior high school students for over thirty years, and her flinty scrutiny evoked a veteran teacher's ability to convey with a glance that she accepted her pupils' ignorance while also prodding them to work harder by suggesting that her patience was limited.

"You need to think of this truck as a character," she instructed. "Observe its behavior. Now what have you noticed about the clutch pedal?"

"It doesn't like to be babied," I guessed.

"That's right!" she said. "It's sticky, so you need to be firm with it."

I restarted the engine, let the clutch out slowly, and we began to move. We stalled several more times, but the distance that I could drive without the truck shuddering to a halt began to increase.

"A good truck behaves the same all the time," Dee declared as she tenderly patted the dashboard of her battered blue and white '68 Mercury M-100 Ranger. "It's boring in a man, but I love it in a machine. This truck's lasted longer than my two marriages and been more dependable than either of my husbands. It acts up every now and then, but at least when I feed a truck gas and oil it does something for me in return. Trucks spoil a woman."

When I was able to successfully drive from the closed cannery to the weigh station and back without stalling, Dee announced that my first truck-driving lesson was finished. "It looks like you've got the hang of second gear," she said.

It's not an exaggeration to say that I felt an immeasurable sense of relief that I hadn't caused an accident or other unforeseen catastrophe. But my contentment was short-lived because my sense of being hounded by bad luck—the star-crossed unease that I walked through life under an archway of ladders as a pride of black cats migrated across my path—returned when Dee said, "Let's go check my net."

The fog started to lift and driving back toward her house, we passed a group of four posted signs that read, "Keep OUT!" and "Private Property" staked in front of a group of bushes and small trees. A smoking chimney and peaked roof rising above the brush revealed a house. It was perplexing that the owner didn't take advantage of the view of the river.

"Who's bothering him?" I asked. "There's no one out here."

"Don't go wandering near there," warned Dee. "Miles has a rifle, and he'll use it."

"It's like he's talking to himself with his signs."

"That's the definition of crazy in Alaska," she said chuckling. "Even when there are no people around, they still get on your nerves."

"There goes my idea that Coffee Point is a little utopia," I said.

"We have our problems," Dee said thoughtfully, "but they're manageable out here. We know who the idiots are and where they live. And we can avoid them. That sounds like paradise to me. I haven't spoken to Miles in ten years, and we're both very happy about that."

At Dee's house, we placed two totes on the back of her truck before she brought out from a storage shed various pieces of fishing gear that she'd inherited from sons and ex-husbands.

"I'm going to pay you five percent of the catch," she announced as I tried to squeeze into a pair of her first husband's waders. Green crewmen were customarily paid five percent of the catch, which didn't sound like much until I calculated that it was probably more generous than the starting pay I'd received in other jobs. I was fairly certain that I had made much less than five percent of the catch working as a busboy or a writer's assistant.

Dee handed me a blue float jacket, which was tight around the arms but she insisted that I had to wear it. As I zipped up the jacket, I realized that the money I would earn was secondary in my mind. I wanted to learn how to fish.

I began to consider that a writer who just knew how to write—no matter how well—was inadequate. I recalled that many of the writers whom I revered could do something else besides writing well. Melville knew how to flense a sperm whale, Mark Twain could pilot a paddle wheel riverboat, and Chekhov could give you your annual physical. I even remembered reading that Oscar Wilde, of all people, was an avid recreational salmon fisherman as a youth in Ireland. Roy had started to fish when he was nine years old, and I thought if a boy could learn to fish at that age then perhaps a clumsy thirty-four-year-old man could also.

Unlike her son, Dee fished from a brand-new, aluminum-hulled boat that she kept parked on a trailer, next to her house. I tried to memorize everything Dee told me and watched carefully as she demonstrated how to attach the trailer to the truck. It took us five minutes to drive down to Dee's set-net site, which she could oversee from her kitchen window. Dee looked over at me before she put the boat into the water.

"Watch the rearview mirror," she advised while expertly backing up the boat into the surf. "You don't want to get in too deep." Looking in the rearview mirror, she slowly drove in reverse. "When the top of the boat disappears under the back of the truck, then stop."

We got out of the truck and she demonstrated how to release the boat from the trailer. "Pay attention," she said while untying a line from a cleat. "You could lose a finger if you're not careful."

At first, I was afraid of working a job where the punishment for negligence or failure could be dismemberment or death. But I discovered that contemplating my extinction greatly improved the focus and quality of my work. I began to speculate on what I might have already accomplished if every job I'd ever had was potentially lethal. If photocopying fatalities were a hazard of office work, I would have been a much better writer's assistant. And if writing carelessly resulted in the loss of a finger, the first draft of my novel would have been flawless.

Once Dee's boat was bobbing in the surf, she waded out and climbed aboard. Then she asked me to push her into deeper water. I could feel the water sloshing outside my waders but was surprised to find that my legs weren't cold—at least, not at first.

"That's deep enough," she said before offering me a hand to climb into the stern. Dee demonstrated how to start and operate the small outboard motor. She let me steer as we putt-putted over to the end of the net farthest from the shore.

Dee reached into the water, grabbed the net, and pulled it up into the boat. Ten tail-wagging salmon were entrapped in the net and she stuck her picking hook into a fish's gills, roughly prying it off, then dropped the salmon into the bottom of the boat.

"Jab it in there, and root around if you need to," she said demonstrating her technique on another fish. Watching her work, I began to think her name was short for Diesel, because she was by far the butchest woman I'd ever met.

We hoisted the net in sections, working our way back to the shore, picking off salmon as we went along.

The fish were big and unwieldy and flopped and thrashed in my gloved hands. "Grab 'em like this," Dee shouted, demonstrating her method of roughly clutching a salmon by its throat. The fish's mouth opened and closed silently, giving the impression that it was afraid to say anything that might piss her off further. Fortunately, my dad had taken me fishing many times, and I wasn't squeamish about handling the slimy fish, although it took me a while to feel comfortable bullying them like Dee did.

I was cautious each time I pulled in the net because our catch wasn't limited to salmon. Other sea creatures became entrapped and they had to be removed and thrown back. The first time, I came face to faceless with a dinner-plate-sized jellyfish, I held the net away from me, as I asked Dee whether jellyfish were dangerous to handle.

"No," she said calmly, reaching over to pluck the blob from the net. "Aren't they beautiful?" she asked, holding the jellyfish in her gloved hands for me to admire. It looked like an enormous vintage Murano glass paperweight, the translucent dome covering a mod sixties pinwheel of yellow and brown. Then, like a woman surprised by the costly price of a bauble she'd idly picked up in an antique shop, she gently returned the jellyfish to the water where it sank from our view.

We returned to the shore with our catch, and Dee announced that she was going to let me transfer the heavy salmon from the boat into the totes. Heaving the large fish was the most exhausting part of the job and when I had almost finished, Roy and Dylan drove past us, slowing down to honk and wave. Waving back to them, I was amazed that I hadn't thought about either of them for the past hour.

At the weigh station, our tote was forklifted off Dee's truck and placed on the scale. Aaron read the dial and announced the weight. "Twelve hundred ten pounds." Dee scribbled down the amount of our catch in a black-and-white spotted notebook. According to Roy, she had a shelf of notebooks in her living room and could tell you exactly how many pounds of fish she'd caught every summer since 1976.

"We did all right," Dee said, turning toward me. I was pleased to be included in her "we" and calculated that I'd earned thirty-four dollars in about an hour and a half. All of a sudden, five percent of the catch didn't seem ungenerous. It was a better hourly rate than I had earned making lattes, and if we made three or four similar catches each day over the next three weeks, I calculated that I wouldn't need to find another job in Anchorage and could spend the rest of the summer working on my novel.

The weigh station crew treated Dee with deference and respect due to her status as a veteran fisherman, but they also enjoyed trying to rile her. They expressed their disappointment upon hearing that she'd hired a crewman.

"Dee," Aaron said, "we never expected you to go soft on us."

"I'm not as soft as you," she replied. "You're young and strong and yet you still need two grown men and a forklift to weigh the fish caught by an old lady. I don't think it's unreasonable for me to have a crewman after thirty-one years."

Her rebuke made everyone laugh.

"How'd Nelson do?" Derrick asked Dee after we concluded our business. I was as eager as they were to hear her answer.

Dee glanced at me and then turned back to them. "He's got the makings of a fisherman."

Her praise made me feel elated. Dee's forthrightness made it clear that she valued the title of fisherman and would never bestow it indiscriminately. And I couldn't easily dismiss her acceptance or cast doubt upon her judgment no matter how much I tried.

"Nelson, we have something for you," Aaron announced as we prepared to leave. "In honor of your first day of fishing." He reached into a tote and removed a king salmon that was almost three feet long. It dwarfed the sockeyes that we caught. I thanked him as he placed the fish in the empty tote on our truck and Derrick shoveled ice over it. I hadn't seen any king salmon in Roy's catches and asked Aaron if they caught many of them at Coffee Point. He explained that they weren't as plentiful as sockeyes in the Egegik River and that he often put them aside when one showed up in someone's catch.

"We usually eat them or I give them away," he said.

I didn't know exactly what to do with my gift. But as we drove away, Dee suggested that we serve it for dinner that night.

"We'll make something special for Wendy," she said. I looked at my watch and saw that I needed to get to the landing strip because her airplane would be arriving in thirty minutes. Before Dee dropped me off at Roy's house, she told me to return to her place at two for my second truck-driving lesson.

"Dee," I said when she stopped the truck to let me out. "I want to thank you for teaching me to drive a standard and for letting me crew for you. I really appreciate it." My words inadequately expressed my gratitude, but I was afraid that I'd come across as a mental case if I told her that I was cautiously starting to believe that my luck was changing for the better because of her.

"You're welcome," she said with a broad smile. "I enjoyed it. I haven't taught someone to drive or fish since I taught Roy. I'm recapturing my youth."

As I walked to the landing strip, it became obvious that the wind on the beach functioned as a mosquito swatter. In the relatively sheltered air of the landing strip, the bugs bit me steadily even though I'd followed Roy's advice and smeared my face, neck, and hands with insect repellent. But it seemed to me that Alaskan mosquitoes savored the carcinogenic taste of DEET in the same manner that tough women enjoyed the taste of nicotine. The buzzing mosquitoes turned my face into a noisy bar, and I almost expected to hear wee slurping sounds from hundreds of tiny straws as the last of my blood was drained from my body.

I recalled the last time I'd picked up Wendy at LAX. She'd flown to New York to visit her aunt and had called me three times to remind me that her plane would be landing at 10:20. Each time she called, she barked, "Don't be late!" I had met her at the baggage claim, standing at the bottom of the escalator, holding up a sign that had the word *Bitch* written in big block letters. Disembarking passengers read the sign and smiled or pointed at it, but I maintained an impassive countenance similar to the bored expression worn by a limousine driver waiting for a passenger at the airport. I knew that I'd nailed Wendy when I heard her scream, "You asshole!" and then her braying laugh.

Wendy's airplane crunched to a stop on the gravel. She looked at me through the windshield and pointed to her forehead and began to shake her head with disbelief. I had almost forgotten about my bandage. The pilot got out and helped her climb down from the cockpit of the small aircraft.

"What happened?" she asked in greeting me.

"I hit my head on the kitchen table, fighting with Dylan over a joint." I braced myself for her inevitable comments on my lack of coordination.

"You should be placed in a plastic bubble and kept out of harm's way."

"It was an accident."

"So was Chernobyl." She threw a large heavy-looking duffel bag over her shoulder.

"And yet because of some klutz, no one can live there for ten thousand years."

The pilot told Wendy to expect him back around the same time in two weeks.

"Ron, thank you," she said warmly. "Because of you I never want to fly again."

"Glad to be of service," he said, playing along with her. We waved good-bye as he climbed inside his plane. The fragile looking airplane barreled down the strip of gravel until the machine, at the last possible moment, lifted free of the earth. It was as astonishing as if a toaster or lawn mower had developed the ability to fly.

"Let me take that," I said, gallantly reaching for the largest duffel bag. My arm was jerked downward by the heavy weight. "What do you have in here?"

"Food," she said. "I wasn't about to depend on you for my meals."

Wendy loved to cook and lived by a complex set of gastronomic rules. Canned vegetables were an abomination except for an obscure, hard-to-obtain brand of corn from Iowa that she insisted was preferable to fresh when used in salads or casseroles. She eschewed frozen foods but under duress would admit that frozen butternut squash could be used to make a satisfactory soup. Her strong dislikes were equally as singular. She had an irrational, almost bigoted hatred of tarragon, although she loved it in béarnaise sauce. And every winter, she lugged back a six-pack of Coca-Cola from Mexico because she claimed that soda made with cane sugar was superior to the disgusting American beverage made with corn syrup. I found being Wendy's dinner guest enjoyable, because she usually concentrated on criticizing the perceived flaws of the delicious food she served, leaving her guests relatively unscathed during the meal.

"I've missed you," she confessed.

"I missed you, too," I said as we both smiled.

"Did you hear my message on the radio?" she asked, waving her hand in front of her face to ward off a persistent bug. She was pleased to hear that I thought her radio announcement was hilarious.

"It's too bad Reina couldn't come," I said.

"I tried to talk her into it. But she can't get away now with her new job." Wendy's last e-mail reported that she was already testing the boundaries of their relationship with her jokes. After Reina's first day working at a new veterinary hospital, she had come home and told Wendy that she had to put a middle-aged woman's beloved cat to sleep because Mr. Mittens had cancer.

"Was he a smoker?" Wendy asked earnestly, causing Reina to laugh and then accuse her of being heartless.

As we started walking toward Dee's house, Wendy informed me that she had fallen in love with Reina and was going to ask her to move in with her at the end of the summer.

"I'm crazy about her," Wendy said, "but I find it hard to talk about her to my therapist, because I'm afraid the therapist will steal her away from me. And my therapist already has a girlfriend."

"Have you talked to your therapist about this?" I asked.

"No," she said. "She'd think I was insane."

"With good reason."

Wendy asked me how I was doing. I filled her in on how I injured myself and how Roy had almost drowned. She didn't appear to be overly impressed by Dylan's heroic rescue.

"I'm sure he enjoyed giving him mouth-to-mouth," she said before suddenly slapping her arm. "Goddamit," she said while examining the blotted bug as if she was reading its entrails. A flick of a finger removed the corpse.

"I forgot how beautiful Alaska is," she said, looking around her. This was her first trip back to Alaska since she had spent the summer in Seward with her ex-girlfriend Mandy. "It makes me feel like I'm the ugliest thing in the landscape. That never happens to me in LA. There's always a dingy motel or a bleak strip mall that makes me feel good about my appearance."

A strap on one of her bags slid down her shoulder, causing the bag to fall and strike her hip, making her sway unsteadily.

"Why didn't you pick me up in a truck?" she snarled when she saw one driving off in the distance.

"Because I didn't think you'd bring so much fucking luggage." I laughed suddenly at the sight of us struggling with her bags on the edge of the tundra. "Can you believe the two of us are in Alaska?"

She smiled. "No, I can't."

I tried to assert my newly minted manly competence of several hours and told her that Dee was teaching me to drive a standard and had hired me to crew for her.

"You're becoming a fisherman?" Wendy asked as her dark brown eyes widened in disbelief.

"I started today," I said proudly.

"It's about time you became some sort of man."

I was about to say the same thing to her but became distracted when I spotted Dylan jogging toward us.

"I thought you might need some help carrying your bags," he said after reaching us. "I would've brought the four-wheeler but Roy's using it."

"Thanks," Wendy said suspiciously, "And to what do I owe this favor?"

"It's part of my plan," Dylan said. "I'm trying to win you over. Because for some strange reason Nelson's fond of you."

Dylan had to be telling the truth. The only reason I could think of his coming out to help her was that he was doing it for me.

Wendy stopped. "I have some news," she announced, setting down her bags and putting on her jacket. Clouds had covered the sun and it felt as if the season had changed.

"What?" I asked.

"Amanda read our sketches," she said. "She really liked them. She raved about them, and she never raves about anything. She wants to hire some new writers for next season. She didn't promise anything, but she wants to meet with us."

My first thought was, what will I tell Roy? I didn't want to have to tell him that I wouldn't be able to finish the season, and I couldn't face quitting on Dee.

I hadn't thought about our sketches in months because Los Angeles is a city filled with tens of thousands of unproduced scripts lying in drawers. I used to say they should be burned as an alternative fuel, because they'd lend a poetic quality to the smog, allowing the city to live under a cloud of dashed hopes. Ultimately, I thought the screenplay smog would be a comforting bond among Los Angeles's inhabitants—the brown horizon giving evidence that the failures in the city far outnumbered the successes.

"Congratulations," Dylan said. "That means Nelson will have to stay in Los Angeles where he belongs."

"You're sure she wants to meet with me, too?" I asked Wendy, thinking that Amanda couldn't have been thrilled to see my name on our scripts.

"Yes," Wendy answered. "She thinks your smoking pot on the job was completely unprofessional, but she doesn't care about the article. She thinks the reporter sandbagged you."

"She'd never say your stuff was good unless she meant it," Dylan said. He seemed to be impressed, and I realized that Agenda's praise of our script added to my stature in his eyes.

"When does she want to meet us?" I asked, resolving not to leave Coffee Point until the end of the season. "I've committed to being Dee's crewman for the next three weeks."

"That's okay," Wendy said. "Fly down for a week when you get done."

I had made my stand and could now bask in the approval of our script by one of Hollywood's sharpest-tongued critics. It had been a long time since I'd received any professional validation for my writing, and it felt terrific.

"What am I going to tell Roy?" I asked. We hadn't discussed our long-term future together beyond my spending the summer in Anchorage. Were we going to stay together? Was I going to move to Alaska?

"Tell him that you're going to become rich," Dylan offered.

Wendy's face became thoughtful. "He'll understand. This could be an opportunity for both of you."

"And an opportunity for *you*," Dylan said spitefully to Wendy.

"For us," Wendy said, sounding annoyed.

"Roy wants to live in Alaska," I explained.

"Let him," Dylan said.

"You could go back and forth," Wendy suggested doubtfully.

"Don't encourage him," Dylan said to her. "Do you want him to move up here?"

"No," she replied. "I'd miss him terribly."

"And you'd be losing your writing partner," he said.

"I know that," Wendy snapped, her eyes flashing angrily. "Why do you care?"

"Hasn't Nelson told you?" Dylan asked. "He's going to become my boyfriend."

Wendy took his comment for a joke until she saw that I blanched. I didn't understand why he was announcing this to her. It seemed like something you'd discuss privately. But Wendy later pointed out he might have spoken to her because he was afraid of saying it to me directly.

She became visibly indignant. "Oh, really? Does Roy know about this?"

"Roy's a summer fling," Dylan said brutally.

"You've got a lot of gall, coming out here as his guest and then trying to steal his boyfriend," Wendy said.

"And your new girlfriend," Dylan returned. "Wasn't she dating someone else when you first met her?"

Oops. I'd mentioned to Dylan and Roy that Wendy had met Reina at a party where Reina had told her that she had a girlfriend but they hadn't had sex in three years. Wendy had made out with Reina at the party, so technically she could be considered a homewrecker.

"What makes you think Nelson would date a drug addict?" Wendy asked.

"First of all, I'm not currently using drugs," Dylan replied. "I've been smoking pot, but I haven't used anything else since I left prison. And I've decided to quit smoking pot when I leave here. Then there's the fact that Nelson is totally into me. I'm certain of that. I can prove it to you, if you want."

He stopped walking as if he was threatening to set down her bags and we were going to fuck right there. His arms bulged from carrying her heavy bags and his face was covered with a photogenic sheen of sweat. I was into him but reserved the right to say that I wasn't totally into him.

Wendy shrugged. "So he thinks you're hot. Guess what? I think you're hot, and you could probably talk me into fucking you—once. But I would never become your girlfriend."

Wendy wasn't bisexual, but in college she had been known to sleep with a beautiful man with the same sense of entitlement that she would visit the newest trendy bar or restaurant. She'd go there once for the bragging rights but, having satisfied her curiosity, would be content to never go there again.

"I'm a better fit for Nelson," Dylan argued. "I've been after him to read his novel and his so-called boyfriend hasn't." He turned to me and said challengingly, "Has he?"

"No," I said. "But he's been busy finishing up with school."

"Yeah, that's a good excuse," he said contemptuously. "Has he read anything you've ever written?"

"No." I said, which hadn't bothered me until Dylan brought it to my attention.

"He hasn't?" Wendy sounded dumbfounded.

"He's talked about reading something, but I never push people to read my stuff," I explained. "And I'm revising the novel."

"That doesn't prove anything," Wendy said to Dylan. "I haven't read his novel since he started on it again."

Dylan reminded us that Roy could have asked to read one of my short stories from college, which was something that had occurred to me also.

"I'd be a better boyfriend for him than Roy," Dylan claimed. "I'm a fellow artist. I understand the ups and downs. The discipline it takes to succeed."

Wendy was temporarily rendered speechless, and in this case it wasn't a sign of confusion but akin to filling a reservoir. She gathered reasons why Dylan shouldn't be my boyfriend that she would release in a deluge.

"You don't have to tell me that I have my flaws," Dylan said, pre-empting her objections. "But I'm working on them."

"*Flaws?*" Wendy snarled. "You've been in jail! I don't know if I'd put that in the flaws category."

Dylan laughed at her sarcasm and admitted that flaws might not be the precise word.

"I think Nelson's just going to get better-looking as he gets older," Dylan said.

Wendy's expression softened and she looked me over once more.

"You know, you do look good," she said. "Other than your head," she added, screwing up her face as she glanced at my bandage.

"Nelson's handsome," Dylan said. "But he doesn't see it yet."

"I've told him that," Wendy agreed. "But he never notices when I compliment him."

I pointed out that properly appreciating her rare praise amidst her nearly constant derision was like trying to find a sweet piece of hay in a stack of needles; the bloody and painful search severely reduced the value of the prize.

"What is going on with you and Roy?" she asked. "Are you moving up here? Please say you're not."

"See?" Dylan said. "Even your best friend thinks it's a bad idea."

"I never said that," Wendy corrected. "I'm just being selfish."

I had no doubt that Wendy wanted me to be happy, although like the sun, she was convinced that life was impossible for her friends unless they lived within her orbit. Becoming a television writer was her ambition, not mine, but I couldn't turn down the opportunity to work on our scripts without hurting her. If Amanda produced our scripts, it could be Wendy's big break, and she was depending upon me to help her succeed. But I didn't want to hurt Roy, either, by committing to a project that would require me to live in Los Angeles. Whatever decision I made would hurt one of them. I felt overwhelmed with indecisiveness and waited for a sucker hole to open in my gloomy thoughts.

Dylan and Wendy waited for me to answer her question about what was going on with Roy.

"We haven't discussed anything beyond the summer," I admitted.

"You haven't been up here during the winter," Dylan warned.

"The winters can't be that much worse than Milwaukee's," I suggested, thinking that I had survived twenty-two years of Wisconsin Februaries without sinking into despair.

"Are you in love with Roy?" Wendy asked.

"I think so," I said. The sight of Roy lying on the beach had been devastating and the thought of losing him had made me believe that I was in love with him. But I was also beginning to think that I was falling in love with Dylan, too. It seemed unfair. I'd been waiting to fall in love, and being hit with two of Cupid's arrows at the same time made me feel like I was being attacked.

"It doesn't sound like it," Dylan said smiling.

"Have you said it to each other?" Wendy asked.

"No."

She raised her eyebrows. "How come?"

"We're not ready yet."

"Why wait?" Wendy said. "He almost died. You don't want to tell someone you love them with a Ouija board."

Wendy was alluding to a stupid argument I'd had with my mother on the morning before she died about my getting a tattoo. I knew that she loved me and I loved her, but it still distressed me that my last words to her were harsh. Of course, she ultimately won the argument, because afterward I couldn't bring myself to get a tattoo.

"I don't know," I said, wondering why neither of us had said it. We'd been dating for almost four months.

"My theory is that for two men, confessing their love for each other has to be orgasmic," I said playfully.

Picking up on my premise, Wendy added, "Prematurely declaring your love is humiliating, and most men wait until they can sense the other guy's getting close."

"Yeah," I agreed. "But you don't want to get stuck in a situation where the other guy seems like he's ready to blow but can't spit it out."

"Ideally you'd both say it simultaneously," she suggested.

I nodded and said, "But bringing two hearts to that point is as dicey as getting two dicks to work in unison."

We were content that we had come to a satisfying conclusion to her question and continued walking.

"You're going to be hired," Dylan declared.

"I think you're right," Wendy said softly, almost as if she was talking to herself.

I knew that she was extremely superstitious about jinxing things, and her admission of confidence convinced me that we probably would be hired as staff writers for *Aftertaste*. The thought should have made me happy, but it didn't. Then I had a revelation, which as an English major, I graded on a descending scale from Joycean epiphany, where I have to encounter for the millionth time the reality of experience and have to forge in the smithy of my soul the uncreated conscience of my race, to the lesser jolt of realizing that hey, I really was versatile in bed and wasn't just trying to avoid being branded as a total bottom. This was somewhere in between: I realized that I no longer looked forward to returning to Los Angeles because I didn't want to leave Coffee Point.

As we plodded along the road, I recalled reading somewhere that using a compass for navigation in the high arctic becomes misleading because the magnetic pole is actually located in Canada, south of the North Pole. Coffee Point was hundreds of miles south of the Arctic Circle but I could pinpoint exactly where I lost my sense of direction.

FIFTEEN

Wendy and I watched Roy carefully unscrew the hand pump from the rusty barrel of gasoline stored within blazing distance of the house. It's universally recognized that storing gasoline in open containers is notoriously unsafe, and I pictured our chain-smoking neighbor, Karen, carelessly flicking a cigarette butt out her truck window as she drove by early one morning, detonating a cinematically explosive fireball that would engulf our house, incinerating us while we slept. Roy had asked me to help him get gasoline for his truck because filling her up was a two-man job. Instead of driving to the cannery's fueling station every time they needed a tank of gas, Roy and the other fishermen transported oil drums filled with gasoline in the back of their pick-ups over ten miles of unpaved, bumpy road. Then after the leaky barrels were unloaded, Roy hand pumped gas into his truck and four-wheeler as needed.

"Why do you store gasoline right next to the house?" I asked. "Why don't you just drive down to the cannery when you need gas?"

"The trip takes too much time," Roy explained as he pressed a plug in the barrel's bunghole. "And driving back and forth twenty miles uses a quarter of a tank." In addition, he also pointed out that we needed gasoline at the house for the four-wheeler.

I helped him lift the slick, greasy barrel, which smelled strongly of gasoline and faintly of self-immolation. I thought *does everything in Alaska have to be dangerous?* I'd already been warned to be on the lookout for bears when I threw out our garbage at the dump and had also been informed that you should never go for a hike without telling someone because people were always getting lost and dying from exposure on what were supposed to be walks in the woods. Storing an oil drum filled with gasoline in your backyard sounded like a reckless tradeoff for con-venience's sake—as crazy as keeping sparking live wires next to the house in case the truck's battery died and needed a jumpstart.

"That's all we need is for Nelson to drop it," Wendy cracked as she watched us raise and set the barrel on the back of the truck. I tried to envision the full barrel slipping from my hands, the heavy drum striking a small stone in the sand, sparking an inferno. But I dismissed the thought because whenever I really could have used a disaster to distract me from my problems, my life proceeded without incident. People die every day with maxed-out credit cards; with gas, electric, and cable bills unpaid; with laundry unfolded; with bosses breathing down their necks; with lovers demanding explanations; with dogs whining to be walked; with important telephone calls, movie rentals, and library books that needed to be returned; with tax audits planned for the next morning; and mammograms and colonoscopies scheduled for the following afternoon—Death mercifully erasing all burdens, decisions, and obligations. But a fiery doom wasn't going to relieve me of having to choose between Los Angeles and Alaska, between writing for television and writing novels, and between Roy and Dylan. I could have dropped lit matches into the barrel all day, and I was confident that nothing untoward would have happened.

Wendy wasn't accompanying us to the cannery as she had volunteered to help Dee prepare dinner. Dee had been whisking a ginger-lime marinade for my king salmon when Wendy arrived at her house, and the two foodies immediately bonded and began to name-drop Basil, Cilantro, and Rosemary as if they shared mutual friends. Wendy also wanted to give me some time alone with Roy because she'd ordered me to speak to him about my going back to Los Angeles to meet with Amanda.

I dreaded telling him the news about our scripts. One of the drawbacks of being a writer is that I could always imagine how Roy would react in any given situation. Accurately predicting his behavior wasn't my strength, but I was accomplished at devising and exhausting a plethora of his possible responses. Often I treated Roy as if he were an actor, and I was an insane playwright who'd expressed an interest in casting him in a part. But I refused to audition him for the role, preferring to run lines with him in my head, then finding fault with his performance.

We drove to the cannery, and I transferred my anxiety about the empty barrel of gasoline exploding to the equally immediate concern that Roy would blow up when he heard that I would be returning to Los Angeles. Unable to think of an ingenious method of introducing the combustible topic, I just blurted out, "Amanda wants to talk to Wendy and me about writing for *Aftertaste*."

I tried to make my announcement sound inconsequential. I emphasized that it wasn't a done deal, stressing that a meeting between a writer and a producer was a mating dance between a horse and an ass, and the odds of producing viable offspring were small.

Roy listened attentively while his mouth and cheeks assumed a solidity that indicated his anger, frustration, and disappointment. He was capable of telling me how he felt but, being male, he elected to stiffen or slacken a piece of flesh to signal whether he felt loving or indifferent. His firm body was a thrilling sight, but it pained me when his face became harder than his arms and chest.

"What does that mean?" he asked as we slowly descended the steep road to the beach. I looked out the rear window of the cab when I heard the barrel banging against the gunwales of the truck. It sounded like the barrel was coming loose, but I could see the bungee cords were holding.

"I'm going to have to fly back to L.A. to meet with Amanda," I announced.

"How long will you be gone?"

"It could be for a week," I said. "Or longer."

"I thought you were staying until September."

"I might be able to come back."

"Might?"

"It depends on whether we get hired."

He didn't respond, and I focused on the barrel rattling in the back of the truck; at that point I would have welcomed its detonation.

"Do you really want to do this?" Roy asked. His ambiguous statement made me unsure whether he was referring to working on the script or talking about leaving him.

"I'm Wendy's writing partner."

Roy continued driving, letting my statement fully sink in, allowing me to understand that I was choosing a writing partner over a possible life partner.

"I'm not talking about that," he said. "Do you really want to write for television?" He pulled the truck over to the side of the road and stopped, waving ahead another truck that had been tailing us.

"I don't know," I said. "I didn't expect Amanda to be interested in our scripts. And to be honest, I'm glad that someone likes something I've written. But I'm also having the best summer I've ever had. I don't want to leave here."

I should have told Roy that I loved being in Alaska, but saying it out loud felt imprudent like happiness was something I could drop and break. But I wasn't taking into account the important lessons about life that bird watching had taught me. Birdwatchers understand that when a beautiful bluebird flies off, it doesn't mean that's it, you'll never see another bluebird again. You might not see one right away, but eventually every experienced birder understands that you're bound to see another spectacular bird. Then I thought of Dylan because birders also understand that happiness isn't limited to bluebirds; sometimes it's a ruthless bird of prey.

"Then don't go," Roy said.

"I made a commitment to Wendy." I knew that Roy believed in honoring your commitments. "She's my best friend, and this is really important to her. I have to see it through for her sake."

"I don't want you to go," he said quietly. Suddenly I was moved to tell him, "You know that I love it here. Coming out here is one of the best things I've ever done."

Roy didn't say anything as the cannery came into view. He slowed down because cannery workers in blue uniforms were walking along the sides of the road. It was disillusioning to discover that my remote

Alaskan wilderness was located down the road from a bustling factory. The cannery's buildings were painted an institutional beige color, but the workers' housing was distinguished by ironic hotel names that had been hand painted in black paint on their outside walls. The "Hilton" stood next to the "Best Western," which was located across the road from the "The Hyatt."

"Wendy knows what she's doing with her life, and she'll do it with or without you," Roy said. "Just make sure you understand what you're doing." I asked him what he was specifically referring to, but he refused to elaborate any further, telling me that he'd said exactly what he meant. Then I made the mistake of accusing him of not communicating enough, goading him into becoming Pandora's chatterbox, giving him permission to release every evil thought he had contained about me.

His face was now wholly elastic with hostility. "Perhaps it's because I'm confused," he said in a low voice. "I'm waiting for you to figure out what you want. First, you say that you want to write novels, that you're finished with Hollywood. Then Dylan shows an interest in you, and I don't know what to think. And now you're ready to go back to work for a woman whom you never really liked before. Why don't you communicate with me as soon as you know what you want?"

I felt like Annie Sullivan when Helen Keller finally connected the finger spelled word *water* with the thing itself. Only in my version of the story, Helen proceeded directly to sarcasm and told Annie in no uncertain terms about her many failings as a teacher—pointing out where Annie had missed several opportunities to connect with her earlier and what she should have done that would have made Helen's life easier. I'd always wondered if during the course of their subsequent years together, Annie had ever been sorely tempted to finger spell "shut up" into Helen's palm.

"You'd live in L.A.?" Roy asked, sounding as if he was thinking aloud instead of asking a question.

"I think I'd have to."

"I couldn't live there," he declared as we arrived at the cannery. Roy no longer appeared to be angry; he looked dejected.

"Even if we get hired, " I said, trying to cheer him up, "it doesn't mean that we won't get fired."

"I'm supposed to root for you and Wendy to fail. I don't want to be that guy." He braked to allow two women in blue uniforms to cross the road. The cannery's workers were mostly Filipino women, and they smiled at Roy when he stopped the truck to allow them to pass.

The fueling station was located a safe distance behind the cannery and workers' dormitories. A skinny, freckle-faced woman with lank brown hair named Lisa dispensed the fuel. Her baggy, stained overalls made her look like a little girl who'd dressed up as a grease monkey for Halloween. She pumped gasoline from an old, blackened fuel truck and diesel fuel from a storage tank buried in the ground. Roy put the cost of the fuel on a tab that would be deducted from the money the cannery owed him at the end of the season.

We lifted the barrel off the truck, and Lisa told us where to set it down. She popped the barrel's plug with a sharply pointed wooden stick, then placed a nozzle in the spout and started pumping. While the barrel filled with gas, Roy announced that he wanted to buy a jar of peanut butter and then check and see if he had any mail.

"Are you going to finish out the season?" Roy asked as we walked back to the cannery.

"Yes," I said, understanding that he must have thought I would be leaving Coffee Point immediately. "I made a commitment to your mom. I'm more afraid of her disapproval than I am of Wendy's or Agenda's."

Roy smiled for the first time since he'd heard that I would be returning to Los Angeles.

"I can't quit now," I declared. "I'm a fisherman."

"After one day?"

"You can lose your virginity in a heartbeat," I said as we entered the cannery's small grocery store, a tiny room attached to the main production facility. A short dark-haired man was opening a carton of ramen noodles. He said hello with a slight Vietnamese accent while his wife glowered at us from behind the cash register. Roy whispered to me that Mr. and Mrs. Phan, the owners of the Happytime Market, took turns greeting their customers. The market was open seven days a week from eight in the morning until eight at night, and Roy claimed that the Phans never smiled simultaneously as if they were trying to conserve their pleasantness, because no one could expect them to be nice to their customers all the time.

The store's three short aisles were dead-ended by two refrigerators and a freezer case. Eyeing the store's limited selection, I grasped that the store's remote location, limited shelf space, and the shortness of the fishing season made offering an assortment of products impossible. At the Happytime Market shopping wasn't so much a matter of choosing an item as it was acquiescing to a brand. If you wanted detergent, it would have to be Tide, just as your soup would have to be Campbell's; although in a concession to varying tastes, chicken noodle and vegetable beef were offered.

It didn't seem that we were shopping in a store as that we were taking items from the shelves of the Phan's house or browsing at a poorly curated art gallery where everything was displayed indifferently, and the steep prices were crudely and baldly stamped on the works of art.

We were disappointed to find that the Phans only carried smooth peanut butter.

"Is crunchy a gay thing?" I asked.

Roy nodded sagely. "Nuts."

We walked a short distance to the cannery's post office. The postal clerk behind the counter was a short, prematurely bald man in his early twenties who responded with a sullen nod after Roy told him his full name. As the sourpuss shuffled in back to fetch his mail, Roy whispered, "He wouldn't last a day in a real post office." The sourpuss returned with a tied bundle of mail and a letter addressed to me, in care of Roy. My father's handwriting—a rugged cursive that reminded me of wrought iron—was instantly recognizable. The stamp on the envelope bore a brightly colored picture of a scarlet King snake. My father didn't write many letters, but he always carefully selected his stamps. He was a bit of a postal dandy and was proud that his electric bill payment always wore something flashy. He couldn't understand why everyone didn't buy interesting postage. "Beautiful stamps don't cost any more than ugly ones," he said. He was a sucker for animal stamps and had posted endangered and threatened species and would, undoubtedly, be first in line to purchase a series featuring archaic, dwindling, or invasive species. He freely bestowed his costly looking postage upon strangers allowing me to think of him as a small-scale patron of the arts.

Roy stood at a counter, sorting through his mail, discarding junk while I opened my letter. Typical of my father's thrifty nature, he wrote to me on the blank sides of advertisements for plumbing supplies. I could hear him saying, "Why waste the paper?"

Dear Nelson,

I received your last e-mail and tried to call before you left for Coffee Point. I must've missed you as the message said you'd left already.

I was glad to hear that you're going fishing with Roy. I knew you'd figure out a way of getting the money. And it's good to hear that you've been writing every morning. I know you hate to show your stuff, but when you're ready I'd like to read something. I'm not nagging though—this is just a gentle reminder.

Your brother came for three days, and I tried to show him and Shari a good time. But it's hard to tell with Cliff because I'm never sure whether he's having fun. He wanted to go to the art museum to see an exhibit of paintings by a 19th century American painter—Martin Johnson Heade. Beautiful stuff— mostly haystacks and hummingbirds. It sounds awful but his paintings are dynamite. (They'd make great stamps!) I spent more time looking for my socks that morning than Cliff did looking at the paintings. Later though, he told me that it was his favorite thing about the weekend. I used to try to figure you two out, but now I've decided that you're both "mental" as you'd put it.

Thanks for e-mailing me the pictures. Alaska looks as beautiful as people say it is. Though if you ask me, Roy's more handsome than the movie star, who looks like he expects to autograph every picture he's in.

You know, I'm not sure if it's any of my business to offer you advice about men. I realize that I've never dated any men, but then I thought about those queer guys on TV giving straight men advice and thought it was only fair that we should be able to turn the tables. After all, straight men would make the best critics of the gays—we can be objective about men because we're never going to date them, but we know all of their devious ways.

*I've been thinking about how you said that this Dylan asked
you to convince Roy to let him go fishing. Something sounds fishy.
(Sorry, I couldn't resist. Maybe I should become a writer? That's
not bad.) I don't see why he needed you to convince Roy to take
him fishing. He's an actor. Isn't it his job to persuade people?
Shouldn't he be able to do his own convincing? It doesn't make
sense. Something's up with him.*

*I look forward to meeting Roy and can't wait to hear about
your adventures. I hope things work out between you two because
I want you to be happy. And, also because I want to come up to
Alaska next summer. (Remember when you asked me to treat your
relationships exactly like your brother's? Well, long family visits
are part of the deal.)*

*Feel free to send me any salmon you can't use. My doctor's
been at me to eat more Omega-3's. Stay in ouch.*

Love,

Dad

I loved that my father signed his e-mails and letters with, "stay in
ouch." Several years back, he had made the typo in an e-mail. It had
become a long-standing joke between us after I had written him back
saying that he had accidentally stumbled upon the perfect phrase to
describe family love.

My father's comments about Dylan disturbed me, principally
because he described exactly what should have bothered me about his
request. After Dylan convinced me that he needed me to be his advo-
cate, it hadn't occurred to me that he could have spoken to Roy directly
about taking him fishing. Dylan certainly wasn't humble, and I didn't
really buy that he didn't think his deep voice coming out of his handsome face wasn't his best means of persuasion.

Roy had received a care package from his friend Diana. She sent him one every year, and this year's package included a new CD from Coldplay and several bars of dark chocolate made with 71 percent cocoa. Roy tore open a bar of chocolate and broke off two pieces, handing me one.

We left the cannery's office and ate the intensely flavored bittersweet chocolate, which tasted like an adults-only confection sold in the no-one-under-21-admitted backroom of a candy store. The sky was mostly clear of clouds, but the sun was content to shine without exerting its strength, reminding me of another lazy star. Suddenly it made sense that Dylan would want me to argue his case with Roy. Acting was Dylan's job, and he probably limited the number of performances that he was willing to give each week. My father was wrong about him. It wasn't necessarily a sign of Dylan's deviousness, but a symptom of his slothfulness that made him want me to talk Roy into taking him fishing.

When we returned to the fuel station, Lisa set the full barrel of gasoline on the back of the truck with a forklift. I was relieved that Roy drove cautiously back to the house with our flammable cargo. He braked when he came to a rough patch on the beach, looking over his shoulder to make sure that the barrel was still secured before proceeding. Every time he slowed down, I looked at Roy and smiled nervously.

"Alaska's license plate should say, 'Live, Freeze, or Die Horribly.'" I suggested.

"A friend of mine said that all of my stories about Alaska end with someone dying," he said. "And she was kind of right. Lots of people die up here."

The return trip from the cannery to the house took twice as long, almost an hour, as Roy carefully avoided potholes in the road. At the house, Roy had to park the truck in the road because Alex and Dylan were playing a game of basketball where we normally parked. Wendy was sitting on an overturned white plastic tote, watching them play. She glanced over at us when we got out of the truck but remained focused on their game.

Without a forklift, the barrel had to be carefully rolled down a plank from the bed of the truck. Roy stood on the truck bed and carefully tipped the barrel over on its side. I stood below him, holding the overturned barrel up at the top of the plank. It took all of my strength to keep the heavy, greasy barrel from slipping until Roy could climb down to stand beside me and help me lower it to the ground. We cautiously rolled the barrel down the plank, and then lifted it upright. My relief at its immobility made me disregard that it was stored three feet from our house.

Roy's automatic assumption that I could do anything that he could do made me think that he was either determined to shatter my belief in my own incompetence or wanted to undermine my faith in his intelligence. But Roy was a smart guy, and his mother was no dummy, and at Coffee Point, I first began to doubt my creed that everything I did would end badly.

"Thanks," Roy said after he reattached the hand pump to the barrel. "That's always my least favorite job."

The basketball game was almost finished, and Wendy scooted over on the tote as Roy and I sat down next to her. "Dylan's good," she said as we watched him slam-dunk the ball. "And so is Alex," she added after he expertly made a layup. Wendy admired athletic ability unreservedly because she was maniacally competitive and was attracted to any activity that indisputably delineated winners from losers. One of the few times that I had wholly basked in her adulation was when we went ice skating at Pershing Square in downtown Los Angeles, and she discovered that I could skate better than she could.

Dylan had stripped off his shirt, and his wide back and dark blond chest hair glistened with perspiration. He dribbled the ball, using his larger body to block Alex. But Alex was faster and more agile and darted around him, harrying him relentlessly, repeatedly shooting out his arms in an attempt to steal the ball. Dylan's defensive posture, almost a standing crouch, reminded me of a mother animal protectively shielding her bouncing baby from a wolf.

Dylan couldn't get a clear shot and hesitated for a moment, before trying to evade Alex by moving to his right, which allowed Alex to reach out and snatch the ball from his hands. Alex spun around and immediately leapt in the air, releasing the ball. Dylan tried to block the shot by jumping up, and they collided in midair. Dylan put out his arms to steady himself while Alex bounced off his chest and fell to the ground as the ball swished through the net.

"Foul!" shouted Roy and Wendy simultaneously.

Dylan remained standing but Alex looked dazed although he appeared unhurt. I was reminded of my grandmother's belief that you could determine a man's character by bumping into him and seeing whether he caught you or looked out for himself. It bothered me that I thought Dylan could have caught Alex if he had tried.

Dylan apologized and offered his hand to Alex, who was seated on the ground. Alex looked skeptically at the outstretched hand but finally clasped it, allowing Dylan to lift him to his feet.

"We're not wrestling," he commented dryly while brushing the dirt from the back of his jeans.

Alex made the free throw and eventually beat Dylan by twelve points. They considered a rematch, but Wendy desperately wanted to play the next game. Dylan agreed to play her, because Alex had hurt his leg from his fall.

Alex hadn't said a word to me or even acknowledged my presence. My remorse for hurting his feelings was offset by the childish ebullience I derived from the terrible joke that I was keeping to myself: an Eskimo was giving me the cold shoulder.

"You're both good players," Wendy said as Dylan threw her the ball. She dribbled the ball and made a few shots, cursing vehemently each time she missed. Alex watched her play, and I walked over to apologize to him. His expression remained unchanged while I admitted that I had been a total asshole, which is possibly the saddest avowal that a man can make because it's never contradicted. Dylan and Wendy stopped playing as they, along with Roy, watched us, waiting to hear Alex's response to my apology.

"I hope that you'll give me another chance," I said finally.

Alex thought about it. Then a smirk crossed his face. "I guess I have to forgive you," he said. "I can't afford to lose a fan."

Wendy informed me later that she hadn't known that Alex was angry with me and when they were introduced, she had told him that I had said that he gave one of the best performances I'd ever seen. She'd laid it on thick, mentioning that in my e-mail I'd raved about his wolverine impersonation, suggesting that he should receive a MacArthur genius award for Yup'ik storytelling. It must have sounded horribly contrived, but fortunately very few artists are immune to being praised.

"There is something you can do to make it up to me," Alex said coolly.

"Sure," I said, willing to do anything to earn back his favor.

"Remember when you talked about the gay salmon swimming upstream?" he asked, referring to my first night in Anchorage at Ship Creek.

"Yeah," I said, remembering that I'd written down our conversation in my notebook the following morning.

"I want to use that," he said. "I'd like to develop it further for my next show." He studied my face, waiting to see how I'd respond. Smiling awkwardly, I tried to hide the feeling of desperation clawing at my stomach. I hadn't expected him to ask me for an idea of mine. That he thought it was valuable immediately established that I should keep it for myself. What if I was giving away the only good idea I would ever have? I resented him asking me for it but knew that it was the price I'd have to pay to reestablish our friendship.

"You can have it," I said, thinking that I wasn't giving him the idea so much as he was taking it.

"Thanks," he said, his smile finally becoming warm again. Alex's generous mood was further explained when he told me that he had just found out that he'd been cast in a small role in Dylan's movie. He was expecting the script to arrive on a plane that day because he would start shooting in two weeks.

I congratulated him and then we watched Dylan wipe the floor with Wendy. She played a good game but he was by far the better player. After they finished, we ate a late lunch at Dee's. She had prepared a pot of her famous chili con carne with two precious jars from her store of canned moose meat. Upon hearing that Dylan, Wendy, and I had never eaten moose, Dee and Roy claimed that they actually preferred it to other meats.

I was uneasy about eating a moose. It was a cartoon animal from my childhood, and my trial taste was hesitant. Moose was as sweetly familiar as beef but as strangely exotic as sampling a tree or a rock. But after a few more bites I decided that Bullwinkle wasn't that funny anyway and asked for a second helping. While I ate the delicious chili, I could almost imagine myself being slowly transformed into an Alaskan bite by bite.

After lunch, Alex and I volunteered to do the dishes while Dee read *Excellent Woman*, Wendy took a nap, and Roy and Dylan went to check Roy's net. I washed while Alex dried, and after we'd worked for a few minutes without speaking, I broke the silence.

"You've been quiet today," I said.

"I'm tired," he said wiping the last of the bowls.

"What have you been doing?" I said, wondering if he was going to mention Dylan spending the night.

"Dylan and I fucked till dawn."

His swagger in bagging that particular trophy revealed Alex's ancestral pride in a successful hunt.

"You seem pleased about that."

"Wouldn't you be?"

I smiled and nodded.

"He thought he was taking advantage of a dumb Eskimo, but I knew that he came over to Egegik to sleep with me. He thought I'd have to accept his apology because his body came with it. But Dylan doesn't know that Yup'ik hunters used to offer their wives to more successful hunters. They believed that you could acquire a great hunter's power by sexual transmission." Alex's face broke into a sly grin. "And I think artists are hunters who believe everything is fair game."

I laughed at the Yup'ik idea of sleeping your way to the top.

"Please don't let the idea that talent can be sexually transmitted get around," I said. "It will only make artists more whorish." I immediately regretted my remark, worrying that it was offensive. "I'm sorry. I'm not putting down your beliefs. I'm actually fascinated by them."

Alex rolled his eyes disdainfully. "I was angry with you because you insulted my grandmother. But if you go all sensitive on me, then I'll never forgive you."

We made a pact that he'd tell me when I was acting like an asshole and give me a heads up before I became a total asshole. We agreed that it's one of the primary duties of friendship.

"What happens if you sleep with someone untalented?" I asked, unable to stop thinking that a lack of talent could almost be considered a sexually transmitted disease.

Alex didn't answer me immediately as he continued to dry the large crock that had held the moose meat chili.

"You wouldn't lose your talent," he said after setting the crock on the counter. "But being untalented is bad luck so I wouldn't advise it."

"Does this talent transmission thing work for nonnatives?" I asked, thinking that it was another incentive to sleep with Dylan.

Alex smiled. "It just might."

SIXTEEN

D inner that night was a feast. In addition to Roy, Dylan, Wendy, and myself, Dee invited Alex, Karen, and Karen's granddaughter Rosalind. We had salmon prepared three ways: baked salmon with wild mushrooms that Dee had picked herself, grilled salmon with a ginger-lime marinade, and Alex contributed a jar of pickled salmon that looked like medical specimens floating in formaldehyde. The pickled salmon turned out to be delicious though, and over cocktails—Roy actually found the ingredients to make negronis—we polished off the entire jar.

Wendy prepared her disgustingly rich and creamy potatoes au gratin, along with haricots verts, corn on the cob, and a supposedly simple green salad where every ingredient had an elaborate rationale for being tossed together.

Roy grilled my steaks and salmon in Dee's yard and we kept him company by passing around a joint. Dee and Karen mildly disapproved of smoking pot and showed their discomfort by drinking red wine in the kitchen. Everyone could relax that evening because there had been an announcement that fishing in the Egegik District would be closed for twenty-four hours, starting at six p.m. Over dinner, Alex and Roy came up with a plan to take a boat upriver the next day to explore Becharof Lake.

The highlight of the meal was Dee's nagoonberry ice cream. I'm not sure whether it was the pot we had smoked or the chunks of dark Vahlrona chocolate she had mixed in, but nagoonberry ice cream was the most delicious dessert that I'd ever eaten.

Nagoonberries are wild and urbane, sweet and tart, heavenly and earthly. It tasted as if thirty-one flavors of ice cream had banded together in a temporary alliance for one night.

After dinner, the four women decided that they were going to have a ladies night and take a sauna together. The four men were relegated to taking a sauna after them, but Alex bowed out because he wanted to cross the river while it was still light out. Judging from the raucous laughter coming from the sauna, the ladies night was a great success. When they were finished, I saw the four women, wrapped in towels and bathrobes, leaving our yard and walking to Karen and Rosalind's house for a nightcap.

It was our turn to wash after the women had finished. Roy and I undressed in our bedroom and, after wrapping towels around our waists, we came downstairs to find Dylan waiting for us in the kitchen. He only began to remove his clothes after we came downstairs. Dylan had been quoted in a magazine interview as saying that he would be willing to do a full-frontal nude scene in a film, and I believed him because he always seemed to be rehearsing for it.

From my first day at Coffee Point, it was apparent that Dylan was an exhibitionist, but his striptease was never routine even though it followed a predictable pattern. He started by unbuttoning his shirt, then pausing to ask a question that demanded a reply. "Should we take beers out to the sauna?" Having gained our attention, he scratched himself, before quickly removing the shirt, allowing us to see his overdeveloped body packed into a tight white wife beater. He questioned the response; in this case, Roy's warning that drinking alcohol in a sauna was a bad idea. "It won't hurt to have one beer," he said while I gaped at him. With one swift motion, he lifted his undershirt revealing his hair-covered six-pack.

Pulling the shirt up and out to reach around his powerful chest, he tugged it hard, ensuring that his face would only be obscured for a moment. Then he argued something else, gesturing broadly with his big arms and shrugging his wide shoulders, making it impossible to ignore his bare strapping torso. "Look, if you pussies start feeling dizzy, then stop drinking," he said. He urgently jerked open his belt as if he was pulling the ripcord on a parachute. His pants plummeted from his slim hips, puddling on the floor. He kept our focus by insulting us. "Although I'm not sure you two queens aren't always dizzy." Dylan stood there in a pair of clinging black athletic briefs, his cock pressed against the fabric, looking like a nervous performer backstage clumsily peeking through the closed curtain before it was time to go on. Then he shucked his underwear and, completely buck-naked, said something else, something flirtatious or provocative: "Let's go get steamy."

He wrapped a towel around his waist.

Dylan told me to grab three bottles of beer from the refrigerator. I did as I was told even though I felt high because Dylan had rolled a fattie that we had smoked while the women were taking their sauna. The three of us ran out to the sauna, trying to evade the mosquitoes that waited for naked men to return to bathe each night with the same anticipatory patience that men waited for the salmon to return to the river each year. We hung our towels on hooks outside the sauna's door, and then quickly slipped inside the sweltering room. Any mosquito biting my arm after I entered would have found my blood a cool and refreshing drink in contrast with the temperature of the sauna. Along the back wall was a ledge, two and half feet above the floor, and I sat down on it while Roy read a thermometer aloud.

"One hundred seventy degrees," he crowed. A small picture window looked out over the beach and the pinkish orange sun hung low in the sky. I still must have been buzzing from the pot because it weirdly resembled a salmon cake returning to the sea.

"It's fucking hot," Dylan grumbled as he sat down next to me.

"Let's get it up to one-eighty," Roy said, dipping a coffee-can ladle into a barrel of water. He doused the rocks piled around the stove, causing a hissing cloud of steam to rise into the air.

"You trying to cook my meat?" Dylan asked.

"It has to be thoroughly cooked to kill any germs," Roy said.

"Sounds like you're going to eat me."

"We just want to make sure whatever you're serving doesn't make anyone sick," I said while glancing furtively at Dylan's dick before the additional steam obscured the view. Checking out another man's penis was similar to observing a celebrity in a restaurant; it was all right to look but to be caught staring was uncool. Dylan's starmeat didn't have any more charisma than Roy's or mine. But then again, most penises are like actors; when they're not performing, it's hard to believe they possess any talent whatsoever.

"Open those beers," Dylan said as he smacked my thigh with his palm, the spot that he touched becoming a new locus of warmth. Opening the three bottles added a fine mist of Alaskan Summer Ale to the room's already stifling humidity. I took an icy swig of my beer and stared at the bleary sun wavering above the ocean's horizon. The sun had the glazed appearance of an overworked employee, exhausted from weeks of overtime, impatient to finish her shift, knowing she'll have to return to work in four hours.

Roy stood up and put on a pair of oven mitts before bending over to add another log to the fire. The flickering light from the wood stove revealed the fine tailoring of Roy's birthday suit, and Dylan whistled at him and said, "Nice outfit." Roy looked fetching wearing nothing but a pair of oven mitts and he was amused when I told him so.

"Do I look hot?" he asked, causing us to groan. He picked up a thick branch and threw it into the stove. He tended the fire as if the logs needed diligent supervision to prevent them from goofing off. His eyes never strayed far from the stove's window and at the first sign of slacking, he'd open the door to prod the burning wood with a poker. He wanted the logs to fear for their jobs—they could always be replaced—and he set an example for any laggards by continually adding more wood to the flames.

"Hey," he asked when he sat on the other side of me, "did you see the whale?"

"No," I said. "I walked down to where you saw it, but I didn't see anything." That afternoon Roy had spotted a beluga whale offshore, and even though we both thought it would be long gone, I had walked down to the beach to see it.

"You walked down to the beach to see a whale?" Dylan asked. He raised his bulging arm to take a sip of beer revealing a tuft of underarm hair.

"Not exactly. I'm not allowed to walk the beach," I said. "Whenever I try, Dee or Mary show up and insist on giving me a ride."

"Really? They never offer me a lift," Dylan said. "They must not like me because they just honk and wave."

When Dylan was naked it was impossible to imagine why he wasn't highly regarded by everyone, but I suspected that they probably did dislike him. I felt sorry for Dylan but was also pleased to think that they liked me better than him.

"They just think you're hardier than Nelson," Roy suggested in an attempt to console him.

"Maybe they're afraid of giving a ride to an ex-con," Dylan wondered.

"Are you kidding?" I asked. "Karen would go out of her way to pick you up. She'd love comparing notes about strip searches and lock-up."

During dinner, Karen had talked about working in the prison pharmacy in Seward. "It's the best job I've ever had," she had said. "There's no pressure; they're not going anywhere. And it's more interesting than filling prescriptions on the outside. I'll read a story about a murderer in Anchorage, then a year later I'm giving him tranquilizers. What's he got to be nervous about? He's the killer; he should be giving us tranquilizers."

Dylan squeezed my leg affectionately as I took another sip of beer. Since I was seated between two handsome, naked men, one of whom had touched me twice, it was reasonable to consider man on man action. Other men talked about sex in steam rooms with panting ardor but the fierce heat obliterated every desire of mine except for my longing to escape. In saunas, the last thing I wanted to do was to have sex. If Dylan and Roy became aroused, I would have asked them to fan me with their stiff cocks before asking them to do anything else.

Roy threw another ladle of water on the rocks, making the sauna more insufferable.

"I'm reading your novel," Dylan said as he lightly patted my leg again. "I love it."

Dylan had kept after me until I gave him the first eighty pages of my novel. To be honest, I'd expected the pages to sit unread in his room and was delighted to hear that he'd already started them. I thought Roy looked uneasy because he hadn't asked to read it.

"It makes me wish that I knew your mother," Dylan said, "Did she really die on your birthday?"

"Yes," I said, nodding, thinking that detail alone would establish me as the narrator in everyone's minds. But I had decided it was too bizarre and darkly comic not to use.

"I loved the description of your ice-cream cake melting in the sun as she dies along the side of the road," he continued. "Then when I thought it was in danger of becoming maudlin, the narrator complains that he'll spend the rest of his life blowing out his birthday candles wishing that his mother was alive. It was perfect."

I explained that I'd made that observation to Wendy one time and she had laughed. We had a tradition where, every year, she always called me up early on the morning of my birthday. "Happy Depressing Birthday!" she'd scream when I answered the telephone. Her birthday salutation always perversely cheered me up, and I found that I looked forward to it each year, as it made a melancholy day almost bearable.

"And I love your dad," Dylan said. "Is he really that cool?"

"Yeah" I replied, not feeling that it was plausible to deny that the father in my book was based upon my dad. I had made him an electrician instead of a plumber, but that didn't really camouflage his identity.

"Oh, and I loved your weeds/wigs story about the guy in the noisy bar who hears like a queen," Dylan said.

Roy had been listening to our conversation and he turned to me and smiled. "Your weeds/wigs story? That's interesting."

Evidently, I'd also loved Roy's story and had incorporated it into my revision of the novel. I really should have asked for his permission before swiping his story. Although I didn't feel too guilty because Roy wasn't going to use it and I had given it an ending.

Dylan turned to Roy. "Have you read it?"

"Um, no," he said, sounding defensive.

"Really?" said Dylan. "If my boyfriend was a writer, I'd be interested in reading what he was working on."

"It's really none of your business," Roy said, his anger flaring up suddenly, making the already hot room seem even warmer. "I'm interested in his novel. I just wasn't sure if I was supposed to ask to read it before it was finished."

"You could have asked me," I said. I had come out fishing with him and was eager to learn all about his life, and I suddenly resented that he hadn't shown a reciprocal interest in my life.

"You send out mixed signals," Roy said, "When I hear you moan, 'I don't know what I'm doing,' it doesn't sound like an invitation to read what you're writing."

"Obviously you've never dated an artist before," Dylan said smugly. "We need to give voice to our doubts. It's part of the process. Another artist would understand that."

"Really?" Roy said, employing the same "gotcha" tone of voice that Dylan had used on him. "Because I'd think an artist might appreciate having the perspective of someone who wasn't so self-absorbed. Most artists don't create their work exclusively for other artists."

"The hardest part of creating something is getting to the point where you're ready to share it with an audience," Dylan said. "After that the opinions of other people don't really matter."

"I can tell," Roy said. "I've seen some of your movies where obviously no one cared about the audience."

I thought Dylan might be offended but he just grinned. "Oh, yeah. I've made some bombs. That's what happens when I don't follow my instincts. For one reason or another, I didn't trust my instincts. Nelson, always trust your gut."

"I never know what that means," I said. "My gut instinct isn't trustworthy because it's always the same. I have butterflies in my stomach about every decision I make and everything I do."

I must have been really wasted because for a moment my mind played with the idea of butterflies in your stomach as an intestinal parasite that artists and performers are particularly prone to—a bohemian tapeworm—but then I focused on Roy who had become awfully quiet. I felt that if I threw a ladle of water on him, he would erupt in a cloud of hissing steam. But he turned to me and placed his hand on my leg. "I'd love to read your book," he said.

"All right," I said, suddenly convinced that he would hate it. I imagined Roy breaking up with me, because he couldn't bear the thought of having to read my writing for the rest of his life.

"I do have one criticism," Dylan said, pausing to see my reaction.

I bridled inwardly but pretended that I wanted to hear a criticism of something that I'd labored on for almost three years. But now that he'd spoken, I would insist on hearing what he had to say. If there was the slightest chance that Dylan, or anyone else, had an idea or suggestion that could help improve my novel then I wanted to hear it.

"You have to change the opening line," he insisted.

I was surprised. "I can't believe you don't like, 'Todd Greco still felt empty inside even with a big cock up his ass.'"

Dylan didn't smile as I had expected. He gave a slight shrug.

"It's funny but it's the wrong tone. Your book's about a family. It's not about sex, it's about love."

He was right and that troubled me. I was, quite frankly, somewhat mystified that I hadn't realized that myself. When a sex addict suggests toning down the sex, you've definitely gone overboard. I had my own doubts about that opening line but had been reluctant to change it because whenever I said the line aloud, it always got a laugh. But in reworking the novel, the narrator's sex life decreased in importance as the father's and brother's lives assumed greater prominence.

"The problem is that I haven't come up with something better."

"You will," Dylan said. "You're really talented."

I was grateful to hear him say that. It's not that I regarded Dylan as a discerning literary critic, but I couldn't dismiss him as a brainless hunk either. (It's hard not to resent intelligent people who also happen to be good-looking, because they seem like members of the elite DNA-list crowd who've been admitted to an exclusive club while the rest of us are kept cooling our heels on the sidewalk.) Dylan was the first person who'd read my novel since I'd started working on it again. I was considering changing my life completely, and I desperately wanted someone to tell me that I wasn't making a huge mistake and that I could become a novelist.

"I'd want to play you in the movie," Dylan said. "But now I guess I'd have to play your dad."

It was a disturbing thought because Dylan was close to my dad's age when my mother had died. Dylan and my father also shared a physical resemblance, as my Dad was a beefy ex-jock who worked out regularly. Pushing the disturbing Oedipal image from my thoughts, I lingered over his praise of my novel. Dylan Fabizak—who was recognized as a talented artist—had said that I was really talented. It's true he was an alcoholic and had other addictions; however, history is chockfull of unsavory artists with great taste. If pigs can be used to find truffles, then why can't a sex pig sniff out talent? "Is it possible for me to be hungry again?" Roy asked.

"We smoked pot, so you could have the munchies," I said.

"Did I tell you that I ate stinkheads last night?" Dylan announced.

"Did you meet Alex's uncle?" Roy asked.

"No," he said, shaking his head. "He had to fly up to Dillingham for the day. Alex wasn't home when I got there so I wandered around town. I got to talking to an old woman, and she offered to let me try some of her stinkheads."

"How were they?" I asked.

"Let me put it this way: I considered rimming her to get the taste out of my mouth."

"C'mon," Roy said skeptically. "How does eating stinkheads help you create your character?"

"I'm not trying to create a character," Dylan said forcefully. "I'm trying to be him. Stanislavski said we're trying to give birth to a new being—the actor in the part." He stood up and poured several ladles of water over his head. The cascading stream made his chest hair billow like seaweed on rocks in the surf.

"I love saunas," he said. "But I have to stay out of them." He took a bottle of shower gel and squeezed a small amount into his right palm.

"Why's that?" I asked.

"They're too tempting," he said. "The last time I used the steam room at my gym in L.A., I ended up having sex with a deaf guy. I don't know whether it was the sign language or what but he gave me the best hand job I've ever had. Better than I could have done myself."

"Did he give you those scratches on your shoulders?" Roy asked.

Dylan turned his head to examine long red scratch marks on the back of each of his shoulders. I hadn't noticed them until Roy pointed them out.

"I don't kiss and tell."

"We know it was Alex," Roy said.

"No wonder he plays all those animals," Dylan said smirking. "He's a tiger. We did it in some deserted shack. On one of those white plastic tubs."

Immediately, I imagined a tote labeled "Sex" in black marker on its sides. Roy stood up to wash next to Dylan.

"Have you two done it outside yet?" Dylan asked as he began to lather up his body, paying special attention to his ass and balls.

"Not here," Roy said. "The mosquitoes would turn it into group sex."

"And what's wrong with group sex?" Dylan asked before pouring several more ladles of water over his body to rinse off.

"Have either of you ever had a threesome?" he asked. I'd been expecting him to bring up the threesome again.

"Sure," Roy said.

"I haven't," I admitted as a trickle of sweat rolled down my back. It felt like my body kept some perspiration in reserve for purely social occasions.

"You're kidding?" Dylan said, sounding as if the natural progression for all men was sex with yourself, sex with another person, then sex with two people and so on. By his reckoning, a man who fucked a thousand individuals but never slept with two people at the same time could still be considered a virgin.

"I was asked once," I said, recalling an incident back in a bar in Milwaukee. "But one guy was a hottie and one guy was a nottie."

"Oh, yeah," Dylan said knowingly. "The hottie and the nottie."

"I'd be afraid that I'd have to keep the conversation going in a threesome," I said, feeling light-headed from the beer and the heat. I proceeded to demonstrate. "'Fred, you're an architect? Well, Bob here's from Chicago and he works in a building designed by Louis Sullivan.'"

"Baby," Dylan said as he patted my knee again. "If you have time to talk, then you've never had good sex."

"Nelson's had good sex," Roy argued.

"The whole idea of being in a threesome seems overwhelming," I said. "I can't imagine deliberately choosing to be in a relationship where it would be even more difficult to pick a restaurant or decide which movie to see."

"Life could be easier in a threesome," Dylan offered. "Maybe you wouldn't have to make any decisions. You might find yourself with two big studs telling you what to do." Dylan began to speak in a dumb-lug Brooklyn accent. "You'll eat Ethiopian food and watch Clint Eastwood movies when we say so, motherfucker."

It was my turn to wash after Dylan sat down. As I stood up from the ledge, I felt slightly dizzy, but pouring dippers of cool spring water from the barrel over myself temporarily revived me. I felt self-conscious about standing naked in front of Dylan and couldn't decide whether to show him my ass or my dick. I didn't have an opinion about which was my best side, which really is something that every gay man should determine at some point in his life. I decided to stand in profile, which was an acceptable compromise, but was also wishy-washy. When I finished rinsing, I moved to take my seat, lurching unsteadily on my feet and Roy sprang up to grab me.

"I feel sick," I said, suddenly overcome with nausea. Spots floated in front of my eyes and my mouth flooded with warm saliva.

"I told you not to drink in a sauna," Roy said as he grabbed me by the arms and helped move me toward the door. Once I was outside, the cool air felt refreshing against my damp skin. Tendrils of steam wafted from our bodies, making us momentarily appear to be the hottest men in Alaska.

Dylan had followed us outside. "We had wine with dinner," he said as he moved next to me.

"Put your head down," Roy ordered. His arm was wrapped tightly around my waist. I sat down on a wooden bench and stared at my ankles. In a few minutes the prickly numb sensation of vertigo was replaced by the distinctive backstabbing pinpricks of mosquito bites. Several of them flew past my ears, screeching, "Yummeeee" and my head shot up in a panic. Being touched by the cold shackles of the food chain has a way of clearing your head and restoring your equilibrium.

"Let's go in," I suggested. "The mosquitoes are eating me alive."

"You're sure you're okay?" Roy asked as I stood up. He told me to put my arms around Dylan and him as they supported me back to the house. The heat from their bodies warmed me as we walked.

Once we reached the kitchen, Roy said, "Help me get him upstairs," as he continued to support me. I tried to reassure him that I wasn't going to pass out. The stairway was too small for more than one person at a time and Roy went ahead of me while Dylan followed behind me in case I fell. I took my towel and wrapped it around my waist to avoid mooning him as we ascended. When we reached the landing at the top of the stairs, I said, "That was embarrassing."

Roy took me by the hand. "I was afraid you were going to hit the stove," he said, watching me closely. I felt much better, almost refreshed, and couldn't decide whether the sauna or almost fainting was responsible for my sensation of well-being.

"You're sure you're okay?" Roy asked.

"I'm okay."

His face softened. "You scared me out there." He glanced over his shoulder to Dylan who was standing behind me, then took me by the shoulders and kissed me tenderly on the lips. I kissed him back as Dylan began to kiss me passionately on the back of my neck. Dylan placed his hands on the back of my arms and pressed his body against mine.

Roy and Dylan switched places by kissing their way around me. When Dylan faced me, he pressed his body against mine. I could smell the shampoo from his damp hair and feel his dick brushing against my legs. "You've fully recovered," he said with a nod down toward my dick.

Dylan's lips covered mine, his beard more bristly and rough than Roy's, and then French-kissed me. His tongue must have been claustrophobic because it panicked, thrashing around in the confined space of my mouth. Immediately I decided that, not only was Roy a better kisser than Dylan, but that I was a better kisser than he was. Somehow it came as no surprise that Dylan was a lousy kisser—he must always be convinced that anyone kissing him was already swooning from his own good fortune.

I tried to tame Dylan's tongue, and after several tries, he let me take the lead.

That night Roy and Dylan made me wonder why having two lovers had never become a middle-class convention in American life, like owning two cars or two telephones. They blew me like an Olympic relay team, passing my dick back and forth like a baton. Roy's mouth was on my dick pushing me toward the finish line when Dylan made his move, kissed me hard, letting my hands roam his chest and shoulders, the scent of him shooting me over the edge, snatching Roy's victory away by a nose.

Afterward Roy ran downstairs to take a leak while Dylan rolled over and lightly ran his finger down my abdomen, tracing the hair between my navel and groin. "Do you think you could go again?" he asked softly. He propped himself up on his elbow, displaying his muscular torso. His body hair was a built-in negligee, fitting him perfectly, revealing and concealing the hard flesh underneath.

"Could you fuck me right now?" he asked playfully.

"I'm not sure," I said as his hand toyed with my stiffening cock.

"This is our getting-to-blow-you sex," he said. "Next time, when it's just the two of us, we're going to fuck."

I reached out tentatively to touch his chest and decided that the combination of hard flesh and soft hair was one of the all-time great combinations, the sum greater than the parts, up there with other classic pleasure-giving teams like cake and ice cream, or gin and dry vermouth.

I heard Roy coming up the stairs and pulled my hand away from Dylan's chest with a guilty start. Dylan calmly rolled onto his back, seconds before Roy appeared around the corner of the alcove-bed, carrying a towel. Dylan and I looked as if we'd been waiting patiently for him, although I hoped Roy wouldn't notice that my dick was stiffer than when he'd departed.

Roy climbed into the bed and he and Dylan swabbed me down, making me feel like a racecar being maintained by a pit crew. Soon I was ready to go again but wasn't sure if it was still my turn. Luckily gay men in a threesome instinctively draw straws and the man with the longest straw is done next. A quick survey revealed Dylan was the winner and, without saying a word, he pulled Roy on top of him.

Roy's eyes met mine as we exchanged a smile at Dylan's presumption. It wasn't until much later that I understood that instant of shared mirth between us was in some ways the most intimate moment of the entire night.

Dylan loved being the center of our attention. I took further advantage of being able to get my hands and mouth on his body. He communicated his likes and dislikes with moans and sighs—harder, softer, nibble here, chew there. At one point he pushed my head around his body like a computer mouse on a trackpad. He took an excessively long time to come, misleading us several times into thinking he was on the brink of an orgasm. At first, I didn't resent the length of time he took because he conveyed how much he enjoyed himself. But after a while, I began to think he didn't want to get off the stage. In my harsh review of Dylan's performance, I'd point out he probably thought he was receiving a standing ovation whenever his dick leapt to its feet.

"We're almost there," Dylan murmured at one point, sounding like the captain of a ship, enjoying the view, oblivious that his crew was slaving away down belowdeck.

When Dylan finally finished, he came with a loud theatrical moan. He immediately swatted away further ministrations, as his penis became too sensitive to be touched. After we rested for a minute, Dylan reached down from the bed to grab a pair of underwear from the floor. I noticed with annoyance that they were mine— we all wore the same brand but I was the only one wearing navy. After using them to wipe himself off, he tossed them back to the floor and rolled over on top of Roy.

"Now I get to fuck the boss," he said gleefully as he pinned him down.

He kissed Roy brutally on the mouth then tenderly on the cheek before nuzzling his neck. Roy chuckled as Dylan's lips moved slowly down to his chest. When his tongue hit his left nipple, Roy moaned appreciatively. The response made Dylan linger a second. A gasp confirmed that he discovered Roy's turn-on and get-off switches. Dylan began to chew energetically. I was unsure about what I should be doing. I awkwardly tried to kiss Roy's neck when suddenly Dylan reached out his right arm and grabbed the back of my head; pushing me down toward Roy's other nipple. Roy growled blissfully. When Dylan placed my hand on Roy's dick, I immediately thought he was trying to get out of another job. But as I began to carpal-funnel Roy, Dylan lifted his head and began to whisper a pornographic story in his ear.

"You're hiking in Chugach Park," Dylan said in a deep compelling voice. "And we meet on the trail." Roy's dick tossed and turned. He loved impulsive sex in the wild. A few weeks before, the blowjobs we'd traded on a hike along the Little Susitna River had forever changed my definition of outdoor recreation.

Dylan continued, "My sweaty shirt sticks to my chest and arms and you check me out. I check you out, too, and I like what I see." As I worked Roy's nipple with my tongue, he began to play with the one that Dylan had abandoned. I felt like an inconsiderate lover because I hadn't immediately taken it over with my free hand. Roy became stiffer as Dylan spun out his tale. When he said, "I'm gonna fuck you," Roy's cock spasmed in my hand like a polygraph needle revealing the truth.

As I listened to Dylan, I thought that if he ever wanted to offer his services to a charity, he should consider reading pornography to the blind. He was a virtuoso of dirty talk; his word play filled with active verbs fucking passive nouns. Meanwhile I started to feel like Dylan's writer's assistant—his amanuensis—furiously scribbling with Roy's pen until either the ink ran out or he finished his story. But as the story progressed, it became apparent that Dylan was also telling me a tale.

"I reach down to pick a wildflower, and you stop me by grabbing my thick forearm." Dylan turned his head and winked at me, before he reached down to grip my hard on. "I make a fist to make my muscles pop. I love that it turns you on—I love making you hard because I want you. I want you more than any guy I've ever wanted."

Dylan didn't take his hand off me as I fantasized that I would keep beanstalking in size. I became so engrossed by Dylan's filthy story that he lost my attention completely. I approached an instant of delightful oblivion where thought's impossible and sensation rules. I ceased analyzing Dylan, Roy, or myself, quit making comparisons, and stopped observing anything or anyone, as my stream of consciousness dwindled to a trickle. I was sans similes, sans words, sans everything.

Although my hand never stopped working, I forgot about Roy until Dylan said, "I'm gonna fuck you. I'm gonna fuck both of you!" Roy came with an anguished gasp and the spray of cum on my hand pushed me over the edge and I came immediately.

One of the virtues of pornographic literature is that the reader can reach a satisfying conclusion long before the author does, and Dylan didn't have to finish his story before we reached Happy Endings. He kissed Roy possessively on the lips, then laid his head on his chest and looked up at me, satisfied, before he closed his eyes.

We lay in bed for a half an hour, draped over each other in a tangle of limbs. "Dudes, that was hotter than the sauna," Dylan said when he removed one of his legs from underneath one of mine. He declined to stay the night, telling us the bed was too small for all three of us to sleep together. He stood up and then bent down to kiss us both goodnight.

Before leaving, Dylan looked at us in turn and then he laughed strangely before he went downstairs.

When we were alone I became aware that I hadn't enjoyed watching Roy have sex with another guy. It felt like we had gone out for an intimate dinner at a restaurant and the handsome waiter had sat down to eat with us. Now you might enjoy his company for an evening but you'd only need to have that experience once to know that you never wanted to repeat it. But Dylan had also said that he loved making me hard and wanted me more than any other guy. It might have been poetic license but it did seem kind of romantic for a fuck story. I was too exhausted to think it through coherently. Perhaps the impulse to sleep immediately after sex was a natural response to prevent our brains from thinking about whether the sex meant something.

Roy turned to me, our heads facing each other on our pillows. It felt awkward for an instant until we both began to giggle.

"You got your threesome," Roy said.

"Did you guys plan that ahead of time?"

"We talked about it down on the beach after dinner. It wasn't definite. Dylan wasn't supposed to do anything unless I started kissing you. That was the signal."

"You could've warned me."

"I'd actually decided against it until I saw you standing there looking dizzy and vulnerable. I really had a sudden impulse to kiss you."

It sounds sickeningly sweet but Roy delivered his confession in a scientific monotone that made his impulsive behavior always sound logical. I was touched anyway and moved over in bed and wrapped my arms around him.

"He's a terrible kisser," I said, which made Roy smile.

"What the hell was he doing with his tongue?" he asked.

"He was demonstrating how a salmon swims upstream."

To clarify my point, I stuck my tongue in Roy's mouth and flippered it convulsively.

"He's a good storyteller," I admitted, still bothered by their love scene where I played the stagehand. I couldn't decide whether my jealousy stemmed from their shared intimacy, or whether I questioned my ability to tell a pornographic story as well as Dylan did. (Although pornography's the only branch of literature where success is measured by losing your reader; if someone finishes a pornographic story, the writer's failed.) The problem I often had with pornography wasn't the sex; it was the poorly constructed narrative. If a hunky telephone repairman came on to me, I'd have to insist that he fix my telephone before we had hot sex, because I couldn't relax and enjoy myself knowing that I might be missing important calls.

"Perfect liars should be good storytellers," Roy said with a yawn.

"I don't think he's lied to us," I said, surprised by his open contempt. Roy reminded me that Dylan had told us his method of telling the perfect lie.

"I thought about that later," he said. "How fucked up is it that he's given it some thought and found a system that works for him?"

"I didn't take him seriously," I said as I reconsidered what Dylan had told us. "I thought he was just entertaining us with a cynical observation about human nature."

Roy looked at me closely then grinned mischievously. "That's the problem with perfect liars: you never know when they're telling the truth."

SEVENTEEN

Around six-thirty the next morning, I awoke to raindrops pattering against the metal roof. Alaskans don't consider rain to be bad weather, and I knew our trip upriver wouldn't be canceled by anything short of a hurricane. Roy had already led me on wet hikes, drizzling mountain bike rides, and drenching kayaking trips where paddling through the air was indistinguishable from paddling through the water.

Adopting Roy's optimistic belief that he was always half-dry, I was grateful to learn that my capacity to be miserable in the outdoors was far less than I had anticipated. Not that I'm claiming to be hardy, but I made my peace with Alaska's climate once I began to regard damp clothing as replacing essential moisture lost to the blood-thirsty mosquitoes.

It still bothered me that Dylan had demonstrated that he knew how to satisfy Roy better than I did. And—this stung bitterly—proved that he was a better storyteller. (At least in first-person narratives where the speaker threatens to fuck you slow and hard.) It was a blunder that made getting stuck in a tar pit pale in comparison; I had willingly arranged for my boyfriend to cheat on me—in front of me—and then had been convinced that he had grounds to look elsewhere.

Roy didn't stir when I slipped out of bed. His expression was tightly focused, making him look like he was concentrating on sleeping and in danger of forgetting how. The house was cold, and after throwing on Roy's University of Alaska sweatshirt, I went downstairs to light the diesel stove. Roy had shown me how to let the diesel fuel drip into a pan at the bottom of the stove, and then how to light a sheet of paper and ignite the fuel in the pan. Diesel fuel doesn't ignite explosively like gasoline but each time I lit the stove, I always felt an outsized sense of accomplishment and relief.

At Coffee Point, I relished knowing that I had no place to go, no calls to be returned, and no e-mails to answer. My obligations were to write every day, learn how to drive a standard, and fish with Dee. I hoarded my mornings like a miser of minutes.

I'd been writing for several hours when Roy joined me in the kitchen. He was still in his underwear and had just poured himself a mug of coffee when we heard a frenzied rapping on the door. Roy yelled, "C'mon in," and Wendy entered the room. "Hi, Gays!" she chirped before pulling back the hood of her sweatshirt from her head, and removing her green rain slicker.

"Dee wondered what happened to you this morning," Wendy said to me. I had skipped my driving lesson, because I had assumed that since we were taking a day off from fishing that we were also taking a day off from my driver's education.

"She's not mad," Wendy said before a frown suddenly appeared on her face. "It stinks in here."

"B.O. or butt?" Roy asked.

"Is one preferable to the other? It smells like men."

Roy had a hierarchy of offensive body odors. Bad breath was more tolerable than B.O., which was preferable to what he termed "stinky balls," which were slightly more bearable than what he called "dirty butt." He insisted that mild funky B.O. generated by three guys living in a small house was to be expected, while maintaining that there was never an excuse for a dirty butt. Wendy listened attentively because his delightfully bonkers reasoning complemented her innate desire to establish a pecking order for everything on the planet. She agreed with him about a dirty butt but argued that bad breath trumped both B.O. and stinky balls because it was more in your face. They were both mental but, when pressed, I sided with her, telling them about a college professor whose breath was so bad that I swore you could smell it when he left a message on my voice mail.

There was a spirited competition to top my story with other anecdotes about reeking faculty.

"Keep your voices down," I said. "Dylan's still sleeping."

Wendy impatiently rolled her eyes. "Shouldn't he be up by now? Or does his character sleep in late?"

Roy rummaged in the sink for a coffee cup for Wendy. "His character does nothing," he said as he washed a cup for her. "I don't think he cleans anything besides his blender."

Dylan made and drank a protein shake every afternoon because he didn't want to lose his prison-made muscle before his comeback role.

Roy shook his head. "He didn't bring any food to share."

"He did save your life," Wendy pointed out. "I think you owe him a few meals."

Roy grinned. "But that's another reason to resent him for being cheap. I feel like he should act heroic, not be counting every penny."

"Is that why your mom never gives him a ride?" I asked Roy.

"Maybe he has stinky balls," Wendy said practically.

Roy and I looked at each other, each of us trying to decide whether we should tell her about our threesome.

"Not really," Roy said causing me to snicker and prompting Wendy to demand an explanation.

"Let's just say we can vouch that his balls are pleasantly scented," I said.

An expression of disgust filled her face. "You had a threesome? Ugh." She gave a brief expletive-filled condemnation of men, memorably describing our stiff pricks as lampposts shadowing streetwalkers.

"Do lesbians have threesomes?" Roy asked.

"Sort of," she said. "We call them, 'couple counseling.'"

Wendy accepted a cup of coffee as Roy announced that he would make us pancakes for breakfast. We watched as he began to assemble ingredients and remove bowls and pans from shelves underneath the kitchen counter. Roy enjoyed cooking but fixed meals as if they had to be repaired. He'd follow a recipe until he got it up and running, then tinker with it by adding or subtracting ingredients. Sometimes his culinary contraptions were inspired (Moroccan-style spaghetti sauce seasoned with cinnamon); at other times you suspected his patched-together food had broken down on your plate (Tofu Stroganoff comes to mind).

"It's pancakes from a mix," he said apologetically. "But we have real maple syrup."

"Sold in an imitation ceramic jug made out of plastic," I added, thinking that the container of syrup could be a symbol of American culture; prized authenticity surrounded by unconvincing phoniness.

Within minutes, gusts of wind slapped the house with sheets of rain. "Alex won't cross the river in this," Roy declared as he poured pancake mix into a large bowl.

"I guess we're not going upriver," I said, looking at the windows, which rattled from the pelting rain.

"It might let up," Roy suggested as he added water and began to stir.

"This rain can fuck me in the ass," Wendy growled.

I didn't want to cancel our trip. Traveling up the Egegik River to Becharof Lake had already become a magical journey in my mind. According to Roy, it was the second largest lake in Alaska, fifteen miles by thirty-five, up to six hundred feet deep in places, with the second largest run of salmon in the world. It was a natural spectacle, he claimed, and wherever you looked down in the water, you would see glowing red salmon swimming below. I pictured Becharof Lake as the world's largest koi pond.

"It's too bad," Roy said. "I wanted to show you an archaeological site that I found last year. As far as I can tell it's not marked on any surveys."

"Can we go there before we leave?" I asked, eager to see a real archaeological site.

He shrugged. "We might not have any more days off. And, chances are, the weather will be worse than this. It's too bad because an untouched site is worth seeing. There are stone tools lying right on the ground."

Roy described a bluff above the lake that was littered with dozens of slate ulus and scrapers. "Without even looking," he said. "I found a beautiful hand axe carved out of greenstone." His deep voice became filled with awe, making him sound entrancing. It occurred to me that Roy was actually quite good at revealing how he felt when he spoke about the things that he loved. I couldn't help but wonder if his voice also became animated when he discussed me.

Dylan's bedroom door swung open and he appeared, bare-chested, wearing a pair of blue flowered surfing shorts. His tousled hair made him look like a satyr with mussed horns.

"I thought I heard Wendy's demure voice," he said sarcastically.

"Good morning, third wheel," she said.

Dylan grinned smugly. "Have you been talking to my bitches?"

"Your *what*?" Roy asked.

"My bitches," Dylan repeated with a smirk, pouring himself a cup of coffee.

"We're not your bitches," Roy said firmly.

"Don't mess with him," warned Wendy. "He's holding a spatula."

"Haven't you heard?" Dylan said to Roy. "In prison the weakest men are always the bitches."

Dylan leaned against the counter, sipping his coffee, letting us take in his muscles and tattoos, serving us notice that the scales of Justice are often tipped by a simple weigh-in between opponents.

"You want a piece of me?" Roy asked, sounding absurdly as if he was quoting a line from a bad movie.

"He had a piece of you," Wendy said. She wasn't paying attention to them because she was reading a supermarket tabloid that was two years out-of-date. "And a piece of Nelson. And you had a piece of him. Blessed are the piece-takers."

At first I thought Roy couldn't be serious about challenging Dylan to a fight. Until he set down the spatula. It was such a ludicrously melodramatic gesture that it convinced me that he was dangerously out of control.

Wendy looked up as Dylan set down his cup of coffee and stepped toward Roy who glared at him.

"I've had you," Dylan sneered, moving inches away from Roy's face. He glanced over at me and smiled, then turned back to Roy. "Nelson's going to be my bitch," he said.

When they started fighting, it never occurred to me that the two of them would trade blows. I wasn't used to men punching each other, because the closest my friends had ever come to physical violence was occasional backbiting.

Roy's first swing missed Dylan's face. He deflected the punch with his arm, causing the blow to land with a wallop on his bare chest. Dylan then decked Roy, his fist connecting solidly with his jaw, knocking him back onto the kitchen table, causing coffee cups to spill while plates and silverware went flying. Wendy cursed at them when she was splashed with coffee. Luckily, Roy landed on a kitchen chair, breaking his fall to the floor. Dylan gazed down at him, amused that Roy had challenged him.

"You took a swing and I took a swing," he said, offering him his hand. Roy refused his help. He stood up and suddenly popped Dylan in the kisser. Dylan's face changed color as he touched his lip to see whether he was bleeding. He grabbed Roy by the collar. Dylan looked incensed, and I recalled that he'd broken someone's arm in prison.

I pushed myself in between them, intending to separate them just as Roy took a poke and hit me painfully in the eye. The intense pain enraged me, and I shouted at them to stop. To my surprise, they obeyed me and stepped away from each other. Roy stood there, rubbing his jaw as I watched Dylan head into the bathroom to check on his lip.

"Great," Wendy said as she came over and examined my face. "Nelson's gonna have a black eye." She got some ice from the fridge and wrapped it in a towel. I sat down and held the ice against my eye.

It still didn't make sense to me why Roy had picked a fight with Dylan. At any other time, Dylan could have called Roy his bitch and they would have both laughed. Wendy must have been thinking the same thing. She turned to Roy and said in a low voice, "What was that all about? You're lucky he didn't kill you."

"He almost broke my jaw," Roy said respectfully as he rubbed the area where he'd been struck, which was red and slightly swollen. "I don't know. He helped himself to a cup of coffee, and somehow I didn't want to give him anything else. He's had our food, my job, my body, and Nelson's body. I'd given him enough. I'm not his bitch."

"All right," Wendy said, "but did you have to start brawling?"

"I didn't have to but I wanted to."

He smiled and so did Wendy. His eyes met hers but avoided mine. She began to clean up the mess as Roy began to pour pancake batter onto an iron griddle. I tried to understand why I hadn't seen Roy's anger coming and why I hadn't seen that Dylan had been deliberately trying to humiliate Roy ever since he came to Coffee Point. He had threatened to kiss me in front of him and then got Roy off to a story that was practically a declaration of love to me.

What disturbed me the most was that Roy hadn't concealed his feelings—I'd sensed his growing rage but I had ignored it because of my own confusion. Perhaps Roy wasn't tack-i-turn and Dylan wasn't being honest with me. And even worse for a writer, maybe I wasn't observant about anything.

Dylan came out of the bathroom and passed through the kitchen. "I'm going back to bed," he announced before returning to his room to sleep for another two hours.

The rain poured down harder after we finished our pancakes. Since our trip upriver was canceled and fishing was closed for the day,

Wendy suggested that the two of us should try to write another sketch before our meeting with Amanda. "It wouldn't hurt to have one more," she said.

I looked at Roy and he told me to go ahead. "I need to replace the radiator on my truck some time," he said. "I might as well do it today."

I asked if he needed any help, not really knowing what assistance I could offer him, as I had no knowledge of auto repair. "No," he said. "You two should write."

Roy smiled and appeared to be satisfied in some way. His fight with Dylan actually seemed to have put him in a good mood. He started whistling as he put on his jacket. Wendy noticed his cheerfulness also. "I love how guys just punch someone to make themselves feel better. It's great unless the guy happens to be the president."

Since our writing sessions tended to be loud and argumentative with frequent outbursts of laughter, Wendy and I decided to work at Dee's house and let Dylan sleep. As soon as we were outside, Wendy began to interrogate me.

"What the fuck were you thinking?"

I explained that Roy and Dylan had decided to start the threesome without discussing it with me beforehand. I didn't really have a choice in the matter.

"Oh, I understand. You were caught between a cock and a hard place."

"That would make a funny title for a gay porn movie," I suggested. But Wendy ignored my compliment, making me aware that she was upset with me. She tended to be her wittiest when she was pissed off, which was sometimes confusing because it appeared that she was trying to entertain the person she was angry with.

"You can't handle one boyfriend, let alone two."

"Dylan's not my boyfriend," I protested, although I found it incredibly exciting that we were even talking about that as a real possibility.

"Good idea. Give up Roy for a sex addict." She sighed. "You and Dylan Fabizak. What the hell do you see in him anyway?"

Her contempt provoked me into arguing in his favor. I considered his obvious physical attributes, suddenly focusing on his ears, which were surprisingly sexy, even though they looked like clamps holding his head in place.

Wendy must have been telepathic. "Don't you dare say because he's hot."

"He's ambitious. He's serious about his work," I said, thinking that they were character traits that he also shared with Roy. "He'd never bore me."

"A psychotic would never bore you either!" she shouted. "Well, maybe after killing thirty people it would start to grow old. . . ."

Even in the midst of a heated argument, we were both unable to resist following a humorous premise to its inevitable conclusion.

"I can't figure him out. I'll start to think that he's the most egotistical man alive, then he'll do something generous or thoughtful."

"Generous?" she sneered. "Because he gave you his dick?"

"He's also smart. He's well-read."

"Does he know what 'virga' is?"

"He might. He grew up in New Mexico."

"He's quick but that's not exactly the same as smart."

"He's disciplined," I continued. "He works out every day."

Dylan had rigged up a chin-up bar on the side of the storage shed and did reps every afternoon until his T-shirt was soaked with sweat.

"He works out because he's vain. That's the absolute minimum I expect from actors. Even if they're untalented, they can have a six-pack."

"Isn't it my obligation as a writer to acquire as much experience as possible?"

"Guess what, loser? You have a great imagination. Use it." Though her words were insulting, her tone was conciliatory.

Dee was working in her office when we arrived. We decided to write in Wendy's bedroom so as not to disturb her either. Wendy went upstairs ahead of me while I stayed downstairs to apologize to Dee for not showing up for my driving lesson at seven. She immediately asked me how I got my shiner.

"Roy and Dylan had a fight and I tried to break it up," I answered sheepishly.

She pondered that before she observed. "Hmm, I've never had two men fight over *me*."

"Me either."

"I'm impressed."

"So am I."

Both of us chuckled at the sound of amazement in my voice.

"I almost knocked on your door," Dee said. "But we can drive on the beach this afternoon. There won't be any traffic today."

"There's something I want to ask you," I said, remembering something that we'd discussed in the sauna the night before.

Dee turned her head in my direction. "Shoot."

"Well, I've noticed that you and Karen always offer me a lift down the beach. But Dylan says you never offer him a ride. Is there a reason for that?"

She bit her lower lip as she thought about my question for a minute.

"Dylan's here to learn how to play a fisherman," she said. "But he thinks we're boring and he hates fishing. The first day he arrived here, he said to Karen and me, 'You do this for four weeks every year?' We laughed but his meaning was clear." She paused to take a whistling teakettle off a burner and to pour hot water over a teabag. "Karen probably doesn't give him a ride because she thinks he's an ass. But I thought I was helping him by not offering him a ride. My truck stinks to high heaven, and I thought walking down the beach would give him a chance to appreciate the beauty of Coffee Point. You have to love something about fishing to keep coming back here each year. I don't know anything about acting, but I can't see how his coming out here will help his performance if he doesn't under-stand that." She laughed. "Maybe that's what acting is: pretending to love something."

I didn't find her comment as amusing as she did, but I gave my own performance and smiled.

Dee picked up her pen and looked as if she was going to resume writing her letter, but she put it down again and turned to me. "Did you know that you're the first friend of Roy's who's ever visited him out here? He's invited people several times but no one has ever made the trip. I know it means a lot to him."

"I almost didn't come," I said, finding it hard to believe then I had seriously considered staying in Anchorage. I couldn't understand how Dylan couldn't see that Coffee Point was marvelous. The mosquitoes and stinky trucks were inconsequential compared to the austere beauty of the land and the sea, the stupendous sight of millions of salmon returning each year, and the temporary but real bonds of trust among the fishermen.

"Roy's glad you came," she said, looking at me with the same blue eyes as her son's. "And so am I."

"I'm glad, too," I murmured. "I'm starting to think that falling in a tar pit was my lucky break."

Dee laughed. It was one of the few times she had laughed at one my jokes. She picked up her pen but held it aloft as if she was considering something.

"I don't want Dylan to feel unwelcome," she said. "I'll offer him a ride the next time I see him walking the beach."

Dee glanced down at her letter, which reminded me of my father's letter. Thinking that I was on a roll with her, I told her about how he signed his letters with "Stay in ouch." After hearing how I interpreted the phrase, she asked, "Isn't your novel about your family?" I hadn't spoken to her about my novel and wondered whether she had heard about it from Roy or Wendy. Dee must have sensed my curiosity because she said, "Wendy's been telling me how much she admires your writing."

I was gratified to hear Wendy's praise but was also disappointed that it hadn't been from Roy.

"You should use 'Stay in Ouch,' for the title," she suggested. "It would seem like you were referring to the bonds of love and loss that a family can share."

It did seem like the perfect title for my book, but I asked whether the title would look confusing on a cover.

"If I saw *Stay in Ouch* in a bookstore," she said, "I'd be intrigued and pick it up."

I told her that I thought the same thing. Dee looked at me glumly. "I wish Roy's father was closer to his sons. They have a yearly breakfast together where Jack cooks for them. But they always have to remind him of their tradition. Jack never remembers to ask them. It's not right that a man's sons always have to ask him to show his love."

When Roy spoke about his father, he began with a sharp intake of breath, which always seemed more revealing than whatever he said about him.

Dee's house smelled delicious because that morning because Wendy had baked a batch of chocolate chip cookies. No matter how successful Wendy would become as a television writer, I always believed that the first line of her obituary should be, "Wendy Haberman made the best chocolate chip cookies."

Dee offered me a cookie from a platter and then took one for herself. She took a bite. "Hmm. Orange zest?" I nodded, but that was the extent of my knowledge of Wendy's secret recipe. Dee took two more cookies and put them on a plate. She resumed writing her letter while I climbed the stairs to Wendy's bedroom. I knocked on the door and opened it to find her sitting on her bed, pecking on her laptop.

"Was the sex bad?" she asked.

"Oh, now you want the details?"

"Of course."

She always wanted to know who did what to whom, and since we had always been candid about discussing our sex lives, I told her. She listened until I finished saying that I found Dylan and Roy's intimacy during our threesome disturbing.

"It made me feel jealous."

"That he didn't tell you a story?"

"No. That I wasn't the one telling Roy a story. I want to be the guy who gets to him like that."

"You just met him a few months ago. Give it time. That's why monogamy's so useful. It takes a lifetime to figure out one person."

"Dylan figured him out in one night."

"He figured out how to get him off. He's a whore. That's what whores do."

She was shortchanging him, I thought. "On some level Dylan gets me."

"On your basest level. He understands your cock."

"That's not true. He read *Diary of a Nobody*."

"So he likes a book that you like? What does that mean? Next you'll tell me that you share the same values because you both love asparagus." She sighed impatiently. "He doesn't get you at all," Wendy said earnestly. "You love Alaska. Roy loves Alaska. Dylan will never come back here."

Her casual syllogism was unassailable. I depended upon Wendy to be my back-up brain when mine malfunctioned, but I resented when she was right.

"I don't want to fall in love with a state," I said, although that was exactly what had happened. "I want to fall in love with a man."

"That's not what I'm saying," she said emphatically. "But part of Roy's appeal is that he's the kind of guy who loves this." She waved her hands around the room to indicate Coffee Point.

I could see what she meant, but I was in one of my peevish moods where because I couldn't pin down exactly how I felt about something, I decided that I was depressed. I could have just as easily decided that I felt happy, but I'd been happy the day before and seemed to observe an unwritten rule that a stylish man couldn't wear the same smile two days in a row.

"Sometimes I think Roy likes me because I can find Bristol Bay on a map."

"That's not why he loves you," Wendy said. "He loves you because you wouldn't let him get trapped at the tar pits. I stood with him that day, and he fell in love with you then."

I'd assumed that Roy had fallen for me when we discussed the stone points found embedded in Bowhead whales. But I could see that my preventing him from getting trapped with me in the tar pits had been instrumental in bringing us together. I couldn't understand why I hadn't made the connection earlier.

"It's obvious," I said. "I don't know why I missed it."

"Because you don't think it's unusual to look out for your friends."

Wendy frowned at her computer screen as she opened a new screen-play file. Once she had made her point, she always grew tired of giving advice or bolstering egos. Of course, she also looked out for her friends but she did it like a grumpy guide dog: it's over there, stupid.

"Let's write," she said.

"Do you have any ideas?"

"Nothing," she said as she stared at her computer screen.

"Let me check my notebook." I grabbed my knapsack and removed my black notebook from the outer pocket. I opened it to read her a few entries to see whether anything triggered an idea for a sketch.

"People are sentimental about baby mammals, but no one loves baby insects," I read. "Nobody ever gushes about a litter of maggots, 'Look at the housefly puppies!'"

She shrugged and told me to continue. I skipped over a few items that had lost interest to me or were baffling ("Cooked bread is called toast/why aren't there special names for other foods after they're cooked?") I came to this entry: "From what I've read and observed, the study of love hasn't achieved any significant scientific progress that I'm aware of. Where is the Sir Isaac Newton who will discover the universal underlying principle of falling in love? Where is the Einstein who will reveal that the speed of a feeling isn't constant but is dependent on the time and the place? Where is the Madame Curie who will give her life studying the radiant power of love, benefiting us with her research while unintentionally revealing that strong, unseen emotions can be fatal? Most importantly, where is the Alexander Graham Bell of love, the man or woman who will invent a cheap portable device that will prevent miscommunication?"

After I finished reading it aloud, Wendy shrugged again and said, "Yeah. Love stinks. Next."

I came to an idea that I'd scrawled months ago in my notebook, "History Channel/old sitcoms."

I explained the premise, asking her to imagine that the History Channel began rebroadcasting old sitcoms, under the guise that the old sitcoms were educational about the lifestyles and values of Americans during the 1950s and 1960s.

"That's a little vague."

"What if the History Channel did their own versions of old sitcoms?" I asked.

"Give me an example," she said from her seat in an overstuffed chair. Her legs rested on the edge of the bed.

"I don't know," I said as suddenly an idea came to me. "What if they remade *I Love Lucy* and Lucy Ricardo's best friend and neighbor wasn't Ethel Mertz but was Ethel Rosenberg?"

Wendy laughed, which I interpreted as a signal to continue.

"It's the right era. *I Love Lucy* first aired in 1951. And the Rosenbergs were executed in 1953. It's conceivable that the Ricardos and Rosenbergs could have been neighbors, since they both lived in New York."

"Lucy was spying for the Russians because she wanted money for acting lessons!" Wendy exclaimed.

"With Lee Strasberg!" I shouted, not exactly sure when he first came to prominence. I made a mental note to do some research online.

We both agreed that the premise was strong enough to allow us to begin writing.

The sketch opened with Lucy asking Ethel to hide the plans for the atomic bomb for her because she doesn't want Ricky to discover that she's been spying for the Russians. "Since Ricky refused to pay for my acting lessons," she says. "I became a real redhead!"

Ethel demurs, arguing that her husband Julius would kill her if he finds out that she's hiding the plans for the atom bomb.

"Oh, you worry too much," Lucy says shaking her head. "No one's going to kill Ethel Rosenberg!" Lucy tries to wheedle Ethel into changing her mind by sweetening the deal.

"You know, Ethel, if I become a big star, I'd be able to hire you and Julius to perform on my show."

The allure of show business proves too tempting for Ethel. She shares with Lucy her own dreams of stardom. "Oh, Lucy, wouldn't it be amazing if someday everyone in the country knew the names of Ethel and Julius Rosenberg?"

Cut to a newspaper headline, "Commie Spies Nabbed for Treason!" Underneath was a black-and-white photo of the chagrined Ethel being glared at by Julius as FBI agents lead them away in hand-cuffs. The camera pulls back to reveal that Ricky is reading the news-paper at breakfast. He does a double take when he sees Ethel and Julius's picture on the front page. Ricky lets out his famous cry of "Ai-yi-yi-yi-yi!" Lucy screws up her face guiltily as she confesses, "Ricky, now don't get mad . . ."

"Loosy, whad you do now?"

Cut to the last scene of the sketch with Ethel in the electric chair while Lucy and Ricky watch as she's executed. "Waaah!" Lucy wails as Ricky tries to comfort her.

It took us almost three hours to write the three-page sketch. Wendy and I repeatedly read aloud the dialogue, rewriting it when we stumbled on a word or phrase, until we felt that the conversations were concise, funny, and idiomatic. We had just noticed the rain had stopped and we were reading the script over again when there was a knock on the bedroom door. Alex had crossed the river, bearing a pizza. During the summer months, a pizzeria operated in Egegik and the return of cheese and pepperoni each season was almost as eagerly anticipated as the return of the salmon. He looked at my black eye as if he had expected to see it.

"Did you fight with Dylan over the script?"

"What?" I asked, confused by Alex's question.

"He didn't fight," Wendy said loudly. "His two boyfriends did after their threesome. He tried to break it up and got clocked."

"Hey!" I hissed, indicating with flailing arms that Dee was working downstairs, and I didn't want her to hear about our threesome.

Wendy grinned and whispered, "Sorry."

"They were fighting over *you*?" Alex asked.

"Which is hard to believe," Wendy said as she stood up from her chair.

"Don't disguise the incredulity in your voices," I said. "It helps my self-esteem."

"What about the script?" Wendy asked Alex, both of us eager to know why he thought reading the script would make me want to punch out Dylan.

"Just read it and tell me what you think."

"What about it?" I asked.

"You've got to read it. I might be wrong."

"Just tell us why reading this script is so important," Wendy demanded.

"I could but I'm not going to," Alex said. "Just . . . read it."

Alex could be as stubborn as Wendy, which she seemed to sense and actually respect.

"All right," I said.

Alex changed the subject and asked us what we were working on. Wendy explained the premise to him and he grinned. "That's really funny," he said. Wendy surprised me when she asked Alex if we could read the sketch to him. My praise of his writing must have really had an impact on her because she almost never asked other people to read our scripts. The three of us took turns playing the various parts and Alex responded with laughter in the appropriate places. After we had finished, he offered us a suggestion for the ending. His idea was great and we immediately decided to use it.

In our final version of the sketch, Ricky comforts the sobbing Lucy but he says to her, "Honey, don't cry. You didn't know they'd be executed. It's not your fault."

"I'm not crying about that," Lucy says through her sniffles.

"Then what are you crying about?"

"I'm crying because now Ethel's more famous than me!" she wails as Ricky lets out another, "Ai-yi-yi-yi-yi!"

"Does anyone under thirty even know who the Rosenbergs are?" I asked, suddenly beset by doubts about the sketch. I wondered if the subject was too esoteric and highbrow for television.

Alex admitted that it could be a problem.

"Do you guys think it's funny?" Wendy asked, turning her head to look at both of us.

"Definitely," said Alex.

"Yes," I said, nodding my head.

"So do I," she declared. "Let's leave it. We'll have plenty of opportunities to write down to our audience later."

We dug into the pizza, which was cold and not very good. Wendy threw her half-eaten piece back in the box. "What are you working on now?" she asked Alex.

"Nelson's inspired me to write the sad story of the poor gay salmon," he said. "I'm thinking of putting together an entire show about queer animals."

"Oh, that'll really bring out the nutjob protestors," Wendy declared before she made a motion with her hand as if she was carrying a placard. "'God Hates Fag Fish!'"

Of course, Alex and I thought that was hilarious.

"When do you start filming?" I asked.

"In two weeks."

"What's your character like?" Wendy asked.

"He's the classic drinks-too-much native who deep-down possesses a spiritual wisdom. I wouldn't mind playing a drunk if the writer acknowledged the appeal of alcohol. People don't show enough respect for alcohol or pot or any mind-altering substance. Alcohol's a *tunghat*." He explained that it was a Yup'ik word for a spirit being that could be good or evil. "Tunghats are dangerous and impossible to control. One of my problems with Christianity is that it ignores the power of alcohol. I've always wanted to know if any of the disciples had a hangover after the Last Supper." He said before giving us a masterful impression of a hungover Judas blaming Jesus for his headache.

"What's Dylan's character like?" Wendy asked.

"It's a good part in a not-so-good script. He befriends this fisherman because he wants to fuck his wife. He plays these mind games with this couple. The wife's a photographer, and when he finds out from the husband that her favorite painter is Frida Kahlo, he hangs reproductions of her work all over his house to impress her. He reads her favorite book. The entire movie is this slow, twisted wooing of her that eventually ruins their lives."

Something was fishy.

"Where's that script?" I asked.

"In my knapsack."

"Would you mind if I read it?"

"Go ahead. But I can't let you keep it. I'm trying to learn my lines."

I reassured him that he would have the script back pronto because I would read it immediately.

EIGHTEEN

As soon as I heard that Dylan's character in his movie won the favor of a woman by reading her favorite book, I suspected that he was preparing for his role by making us his unwitting rehearsal partners. Alex dug the script out of his backpack, handing me a pale blue binder. I started to read it but couldn't concentrate because Alex and Wendy had decided to assemble a twelve-hundred-and-fifty-piece jigsaw puzzle of a photograph of Denali. They began to bicker over an assemblage strategy, whether to start with the sky or land first, and I quickly decided that I couldn't read the script in front of anyone. If Dylan had lied to me, I wanted to discover it privately back at the house. I felt ill, queasy with incipient disappointment, convinced that reading *Violet*

Cryderman would confirm Dylan as a lying fraud. It would be devastating to learn that he couldn't be trusted, throwing into doubt whether he really admired my writing, really wanted to be my boyfriend, and really thought that my arms looked noticeably larger. I excused myself to Alex and Wendy telling them that their squabbling was preventing me from concentrating on the script.

The rain had stopped and the clouds were breaking up. A sucker hole appeared in the sky, the deceptive shaft of fool's gold falsely promising fair weather. Trudging slowly back to the house, holding the script in my hand, I resolved never to trust the sun, or any other lying star, ever again.

At the house I made a cup of Roy's green tea, not really wanting anything to drink but needing something warm and comforting to hold, then I went upstairs to our bed and slipped under the patchwork quilt.

After reading the first ten pages, it was obvious that Dylan had used the script of *Violet Cryderman* as a blueprint for his courtship of me.

The story is set in the fictional Alaskan fishing village of Dodson. Dylan's character, Seth Tockley is intent on sleeping with a married woman named Violet Cryderman. Seth's a devious man, incapable of telling the truth, and his cunning method of achieving his goal includes earning the trust of her husband. Seth's revealed as a liar in the first scene, when he takes three years off his age—on his fishing license—making me think the screenwriter had spent too much time in Hollywood.

Oh, brother . . . their mutual attraction is triggered when they meet at the post office and discover that they both subscribe to the *New Yorker!* Afterward Seth meets Violet while walking in the woods. She inquires about the coiled rattlesnake tattoo on his forearm, timidly confessing that she's always been afraid of snakes. Boldly placing her hand on his tattoo, he tells her that she has nothing to fear. As far as I was concerned, Violet would have been more appealing and believable if she had asked Seth if he had ever considered that when he was an old man, the coiled snake tattooed on his arm would resemble a pile of dog shit. During their stroll, Seth asks Violet to speak to her husband Bing Cryderman about giving him a job on his fishing boat, telling her a sob story about losing his brother in a fishing accident and his need to overcome his fears of returning to the sea. At this point, I wanted to re-title the film: *Hook, Line, and Stinker.* The gullible husband hires Seth on his wife's recommendation, offhandedly mentioning that Violet's favorite painter is Frida Kahlo. I immediately wanted to know if Roy had told Dylan that my favorite painter was Marsden Hartley. (Roy later confirmed that he had.) Seth hangs a Frida Kahlo poster in his kitchen, pretending to Violet that he's always admired her work.

Seth surprises Violet and wins her admiration when he reads her favorite book—*Anna Karenina*—the obvious choice for a woman with a wandering eye, but Violet's too bland to be tragic, really; she's more of a Pollyanna Karenina. Seth encourages Violet to think of herself as an artist, praising her photographs of forlorn and battered fishing boats. The net motif is overworked. We get it; she's trapped in her marriage and in a small town. Seth continually disparages life in Dodson to Violet, citing the usual small town bugaboos of isolation and narrow-mindedness, along with the additional hardship of Alaska's long, dark winters. This was the low point of a weak script. Living in Alaska is like living in a castle; it's damp, cold, and inconvenient, but it's also majestic and romantic and beats the hell out of living in a centrally-heated-box state. For the most part, the Alaskans I'd met were fascinating individuals, gaining a leg up on avoiding dullness merely by choosing to live in Alaska. There are bores in Alaska, but at least they possess the novelty of being dull about subjects I'd never yawned through before. They replaced standard snooze topics such as the comic behavior of their young children, their favorite television programs, and the rising price of real estate in their area, with fur trapping, jade mining, and completely selfish reasons for drilling in the Arctic National Wildlife Refuge.

It was particularly insulting to learn that Dylan considered me to be a silly, fatuous woman named "Violet." Oh, and get this—she's the villain in the film. The writer skillfully makes the case that adultery is a white-collar crime, an inside job of betrayal. We're shown, scene by scene, how Violet becomes unfaithful to her husband. In the beginning she innocently flirts with Seth. ("I always read The Talk of Town section first, because someday I'd like to be the talk of the town.") Their flirtation becomes inappropriate though when she begins to discuss her husband's flaws with Seth. (The husband was being played by the same buffed-out actor who played Leif Eriksson's hotheaded brother in the previous summer's blockbuster film, *Leif Eriksson*.) Her major complaint about her husband is that he prefers reading history to fiction! Considering that he's a total hunk who reads books of any kind, it was hard to sympathize with her lament that "he lives in the past, and I'm in the present."

It was chilling to read the scene on page sixty-four where Seth gleefully whispers to Violet that he's going to fuck her. Violet sees Seth changing his shirt down at the dock, and her eyes are described as being "inflamed with lust." Which sounded like a medical condition that can be treated by cold showers of eyedrops. Eventually Violet makes a pivotal decision and tells her husband a pointless fib, claiming that she spent the day doing research online when she actually spent it in her darkroom. You watch her face change as she realizes that he believes her. It wasn't hard; she begins to think that she can get away with having an affair. She becomes a thief, robbing her partner of the love and respect that he deserves.

Seth and Violet have sex for the first time when he swats a mosquito on her arm, touching her, sparking the contact that leads to their having what the script describes as "passionate and beautiful lovemaking."

I didn't read past page seventy-seven because, after reading the page twice, I shouted, "That fucker!" and threw the script across the room. On page seventy-seven, Seth "accidentally" pushes Violet's husband overboard then "saves" him from drowning to win Violet's admiration.

The script hit the window ledge, striking the oosik, which popped up in the air and landed on my desk, where it struck my lucky blue coffee cup, which exploded into shards of pottery. The destruction of my lucky writing charm seemed ominous. An artist might have construed my coffee cup's death as symbolic—a penis bone obliterating the repository of my muse—but I quickly decided that it was just an accident. I refused to see it as being symbolic of anything because I wanted to have nothing more to do with art or being an artist. If the destruction of my coffee cup was symbolic of anything, I thought as I threw off the quilt, it's symbolic of how dick can mess up your life.

I left the broken cup and went downstairs, looking to see if Dylan was in his bedroom. He wasn't there but the Marsden Hartley poster was hanging on his door and I shocked myself when I ripped it down.

It was inconceivable that, as an acting exercise, Dylan deliberately pushed Roy off the raft to rescue him. But the circumstantial evidence in the script was enough to convict him. What would he do if he ever played a Nazi? Conquer Poland? I understood that he wanted to give a great performance in his comeback role, but how could he justify hurting or killing Roy to create a work of art?

Dylan's despicable behavior couldn't be excused even if he gave a masterful performance and *Violet Cryderman* came to be regarded as a classic film. But Roy almost died for the sake of a film that was destined to earn a permanent berth in the $1.99 DVD bin at supermarkets and drug stores.

I stared out the kitchen window, trying to figure out what I would do or say to Dylan. Gray clouds moved aimlessly across the sky, looking for something to rain upon. My hands trembled as I envisioned punching him in the face. I could see the blow landing and no joke or dismissive comment appeared in my head. I couldn't forget Dee's shaking hands that day on the beach. I'd experienced grief but couldn't imagine the heartache of a mother losing a child. Suddenly the image of hooded Death swinging a sickle made sense again, because when Death swings his blade, his sloppy stroke always goes wide, slashing the people closest to his victim. Equally as painful was acknowledging my unwitting complicity in Dylan's attempted murder. I was the one who had forced Roy to invite him out to Coffee Point. I was the one who couldn't hide my infatuation with Dylan. And I let Roy procure Dylan for our threesome because I longed to gain something called "experience." Two selfish men put Dee and Roy through a brutal, traumatic experience. I recalled that Dylan threw up when we drove back from the beach. I wondered whether he became sick when he realized the full horror of what he had almost done. I wanted to think that he did but wasn't sure because it seemed that I'd never known him.

Disenchantment sounds like a childish word but, for adults, disenchantment is a witch's curse, where every prince is secretly slimy. There wasn't a looking glass handy but I knew if I gazed into one, I'd see a frog.

I decided to go out and find Dylan. I walked toward Dee's house to return the script to Alex, but as I thought about what Dylan had done, I considered that writers use the people in their lives to "feed their work," a term that brought to mind being devoured.

I really was Violet Cryderman.

What was disturbing was that I didn't completely regret my behavior. The threesome had been a disaster and I had no desire to repeat the experience, but it was my decision, and I could live with it. That was new for me. Normally, I would have tortured myself with contrition, penitence, or remorse, selecting one of them from my wardrobe of hairshirts.

At Dee's house, I found Alex and Wendy had abandoned the uncompleted puzzle, leaving Denali without its snowcapped summit. Alex asked me to stuff the script in his backpack, as he and Wendy dressed to go four-wheeling, donning goggles along with waterproof jackets and pants.

"So?" Wendy asked as we walked downstairs.

I started to explain to her that Dylan had almost killed Roy as an acting exercise but choked up when I began to speak. I was on the verge of tears, but my freshly minted butch fisherman persona refused to sail on that saltwater.

"Are you all right?" Wendy asked.

"It's fucked," Alex said slowly shaking his head.

I carefully recounted my reaction to the script and in the telling became disgusted by how easily I'd been duped.

Alex was surprised to learn about the Marsden Hartley poster and that Dylan had also made a point of reading a book I had recommended.

"Are you sure it's not just a coincidence?" Wendy asked, reminding me that I tended to be paranoid, recalling the time that I'd been convinced that Agenda was going to fire me when she had actually been testing my mettle, before promoting me to the position of script coordinator.

"It's not a coincidence," I said.

"He'll do whatever he needs to do to survive," Alex said.

"What the hell would make him take method acting to this extreme?" Wendy asked. "He must be psycho."

"Or scared," Alex suggested. "Can you imagine the pressure he feels? It's his first film since he got out of jail. Everyone in Hollywood is curious to see how he does. He needs to astonish them because, right now, no one wants to hire him. He's terrified that he'll never work again, and he doesn't know how to do anything else."

"His entire career rides on this one performance," I said. "And he'll say anything and use anyone to make it happen."

"If he fucks up, he'll be lucky to get an infomercial," Wendy declared.

Alex shook his head sadly. "He never uses drugs when he's working. But he told me if he couldn't act, he'd probably start using and find himself back in jail."

"I might lie and use people if my career depended upon it," Wendy said.

"Might?" I asked scornfully.

She erected the middle finger of her right hand. "We all might."

"Survival turns everyone into a hunter," Alex said.

"That doesn't excuse his behavior," I insisted. "He almost killed Roy. He's completely selfish."

"Not completely," Wendy argued. "All three of you slept with him. He gave you a chance to fulfill what seems to be the secret dream of every homo: to have sex with Dylan Fabizak. When you're old queens, spilling your negronis at cocktail parties, I'm sure you'll still be bragging about it. Yeah, he's an egomaniac, but what did you expect?" Her face became an exaggerated pout, reminiscent of a hurt child's. "'Gee,' she said in a spoiled little girl's voice. 'I never thought a movie star would behave like that.'"

Alex smiled and said, "That's true."

"It's not like he's done any lasting damage," she added. "I assume you idiots played safely."

We assured her that we had been careful. Roy and I had treated Dylan as a triple threat because, as an ex-con, former IV drug user, and gay slut, he had three winning lemons on the HIV slot machine.

"He said he liked my writing." I immediately felt ashamed of myself because I was close to admitting that I had believed him when he said that he wanted to be my boyfriend.

Wendy waved her hand dismissively. "Why do you care what he thinks? You can't trust him. He's a liar."

I understood that, but I wanted to know if he had lied about everything; liars have to let slip an occasional honest remark so you'll believe them, even if it was something as innocuous as "I'm hungry." Dylan's character did genuinely admire Violet's photography in the script. It was childish but I really wanted to know whether Dylan actually liked my novel or whether that was also a lie.

"What do you think Roy will do?" Wendy asked. "He really has a reason to punch him out now."

I couldn't predict how Roy would react. He was capable of the full amplitude of male emotional responses, ranging from public brawling to shutting down completely.

Assuming that Alex's position as Roy's best friend conferred expertise on his conduct, I sought his guidance.

"What do you think he'll say?"

"Good-bye, Dylan," Alex said confidently as he used his hand to wipe raindrops from the four-wheeler's leather seat. "He'll be on the next plane. Roy won't live with a liar. He did that once, and he vowed that he'd never do it again."

My heart jumped as I suddenly thought that he'd ask us both to leave. I decided to speak to Dylan alone before I revealed his duplicity to Roy. I didn't consider this to be deceptive, telling myself that my life was a large and complex jigsaw puzzle and that I was giving precedence to the harder-to-figure-out Dylan than the easier-to-understand Roy.

"You know what's funny?" Alex said. "After Dylan's gone, Roy will be the first one to sympathize with the position he was in. Roy's almost as obsessive about archaeology as Dylan is about acting."

"I don't think so," Wendy said as she climbed behind Alex on the four-wheeler. "Roy would never try to kill someone to get ahead."

"That's because in archaeology everyone who can help your career is dead," Alex declared.

"All right, enough about Dylan trying to murder Roy," Wendy said. "What I want to know is, is the script any good?"

"The dialogue's terrible," I said, before quoting a line of Violet's, "My heart is like a stuck jar; I need a strong man to help me open it."

"Ewww," said Wendy.

"I'd love to rewrite the script," Alex said. "The situation has the makings of a good small film."

Wendy and Alex had a short scuffle of swatting hands after she goosed him. He gripped her arms, wrapping them around his waist, then they both beamed, making them look like a queer but adorable biker couple.

"What are you going to do?" Alex asked me.

"I'm not sure." I said. I had no plan other than the old standby of human interaction: say something that will trigger a reaction, hoping that the other person's response will clarify how you feel. It's the basis for all human relationships. Well, that and getting laid.

"Have you seen them?" I asked.

"We saw Dylan walk down to the weigh station a while ago," Alex replied. "But we haven't seen Roy. I think he's gone off to think things through. He gets all quiet and then has to go off by himself."

"Whatever you do, don't get caught between them if they start fighting again!" warned Wendy before they roared off down the road.

I walked down to the weigh station, determined to confront Dylan about the screenplay. The crew lived behind the station in a corrugated steel Quonset hut that was nicknamed, the Can. Peals of stoned laughter could be heard coming from inside the building, large outbursts of hilarity followed by confused nervous chuckles, as if what had appeared to be hilarious a second ago, suddenly seemed ominous on second thought.

Aaron spotted me though the kitchen window and waved for me to come inside. The kitchen was hazy with smoke, the pungent aroma of marijuana instantly recognizable. Everyone huddled around the bong as if the burning bowl was a tiny hearth. Dylan had taken the most comfortable seat, a large dilapidated upholstered armchair, each arm wearing dirty corsages of stuffing. Roy sat next to him, perched on a barstool. He looked at me when I strolled in, but his face wore the vacant expression of someone who was either completely stoned or deeply depressed.

"Here comes Sugar Ray Nelson," Aaron announced when I entered the large kitchen. He shadowboxed with me, causing me to awkwardly throw up my hands. I resented sham fighting more than real punches because no one wants to look like a lightweight at an *imaginary* sport. The crew members all took verbal pokes at me, making sucker punch remarks about my fighting skills, until I threatened them with a beating if they kept it up.

In addition to the bong, a burning roach was being passed around the room, and when it reached Dylan, he shooed it away as if it were a pesky firefly. Handsome Derrick picked up the unusual bong, which was a ceramic effigy of a bright red devil. He clicked a cigarette lighter and held the flame to the bowl while sucking on the devil's head. Then he blew smoke out his ass. After taking his hit, Derrick passed the bong to me.

"No, thanks," I said, waving it off. I was determined to have a clear head when I spoke to Dylan about the script.

"Why didn't you tell us you were famous?" Aaron asked as I passed the bong to him. Roy looked at me, shaking his head disapprovingly as Dylan averted his gaze, leading me to believe, correctly, that he had spilled the beans about my night in the tar pits.

"I can't believe we didn't recognize you," Derrick said. The weigh station crew began to tease me, wringing every possible variation on the words: stuck, sinking, sunk, and trapped. It was a minor ordeal that made me wish that they were cleverer and could come up with at least one variation that I didn't see coming. I planned on leaving as soon as possible—I decided that I could talk to Dylan later—but had to wait because I didn't want to be perceived as a poor sport.

"Nelson was more worried about me than he was about himself," Roy said, his voice raspy with impatience. "He kept telling me to leave because he didn't want me to get arrested. So give him a break because you're pissing me off and I've already been in one fight today."

"Don't mess with Roy," Dylan warned as he rubbed his lip for their benefit. "He's got a mean right hook."

Roy stood up to leave, prompting me to follow suit.

"You're not leaving yet," Aaron said, "We still have to ask the question of the day."

The lack of enthusiasm in the room was palpable and people shifted in their seats uncomfortably. Roy announced that he was going to pass but Aaron browbeat him until he agreed to stay.

"Make it quick," Roy snapped as everyone looked at Aaron.

"What have you done that completely backfired on you?" he asked.

Aaron's eyes darted around the room but no one made a motion to speak up. I decided to go first because my answer was obvious. "I visited the La Brea Tar Pits." The group chuckled appreciatively then Aaron turned toward Roy. "Your turn."

"You don't want to know," Roy said as he looked at Aaron. He glanced at me briefly, which made me feel anxious. People who wanted to be coaxed into revealing something that they were eager to confess often used that statement, but ordinarily Roy didn't play those kinds of games. He sighed heavily and shrugged, the two actions forming the universally understood sign for "what the hell."

"I arranged a threesome, because I thought it would make my boyfriend happy."

His answer demanded an explanation, but everyone in the room appeared to be horrified that he'd violated the social convention that when gay men and straight men socialized together, they never talked seriously about gay sex; they were only allowed to make lewd allusions to the subject. Roy's face wore an expression of satisfaction. "See? I warned you."

His answer shocked me, because Roy's regard for his privacy was frequently misinterpreted as being taciturn, and for him to discuss an intimate matter in a room full of acquaintances was a sign that he had become unhinged.

"Oh-kay," Aaron said lightly. "We're not going to inquire too deeply into that." He moved on to Derrick who said that he had introduced his high school girlfriend to his best friend and within six months they were dating each other.

Weird Walt told us about his informing a friend beforehand that he was going to bid on a rare pair of latex pointy ears being auctioned on eBay, and the friend outbid him for them.

Aaron revealed that, after college, he'd threatened to join the Peace Corps, and to his surprise, his parents thought it was a great idea, so he ended up spending two years in Gambia.

Dylan was the last one in the room to answer. He appeared nervous and cleared his throat twice before he spoke.

"I pretended to fall in love with someone only to discover that I'd fallen in love with him."

I thought Dylan had to be lying again as he caught my eye, his intense focus unmistakably signaling that he was speaking about me. But I remained indifferent because I was still angry with him. I could sense Roy sitting motionless beside me, watching us intently. But then I felt perplexed. Dylan had admitted that he had been using us but there wasn't a comparable incident in the script of Seth confessing his love for Violet in front of her husband. Possibly, in this instance, Dylan was telling the truth.

Roy stood and zipped up his sweatshirt; he looked distraught. Dylan also rose from his seat, thanking Aaron for his pot, prompting Roy and me to do the same, making us sound like polite guests thanking our hostess for a lovely afternoon of bong hits.

Aaron asked Roy if the weigh station crew could use the sauna that night. "Sure," he said. "But do you mind bringing sauna wood?" They discussed how much wood to bring, settling upon all they could carry.

Walking outside, we saw that the sky had mostly cleared. The sun shone brightly, causing tendrils of steam to rise from the clumps of

grasses growing around the weigh station. The three of us stood awkwardly, dazed by the bright sunshine, which contrasted strongly with
the dark interior of the Quonset hut. We waited while Dylan tried to
light a cigarette, the wind off the river blowing out his first two matches.

"You're upset about the threesome?" Dylan asked Roy as he slowly
exhaled cigarette smoke.

"Yes," he said.

"Why?" Dylan honestly looked confused. Roy glanced at him, then
looked at me, his face somber but determined.

"You arranged it," Dylan said.

"I know, and I regret it."

"That's not fair."

Roy began to fiddle with his watchband. "There's something else,"
he said. "I want you to leave. As soon as possible."

Dylan appeared to be stupefied by his request.

"Why do I have to go?"

"Because you're my guest here, and I've asked you to leave," Roy
said, trying not to become angry.

"What have I done?" Dylan asked.

"Look," Roy said harshly, "I invited Nelson to come to Alaska to
spend the summer with me. I didn't invite you to spend the summer
with me. But somehow this summer's all about you."

"It's going to cost me money to change my plane ticket."

Roy smiled coldly. "A hundred dollars," he said. "Think of that as
the money you didn't spend on food or drink while you were out here."

Dylan's eyes darkened. "Let me understand this," he said. "You
let me blow your boyfriend and then, because he liked it, you're
pissed off."

"That's right."

Dylan tossed his cigarette to the ground, crushing it beneath his boot while Roy stared at him, his blue eyes like two icy ponds.

Dylan turned to me. "Do you want me to leave?" he asked. My face changed color because I hadn't expected his question. They both watched me, waiting for my answer.

"We hadn't talked about it," I said, experiencing a sinking sensation that I was intimately familiar with.

"Yes or no," Dylan said impatiently.

I wanted Roy to jump in and say something, but he was content to examine me with scientific detachment, staring at me as if I were a specimen that he was trying to identify. Dylan's smug confidence that I would immediately come to his defense made me indignant.

"Yes," I stammered.

Dylan looked angry and then sad, his blazing eyes suddenly extinguished by tears. "I'm sorry to hear that."

"I am, too," I muttered, thinking that if he was still acting I had never witnessed a greater performance.

Dylan turned from us and trudged toward the house.

Nineteen

When Roy and I returned to the house, we were reluctant to go inside, where I assumed Dylan was packing his clothes and unfinished protein drinks. Roy began to tidy up the yard, picking up a fishing net that had been sitting on the ground since I arrived and putting it, along with a set of weathered buoys, in a ramshackle storage shed that looked like it should be thrown out. I asked Roy what I could do to help. He surveyed the yard and then pointed to a rusty length of wire poking out of the grass, telling me to coil it up and place it in the old oil drum that served as our garbage can.

"We need water for the sauna," Roy announced, before asking me to help him load two white totes marked "Water" onto the back of the truck.

"You don't have to come with me," he announced after the totes were loaded. "I can do this by myself. Why don't you stay here and write?"

I considered working on my novel but my computer was upstairs in our bedroom and I'd be alone with Dylan inside the house. I'd lost my desire to privately confront him about the screenplay. What was I going to learn from hearing him say that he had duped us? I was angry with him, and I also felt betrayed. I'd grown to believe that Dylan and I were becoming friends and his pretending to be sexually attracted to me didn't hurt nearly as much as his faking our friendship.

Roy opened the door to his truck and then he paused. I could see an idea scurrying behind his face as he curled his lips and wiggled his eyebrows. Looking at me, he grinned and asked, "Why don't you drive?"

I returned his smile. "All right." My moving behind the wheel of Roy's truck was a noteworthy milestone and his eyes gleamed with amusement and, I thought, pride as he handed me the keys. I was grateful that he refrained from throwing them at me, because missing the catch and dropping them would have spoiled the moment.

"I feel like my father's letting me drive his car for the first time," I said as we switched places.

"Father?" Roy asked as he climbed into the passenger side. He was only one year older than I was.

"Hot daddy?" I responded, seeking to placate him.

"Rewrite that one," Roy said, shaking his head, which made me happy. His lighthearted censure was more satisfying than other people's earnest approval would have been. It's one of the classic diagnostic tests of love, but it didn't register with me because I was busy congratulating myself for learning how to drive a standard.

I adjusted the rearview mirror and felt confident that I could handle driving down to the spring for water even though I had to suppress my urge to squeal, "Oh my God!" I had just put the key in the ignition when we heard Karen shout, "Hold up!" Turning my head to the right, I saw her strolling down the road, a lit cigarette dangling from her lips. Her cigarette reminded me of the exhaust pipe on an old car, the constant puffing of gray smoke, a disturbing sign of engine trouble.

Roy rolled down his window while we waited for her to reach us. She removed the cigarette from her mouth. "Can I borrow one of you guys?"

"Sure," replied Roy, while I nodded and said, "Yes."

"Rosalind's moving her bedroom upstairs," Karen explained. "She's over there now lifting chairs like a stevedore." Karen's expression was a mixture of admiration and dismay. "She got the chairs up by herself, but now she's trying to do the bed and dresser." Karen wheezed slightly as if just talking about her granddaughter's exertions put her out of breath. "She doesn't want any help, but I want one of you to pretend to drop in and give her a hand." Karen glanced down at her cigarette and discovered that it had burned down to the filter. She dropped the butt to the ground, then stubbed it out under her boot.

"We'll both go," Roy said before opening the door to his truck.

"No, no," Karen shouted, waving her hands at us. "I'll never hear the end of it if she finds out I asked you to help her. Only one of you should go."

Roy thought for a minute, as Karen seemed perfectly content to wait until we decided which one of us was going to help Rosalind.

"I want to borrow your saw," Roy said with a shrug. "That's a reason to stop by." He had started building a small shelf out of scrap wood for the sauna, because he thought we needed a place to store bottles of shampoo.

"Great," Karen said as she pulled a pack of cigarettes out of her pocket, removed one, and lit it with a blue disposable lighter.

Roy looked at me. "Can you get the water by yourself?"

"Yes," I said, feeling slightly apprehensive about driving down to the spring and filling the totes by myself.

"You're sure?" Roy asked.

"Roy," Karen coughed, before releasing a small cloud of smoke. "If he's too stupid to catch falling water. . . ." She shook her head to indicate the hopelessness of such a person.

We laughed as Roy got out of the truck.

"Cut him loose if he is," Karen advised as she winked at me.

I started up the truck and watched Roy cross the road to Karen's house while she continued walking down to Dee's.

A natural spring located a half a mile further up the river from the weigh station supplied Coffee Point with water. A plastic pipe, four inches in diameter, supported by a wooden trestle, had been inserted into the side of the bluff, tapping the spring. Icy cold water fell continuously in a gentle trickle down to the river. (Roy, claiming it was the best water he had ever tasted, described the flavor as "fresh air in a glass.")

For me, the difficult part of filling the totes with water was maneuvering the truck underneath the pipe. Karen's comment, "If he's too stupid to catch falling water . . ." echoed in my ears as I did a three-point turn in the road and prepared to put the truck in reverse. I kept looking over my shoulder as I gingerly pressed the gas pedal until I finally heard the reassuring sounds of the water hitting the metal truck bed and then splattering against the sides of the plastic tote.

I got out of the truck while I waited for the first tote to fill. It usually took about forty minutes for the dribbling water to fill a tote, and I had to fill two of them because we needed enough water for six men and four women to bathe with. The sky had mostly cleared, and I grabbed my book from the front seat of the cab, looking for a place to read in the sunshine. A sandy ridge sheltered the spring, and I touched the long grasses that grew along it to see whether they were still wet. They were dry enough and, once seated, I noticed the green stems and lavender flowers of wild geraniums snaking through the brown grasses. It was warm, almost hot and I removed my sweatshirt. After I settled into my grassy bower, I looked down the river to the sea. The light hit the water brilliantly, and I had to squint to see the fishing boats beyond the mouth of the river.

I was reading the one-volume selection of Chekhov's letters. The photograph of the handsome author on the cover reminded me that Dylan had suggested that I should read them. I'd reached the section where Chekhov wrote about traveling across Siberia to Sakhalin Island. It was amazing to think that Sakhalin Island was somewhere across the sea that I gazed out upon. A long-tailed jaeger flew low over the water and I became vividly aware that having an adventure wasn't something that only happened to people in books.

A blond-haired man in a blue jacket walking along the riverbank came into view. As Dylan approached, I could see that he looked forlorn, his downcast eyes reminding me of the pivotal moment in his shot-putter movie when he led the Pledge of Allegiance at a pep rally, and the other students laughed as he stuttered on, ". . . and to the repub-pub-pub. . . ."

I heard Dylan's feet crunching in the sand before I saw him standing over me. I looked up at his distraught face and waited for him to speak.

"I need an explanation from you before I go," he said.

"I read the script."

Dylan looked momentarily guilt-stricken but then he almost appeared to be pleased.

"I was going to tell you about it," he said as he sat down beside me in the grass. "I was just waiting for the right time."

"Did you push Roy in the water?" I asked, my anger returning as I recalled Dee's devastated face when she saw Roy lying on the beach.

Dylan's face became grave as he considered my question.

"I didn't know he couldn't swim," he said softly.

"You're sick," I snarled.

"I wish I was," Dylan said as he sat up and removed his jacket, revealing a red sweatshirt. "Unfortunately my only excuse is that I was thinking of myself."

"You've lied to us the entire time."

"I'm sorry I lied to you," Dylan said. "You don't know how much I regret that now."

His bid for my sympathy didn't move me, but I unexpectedly felt exhausted from thinking about him. I really did want him to go away.

"I don't understand why you needed to take it this far," I said weakly.

"Do you understand everything about Roy?" he asked.

"No. But I believe him when he tells me something. I don't always understand him, but I always trust that he's telling me the truth. Roy's not a liar."

"I always told you what I was doing here," he said. "I was getting into character. I just didn't explain that my character was devious and manipulative."

"You didn't tell us that you'd try to kill Roy. We might have appreciated the heads up."

Dylan's back was to the sun and I squinted at him as the bright light shone in my eyes. I was beginning to feel hot in my T-shirt. Dylan unzipped his sweatshirt and removed it. He was wearing a black tank top.

"My character doesn't explain his motives. He just acts upon them," Dylan said. "Great actors never judge their characters. To play Iago, you can't judge him."

"Iago's fictional! As far as I know, he's never actually killed anyone. Never. It's make-believe. All art is make-believe. But you almost killed Roy. An artist makes sacrifices for his art; he doesn't sacrifice other people for his art."

"That's funny," said Dylan as he smiled affectionately at me. "I'm an acting *fiend*," he declared, imitating my imitation of the champagne fiend. "I can't even have friends anymore. They've all become fodder for my characters. Oh, it's *not* a pretty picture."

I refused to smile at what I had to admit was a superb rendition of a queen.

"You used us."

"Really? What were you doing with my ass last night?"

"It's not the same thing."

"It started out as an acting exercise," Dylan said. "But then I began to discover that I liked you. You're smart and funny and handsome. Then I read your novel and I began to admire you. Your book's funny but it's also thoughtful, and you're not afraid to be sad and vulnerable at times. Last night, I wasn't acting or getting into character. I really wanted to sleep with you."

He looked at me with his glistening eyes and I almost believed him. Dylan sat up again and stripped off his wife-beater. Seeing him shirtless once more reminded me that I still couldn't believe that I had actually slept with Dylan Fabizak. Wendy was right; I'd be bragging about that when I was an old queen.

"I've never really had a boyfriend," Dylan said. "For a long time, I was afraid to have one because I didn't want the press to find out I was gay. Along with being just too crazy and fucked up to have a boyfriend. But I'm ready for a boyfriend now and I think you're the guy."

I rolled my eyes at him because I didn't trust him.

"How do I know that you haven't accepted a part in another film playing a nice guy who wants a boyfriend?" I asked. "You could be preparing for your next role."

He laughed, reaching over to grab me by the shoulders, pulling me closer to him, moving his face inches away from mine. "You'll never know. I'll always keep you guessing."

"That's hardly an inducement to run off with you," I said, disturbed and, yes, flattered by his persistence.

Dylan abruptly rolled over on top of me. His muscular bulk pressed me deeper into the grasses as he straddled me around the waist.

"All right, get off of me," I said, raising my hands to his arms to push him off me. Dylan appeared to be supremely confidant that I would fail to dislodge him, as he outweighed me by at least fifty pounds. He smiled as I struggled, then he pushed back, his flexed biceps filling my palms. Suddenly, I was confused whether I was fighting him or whether we were wrestling as a prelude to sex. Dylan waited until I removed my hands from his arms before he spoke again.

"I don't think it's just my body that excites you, although it clearly does," he said, leaning down closer to my face, glancing at my hands, which I had to admit were eager to touch him again.

"You're trying to figure me out because you're a writer. I might drive you crazy, but I also excite your imagination. But when you write about me, I'll never accuse you of using me. I get it. I read your novel and it's the work of a very ambitious writer. You should take advantage of me. I could be the opportunity of a lifetime for you. Who knows? Maybe I'll turn out to be your Sally Bowles or your Sebastian Flyte."

I must have looked surprised by his literary references, but my star-tled facial expression was caused by his conviction that I would write about him someday. It was absolutely clear that I had been observing Dylan closely because he fascinated me and I knew that he would make a great character.

"That's insulting," Dylan said angrily, mistaking my look of inspira-tion for disbelief that he had read Isherwood and Waugh. "I told you that I like to read. I'm not just a stupid hunk."

"I haven't thought of you as stupid for a long time," I said, which was true.

Dylan stared down at me and smiled. "Do you still think I'm a hunk?" he asked leaning on me, letting me feel his full weight as he kept his eyes locked upon mine.

I grinned but refused to give him the answer that he wanted to hear.

He tried to kiss me on the lips, but I turned my head away because I could feel myself becoming aroused. Dylan wasn't deterred by my attempt to thwart him, because he reaimed his kiss for the nape of my neck, hitting me directly upon my sweet spot. I squirmed underneath him but he grabbed my arms, pinning them at my sides as he kissed my neck until my toes curled. Once he sensed that I had stopped fighting him, he let my arms go and moved his mouth to my lips. This time he kissed me without his tongue turning into a sockeye. We kissed for a long time until I was completely hard. I suddenly turned my head, breaking off our kiss, renewing my determination that we weren't going to go any further.

Dylan looked satisfied, happy that I had stopped pretending that I wasn't interested in him. He rolled off me for a minute and lay on his back on the grasses. Arching his back, he reached underneath his ass to remove my book. Dylan looked at the cover photograph of Chekhov, sitting at his desk.

"Aren't these wonderful?" he asked.

"I've been reading them because you recommended them," I said, not really in the mood to talk about books when I was raring to have sex.

"He was a great man," Dylan said. "He gave advice to young writers, he built schools, tried to help the brother of a political prisoner. . . ."

"You read a lot but it doesn't have much of an impact on you," I said, annoyed that Dylan got me all worked up for him and then started a book group. "Did you forget that Chekhov wrote that a great artist should be free from violence and lies, no matter what form the latter two take?" I kept my eyes on him because I wanted to see his reaction.

"Does that ring a bell?"

I looked into his broccolate-colored eyes and he appeared to be genuinely abashed. His pupils were huge.

"Yes," Dylan said softly. "But he also wrote, 'I would like to be a free artist and nothing else, and I regret God has not given me the strength to be one.' I've been trying to find the strength to be a free artist. But I'm starting to think that maybe I can't do it by myself."

He looked at me meaningfully. Actors have always been accused of being egotistical: eager to draw attention to themselves; but the true measure of a great actor is his ability to focus on other people. When Dylan gave me his full attention, he made me feel that I was center stage.

"Think of how much fun we could have together in L.A. We could work out together. We could go hiking. We'd go to parties. We could go to bookstores and movies and plays. We could even go bird watching." He moved closer to my lips. "We could read in bed. . . ."

I considered his proposition and tried to picture him as my boyfriend, finding the sex easy to envision but finding it more difficult to imagine him cleaning up after our dog or making our bed. That I didn't immediately dismiss the thought was a sign of how seductive Dylan could be.

He suddenly smacked my arm, killing a mosquito. He gingerly picked up the crumpled corpse, displaying it for my inspection. It appeared to be a bent staple that had failed to bite through the paper.

"I know this is in the script," he said grinning wickedly, "but there was a mosquito on you." He tossed the mosquito aside and then reached out to pick a wild geranium from above my head.

"What did I tell you about picking wildflowers?" I asked.

"I always take want I want," he said as he slowly traced the stalk of the pale lavender flower around my lips. It tickled, and I brushed the stem away from my face with the back of my hand. Dylan suddenly became distracted and paused for a moment to look down at his feet. He shook his left leg.

"My foot's asleep," he explained.

"I hope I'm not boring it," I said.

"No," he said, as he placed his hand on my crotch, patting me possessively.

"Come back with me to Anchorage. We'll leave tomorrow. You can stay in my hotel while I shoot the film. You'll write every day and then when I get home—"

He proceeded to tell me, in salacious detail, an adult bedtime story whose purpose was to prevent the listener from falling asleep. He outdid the tale that he had told Roy the night before, making me a mythic figure whose seven Herculean labors were far filthier than cleaning the Augean stables.

When Dylan finished his story, he winced for a second as he crossed and recrossed his legs to find a comfortable position.

"Come with me," he repeated as I marveled at his torso, wondering how someone could develop muscles between his ribs.

"I can't leave."

"Why not?"

"Did you forget about Roy?" I asked. "And Dee hired me to work for her for the rest of the season." I laughed at him.

He didn't take offense, but his face became grave as he reached out and rubbed my shoulders.

"So what? I want you. I don't care about anyone else but you. And you want me, too." Dylan looked down at my dick, which corroborated his assertion. He leaned over quickly and kissed me on the lips. I made the mistake of moving my hands over to his thick, hard, hairy chest in an attempt to keep him from getting closer to me.

Dylan unbuttoned my pants with swift assurance, a task that he could presumably have performed in his sleep. He reached into his back pocket and pulled out a condom.

"Don't tell me that you don't want to," he said when I frowned. He reached down into my underwear, releasing the part of me that lacked a backbone but always had conviction.

He lowered his face down to mine and kissed me on the mouth and I didn't even try to pull away. Dylan broke off our kiss and said, "I'll change your plane ticket. You can pay me back later."

The fucking cheapskate. Why couldn't he have lied and told me that he would pay to change my plane ticket? He only reminded me that Roy had given me a three-hundred-dollar plane ticket to come to Alaska with no expectation of ever being paid back. But Dylan wanted me to be his boyfriend even though he was unable to fork over a hundred bucks to change my plane ticket. I foresaw unwrapping anniversary, birthday, and Christmas presents from him, knowing that whatever gift Dylan gave me, he had always picked the least expensive choice.

His face contorted into a grimace.

"Bowf my feet are asleep," he said, slurring the word "both."

His forehead shone with sweat as he shook his legs vigorously. He looked terrified.

"Are you all right?"

"Shumthing's wrong," he slurred. "All of a shudden, I feel shick. I'm having trouble talk—" his tongue stumbled drunkenly in his mouth until he righted it and spit out, "—talking."

"Let's go back to the house," I said, as he rolled off of me onto the grasses. He looked frightened and as I stood up, I decided that we needed to get him to Dee's. I helped him get dressed then I had to help him stand up because he had trouble walking. He needed to lean on me to make it to the truck.

"I don't know what's wong," he said, sounding ludicrously like a Caucasian actor from a Thirties film doing a racist Asian accent. I started the truck and could hear water slopping out of the tote as we raced down the road and sped up the bluff. While I drove, I kept one eye on Dylan, his face contorted into a rictus. He mumbled that his calves were numb. I parked next to Dee's house and left Dylan sitting in the truck, explaining to him that I would be right back. He nodded but made no attempt to speak. Rapping quickly on Dee's door, I opened it to find her seated at the kitchen table, reading Barbara Pym and drinking a cup of tea.

"Dylan's sick," I shouted. She put her book down and hurried outside with me while I explained that his legs had gone numb and he was slurring his words.

Dee looked increasingly worried as I described his symptoms.

"Has he eaten any native foods recently?" she asked.

"He tried stinkheads yesterday."

"Oh, shit."

It was the first time I'd ever heard Dee curse.

Dylan could barely walk and it was a struggle for us to get him from the truck to the house. We put him on the couch in Dee's office. She motioned for me to step into the kitchen with her. "I think it's botulism," she said in a low voice, explaining that Alaska had the highest rate in the country for food-borne botulism because the native population ate fermented foods such as stinkheads. The risk was low when they were prepared in the traditional manner in grass-lined pits but allowing stinkheads to ferment in closed plastic containers was dangerous.

"They've warned people but everyone thinks it won't happen to them because they know how to prepare them properly," Dee said. "It's their neighbors who are incompetent."

My knowledge of obscure subjects failed me as I tried to recall what I knew about botulism. I didn't really know anything about it except that it could be fatal.

"Could he die?" I asked in a whisper.

"Not if he's treated promptly, but we need to get him to a hospital." She explained that botulism affects the nervous system and that the chief danger was that Dylan might stop breathing from muscle paralysis. She used her radio to call Mary in Egegik, informing her that there was a medical emergency and then explained the circumstances.

"We're going to need a plane to take him out," Dee said into her microphone. Mary told Dee to make Dylan comfortable and she'd call her back when she had an airplane confirmed.

Within minutes, Mary called back and said an airplane would be arriving within an hour. While waiting for the plane to arrive, Dee tried to make sure that Dylan was comfortable, but there wasn't much she could do for him. He lay on the couch, his head propped up by a pillow, seemingly unable to talk, his eyes wide open, looking bewildered and terrified. I walked to our house and discovered Roy, lying in bed, reading the copy of Willa Cather's *The Professor's House* that Lloyd had given him. Until then I wasn't sure if he had brought it out with him, and I was glad to see him reading it.

Roy looked up at me when I entered our bedroom.

"What's wrong?" he asked before I had a chance to say anything.

"Dylan has botulism," I cried. Roy set down his book and then followed me downstairs. On the way to Dee's house, I explained what had happened to Dylan without mentioning that his feet became numb after he kissed me and or that his speech started to slur after he had removed my dick from my underwear. We were in a hurry, and I felt that bringing myself into the story when someone's life was in danger would have been the height of selfishness.

Outside her house, we met Alex and Wendy. They had returned from four-wheeling, and their clothes and faces were splattered with mud. They followed Roy and me into Dee's mudroom as I explained the situation. They cleaned their boots by banging them repeatedly against a wood post and then skinned the remaining caked mud off their soles with a screwdriver.

"Is he going to be all right?" Wendy asked.

"I don't know," I said, suddenly afraid that Dylan would die. I would miss him terribly, but I also realized with calculated, cold-blooded heartlessness that I wanted Dylan to live, because I wanted to write about him. I might have questions about him later that only he could answer.

That was the moment when I quit being a writer's assistant and became a writer.

Our faces assumed suitably solemn expressions of concern although my expression was the poker face of a writer trying not to let other people know that he was thinking about his next book and wasn't really paying close attention to them.

Dee took charge of us when we returned to her house. Roy had already retrieved a stretcher that she kept in a storage locker. She directed Roy, Alex, Wendy, and me to lift Dylan and place him on the stretcher. We were going to put him in the back of Dee's truck and drive him down to the landing strip. Outside in the yard, Dylan stared at me and suddenly grabbed my right hand with his hands, which made my face flush as everyone, including Dee, stopped talking and watched us. Dylan gripped my hand tightly and I looked down at his handsome face. He was shiny with perspiration and his terrified eyes remained fixed on me as I squeezed his hand back.

"You'll be all right," I said, hoping that my acting ability was competent enough to convince him of something that I wasn't sure I believed.

"C-c-come wid me?" he asked, barely able to garble the words, as I involuntarily flashed upon the shot-putter with the stutter.

Four pairs of hard eyes fell upon me, making me feel that I was being stoned for adultery by a small mob of my friends. For an instant, it crossed my mind that Dylan's botulism was a ruse to get me to leave with him. When the plane touched down in Anchorage, he'd sit up on his stretcher. "It was the only way I could get you to come with me."

But Dylan's face was ashen and, for once, I was certain that he wasn't lying. I didn't know whether Dylan had really fallen in love with me, or even considered me to be his friend. But I still felt that he was my friend—a friend who had fucked up big time—and I couldn't abandon him.

I looked at Dee because I didn't want to leave her without a crewman. She nodded her head.

"I'll come with you," I said.

Dylan smiled weakly and released my hand. Roy looked concerned but I couldn't tell from his expression whether he was concerned for Dylan's health or concerned that I was leaving Coffee Point with Dylan.

Roy, Wendy, Alex, and I carried Dylan's stretcher and laid him in the back of Dee's truck. She got in the cab with Alex and Wendy while Roy and I climbed in the back to ride alongside him.

Roy and I looked at each other, but our faces remained expressionless. Once more we had become the salmon people, silently moving forward, filled with unspoken passions. Suddenly Dylan reached out with both arms and put his hands in ours. We rode to the airstrip holding his hands. We didn't have to wait long for the airplane to arrive, and after it landed the pilot and a paramedic took charge of Dylan. Roy and I stood awkwardly on the airstrip as the paramedic placed an oxygen mask on his face and quickly examined him in the back of the truck. I wanted to talk to Roy but the situation seemed so weird. There were too many people around, and I was also worried about Dylan. Then I realized that I was traveling back to Anchorage with no luggage except for my wallet.

"How do I get back here once I get to Anchorage?" I asked.

Roy's face had the stalwart expression of a man heading into battle or scooping his dog's poop from a sidewalk.

"I love you," he blurted out. At first, my heart felt cornered in my chest but my panic gave way as I remembered my mother's question, "If a friend asked you to jump over Niagara Falls, would you?" For once, I wasn't beset by qualms, full of misgivings, or troubled by uncertainty. I was supremely confident that if my mother knew Roy like I did, even she would be pushing me to take the plunge. I repeated his words back to him and we kissed.

"Uh, we're ready to put him in the plane," the pilot said awkwardly when we separated from each other.

We helped carry Dylan to the cargo hold and then I quickly said my good-byes. The paramedic announced that he was going to stay in back with Dylan during the flight, which meant that I would sit in the cockpit next to the pilot. The pilot's shocked expression from our public display of affection made me expect that there wouldn't be too much conversation during the flight. As I walked to the plane, my foot slid on a patch of mud. It brought back memories of stepping into the tar pit but didn't alarm me. I'd survived one widely acknowledged, internationally headlined act of incredible stupidity but had the contentment of knowing the odds were infinitesimally small that I would ever tumble into a tar pit again. And so what if I'd completely fallen for a sex and drug addicted movie star hottie who bookwormed into my heart and made me believe that we were two artists embarked on a journey together. The odds were slightly better that someday my head would be turned again—and my genitals would weathervane along with it—by another handsome face and seductive body.

As the plane lifted off, I watched Alex, Dee, Wendy, and Roy wave good-bye and suddenly I felt bouyant because I knew that I would never be able to accuse Roy of being tack-i-turn again.

EPILOGUE

D ylan was flown to a hospital in Anchorage where he was placed on a respirator. For three days he was in critical condition. Every night I called Coffee Point to give an update on his condition. The crisis passed four days after we arrived. Dylan would live, although his full recovery could take several months.

The bad news was that Graham Lemoore couldn't afford to stop production on his film, and Dylan had to be replaced with another actor. Dylan took it hard, he actually started to cry, but I thought his illness was a lucky break for him, because the terrible script made me think that the writer of *Violet Cryderman* deserved to get botulism.

In fact Dylan received a shitload of publicity about his brush with death. Offers began to come in and in his next film, he played the young Oscar Wilde traveling in the American West. It was preposterous casting. Dylan dyed his hair black for the part, and I found it hard to believe Oscar Wilde had a six-pack, which was revealed when a two-spirited *winkte* Sioux shaman initiated Oscar into gay sex after Oscar participated in the sacred Sundance ceremony. But Dylan managed to make his portrayal of Oscar Wilde riveting and was nominated for an Academy Award for best actor, firmly reestablishing his career. (Ironically, he lost to another studly actor, who played the young gay Abe Lincoln.)

The most extraordinary side effect of Dylan's illness was that it helped him become clean and sober. After he was released from the hospital, Dylan rejoined a 12-step program and was able to finally quit every drug, including marijuana. Roy and I learned this in the mandatory letter Dylan sent out when he tried to make amends to people he might have hurt when he was an addict.

"I notice there's no mention of his overcoming his sex addiction though," Roy said after he read the form letter.

I returned to Coffee Point as soon as possible. Wendy was leaving the next day, and she was spending her last day in Egegik with Alex. When I arrived Roy met me at the airstrip. It was the last sunny day we had that summer. A few fat clouds lounged in the blue sky and millions of tiny green tundra leaves rustled in the breeze, causing a steady sibilant blustering noise.

"It's too nice to stay inside," Roy said after we stopped at the house. He suggested that we go for a walk. Instead of hiking along the beach, he recommended walking the double rutted snow machine trail that ran along the top of the bluff. We set out from Coffee Point, following the sandy road until it gradually became the snow machine trail. (No one ever did explain to me why snowmobiles are called snow machines in Alaska but trust me, they are.) I had read enough environmental articles to understand that the parallel tracks in the tundra were a sign of environmental damage, but they also looked appealingly picturesque. The tracks were a sign that we weren't living in the wilderness; we were living in a fishing community, tenuously able to "stay in ouch" with the world.

As we strolled along the bluff, I looked to my left, down on the beach. There was no activity because fishing had been closed for another day. Fishing nets were pulled up high above the tide line, and a string of fishing boats idled offshore. Behind us were thirty or so houses and ahead of us, still out of sight, was the cannery. To my right was the gently rolling tundra, puddled with ponds, the land too wet to walk on, but too dry to swim. At that moment, I experienced the magisterial sensation, a common delusion of writers, that I could know and encompass an entire world, at least the world north of Egegik and south of Naknek. I knew that someday I would write about Coffee Point.

As we walked, Roy and I discussed how Dylan had deceived us. In my absence, Wendy and Alex had explained everything to Roy, who didn't seem to be surprised that Dylan had pushed him off his raft.

"I didn't expect you to take it so calmly," I said.

"How can I be angry with him? He told us from the beginning that he was a perfect liar."

Roy also pointed out that I was angry with Dylan because I'd been a perfect idiot.

"He figured out your flaw and used it against you. 'I'm romantic. I'm artistic.'" Roy said as he mincingly imitated me. "'I love art and books and artists.'" Roy rolled his eyes and shook his head after he finished his impression of me. "All Dylan had to do with you is take off his shirt and tell you about the hardships of being an artist and you became his patsy."

I laughed because I couldn't deny anything he said. "Aren't you at least a little bit mad that he almost killed you for the sake of his art?"

"No," he said. "It serves me right for hanging around with artists."

His tolerance faded, though, when I told him that Dylan had asked me to become his boyfriend. I wasn't going to keep that to myself because I wanted Roy to know that I was a sought-after guy. I decided not to tell Roy about Dylan pulling down my underwear because nothing happened beyond that. I'm sure that even Chekhov had to draw the line on honesty somewhere. But I admitted that Dylan had been trying to seduce me when Roy questioned me about it.

"You were going to have sex with him, weren't you?" he asked.

"I thought about it," I admitted, feeling ashamed of myself. I told him that I changed my mind after Dylan offered to loan me the money to change my plane ticket.

"Let's hear it for tightwads," Roy said, raising his hand in a mock-salute.

"Yep," I said, "Dylan's flaw is that he's cheap."

"Damn," Roy said. "Why didn't I think of that earlier? That's how I could have gotten rid of him. I should have told him that you were in debt up to your ears and owed a fortune on your credit cards. He would've run from you like a man being chased by a bear."

We stopped walking when we reached the shore overlooking Roy's site. I stood near his chartreuse sign admiring the view of the beach. Roy sat down on the tundra and began to unlace his boots. "Take off your boots and socks," he said. "You have to walk barefoot on the tundra. It feels incredible."

I removed my boots and socks and stood up. The spongy tundra felt prickly against the soles of my feet but it also felt surprisingly warm and dry.

"How come it's not wet?" I asked.

"The bluff is all sand. The water drains off."

The plants felt soothing as I walked across them. "It's like getting a foot massage," I said. Roy compared the ground to a loofah but I told him that I liked to think we were walking across the stubble-covered face of the earth.

"It's a hotter metaphor," I said.

"Whatever," he said, indulging me in my silliness.

As we walked around the edge of the bluff, I thought that it never would have occurred to me to walk barefoot on the tundra. I would have been afraid that it would have been too cold or rough or that I would stub my toe on a caribou antler or the oosik of a walrus. Suddenly curious, I asked Roy how he discovered the joys of tiptoeing on the tundra.

"I didn't have any friends out here as a kid," he said as he bent down to examine a small rock on a stony patch of ground. "To pass the time, I'd devise all sorts of experiments. I'd see how long I could keep my bare feet in the water or try to see how close I could creep up to a Bald Eagle. One day, I decided to try walking barefoot on the tundra."

Roy asked me to come over to where he was standing. He pointed toward a dark gray quarter-sized rock on the ground.

"Would you pick up that stone for me?"

I thought his request was odd but I bent down and picked it up. I saw that the edges of the stone had been rounded off and a tiny pie-wedge notch had been incised in the upper right-hand corner.

"You just found this?" I asked, thrilled to think that other people had fished at Coffee Point long before us.

"There's probably more here if we look around," he said.

I scanned the ground looking at the stones until I found a net-stone also. "I can't believe it," I said. My net stone wasn't as finely made as Roy's, but it had the unmistakably man-made notch on its upper right-hand side.

"I love this," I exclaimed as I held the stone in my palm.

A smile crossed Roy's thick lips. "You said that you wanted to find an arrowhead."

A surge of affection suffused my body with warmth and I carefully examined his unshaven, deeply tanned face, trying to picture the inquisitive, imaginative boy who used the tundra as his playground. Standing barefoot on the tundra in the warm sunshine, near the edge of the bluff, I knew then that I loved Roy as a man, loved him as a boy, and would love him when we were old men, drinking negronis.

Roy was a masterpiece of the boyfriend genre, capable of becoming my favorite book. He was funny, smart, deeply satisfying, profound, and beautiful but also difficult and challenging. Oh, there were occasional obscure passages, but that was due to his complexity. But I was certain that Roy would always be worth rereading. There would always be something new to discover, and I'd gain a better appreciation for the parts of him that I'd overlooked before.

For Wendy's last night, Dee prepared another salmon feast and afterward, Alex, Roy, and I planned on taking a sauna together. But Wendy refused to be separated from us and invited herself along. Alex and Roy looked unsure but I explained to them that when Wendy and I were roommates, she would frequently walk in the living room, topless, to ask me, "Do you like this shirt?" She was almost as much of an exhibitionist as Dylan.

While Wendy and Roy were building the fire in the sauna, I asked

Alex if Dylan's illness had been some sort of Yup'ik payback for insulting his grandmother.

"I didn't do anything," Alex said. "But I can't vouch for my grandmother."

Since Dylan had almost died and lost a major part in a movie, I asked Alex what lay in store for me.

He didn't have to think about his answer.

"You've had your payback," Alex said.

I couldn't think what he was talking about and asked him what he meant.

"You'll never know if you and Dylan could have been boyfriends," Alex said. "That's your payback."

(A year later, another form of payback occurred when Alex used my gay salmon idea in a television commercial for a telephone company that wanted to target the gay market. Alex eventually earned six figures for the deal when the commercial became one of those television touchstones that catches the fancy of the country. People of all sexual orientations started to repeat the catchphrase of Alex's gay salmon, "Too laaatte!!!" It didn't help assuage my feelings of being used that the salmon was named Nelson, in homage to his creator.)

Dylan was still in the hospital in Anchorage two weeks later when we returned from Coffee Point. It was Roy who insisted that we should visit him on the day we arrived. His hospital room was filled with flowers. Dylan was sitting up in bed, wearing his eyeglasses, reading *Vile Bodies* when we entered. He smiled at us, but I was startled by his appearance. He'd lost the twenty pounds of muscle he gained in prison and while he was still handsome, he also looked sickly and vulnerable.

At first, we discussed Dylan's treatment and recovery, but our conversation was stilted until Dylan eased the tension by asking Roy how the rest of his fishing season went.

"I've had better seasons," he said. "But it was the most fun I've ever had out there."

Roy glanced slyly at me as we recalled that it had rained for the past six days and we had spent most of our free time engaged in rugged cuddling in our cozy bed.

Dylan complained that he was bored out of his mind and couldn't wait to get back to Los Angeles.

"When do you get out?" Roy asked.

"On Friday," Dylan said. "I'm leaving the next day because I have an audition for another part on Monday."

"You're lucky," Roy said. "I've heard that some people take months to get better."

"When do you leave for L.A.?" Dylan asked me.

Wendy had arranged our meeting with Amanda, and I was flying back to discuss our scripts with her. Roy and I had made a plan; we would see what happened with the show while Roy finishes school. One thing was certain: I was going to finish my novel.

"Do you need a place to stay?" Dylan asked. "You can stay with me if you want."

He looked at me innocently but there was a devious sparkle in his eyes.

"No, he can't stay with you," Roy said. "You two aren't allowed to see each other." Roy looked directly at Dylan. "And if you try to see him, you'll be falling off a raft." Roy waited a second before grinning wickedly.

Dylan looked surprised by his vehement response but then he laughed.

"So are you moving up here?" Dylan asked me.

"We don't know yet," I said, having already told Roy that I wanted to live in Alaska at some point. "We're definitely going fishing next summer, no matter what happens." Dee had already asked me to crew for her again, but I told her she was going to have to raise my share of the catch because I'd no longer be a greenhorn. She argued that I still couldn't get the boat in the water by myself but when I countered that she couldn't fish by herself anymore, she finally agreed to raise my pay to a third of the catch.

"You couldn't pay me the whole catch to go out there again," Dylan declared. "I've had enough salmon to last me."

I understood his reaction, but it wasn't my experience. For at least ten or twenty years, I hoped to forestall blurting out to complete strangers at cocktail parties, "I'm an Alaska *fiend!*" and then launching into a rambling soliloquy about the bears, forests, mountains, people, salmon, and tundra of our forty-ninth state.

However, resisting the urge would require extraordinary willpower, because that summer I had fallen in love as swiftly as the term suggested. My heart had dropped from a great height and landed in Coffee Point.

ACKNOWLEDGMENTS

I'd like to thank the following people who were instrumental in helping me write this novel: John Arnold, Chloe Brushwood-Rose, Maggie Cadman, Chris Chisholm, Jaffe Cohen, Liz Craft, Dan Davis, Greg Davis, Jeffrey Epstein, Sarah Fain, Michael Hart, Hank Hodges, Chuck Kim, Eric Kornfeld, Richard Kramer, Elvira Kurt, Tom Lasley, David Masello, David McConnell, Bill Oliver, Matthew Richmond, Glenn Rosenblum, Mark Salzwedel, Mark Solan, and Rob Weisbach.

I'd also like to thank a few of the many Alaskans (and former Alaskans) who've been extremely kind and generous to me: Ben Bohen and Peter DuBois, Greg Kramer, Dr. Ken Peterson and Dr. Robert

Burgess, Vic Carlson and Jerry McEwen, Pete Pinney, Jeff Walters, and Jim Wilkins.

My experiences in Alaska were made especially memorable by the following people: Jennifer Bersch, Gretchen Bersch, Chris Beanes, Jeremy Neldon, MK MacNaughton and Susan Haymes, Rorie Watt, Tim Stallard and Bob Burgess of www.outinalaska.com, and the man who first insisted that to understand Alaska I had to get out in the bush: Brad Williams.

Of course, I want to thank my patient and supportive agent Elaine Markson and her terrific associate Gary Johnson.

And I'd especially like to thank: Eddie Sarfaty, Patrick Ryan, Michael Zam, and my insightful editor and friend Don Weise.